LAST PICK

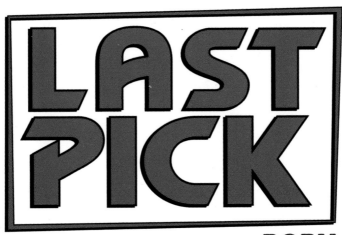

BORN TO RUN

LAST PICK

BORN TO RUN

JASON WALZ

Color by **Jon Proctor**

:01
First Second
New York

For Oskar and Ingrid. Your dad was many things, but at his core,
he was a storyteller and a dreamer. Live *your* best dream.

So many people to acknowledge, and so little space to do so. Lionsgate Academy let me spend
years getting to know so many amazing students who have helped to shape Wyatt. Matt
Daigle and Marian Lucas have been patient teachers to me and have tried their best to make
sure that Harper's sign language is appropriate. Connie Hsu, Robyn Chapman, and the entire
First Second crew have done a spectacular job shaping the story you're now holding. Jon
Proctor continues to breathe life into each page with his beautiful colors.

Most of all, a huge shout-out to Emily. Our lives together
will always be the best story we work on.

First Second

Copyright © 2019 by Jason Walz

Published by First Second
First Second is an imprint of Roaring Brook Press, a division of
Holtzbrinck Publishing Holdings Limited Partnership
120 Broadway, New York, NY 10271

Don't miss your next favorite book from First Second!
For the latest updates go to firstsecondnewsletter.com and sign up for our enewsletter.

Library of Congress Control Number: 2018953560
Hardcover ISBN: 978-1-62672-892-9
Paperback ISBN: 978-1-62672-893-6

Our books may be purchased in bulk for promotional, educational, or business use.
Please contact your local bookseller or the Macmillan Corporate and Premium Sales Department
at (800) 221-7945 ext. 5442 or by email at MacmillanSpecialMarkets@macmillan.com.

First edition, 2019

Edited by Connie Hsu and Robyn Chapman
Cover design by Andrew Arnold and Molly Johanson
Interior book design by Dezi Sienty, Gabriel Guma, and Molly Johanson
Cover color by Shelli Paroline and Braden Lamb. Interior color by Jon Proctor
Printed in China
Paperback: 10 9 8 7 6 5 4 3 2 1
Hardcover: 10 9 8 7 6 5 4 3 2 1

Penciled with a light blue Prismacolor Col-erase, inked with a Pentel Brush and
Alvin Penstix in a variety of sizes, and colored digitally in Photoshop.

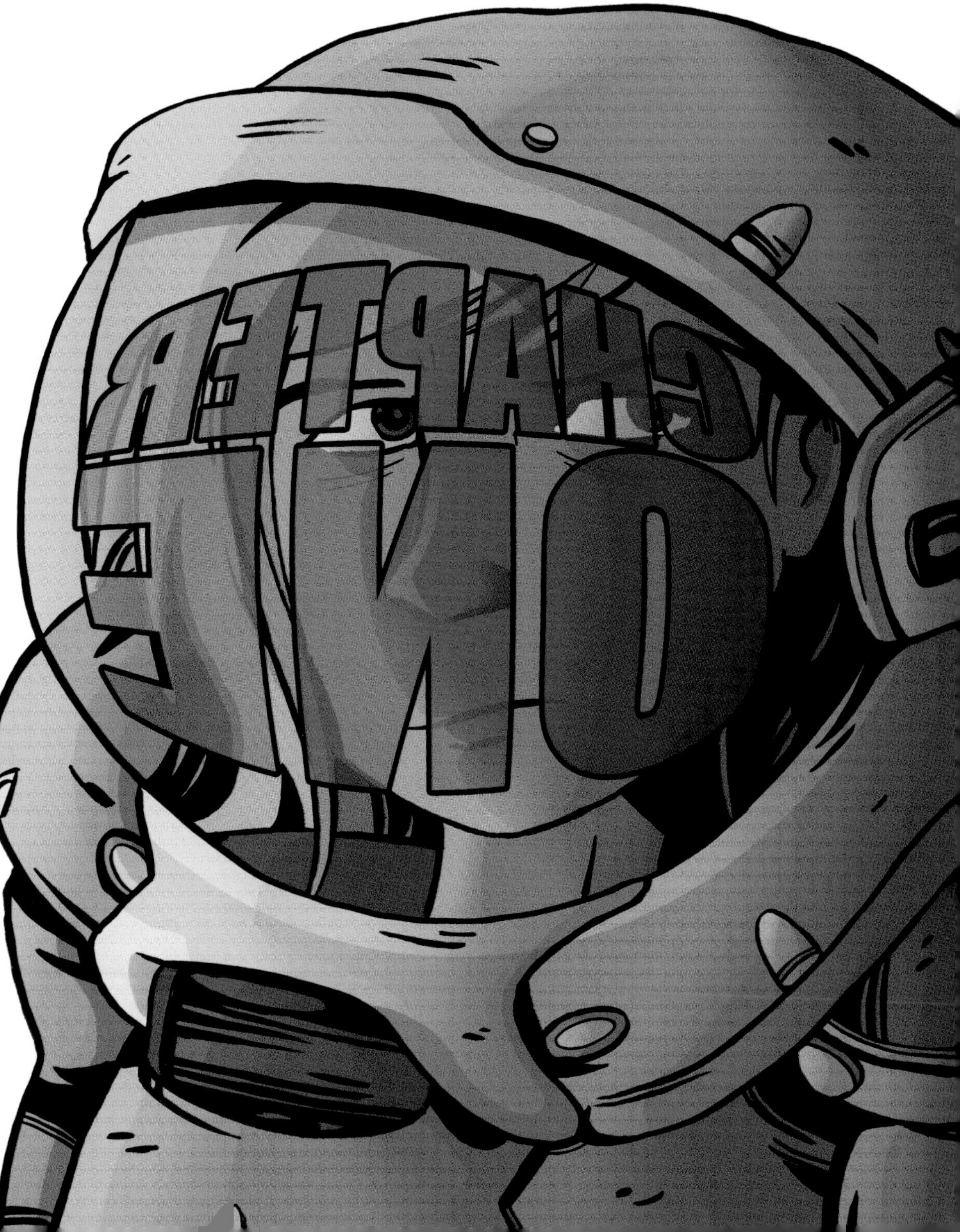
CHAPTER
ONE

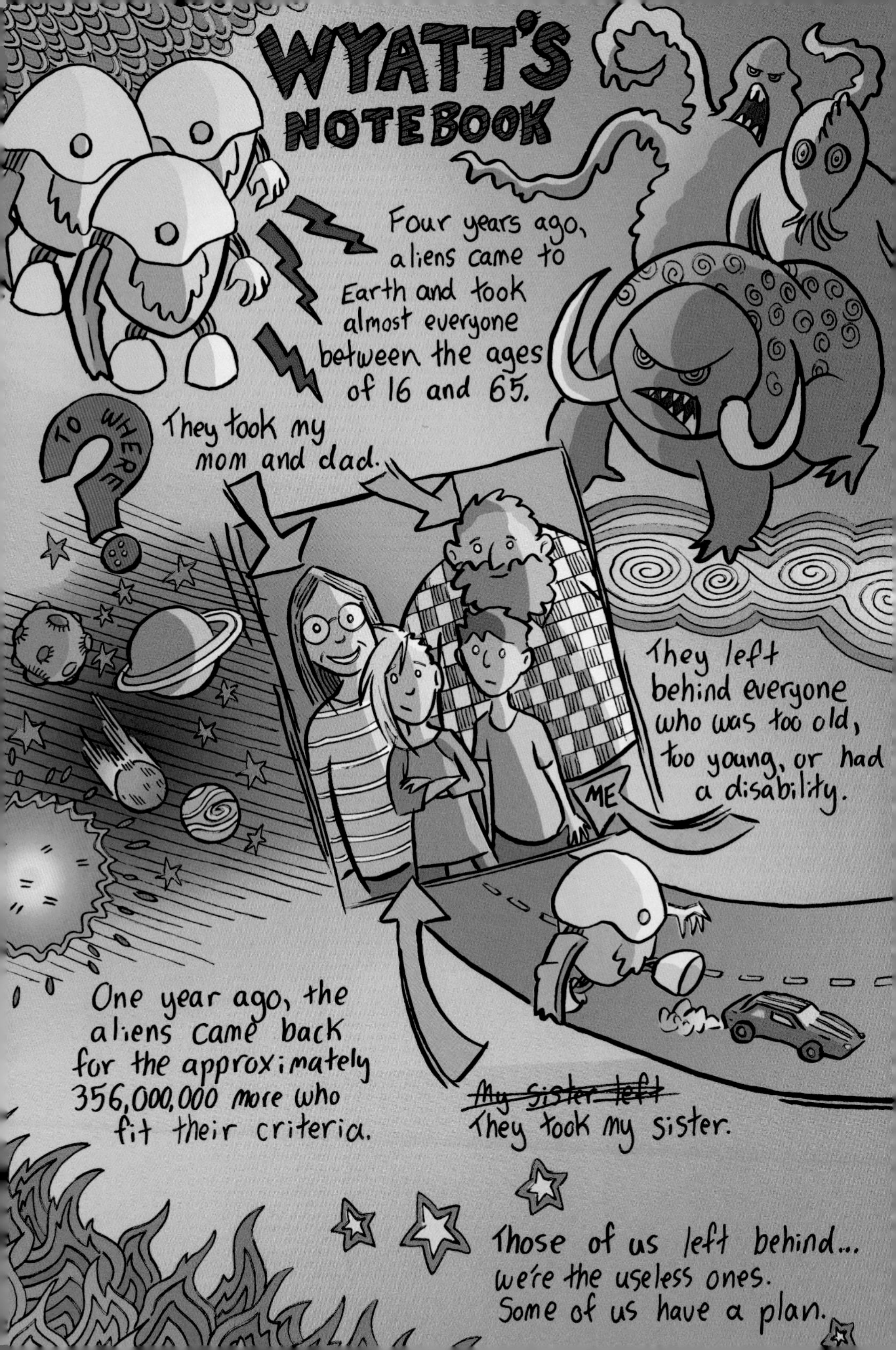
WYATT'S NOTEBOOK
Four years ago, aliens came to Earth and took almost everyone between the ages of 16 and 65.
TO WHERE
They took my mom and dad.
They left behind everyone who was too old, too young, or had a disability.
ME
One year ago, the aliens came back for the approximately 356,000,000 more who fit their criteria.
~~My sister left~~
They took my sister.
Those of us left behind... we're the useless ones.
Some of us have a plan.

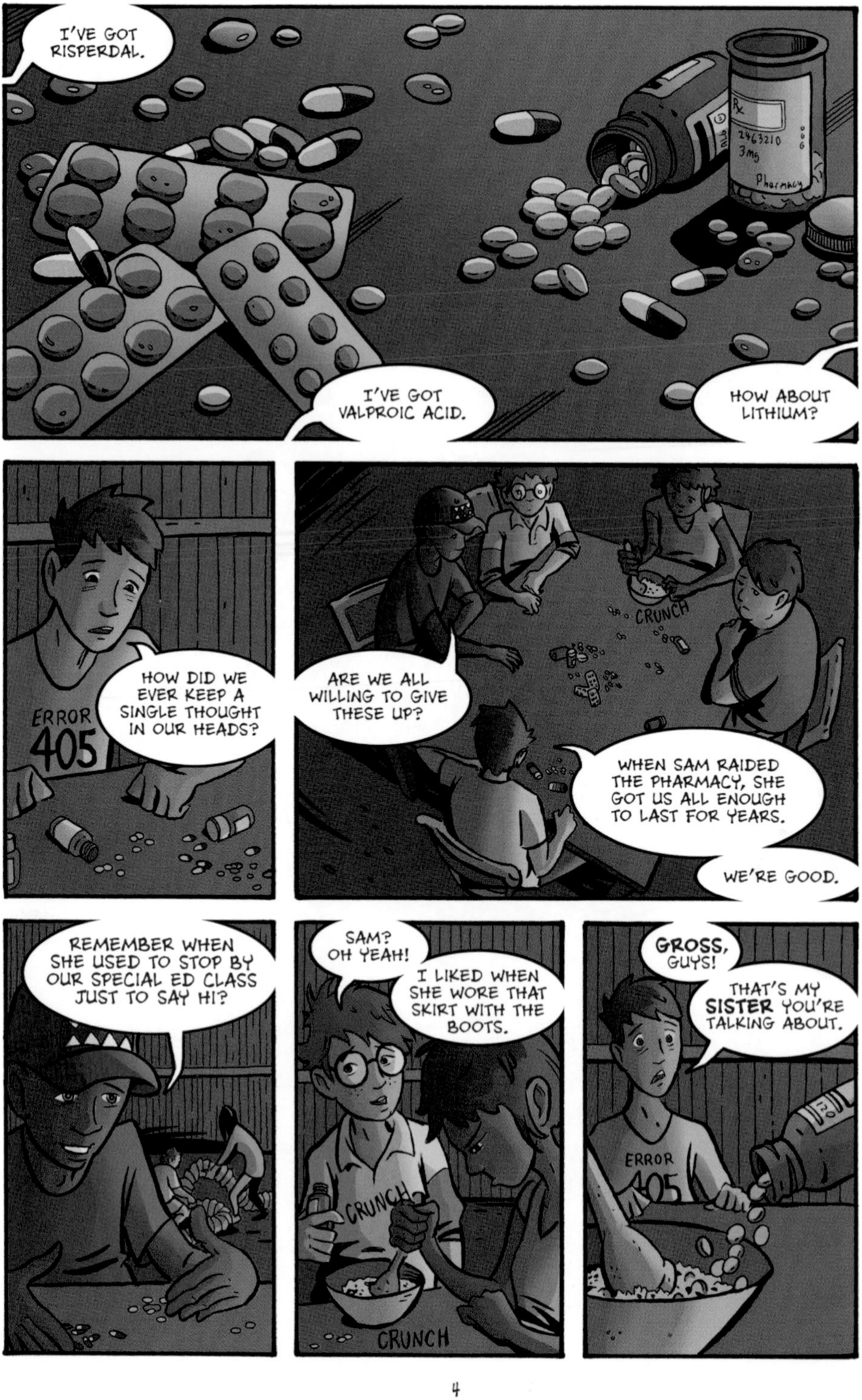
I'VE GOT RISPERDAL.
Rx 2463210 3mg Pharmacy
I'VE GOT VALPROIC ACID.
HOW ABOUT LITHIUM?
ERROR 405
HOW DID WE EVER KEEP A SINGLE THOUGHT IN OUR HEADS?
ARE WE ALL WILLING TO GIVE THESE UP?
CRUNCH
WHEN SAM RAIDED THE PHARMACY, SHE GOT US ALL ENOUGH TO LAST FOR YEARS.
WE'RE GOOD.
REMEMBER WHEN SHE USED TO STOP BY OUR SPECIAL ED CLASS JUST TO SAY HI?
SAM? OH YEAH!
I LIKED WHEN SHE WORE THAT SKIRT WITH THE BOOTS.
CRUNCH
CRUNCH
GROSS, GUYS!
THAT'S MY SISTER YOU'RE TALKING ABOUT.
ERROR 405

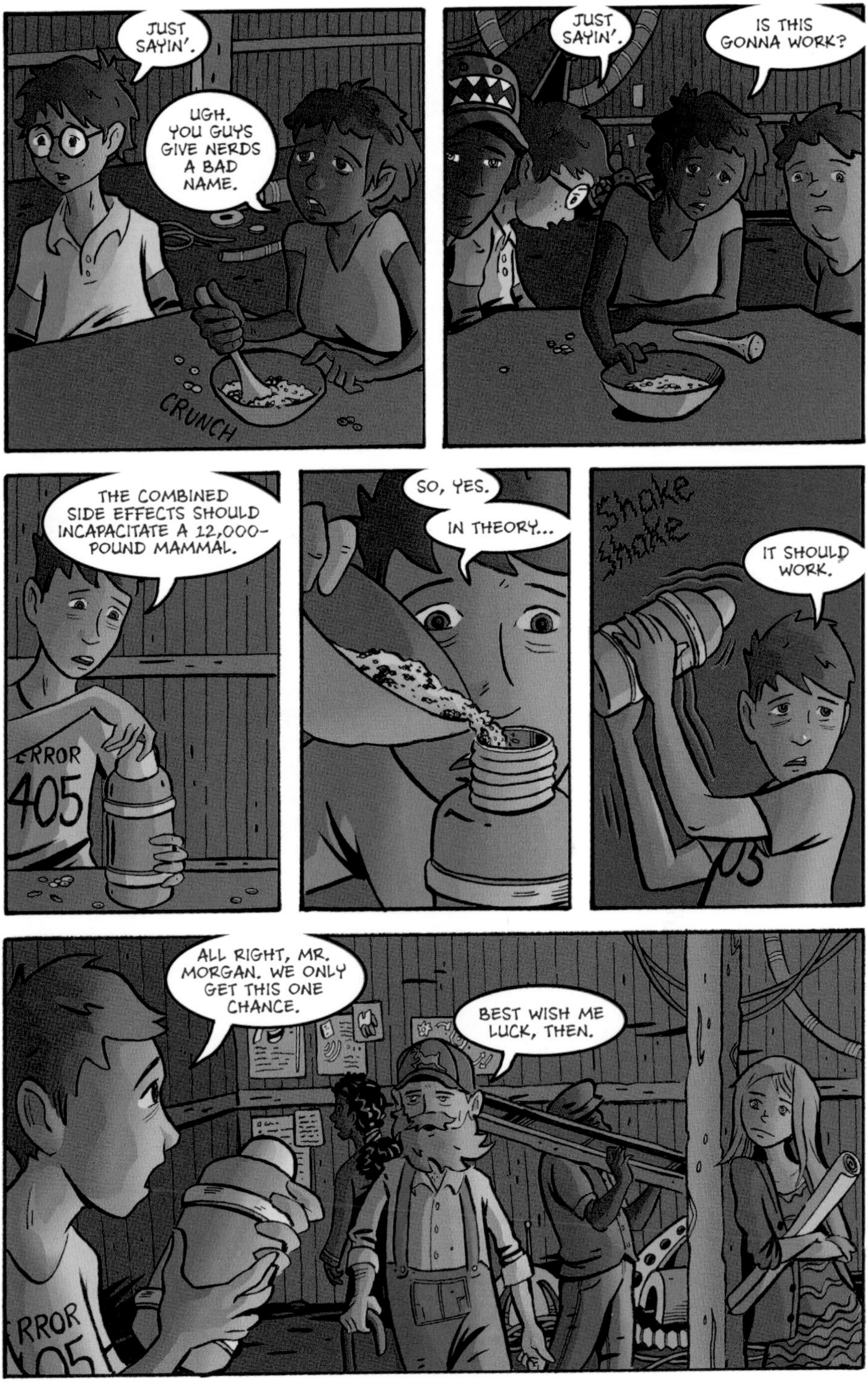
JUST SAYIN'.
UGH. YOU GUYS GIVE NERDS A BAD NAME.
CRUNCH
JUST SAYIN'.
IS THIS GONNA WORK?
THE COMBINED SIDE EFFECTS SHOULD INCAPACITATE A 12,000-POUND MAMMAL.
ERROR 405
SO, YES.
IN THEORY...
Shake Shake
IT SHOULD WORK.
ALL RIGHT, MR. MORGAN. WE ONLY GET THIS ONE CHANCE.
BEST WISH ME LUCK, THEN.
RROR 05

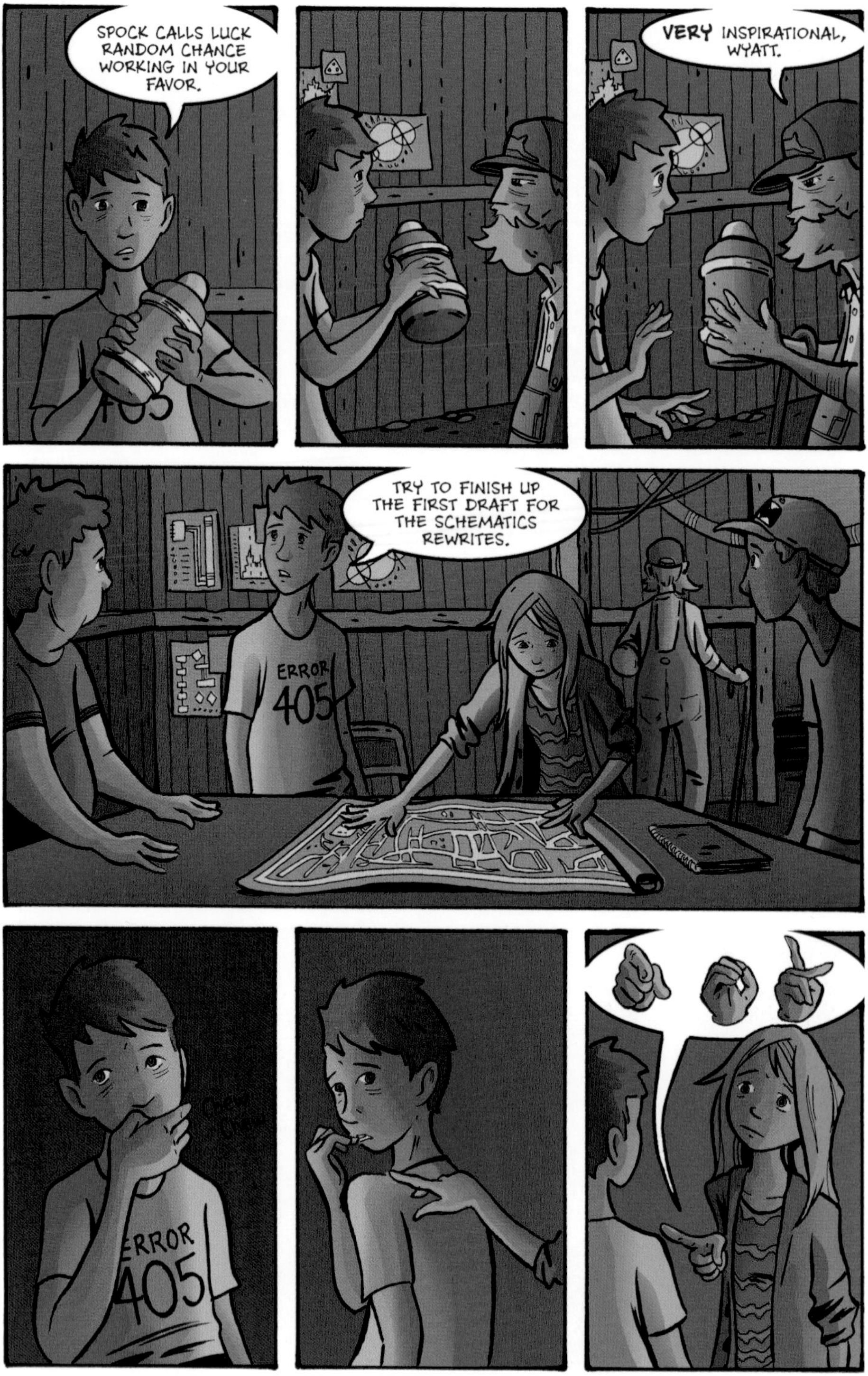
SPOCK CALLS LUCK RANDOM CHANCE WORKING IN YOUR FAVOR.
VERY INSPIRATIONAL, WYATT.
TRY TO FINISH UP THE FIRST DRAFT FOR THE SCHEMATICS REWRITES.

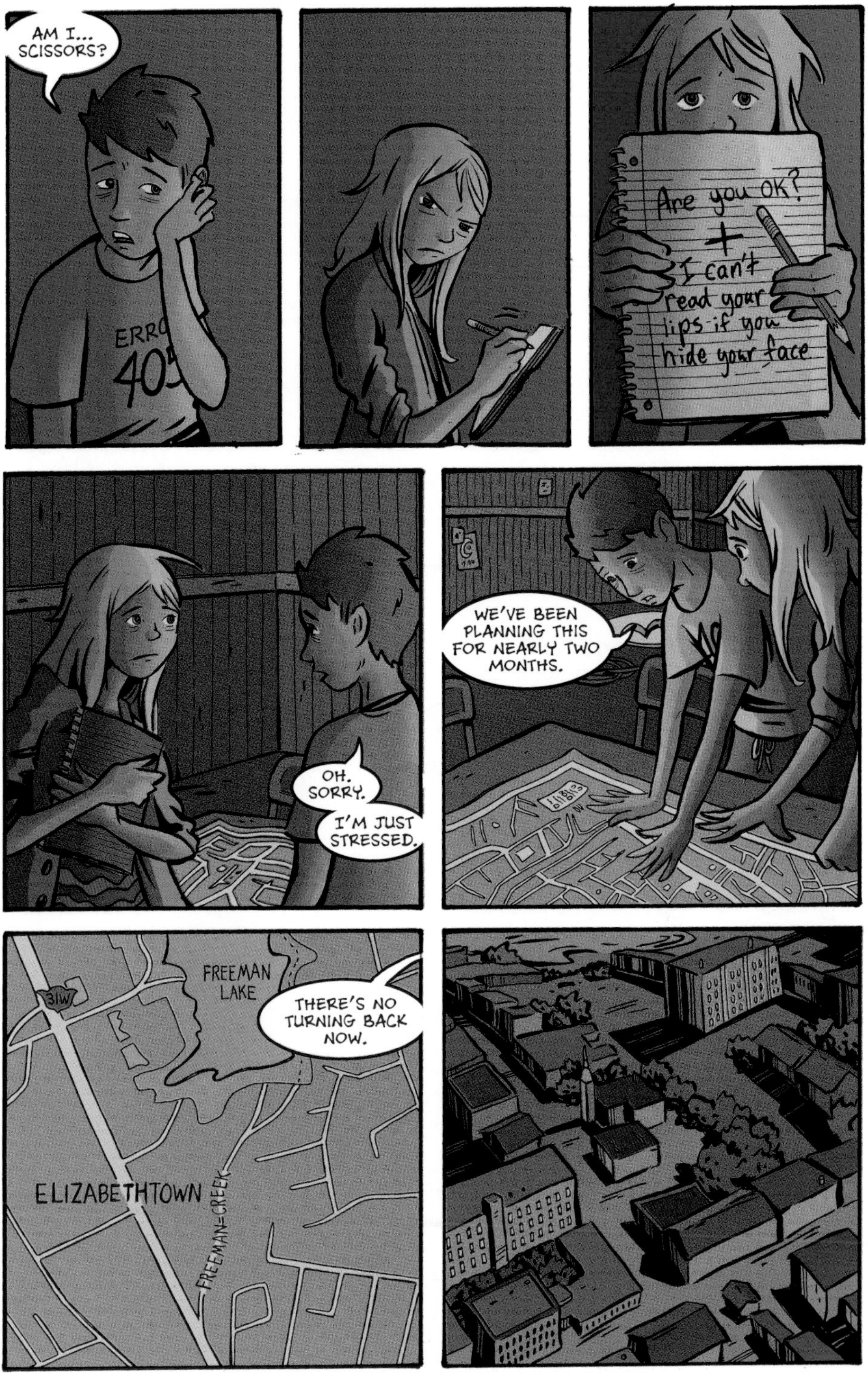
AM I... SCISSORS?
ERRO 40
Are you OK? + I can't read your lips if you hide your face
OH. SORRY.
I'M JUST STRESSED.
WE'VE BEEN PLANNING THIS FOR NEARLY TWO MONTHS.
FREEMAN LAKE
31W
ELIZABETHTOWN
FREEMAN CREEK
THERE'S NO TURNING BACK NOW.

KEEP OUT

MORNIN', BOYS.

FINE DAY. AM I RIGHT?

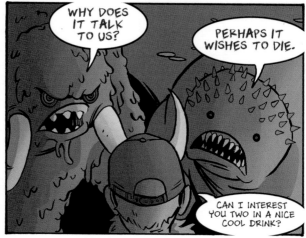

WHY DOES IT TALK TO US?

PERHAPS IT WISHES TO DIE.

CAN I INTEREST YOU TWO IN A NICE COOL DRINK?

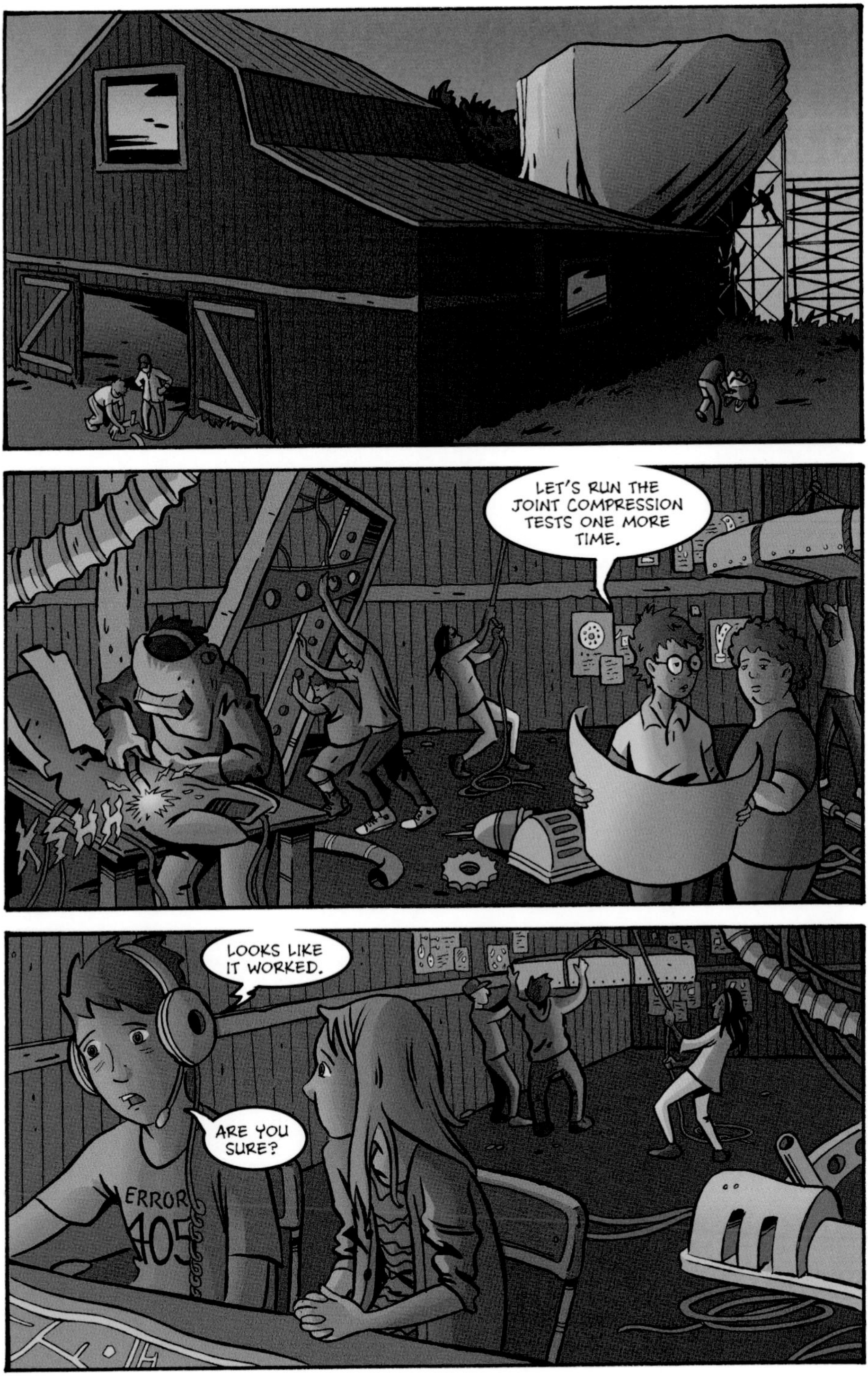
LET'S RUN THE JOINT COMPRESSION TESTS ONE MORE TIME.
KSHH
LOOKS LIKE IT WORKED.
ARE YOU SURE?
ERROR 405

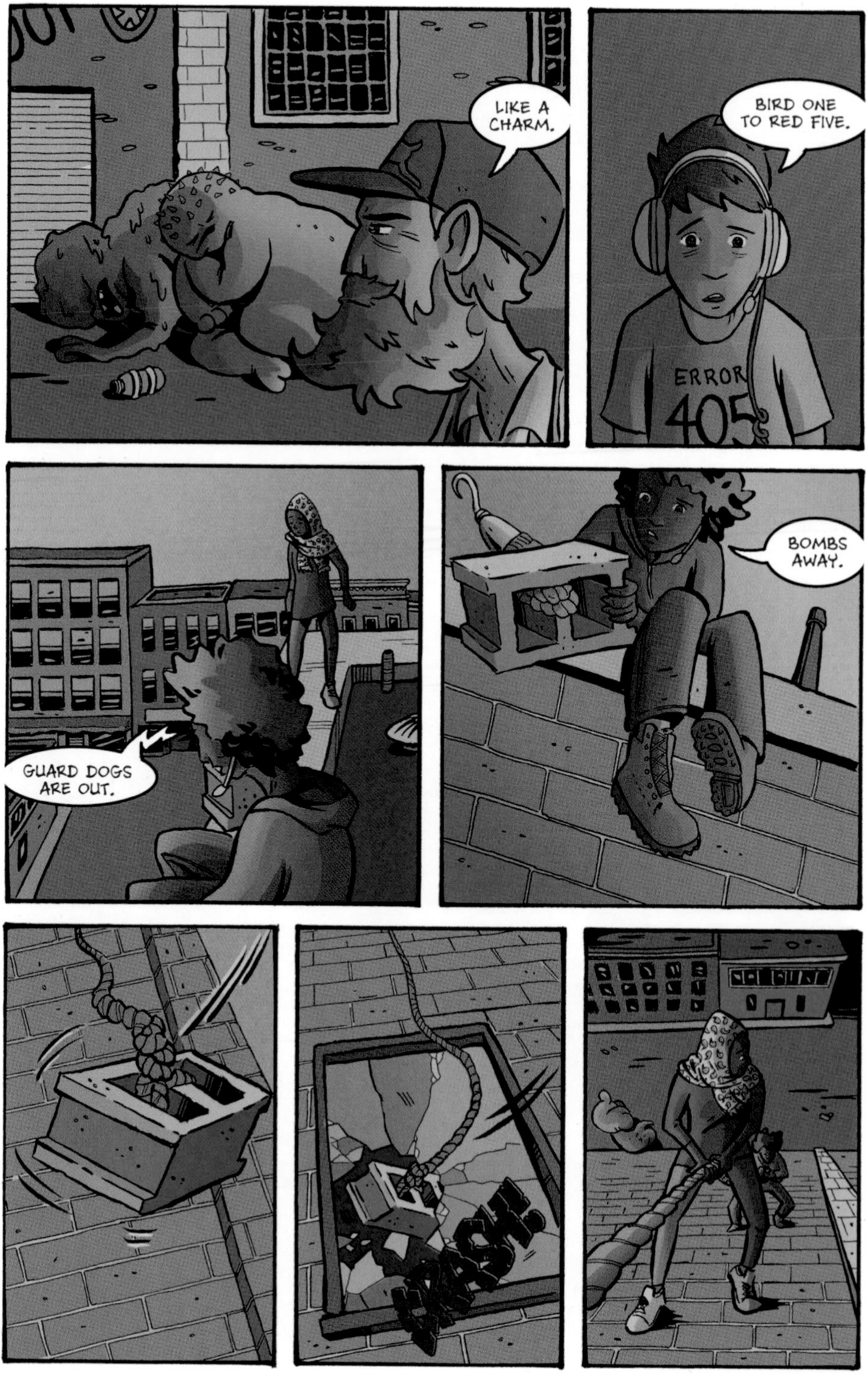
LIKE A CHARM.
BIRD ONE TO RED FIVE.
ERROR 405
GUARD DOGS ARE OUT.
BOMBS AWAY.

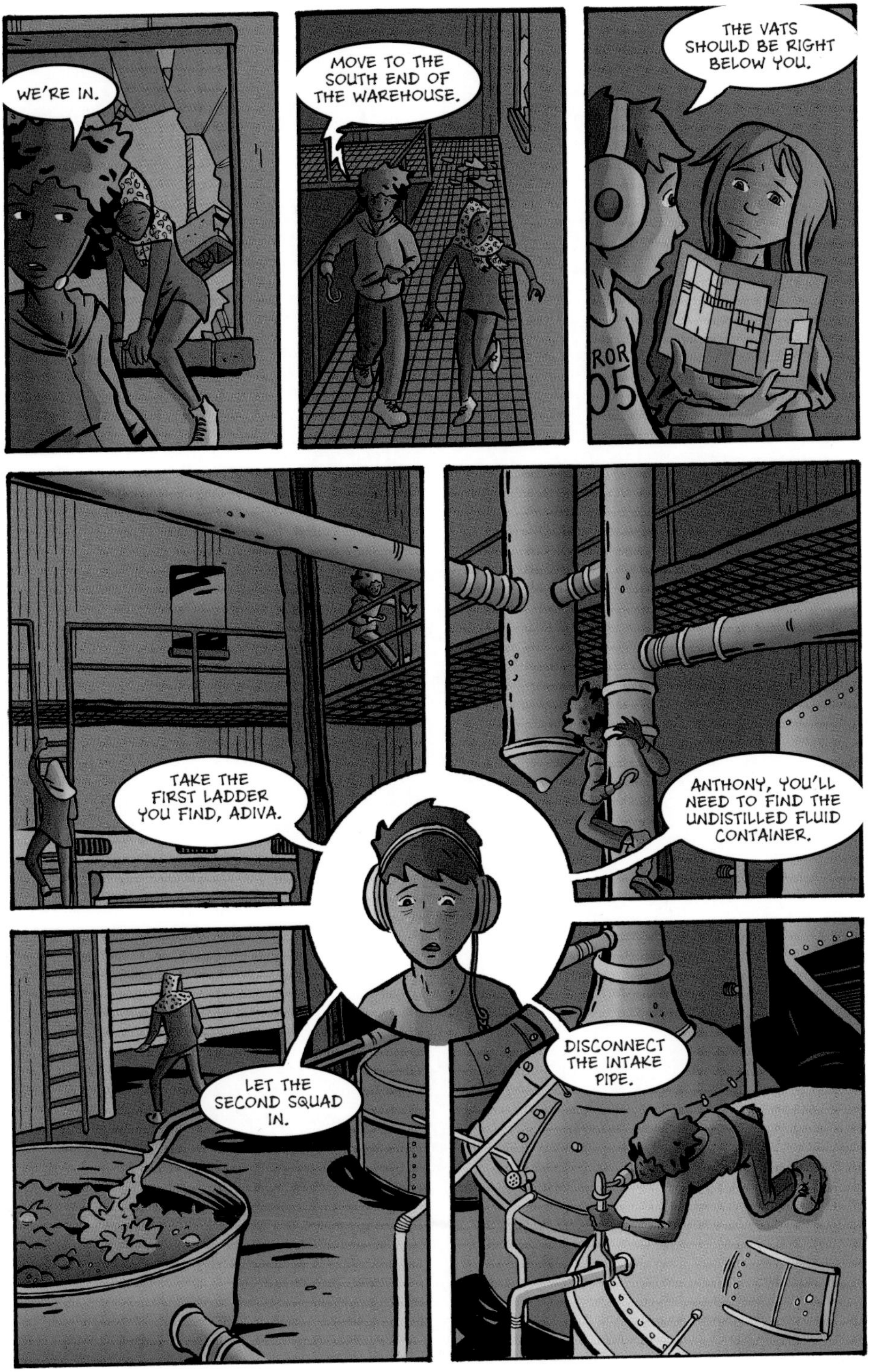
WE'RE IN.
MOVE TO THE SOUTH END OF THE WAREHOUSE.
THE VATS SHOULD BE RIGHT BELOW YOU.
ROR
05
TAKE THE FIRST LADDER YOU FIND, ADIVA.
ANTHONY, YOU'LL NEED TO FIND THE UNDISTILLED FLUID CONTAINER.
LET THE SECOND SQUAD IN.
DISCONNECT THE INTAKE PIPE.

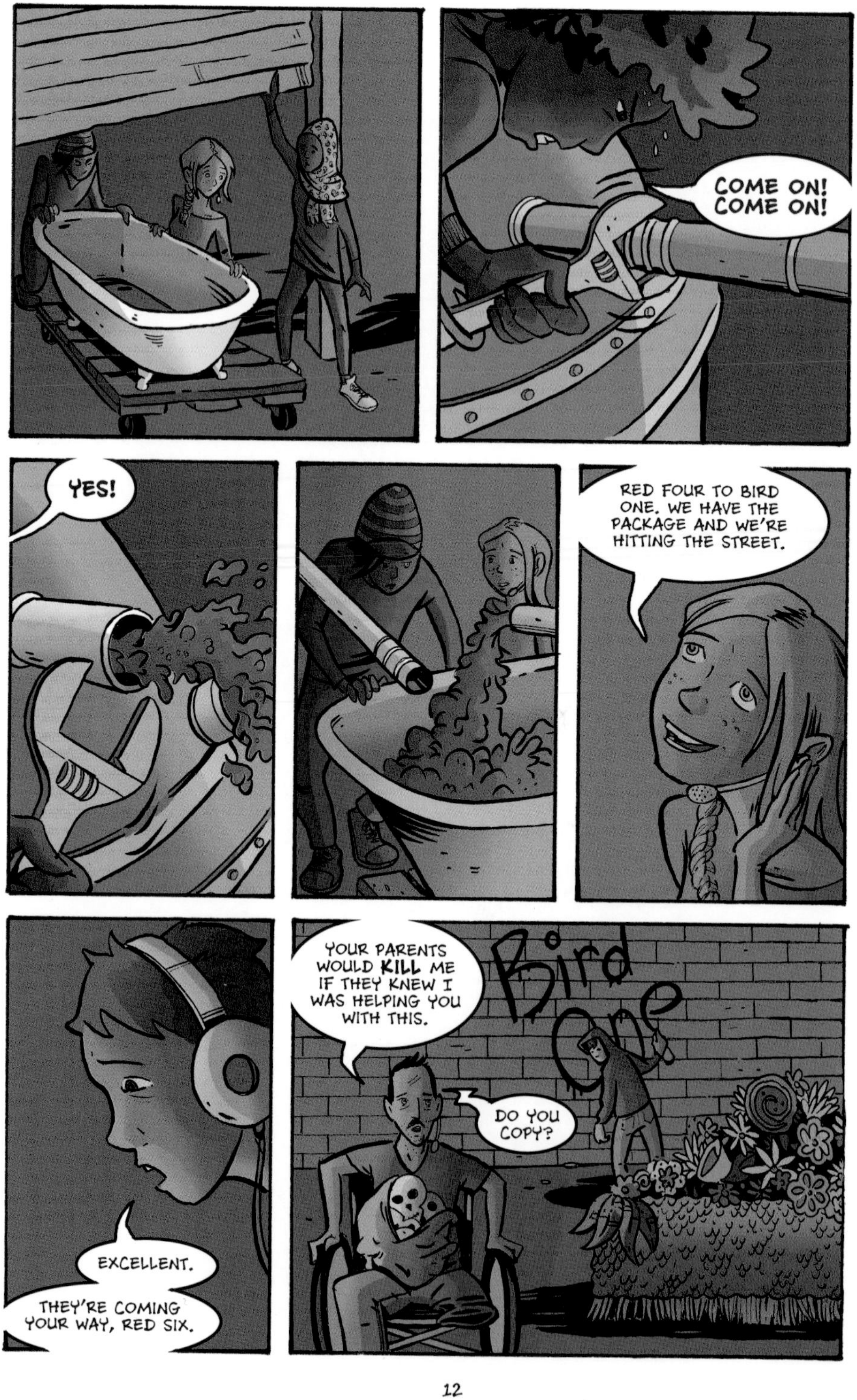
COME ON! COME ON!
YES!
RED FOUR TO BIRD ONE. WE HAVE THE PACKAGE AND WE'RE HITTING THE STREET.
EXCELLENT.
THEY'RE COMING YOUR WAY, RED SIX.
YOUR PARENTS WOULD KILL ME IF THEY KNEW I WAS HELPING YOU WITH THIS.
Bird One
DO YOU COPY?

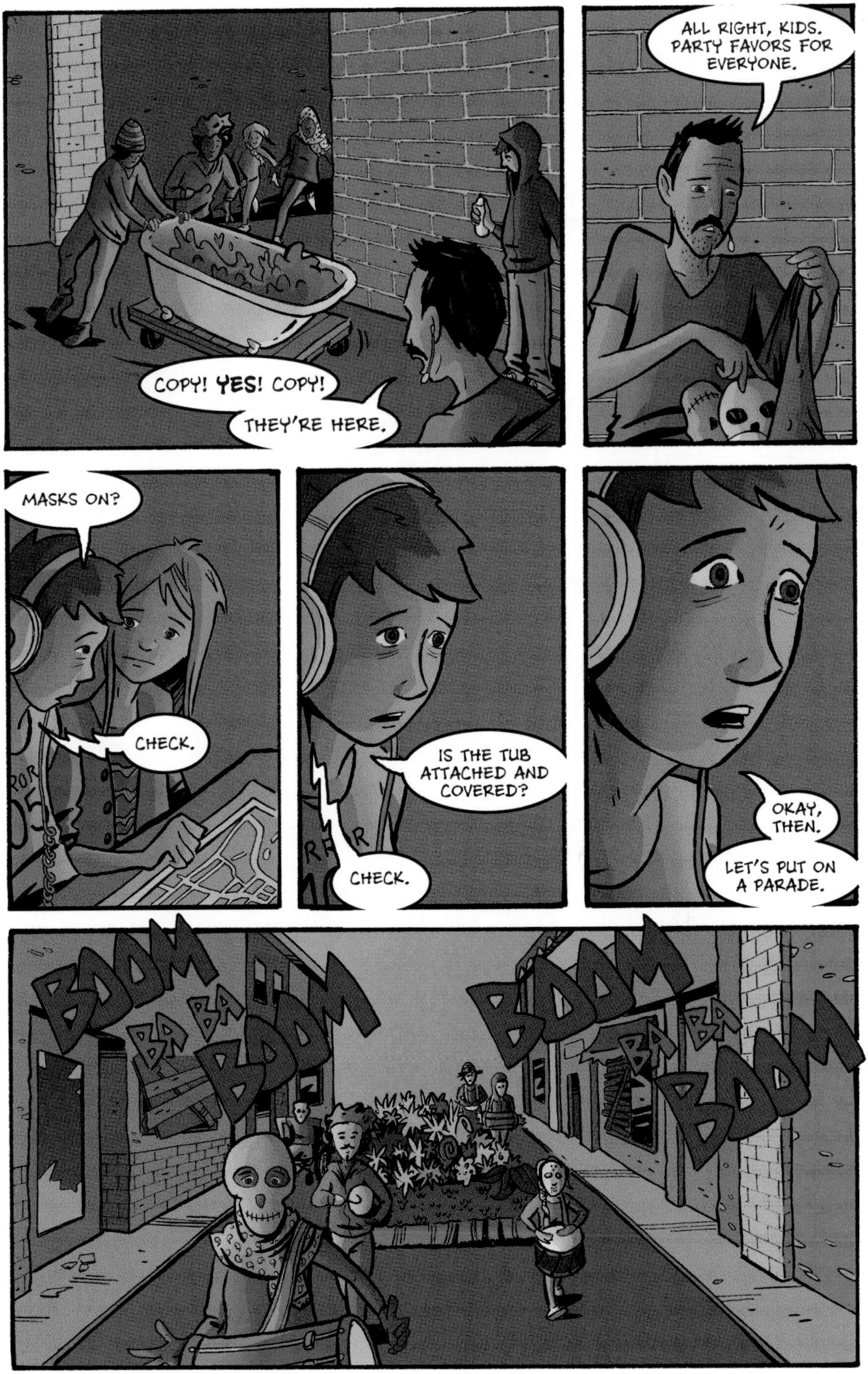
COPY! YES! COPY!
THEY'RE HERE.
ALL RIGHT, KIDS. PARTY FAVORS FOR EVERYONE.
MASKS ON?
CHECK.
IS THE TUB ATTACHED AND COVERED?
CHECK.
OKAY, THEN.
LET'S PUT ON A PARADE.
BOOM BA BA BOOM
BOOM BA BA BOOM

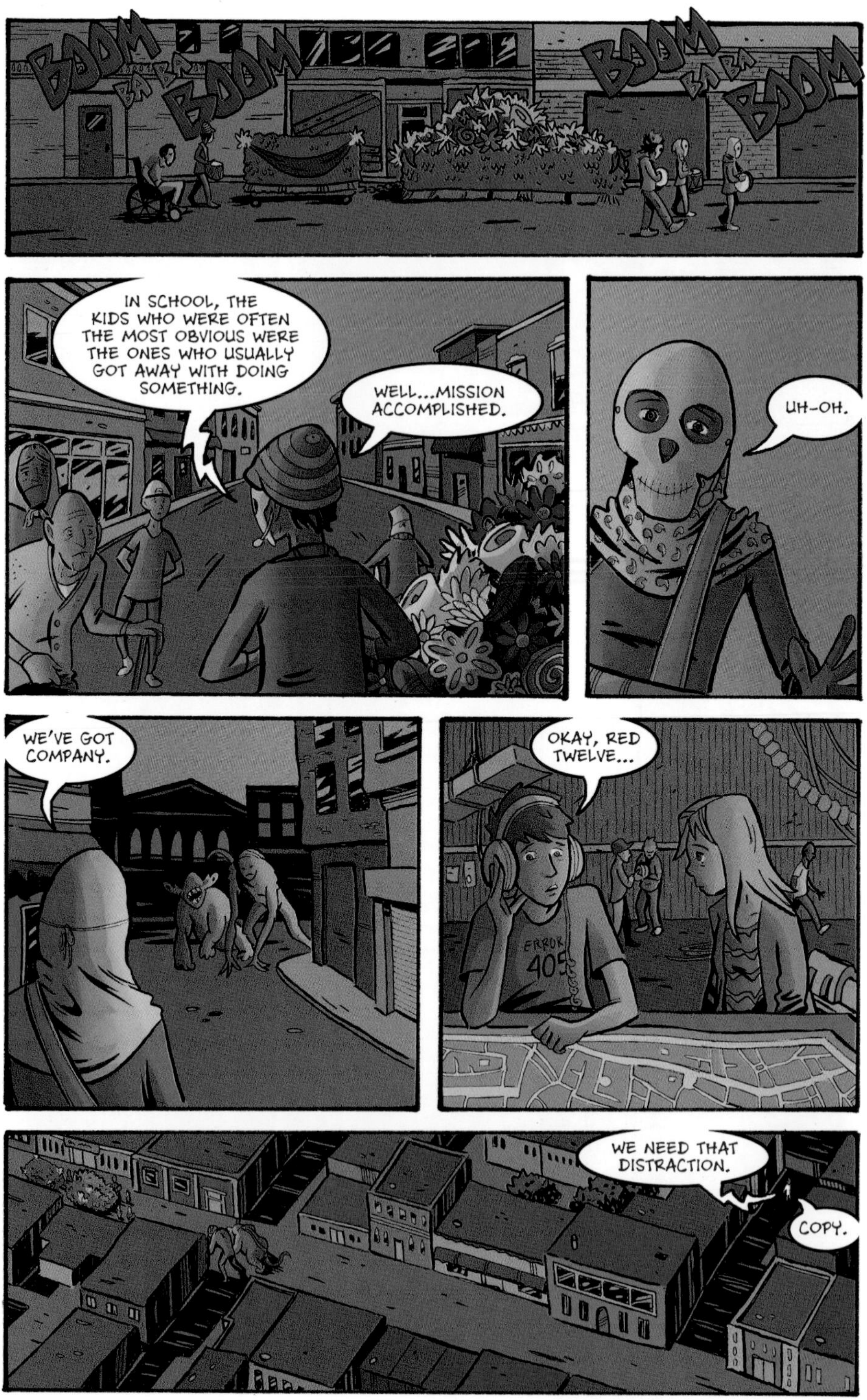
BOOM BA BA BOOM
BOOM BA BA BOOM
IN SCHOOL, THE KIDS WHO WERE OFTEN THE MOST OBVIOUS WERE THE ONES WHO USUALLY GOT AWAY WITH DOING SOMETHING.
WELL...MISSION ACCOMPLISHED.
UH-OH.
WE'VE GOT COMPANY.
OKAY, RED TWELVE...
ERROR 405
WE NEED THAT DISTRACTION.
COPY.

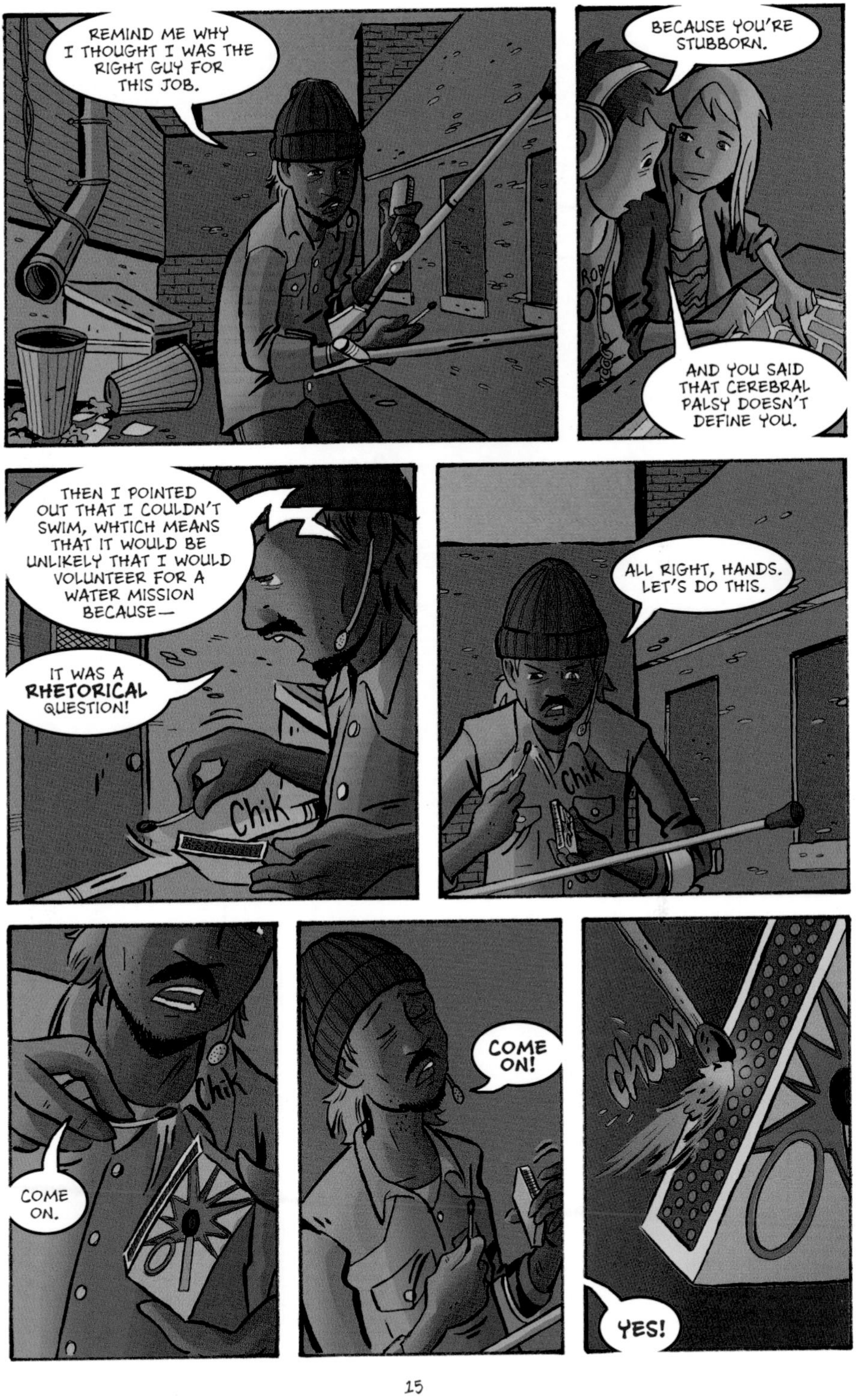
REMIND ME WHY I THOUGHT I WAS THE RIGHT GUY FOR THIS JOB.
BECAUSE YOU'RE STUBBORN.
AND YOU SAID THAT CEREBRAL PALSY DOESN'T DEFINE YOU.
THEN I POINTED OUT THAT I COULDN'T SWIM, WHTICH MEANS THAT IT WOULD BE UNLIKELY THAT I WOULD VOLUNTEER FOR A WATER MISSION BECAUSE—
IT WAS A **RHETORICAL** QUESTION!
Chik
ALL RIGHT, HANDS. LET'S DO THIS.
Chik
Chik
COME ON.
COME ON!
choom
YES!

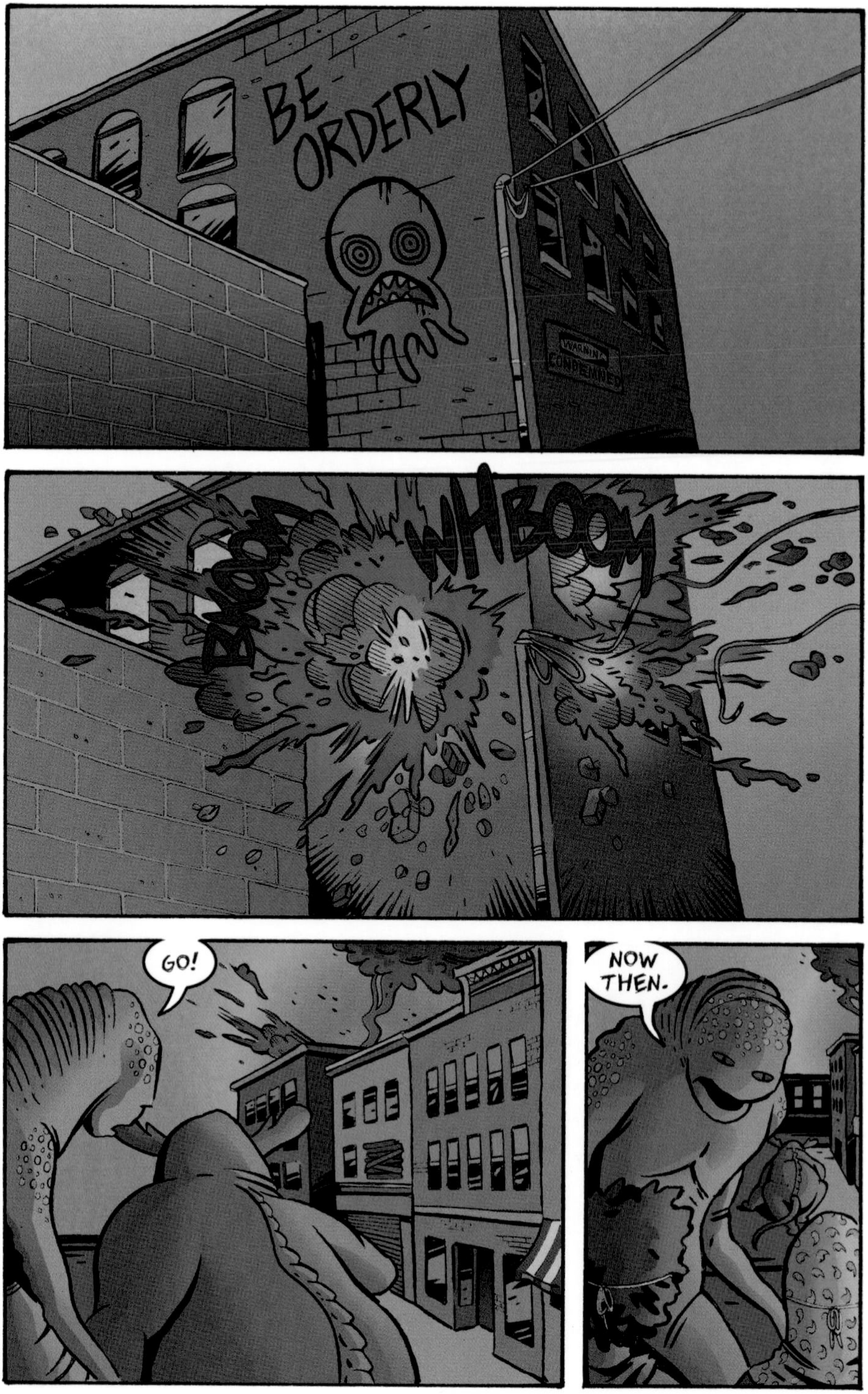
BE ORDERLY
WARNING CONDEMNED
WHBOOM
GO!
NOW THEN.

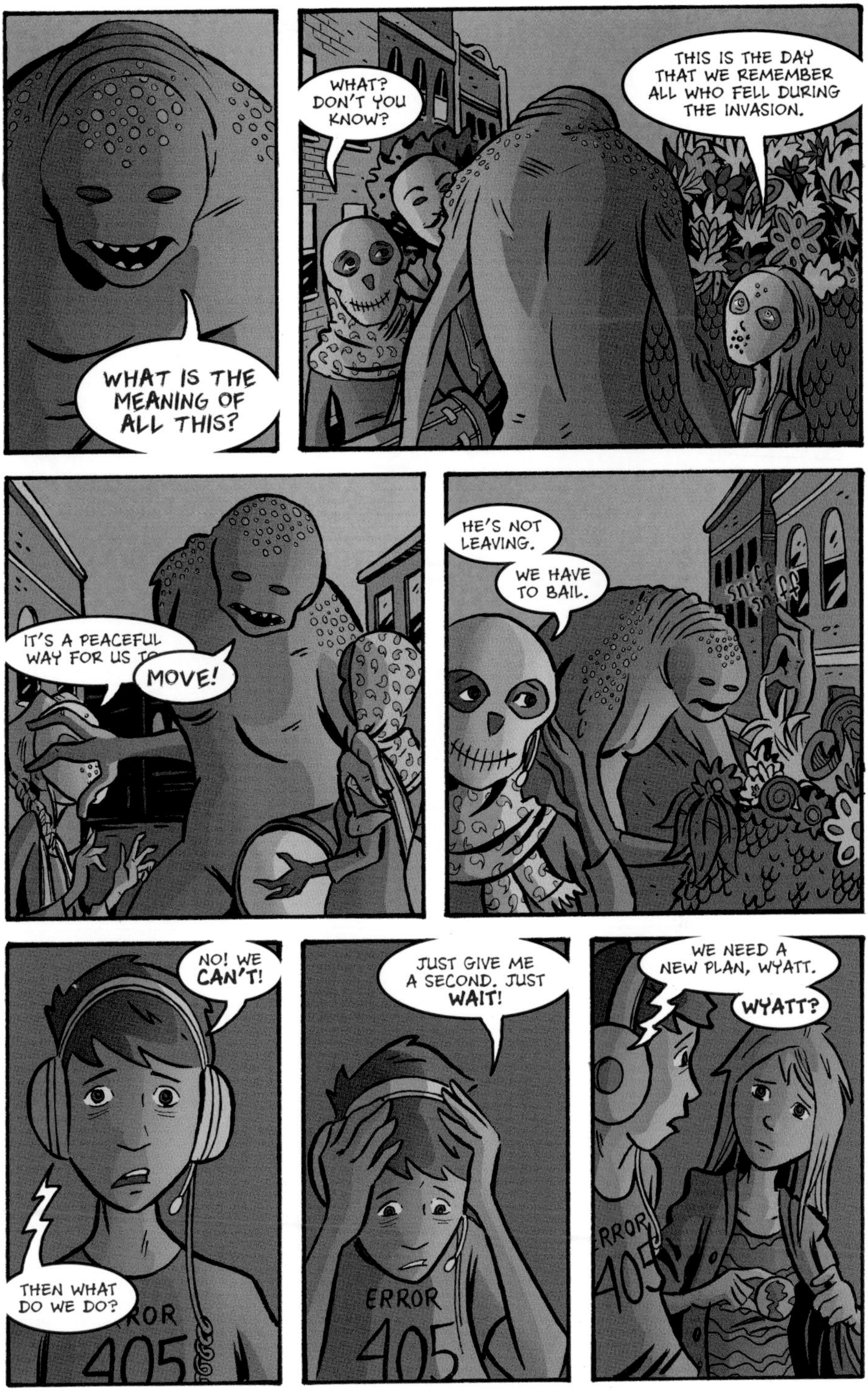
WHAT IS THE MEANING OF ALL THIS?
WHAT? DON'T YOU KNOW?
THIS IS THE DAY THAT WE REMEMBER ALL WHO FELL DURING THE INVASION.
IT'S A PEACEFUL WAY FOR US TO
MOVE!
HE'S NOT LEAVING.
WE HAVE TO BAIL.
sniff sniff
NO! WE CAN'T!
THEN WHAT DO WE DO?
ERROR 405
JUST GIVE ME A SECOND. JUST WAIT!
ERROR 405
WE NEED A NEW PLAN, WYATT.
WYATT?
ERROR 405

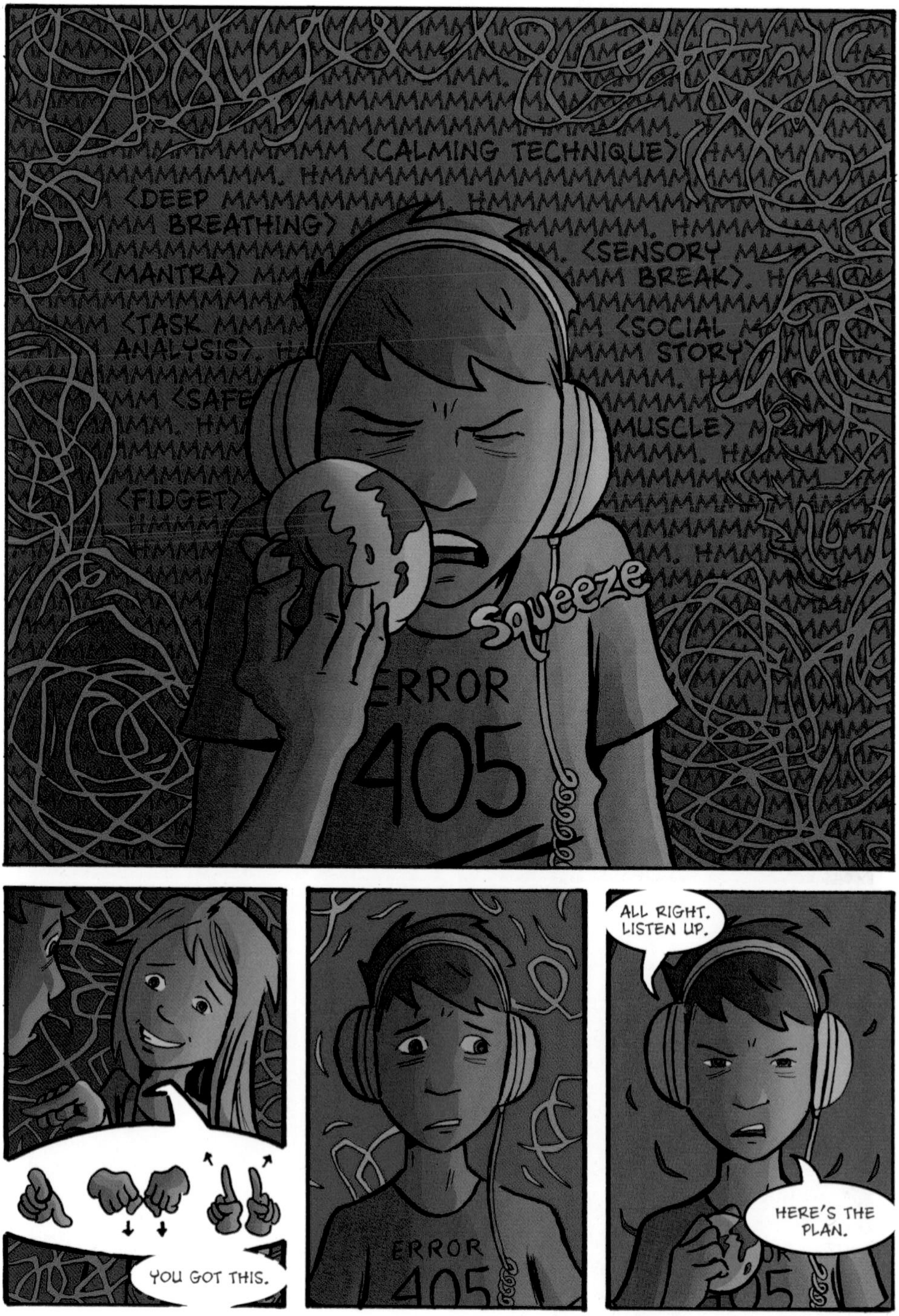
<CALMING TECHNIQUE>
<DEEP BREATHING>
<SENSORY BREAK>
<MANTRA>
<TASK ANALYSIS>
<SOCIAL STORY
<SAFE
MUSCLE>
<FIDGET>
SQUEEZE
ERROR 405
YOU GOT THIS.
ERROR 405
ALL RIGHT. LISTEN UP.
HERE'S THE PLAN.

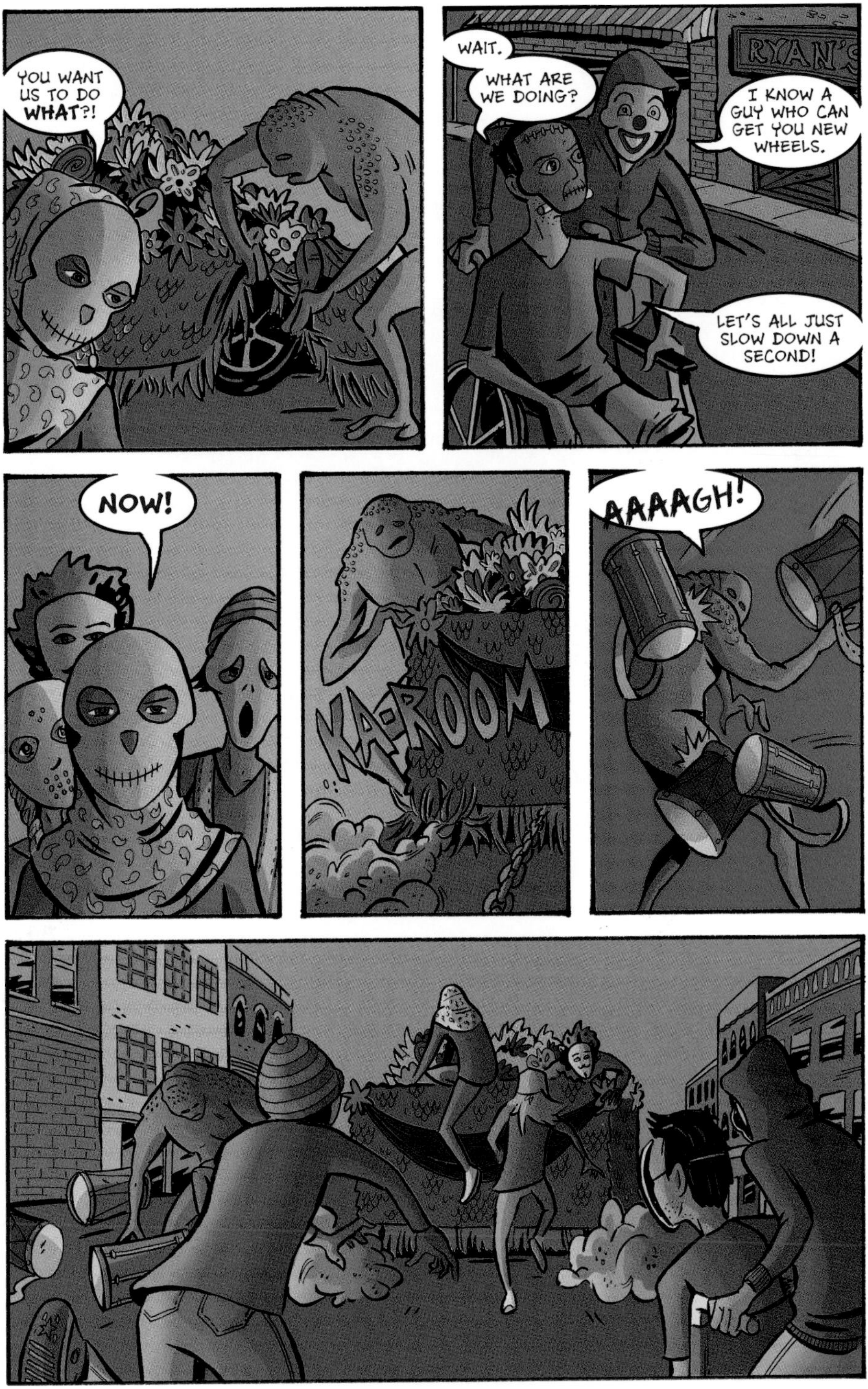
YOU WANT US TO DO **WHAT**?!
WAIT.
WHAT ARE WE DOING?
RYAN'S
I KNOW A GUY WHO CAN GET YOU NEW WHEELS.
LET'S ALL JUST SLOW DOWN A SECOND!
NOW!
KA-ROOM
AAAAGH!

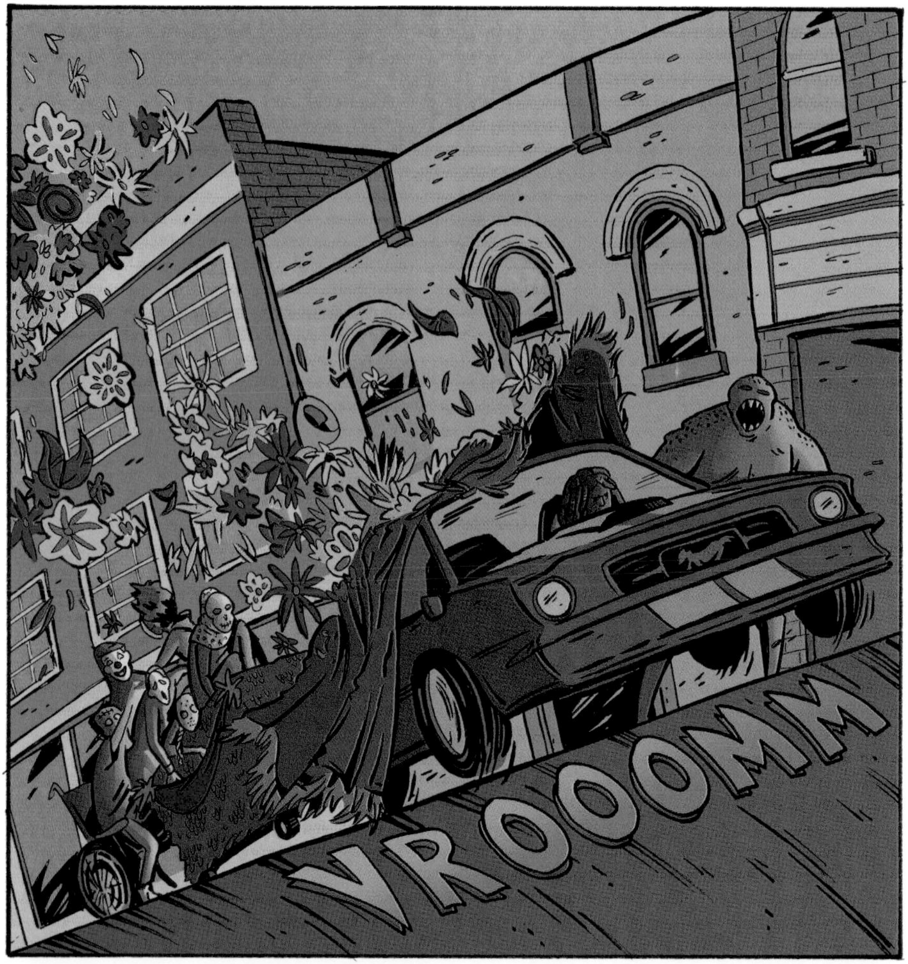
VROOOMM

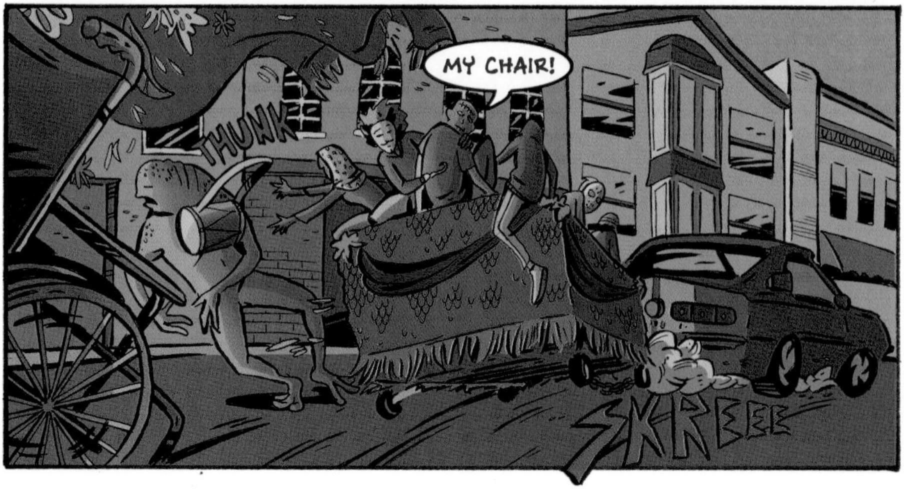
MY CHAIR!
THUNK
SKREEE

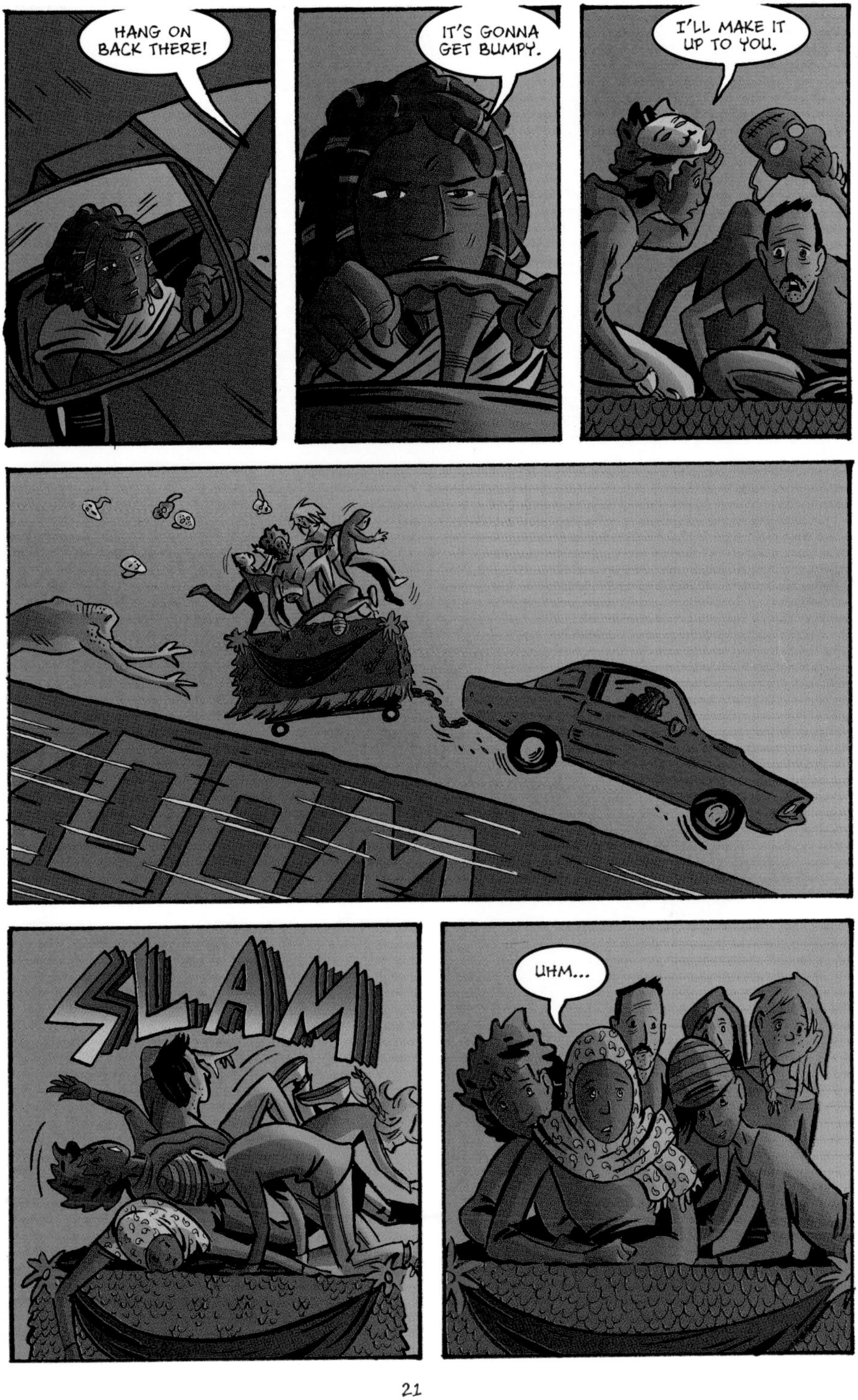
HANG ON BACK THERE!
IT'S GONNA GET BUMPY.
I'LL MAKE IT UP TO YOU.
VROOM
SLAM
UHM...

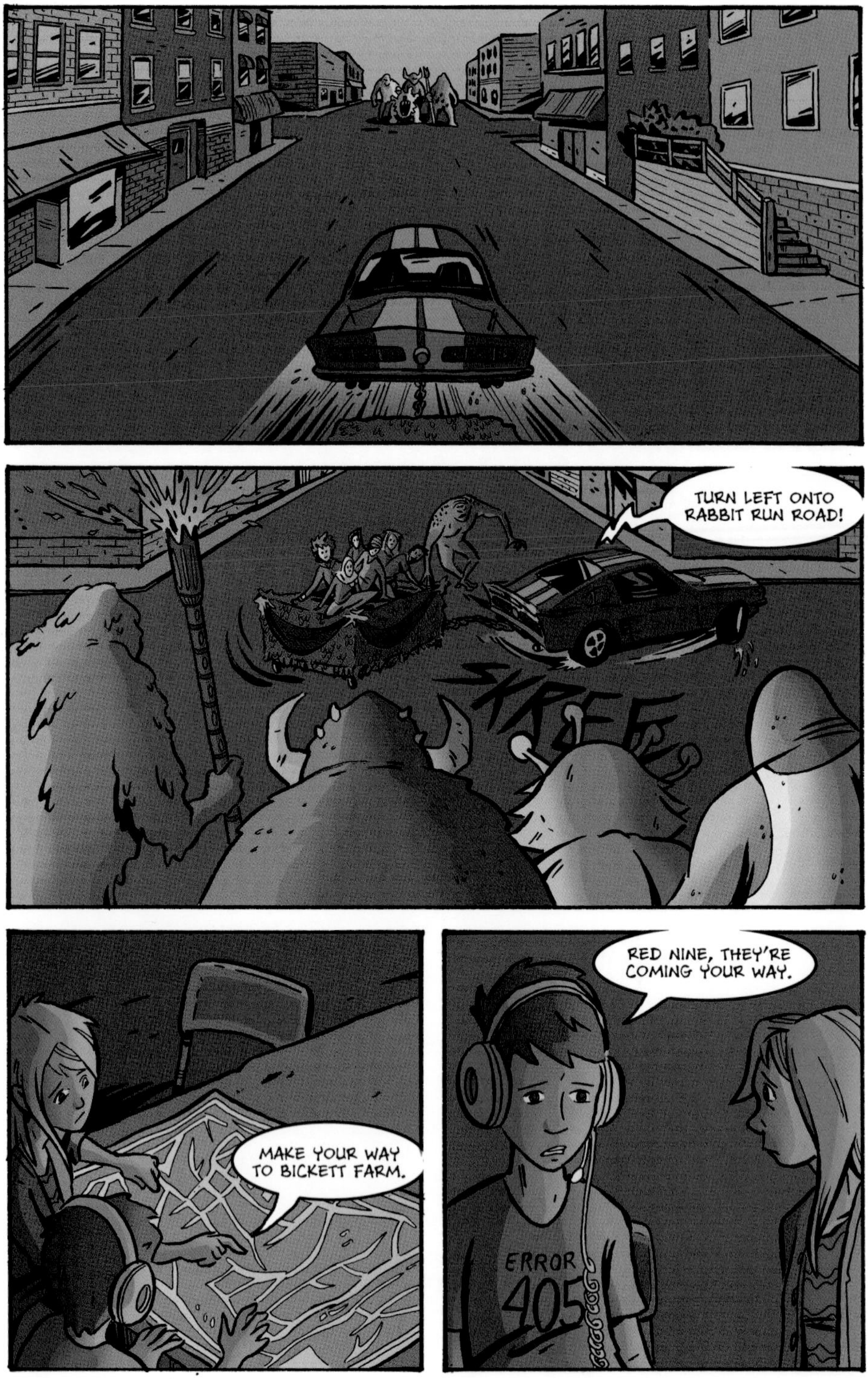
TURN LEFT ONTO RABBIT RUN ROAD!
SKREE
MAKE YOUR WAY TO BICKETT FARM.
RED NINE, THEY'RE COMING YOUR WAY.
ERROR 405

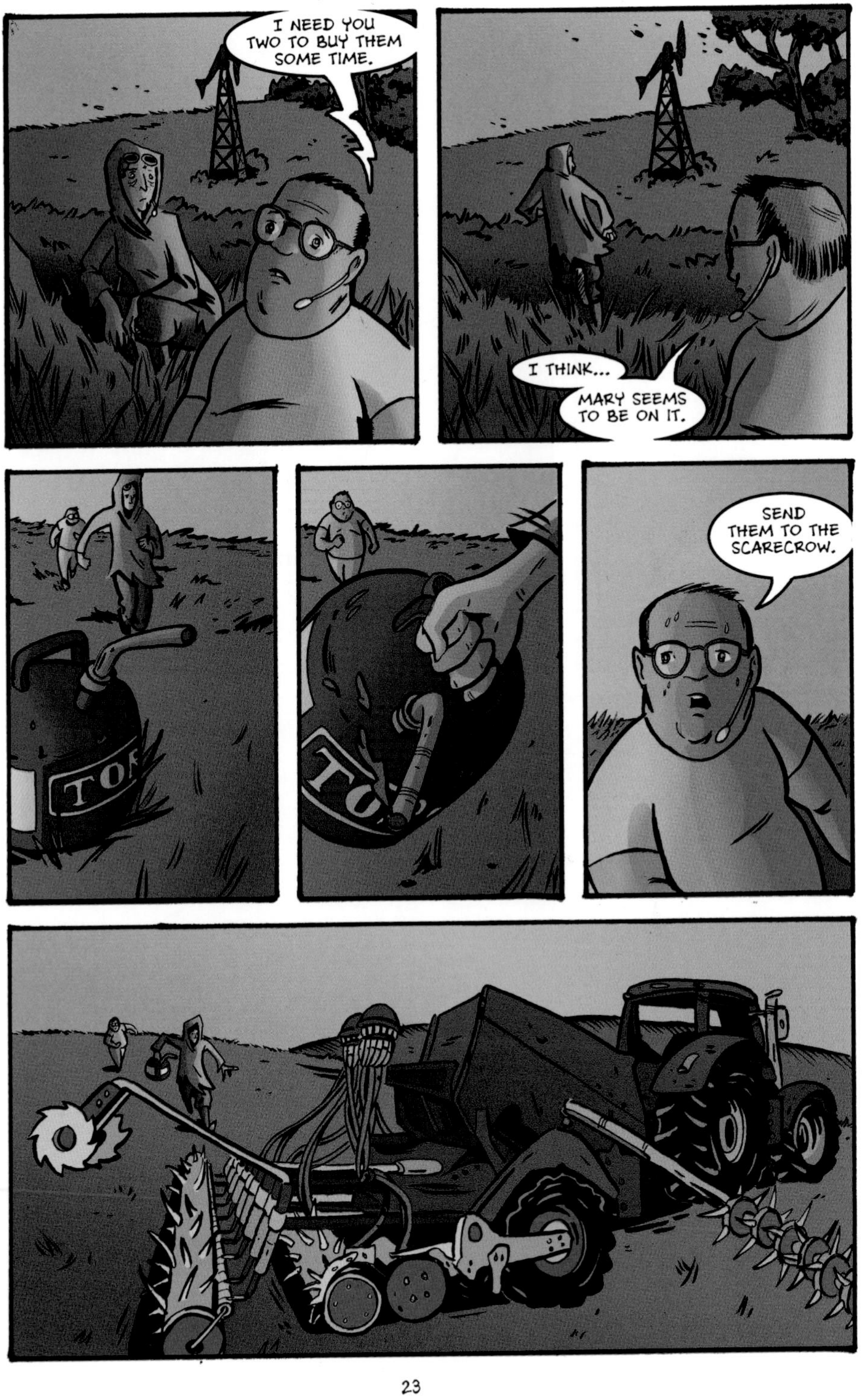
I NEED YOU TWO TO BUY THEM SOME TIME.
I THINK...
MARY SEEMS TO BE ON IT.
SEND THEM TO THE SCARECROW.

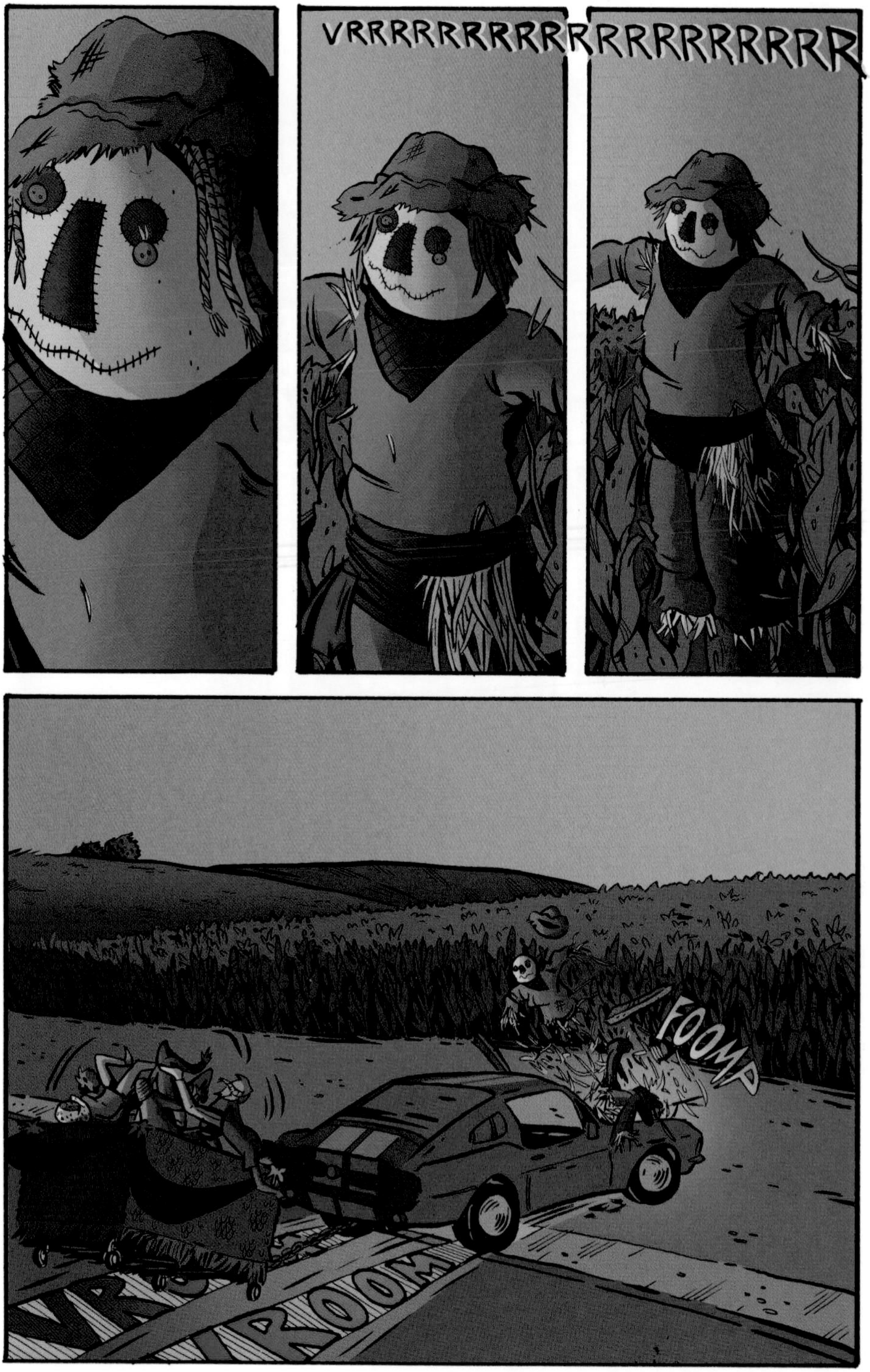
VRRRRRRRRRRRRRRRRRRRRR
FOOMP
VROOM

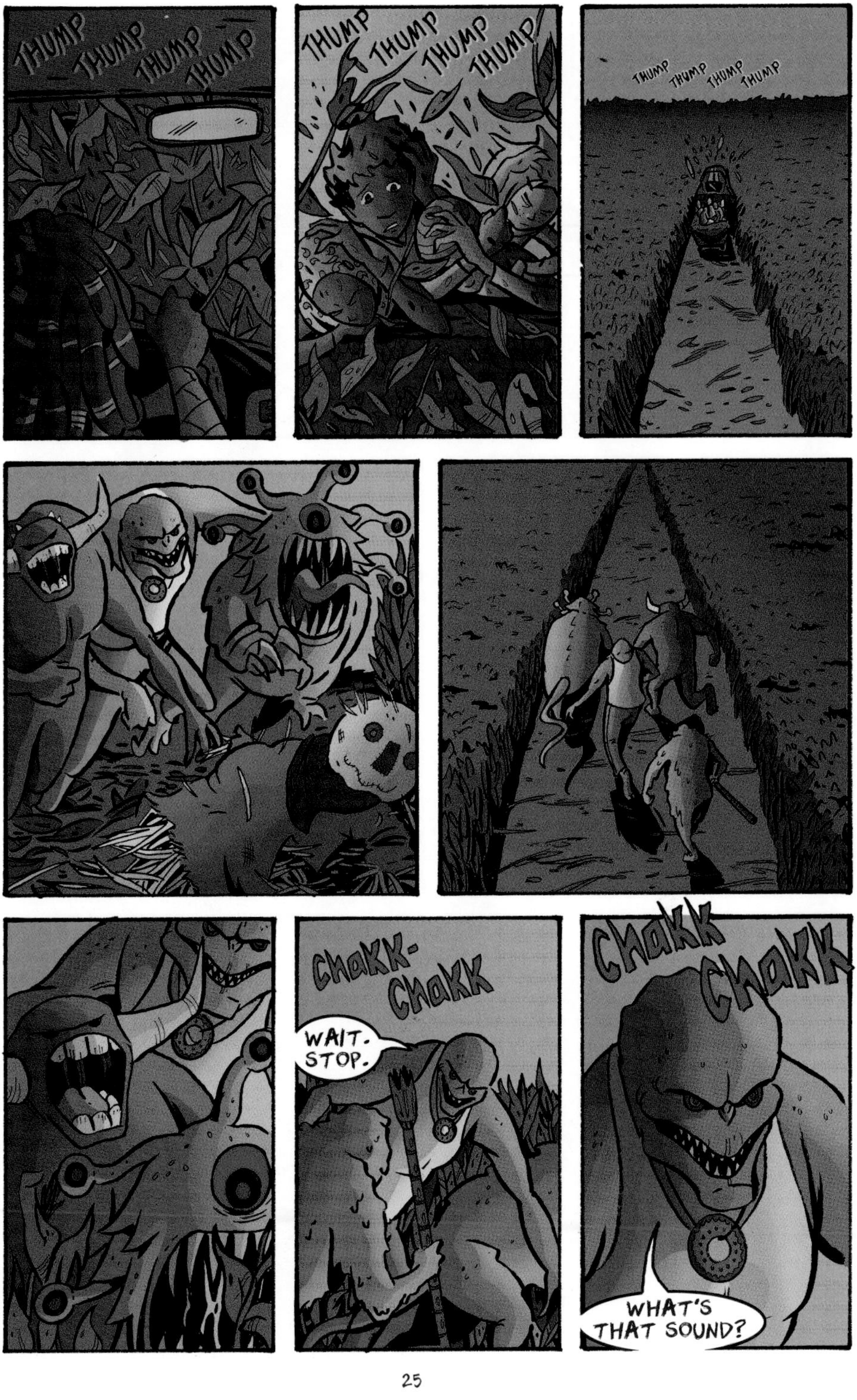
THUMP THUMP THUMP THUMP
THUMP THUMP THUMP THUMP
THUMP THUMP THUMP THUMP
CHAKK-CHAKK
WAIT. STOP.
CHAKK CHAKK
WHAT'S THAT SOUND?

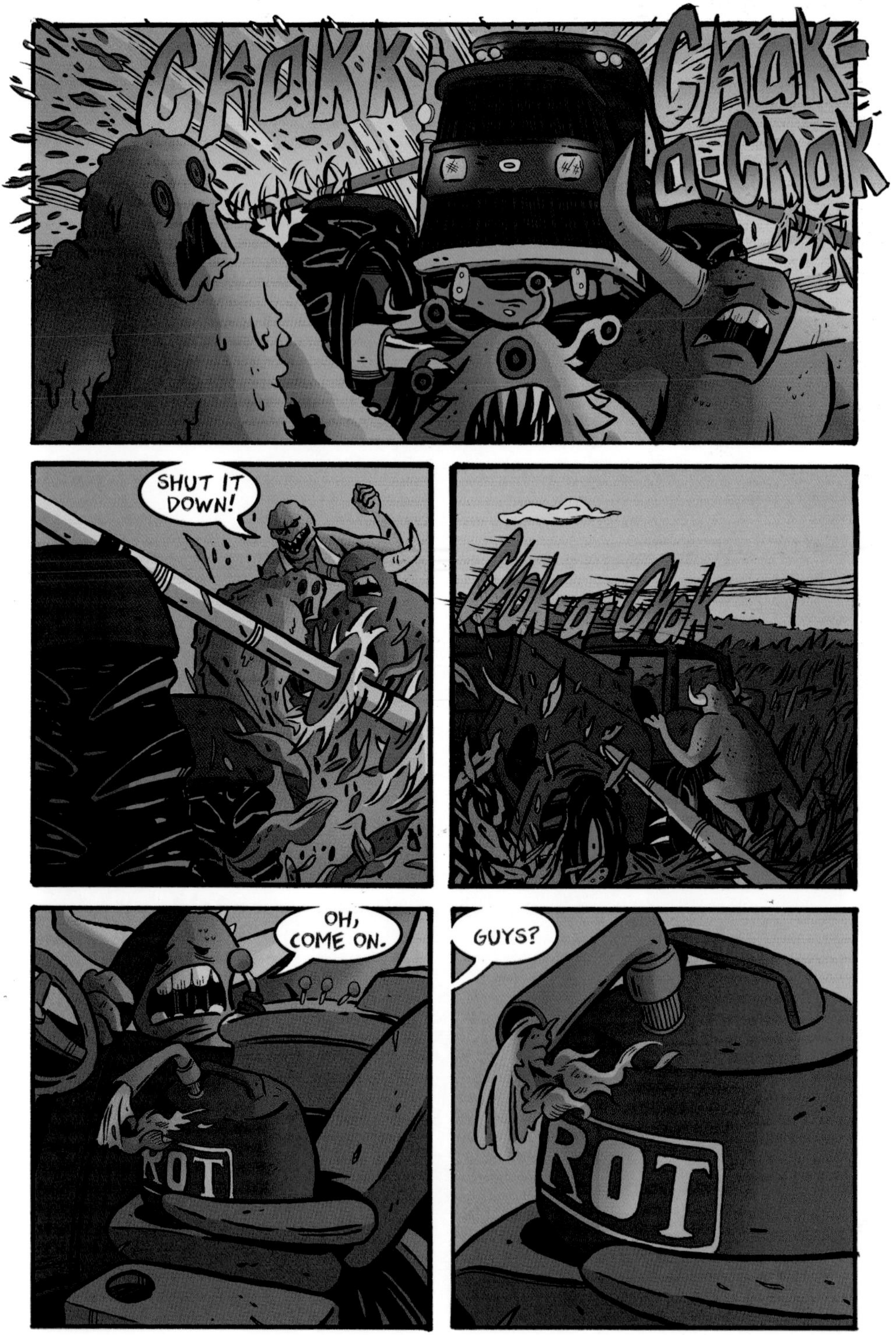

CHAKK!
CHAK-A-CHAK
SHUT IT DOWN!
CHAK-A-CHAK
OH, COME ON.
ROT
GUYS?
ROT

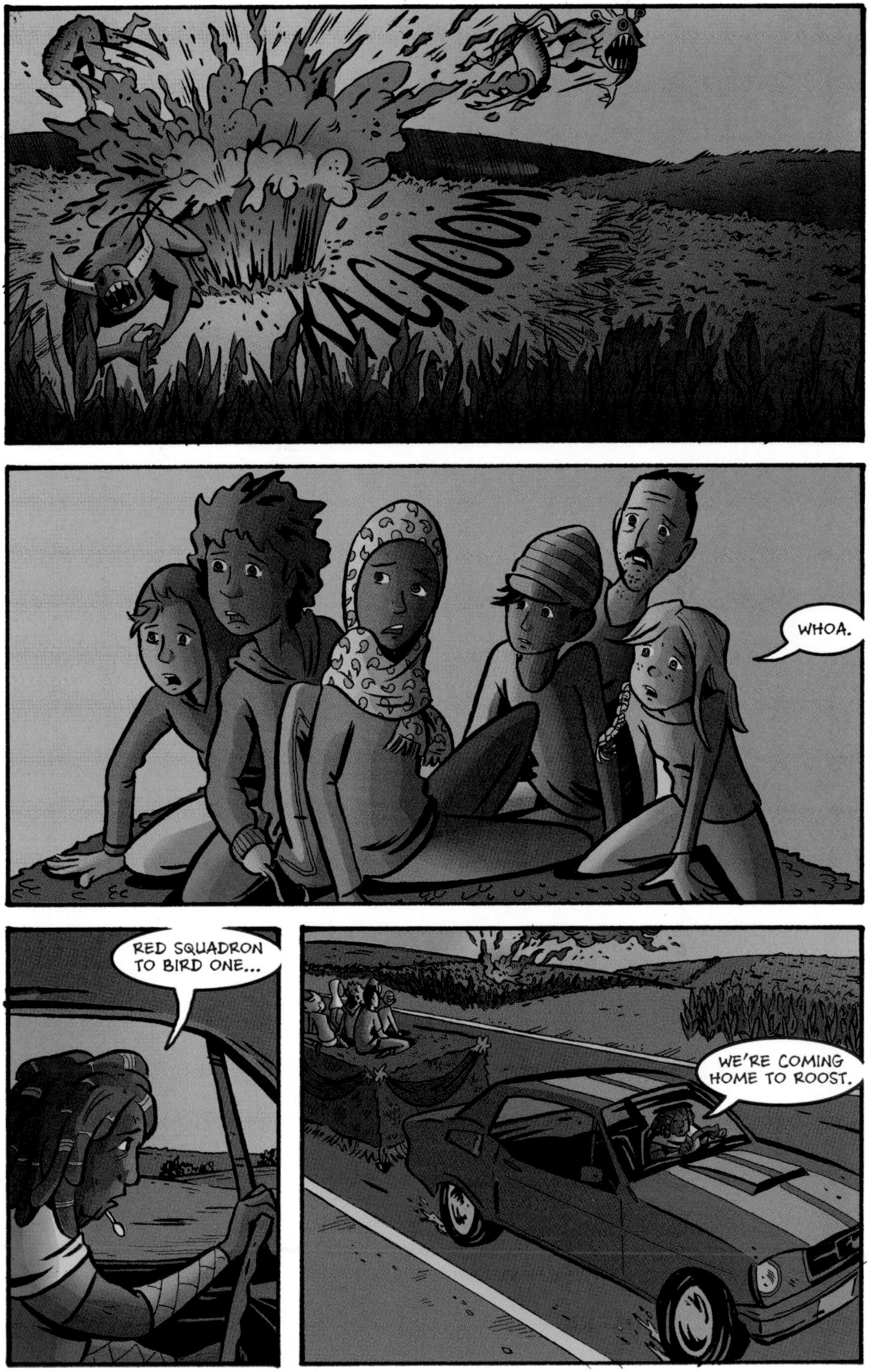
KA-CHOOM
WHOA.
RED SQUADRON TO BIRD ONE...
WE'RE COMING HOME TO ROOST.

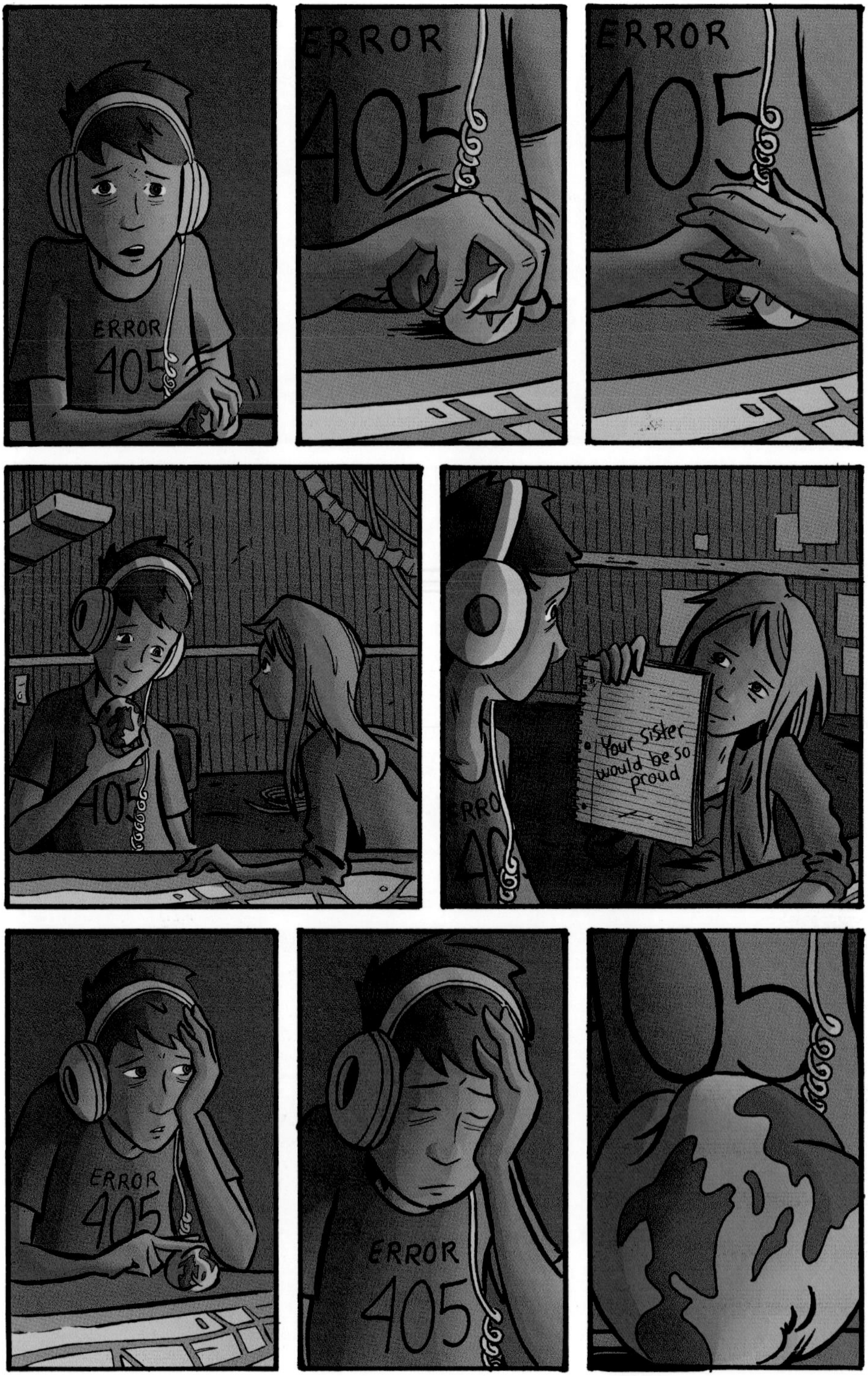
ERROR
405
ERROR
405
ERROR
405
405
Your sister would be so proud
ERROR
405
ERROR
405

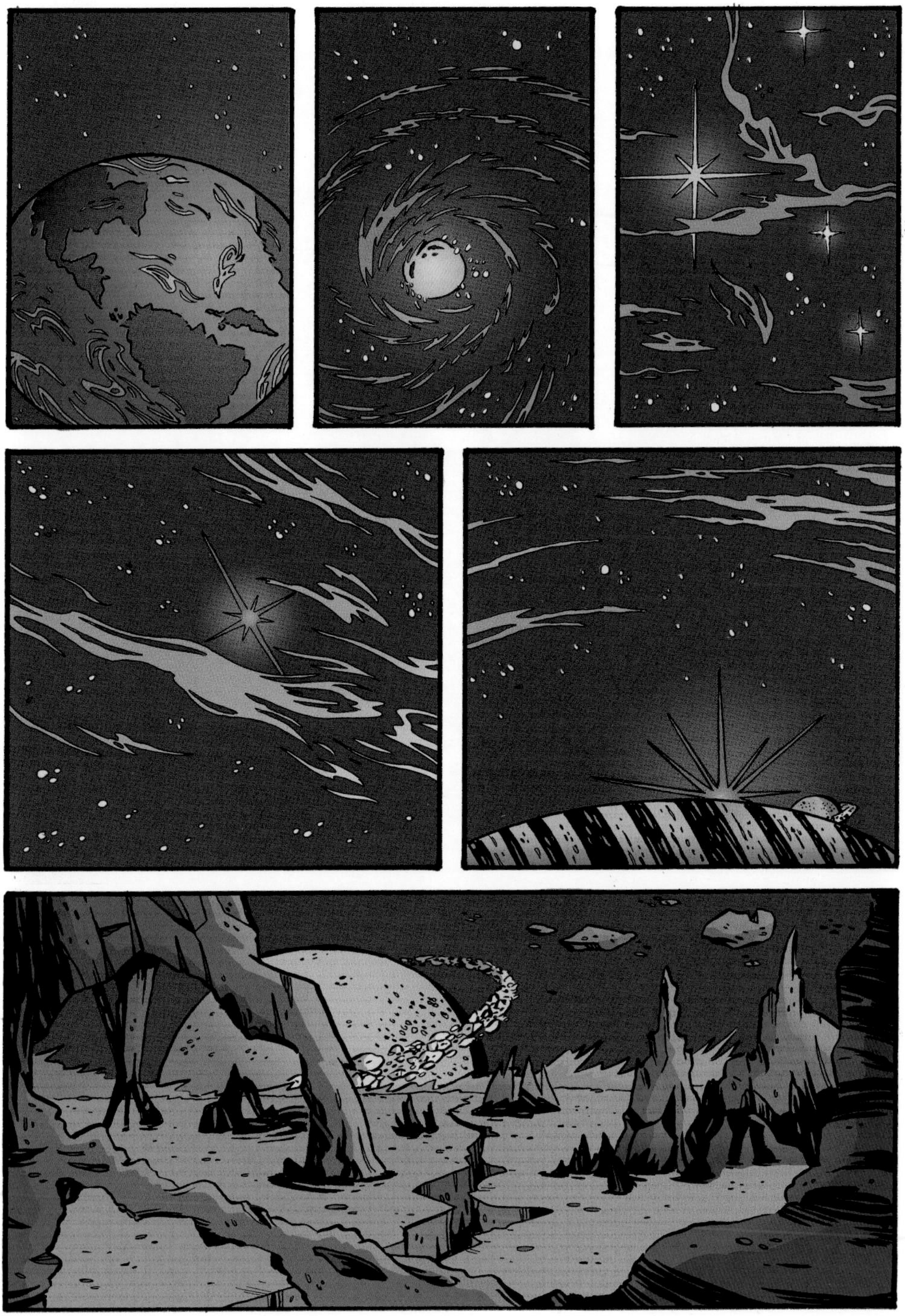

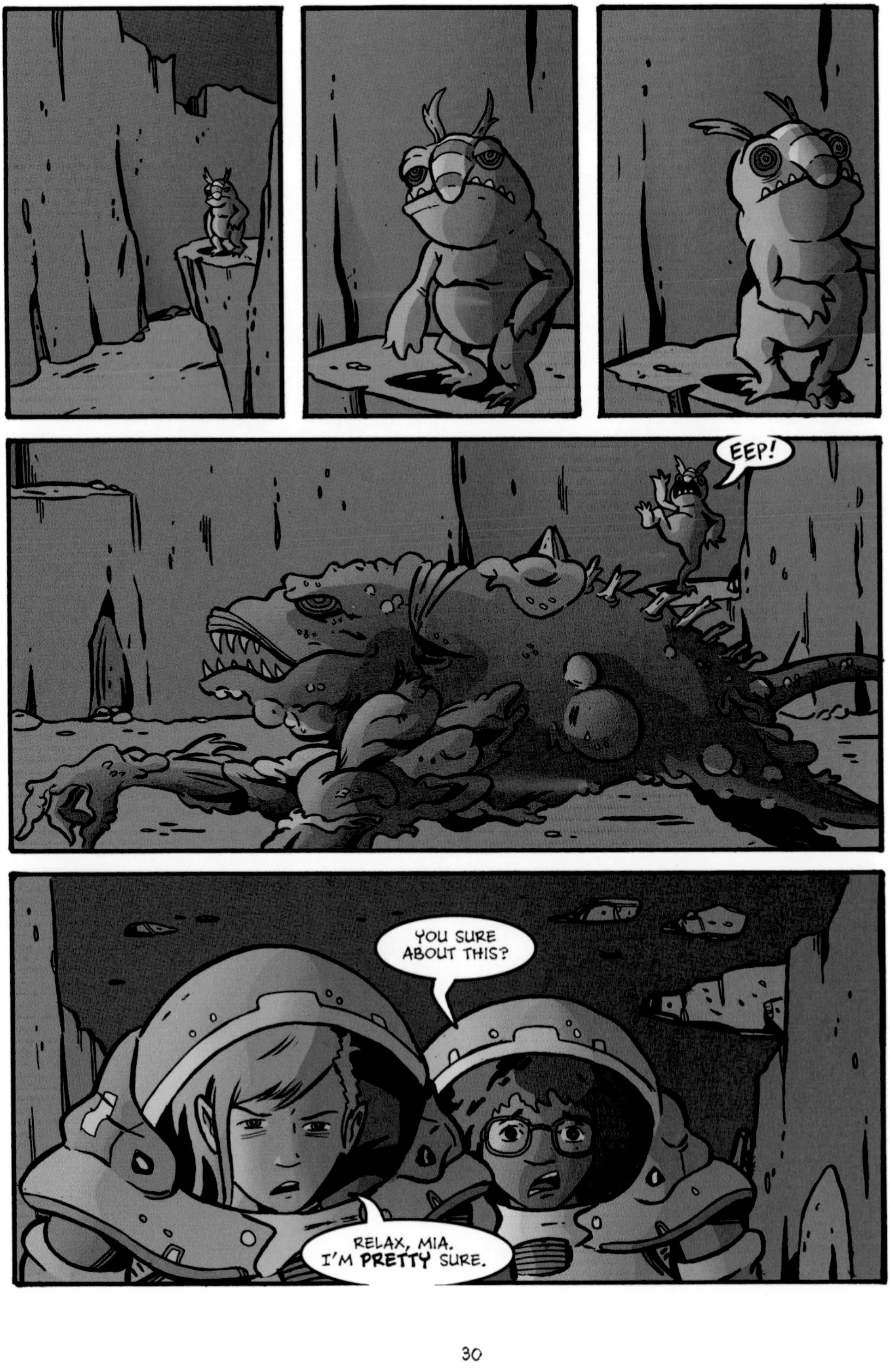
EEP!
YOU SURE ABOUT THIS?
RELAX, MIA. I'M PRETTY SURE.

"PRETTY SURE"?!

ARE YOU KIDDING ME?

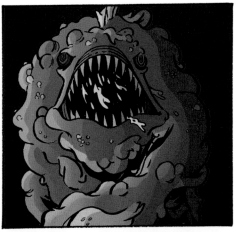

IF I'M "PRETTY SURE" I DON'T LIKE PINEAPPLES ON PIZZA, AND I FIND OUT I'M WRONG...

I DON'T END UP DEAD.

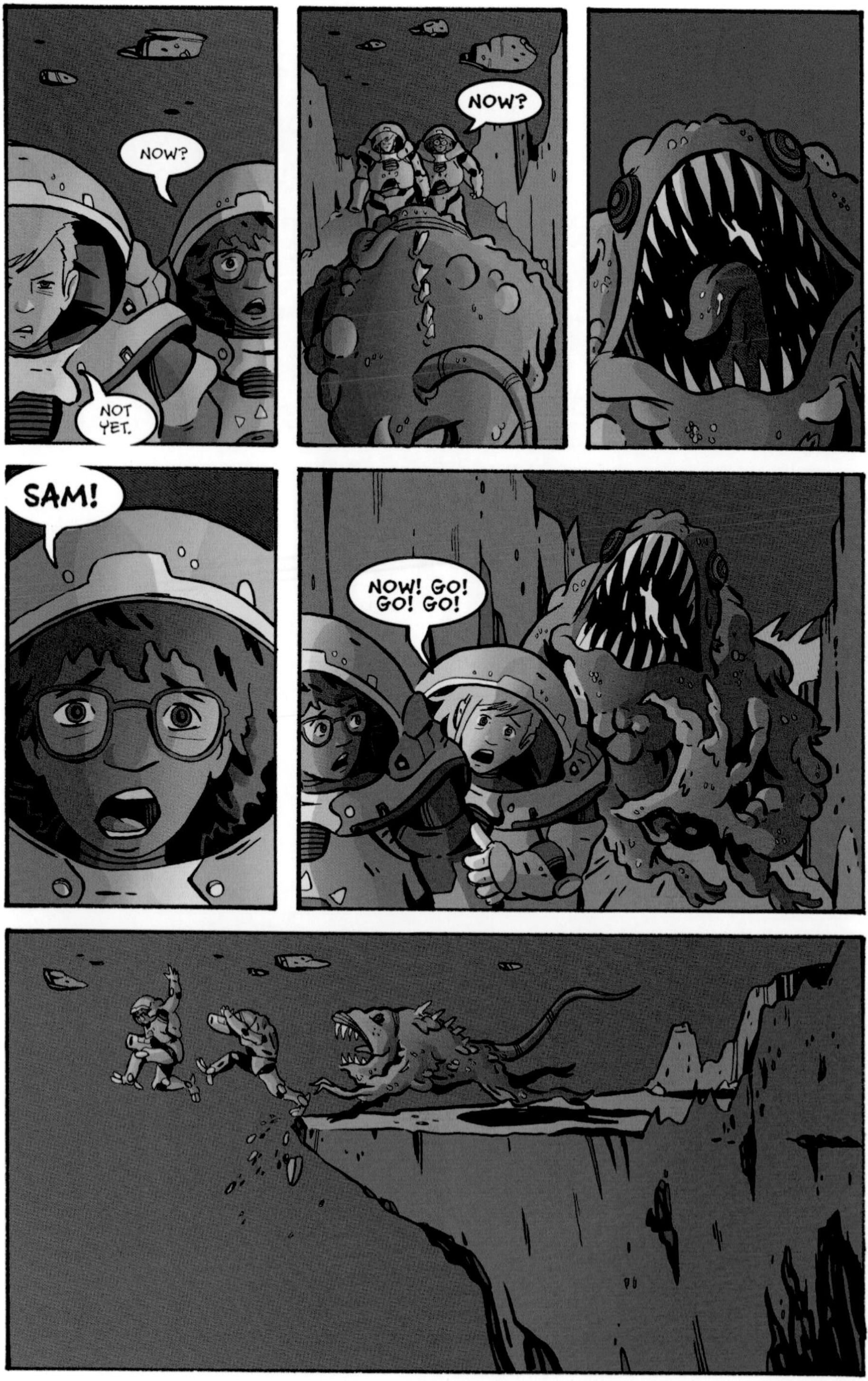
NOW?
NOT YET.
NOW?
SAM!
NOW! GO! GO! GO!

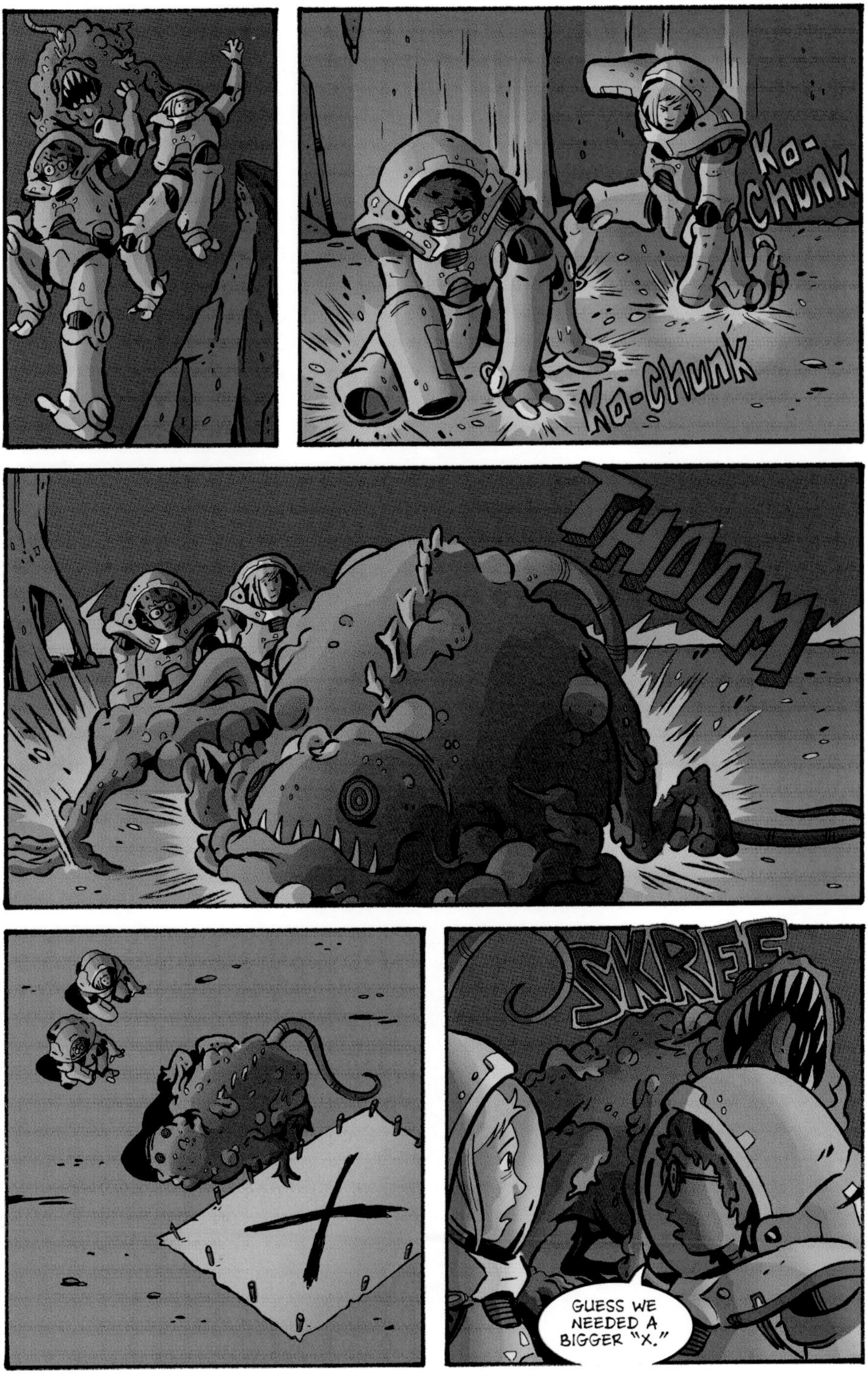
Ka-Chunk
Ka-Chunk
THOOM
SKREE
GUESS WE NEEDED A BIGGER "X."

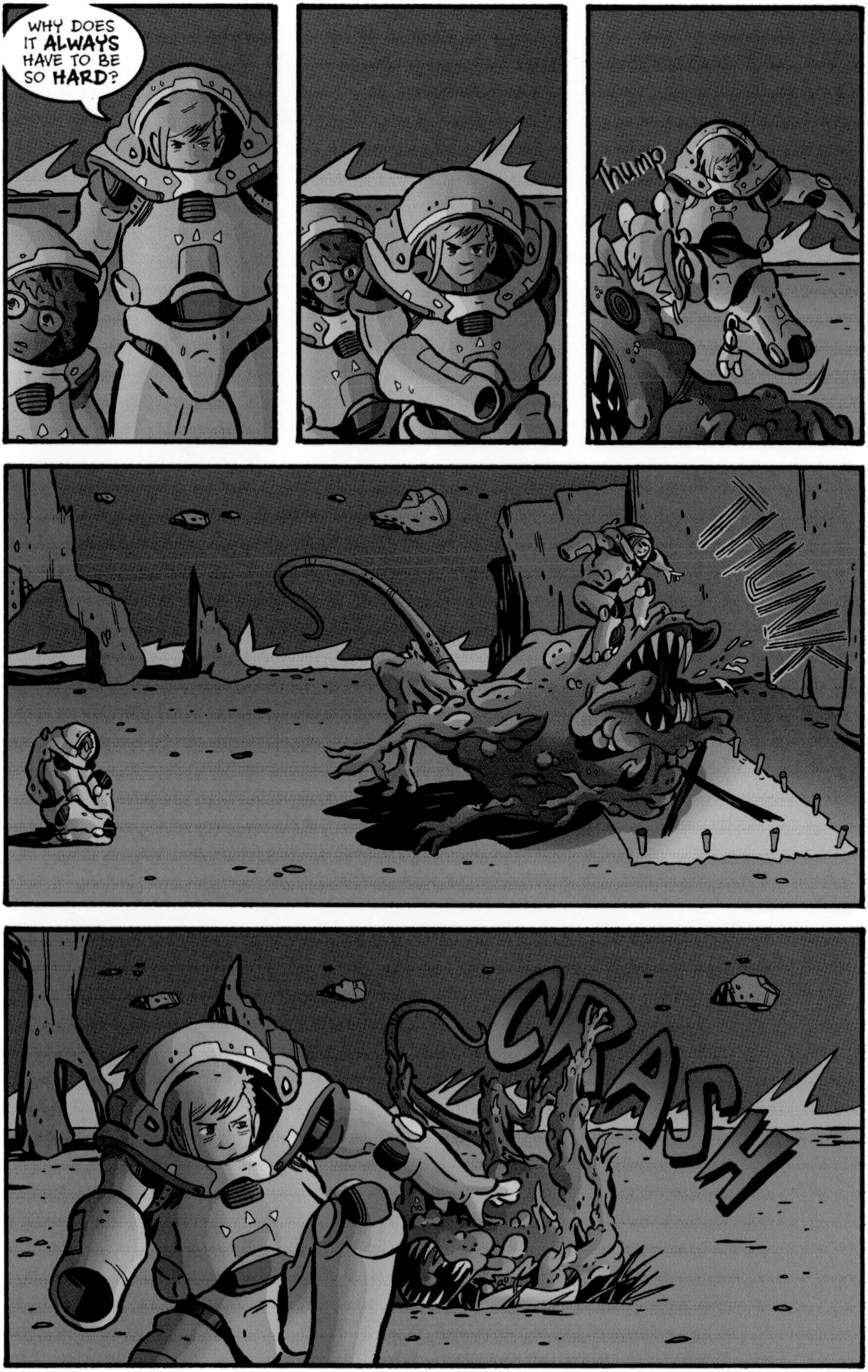

WHY DOES IT ALWAYS HAVE TO BE SO HARD?
Thump
THUNK
CRASH

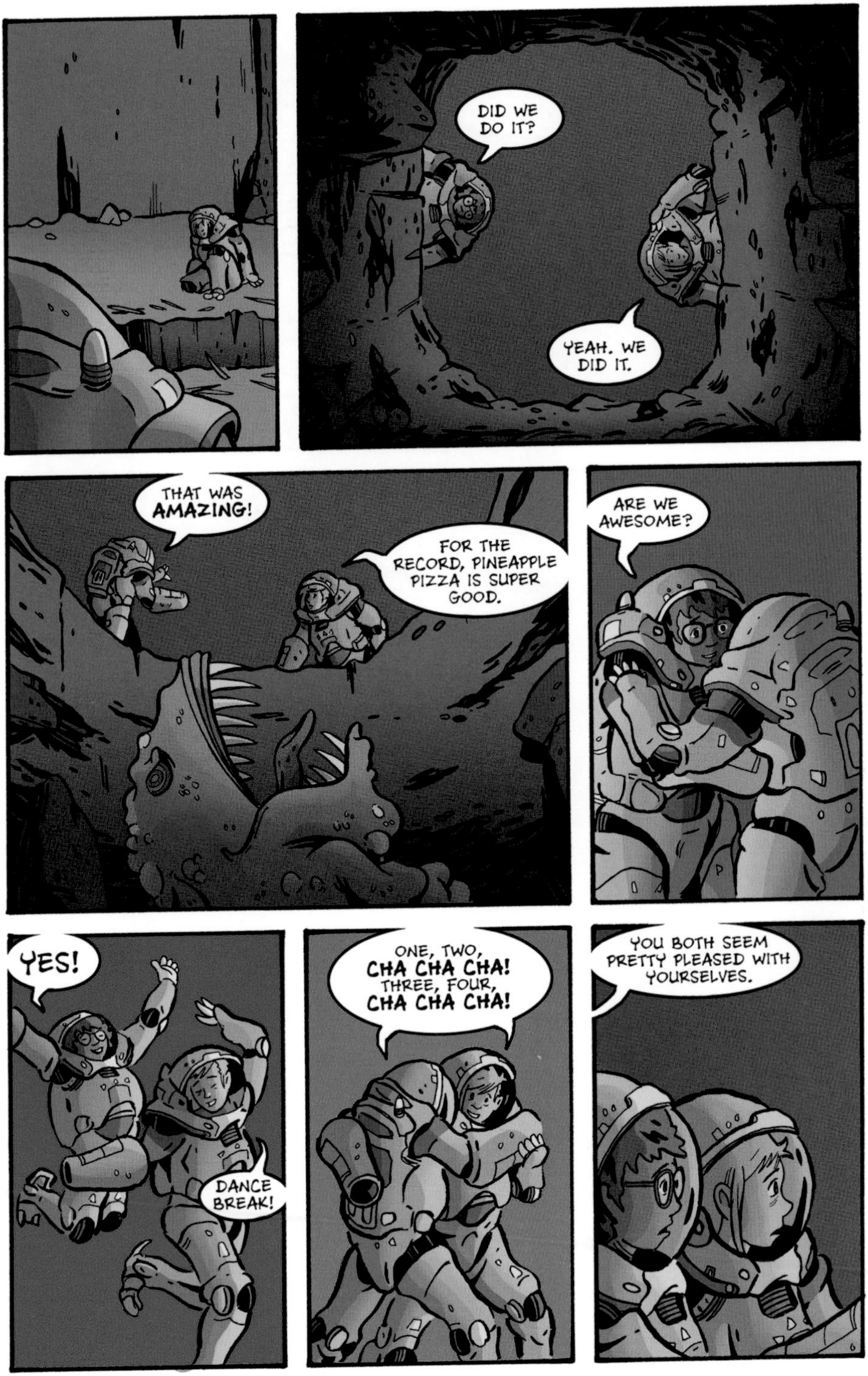

DID WE DO IT?
YEAH. WE DID IT.
THAT WAS **AMAZING!**
FOR THE RECORD, PINEAPPLE PIZZA IS SUPER GOOD.
ARE WE AWESOME?
YES!
DANCE BREAK!
ONE, TWO, **CHA CHA CHA!** THREE, FOUR, **CHA CHA CHA!**
YOU BOTH SEEM PRETTY PLEASED WITH YOURSELVES.

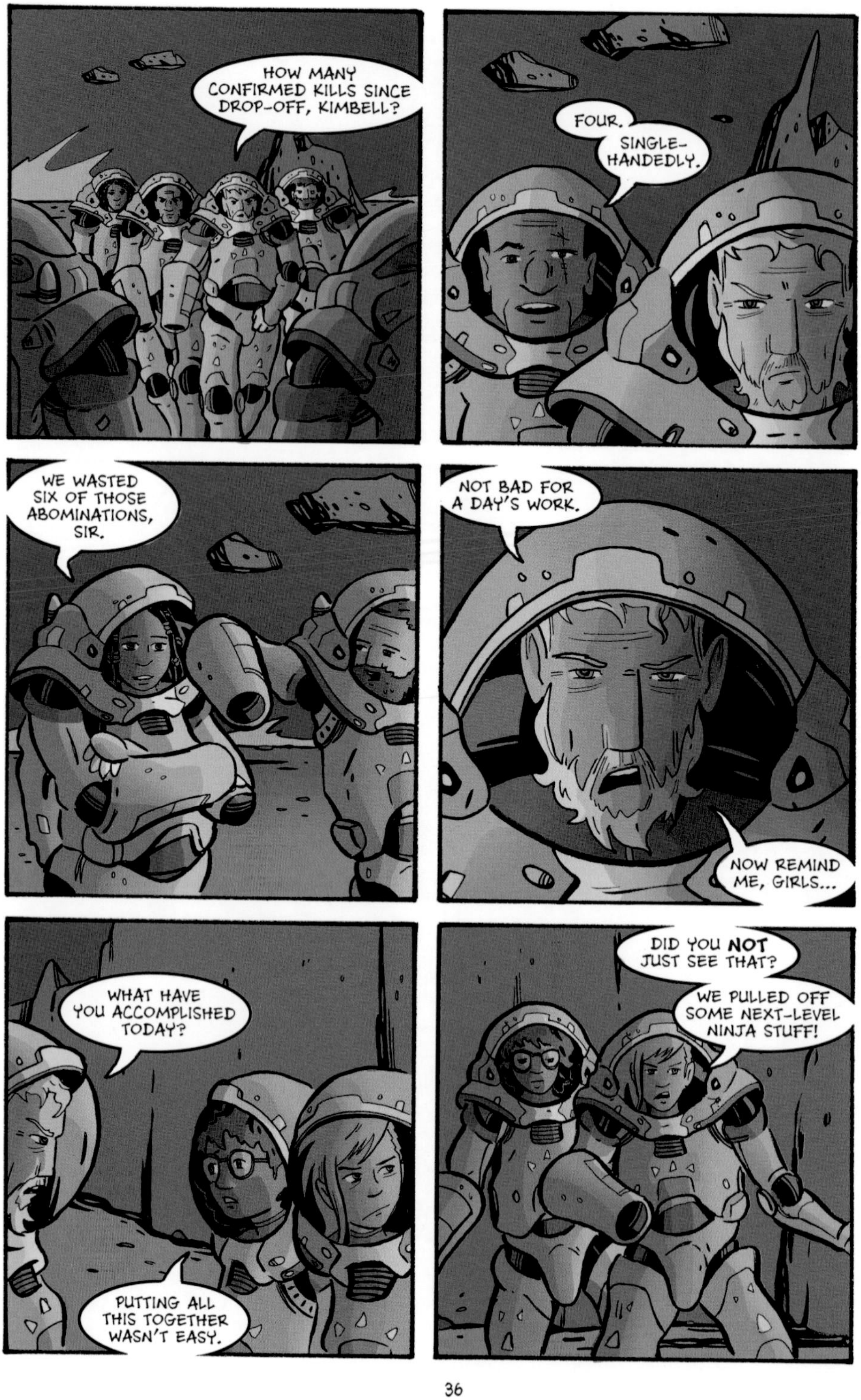
HOW MANY CONFIRMED KILLS SINCE DROP-OFF, KIMBELL?
FOUR.
SINGLE-HANDEDLY.
WE WASTED SIX OF THOSE ABOMINATIONS, SIR.
NOT BAD FOR A DAY'S WORK.
NOW REMIND ME, GIRLS...
WHAT HAVE YOU ACCOMPLISHED TODAY?
PUTTING ALL THIS TOGETHER WASN'T EASY.
DID YOU **NOT** JUST SEE THAT?
WE PULLED OFF SOME NEXT-LEVEL NINJA STUFF!

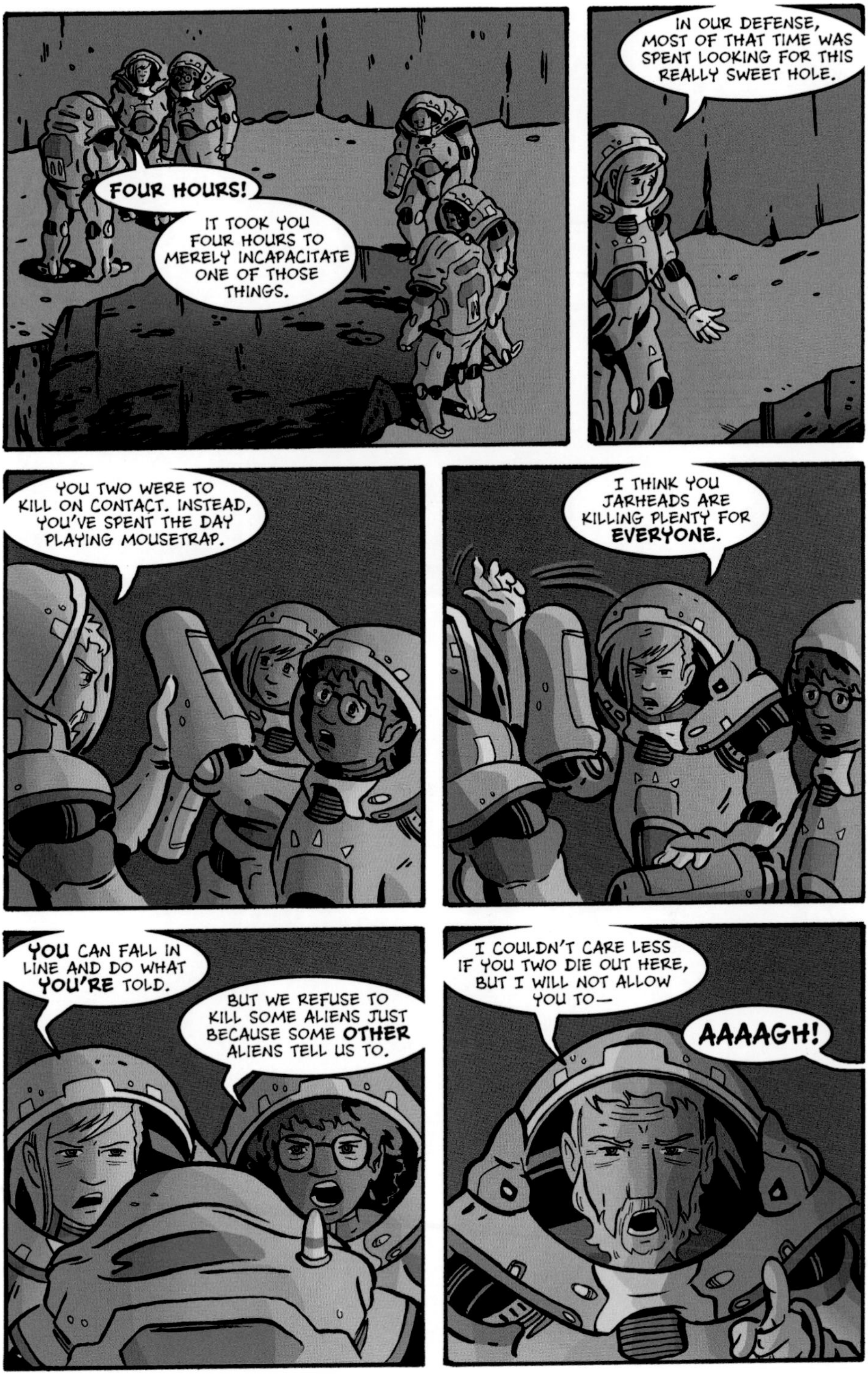
FOUR HOURS!
IT TOOK YOU FOUR HOURS TO MERELY INCAPACITATE ONE OF THOSE THINGS.
IN OUR DEFENSE, MOST OF THAT TIME WAS SPENT LOOKING FOR THIS REALLY SWEET HOLE.
YOU TWO WERE TO KILL ON CONTACT. INSTEAD, YOU'VE SPENT THE DAY PLAYING MOUSETRAP.
I THINK YOU JARHEADS ARE KILLING PLENTY FOR EVERYONE.
YOU CAN FALL IN LINE AND DO WHAT YOU'RE TOLD.
BUT WE REFUSE TO KILL SOME ALIENS JUST BECAUSE SOME OTHER ALIENS TELL US TO.
I COULDN'T CARE LESS IF YOU TWO DIE OUT HERE, BUT I WILL NOT ALLOW YOU TO—
AAAAGH!

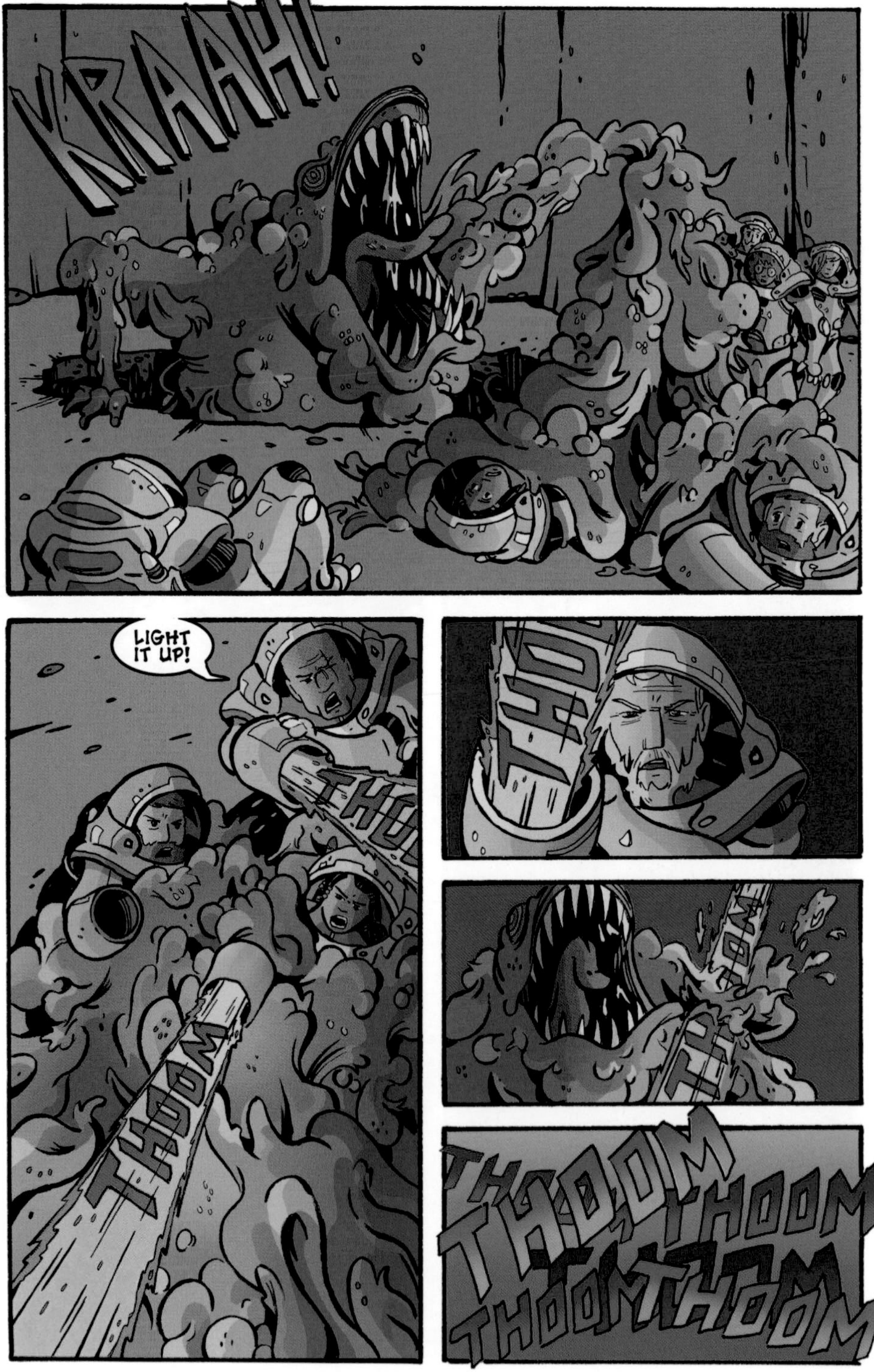
KRAAAH!
LIGHT IT UP!
THOOM
THOOM
THOOM
THOOM THOOM

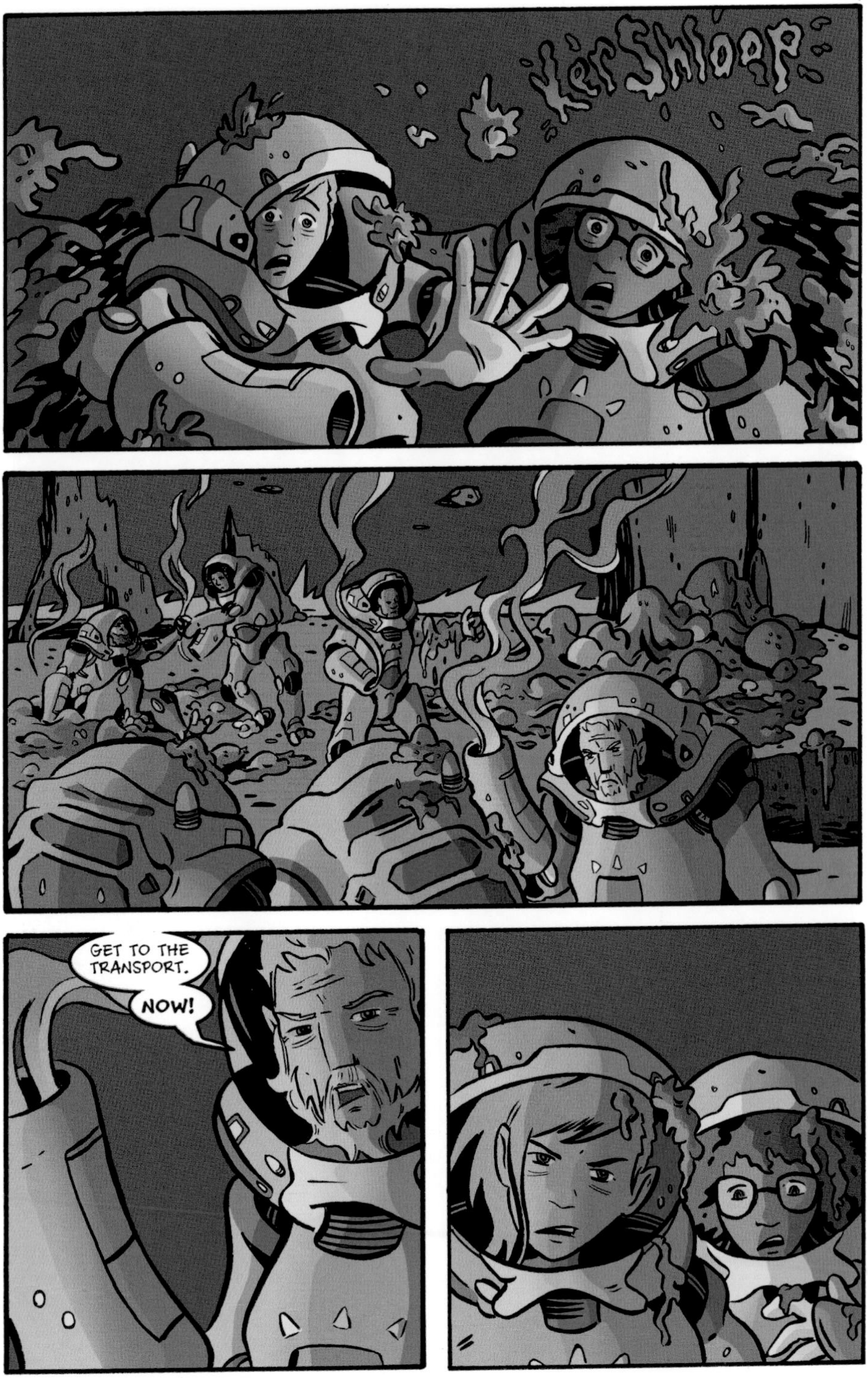
KERSHLOOP
GET TO THE TRANSPORT.
NOW!

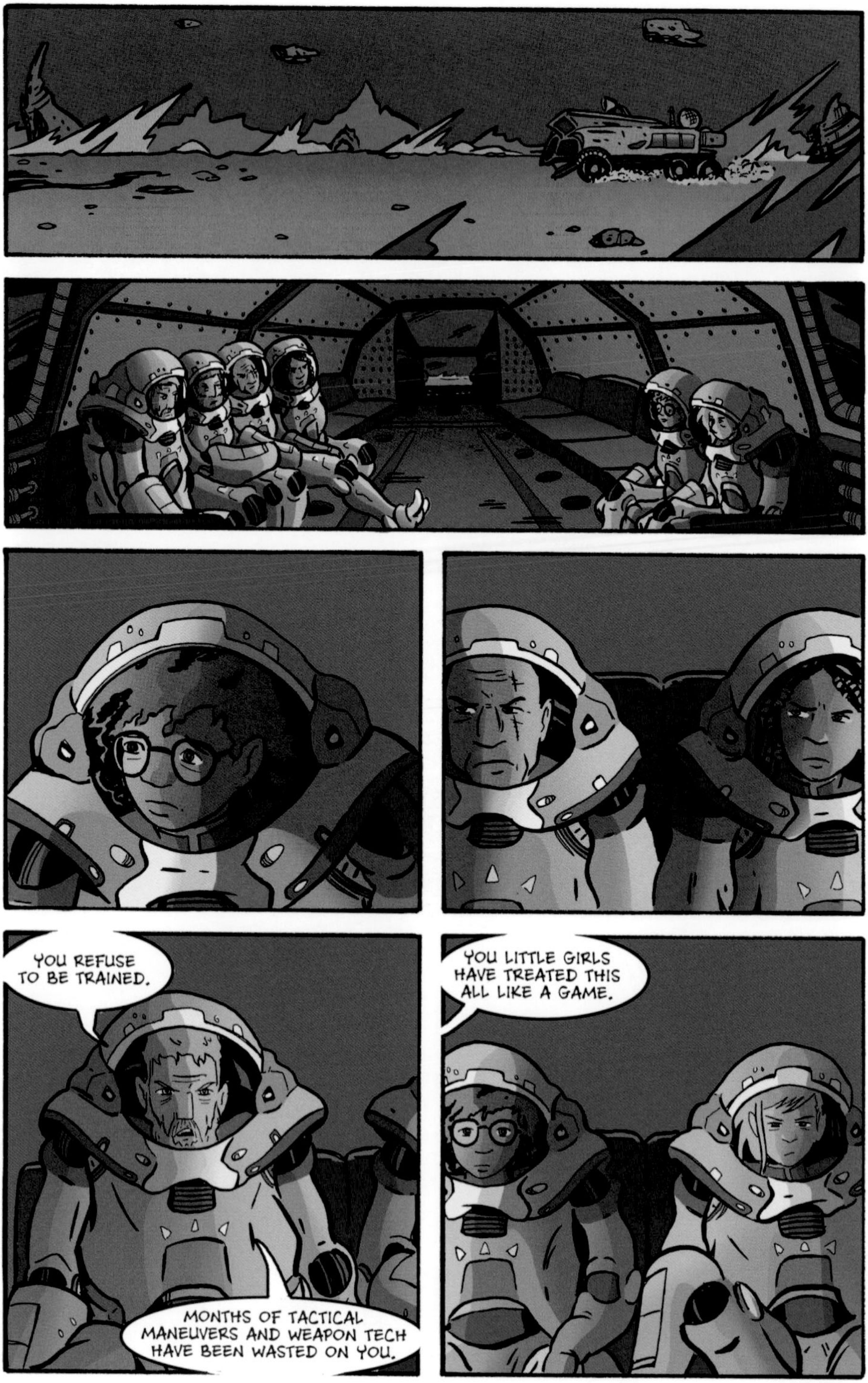
YOU REFUSE TO BE TRAINED.
MONTHS OF TACTICAL MANEUVERS AND WEAPON TECH HAVE BEEN WASTED ON YOU.
YOU LITTLE GIRLS HAVE TREATED THIS ALL LIKE A GAME.

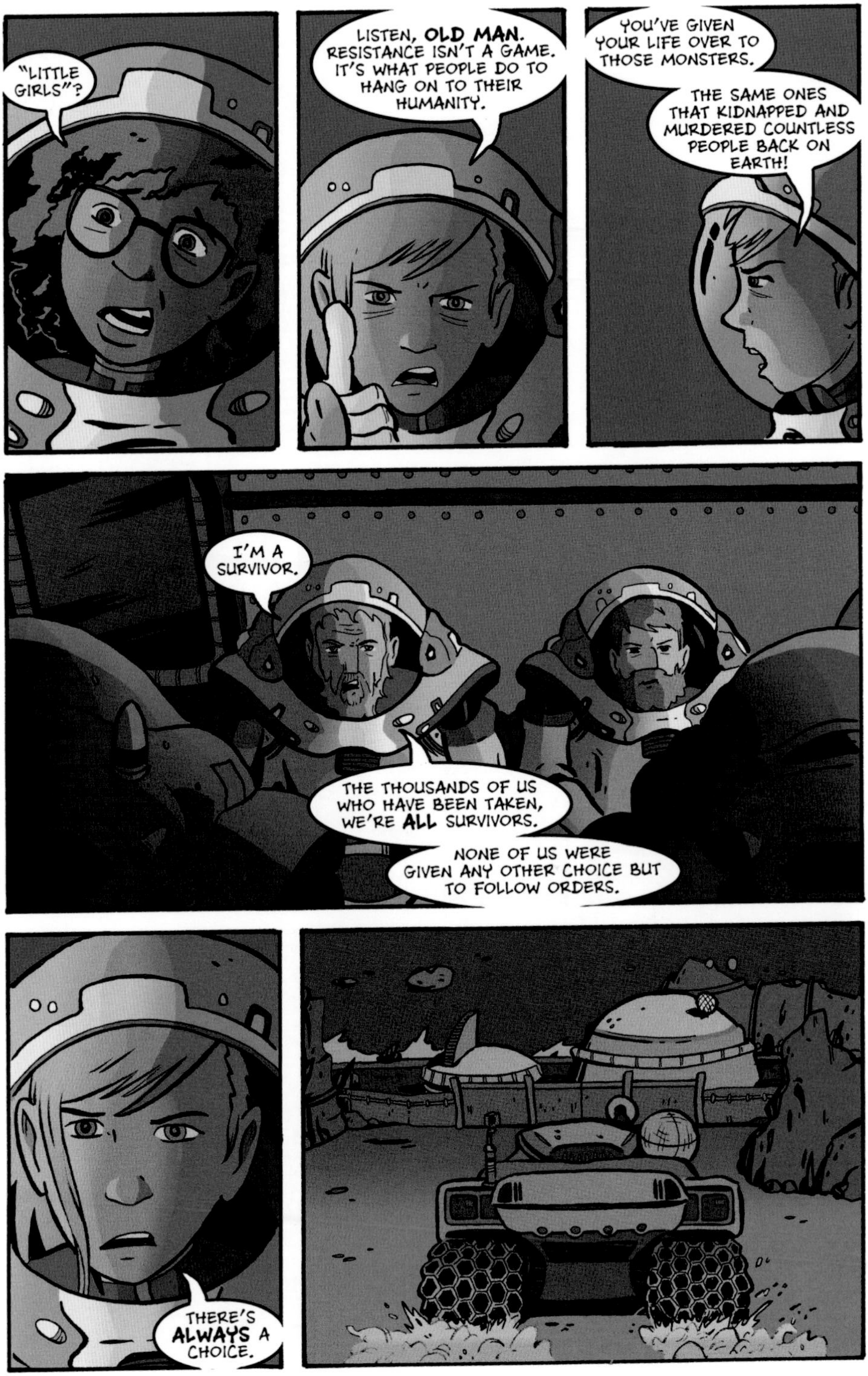
"LITTLE GIRLS"?
LISTEN, OLD MAN. RESISTANCE ISN'T A GAME. IT'S WHAT PEOPLE DO TO HANG ON TO THEIR HUMANITY.
YOU'VE GIVEN YOUR LIFE OVER TO THOSE MONSTERS.
THE SAME ONES THAT KIDNAPPED AND MURDERED COUNTLESS PEOPLE BACK ON EARTH!
I'M A SURVIVOR.
THE THOUSANDS OF US WHO HAVE BEEN TAKEN, WE'RE ALL SURVIVORS.
NONE OF US WERE GIVEN ANY OTHER CHOICE BUT TO FOLLOW ORDERS.
THERE'S ALWAYS A CHOICE.

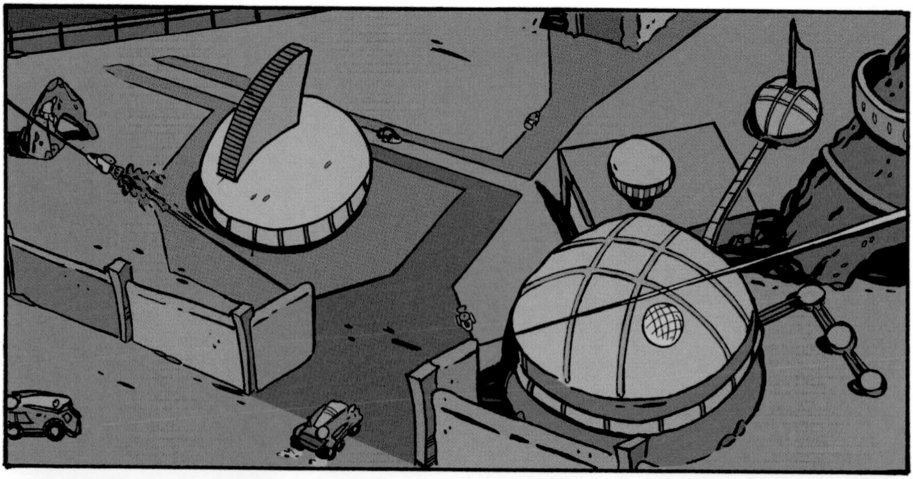

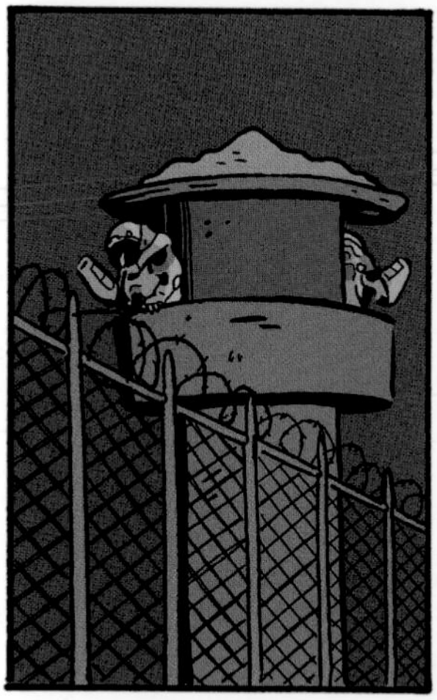

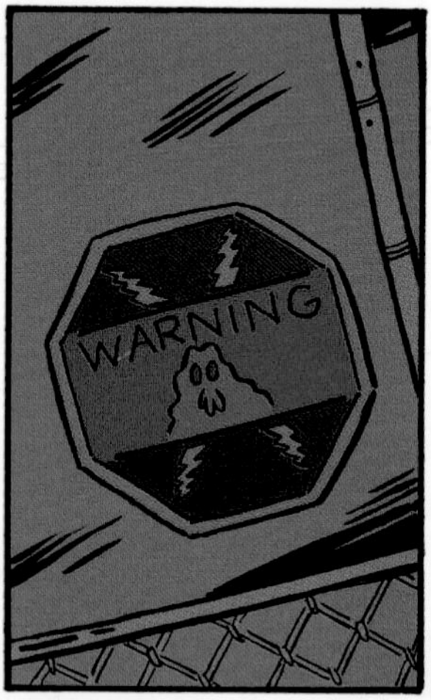
WARNING

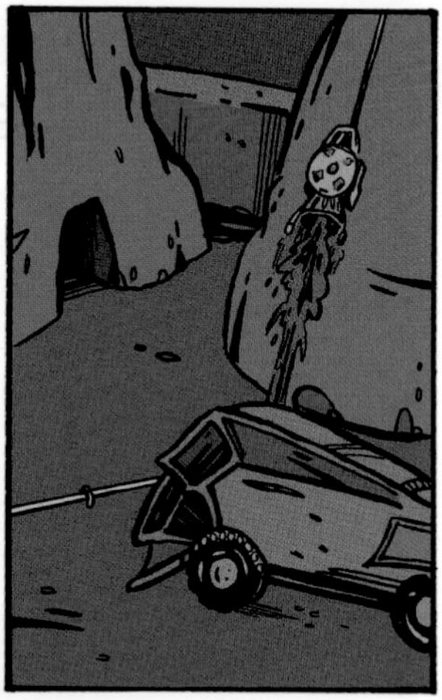

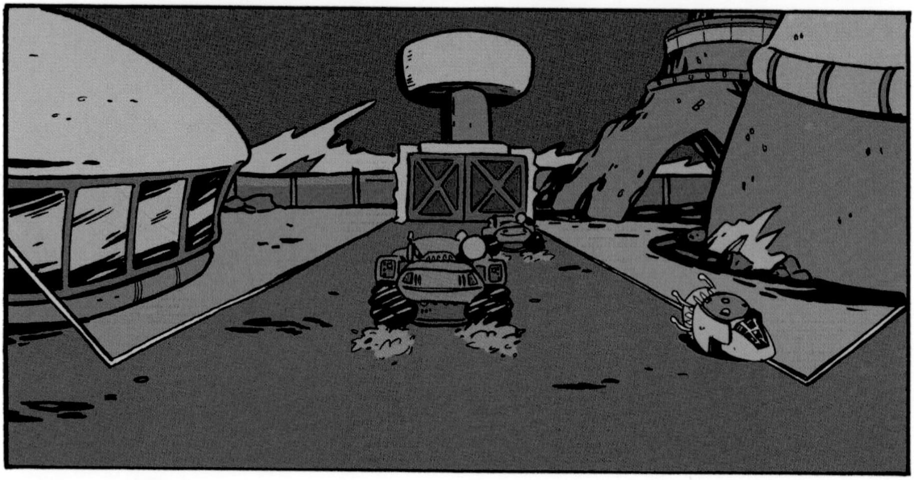

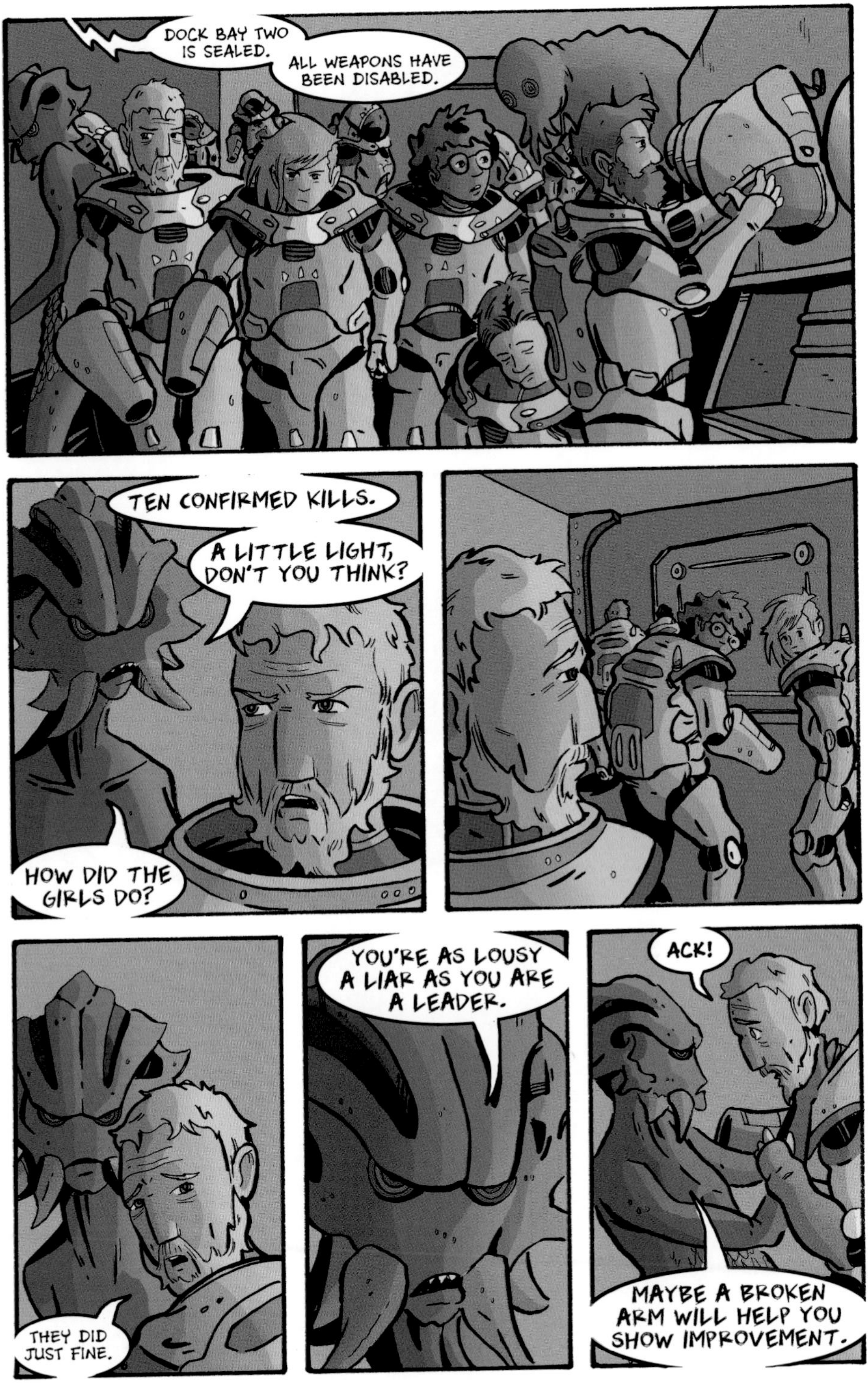
DOCK BAY TWO IS SEALED.
ALL WEAPONS HAVE BEEN DISABLED.
TEN CONFIRMED KILLS.
A LITTLE LIGHT, DON'T YOU THINK?
HOW DID THE GIRLS DO?
THEY DID JUST FINE.
YOU'RE AS LOUSY A LIAR AS YOU ARE A LEADER.
ACK!
MAYBE A BROKEN ARM WILL HELP YOU SHOW IMPROVEMENT.

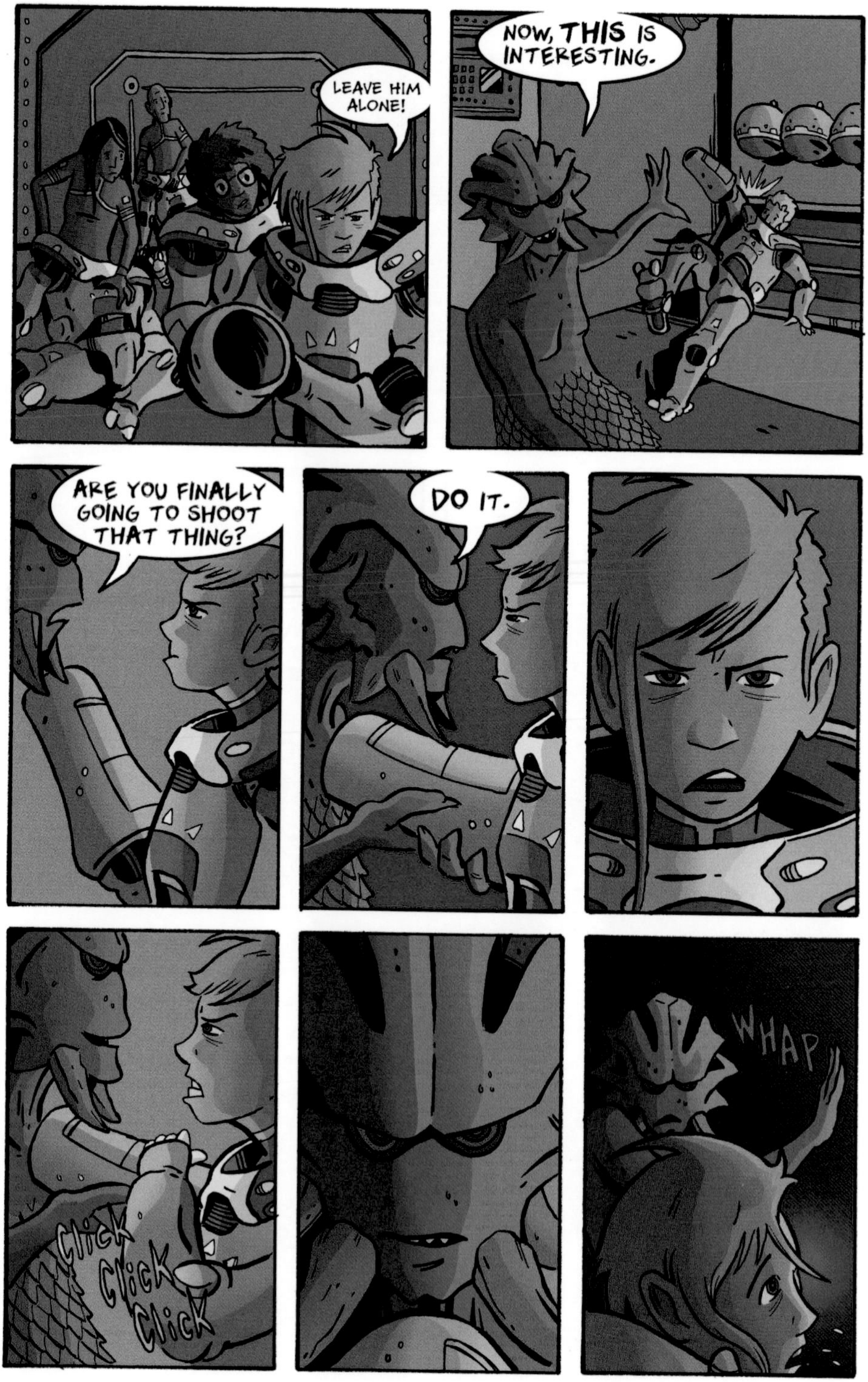
LEAVE HIM ALONE!
NOW, THIS IS INTERESTING.
ARE YOU FINALLY GOING TO SHOOT THAT THING?
DO IT.
CLICK CLICK CLICK
WHAP

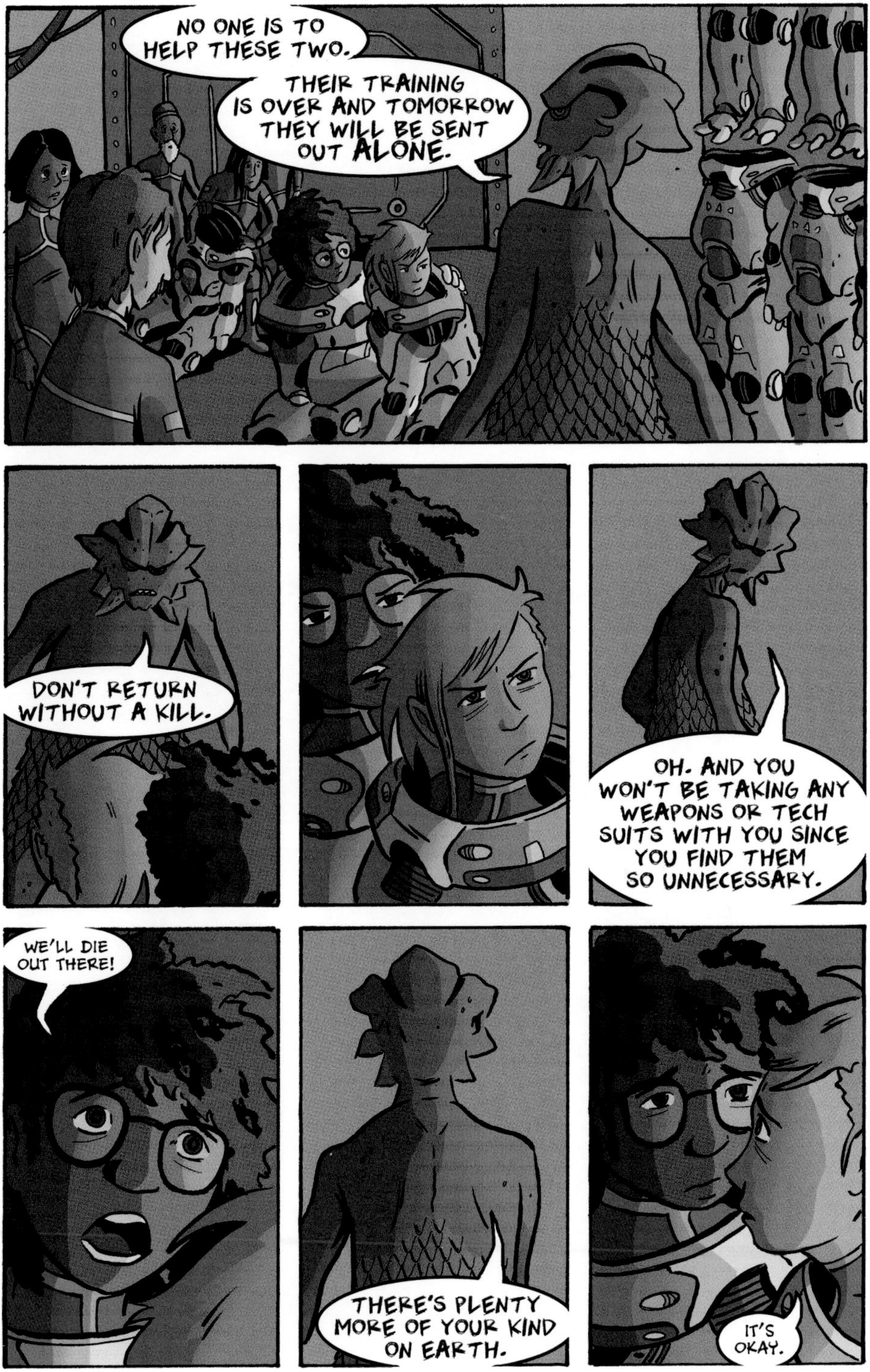
NO ONE IS TO HELP THESE TWO.
THEIR TRAINING IS OVER AND TOMORROW THEY WILL BE SENT OUT ALONE.
DON'T RETURN WITHOUT A KILL.
OH. AND YOU WON'T BE TAKING ANY WEAPONS OR TECH SUITS WITH YOU SINCE YOU FIND THEM SO UNNECESSARY.
WE'LL DIE OUT THERE!
THERE'S PLENTY MORE OF YOUR KIND ON EARTH.
IT'S OKAY.

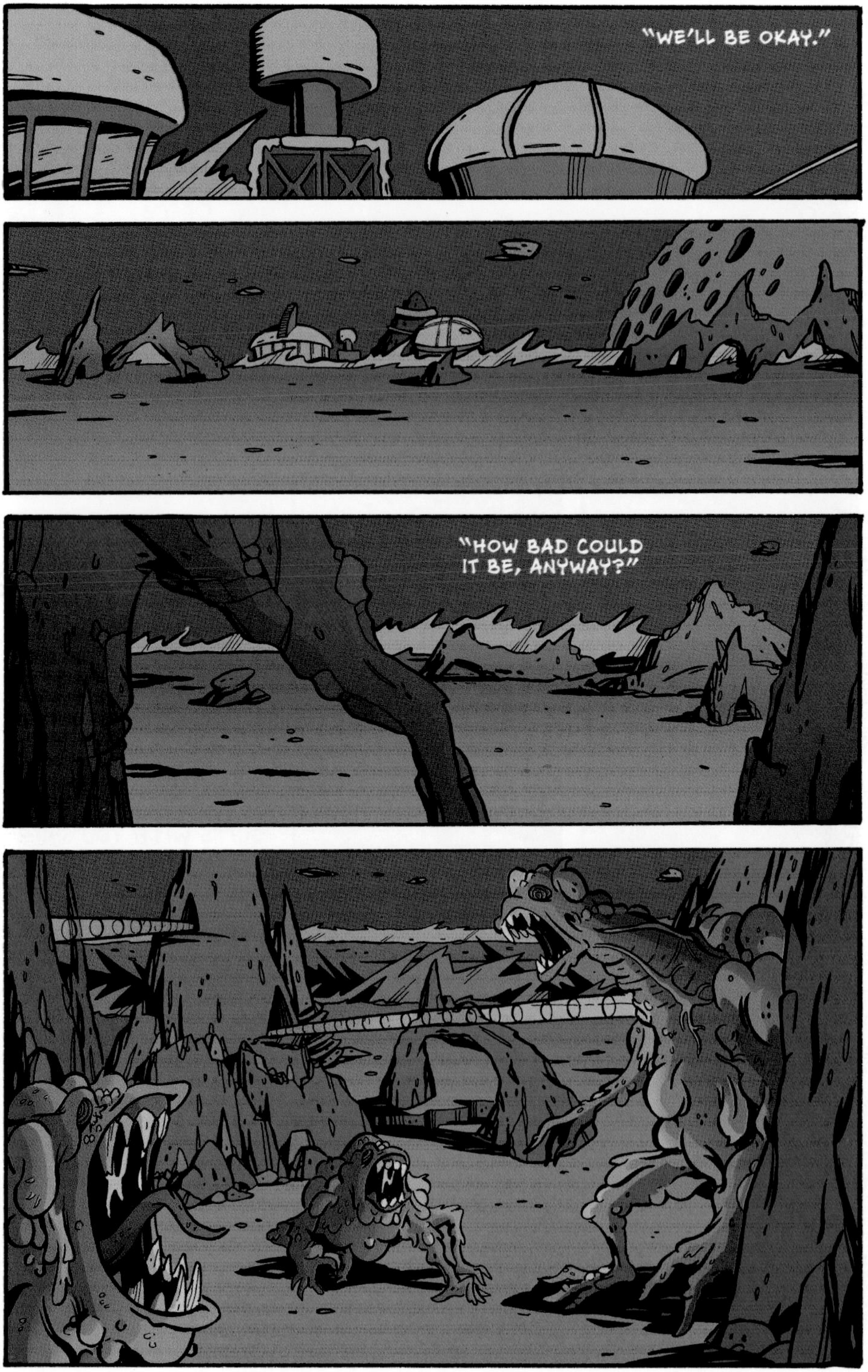
"WE'LL BE OKAY."
"HOW BAD COULD IT BE, ANYWAY?"

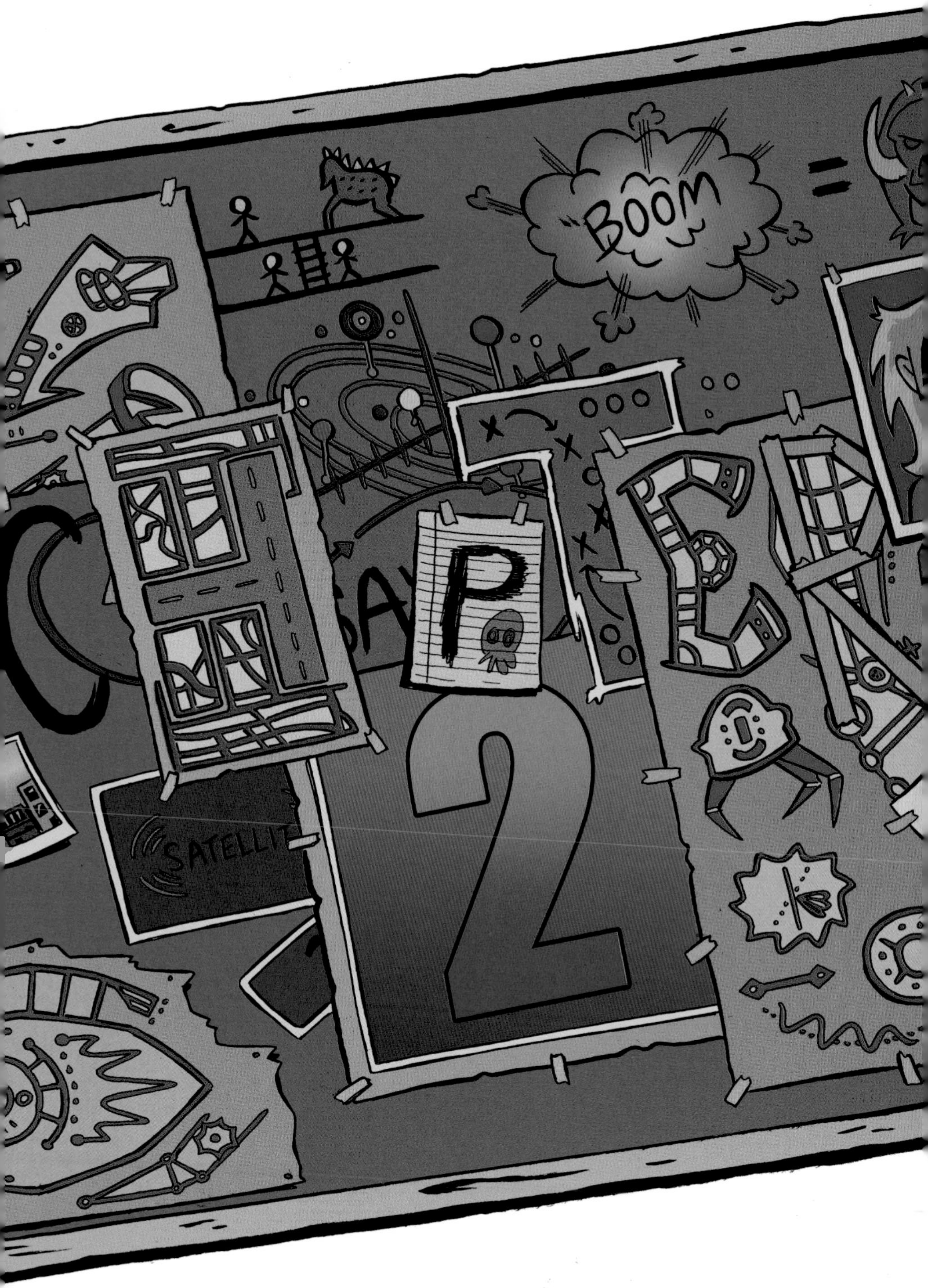
BOOM
P
2

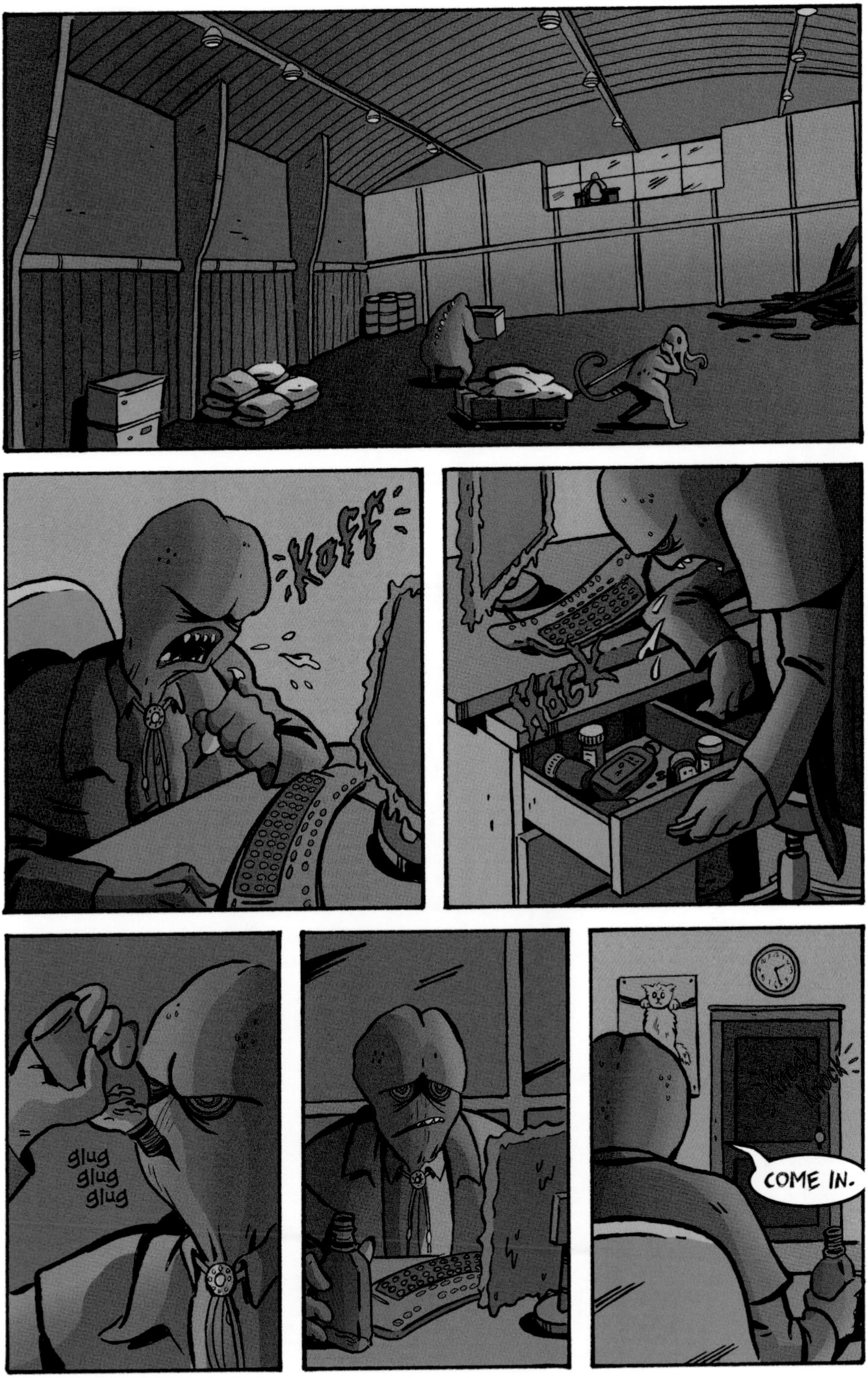
KOFF
HACK
glug glug glug
KNOCK KNOCK
COME IN.

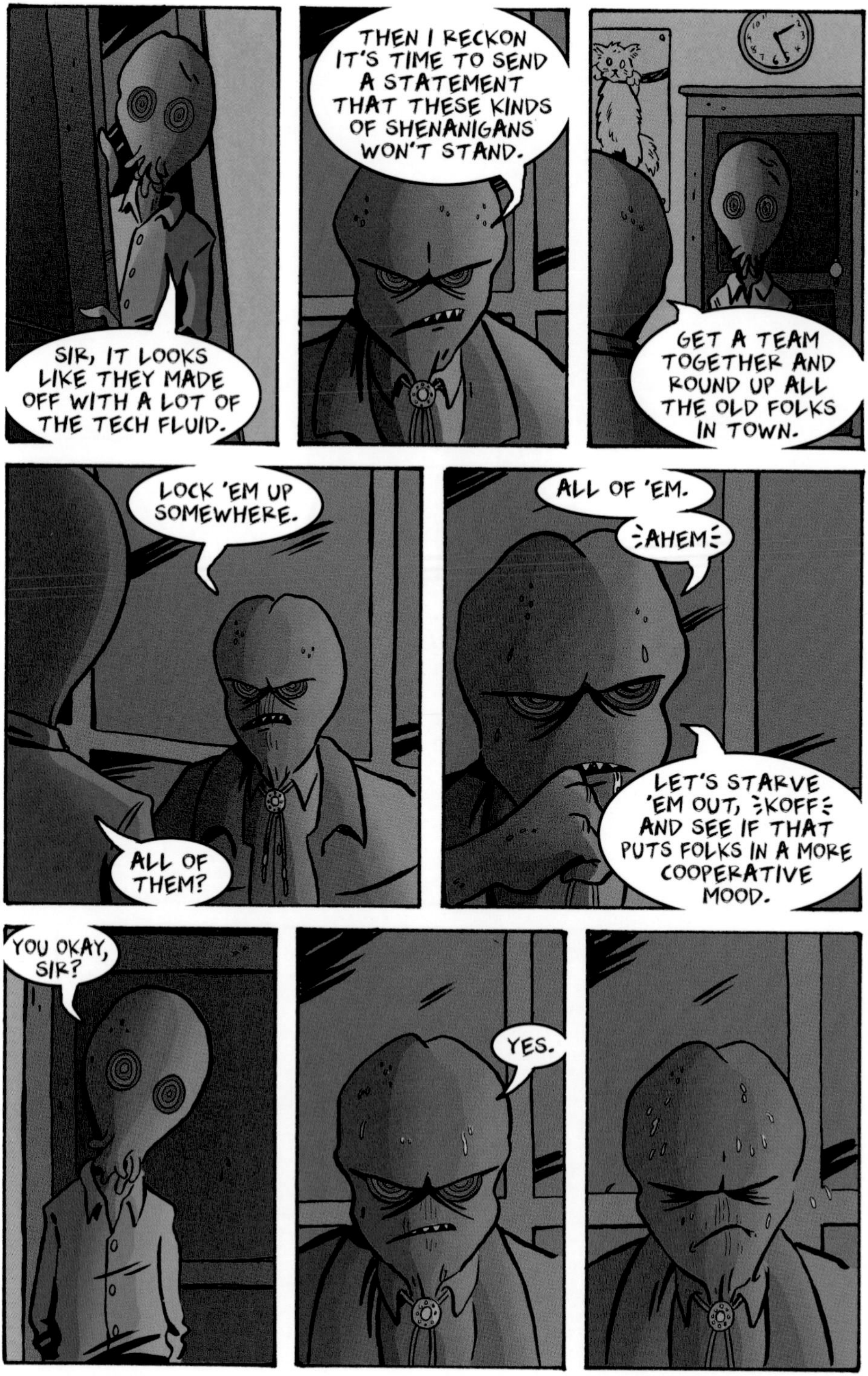
SIR, IT LOOKS LIKE THEY MADE OFF WITH A LOT OF THE TECH FLUID.
THEN I RECKON IT'S TIME TO SEND A STATEMENT THAT THESE KINDS OF SHENANIGANS WON'T STAND.
GET A TEAM TOGETHER AND ROUND UP ALL THE OLD FOLKS IN TOWN.
LOCK 'EM UP SOMEWHERE.
ALL OF THEM?
ALL OF 'EM.
AHEM
LET'S STARVE 'EM OUT, KOFF AND SEE IF THAT PUTS FOLKS IN A MORE COOPERATIVE MOOD.
YOU OKAY, SIR?
YES.

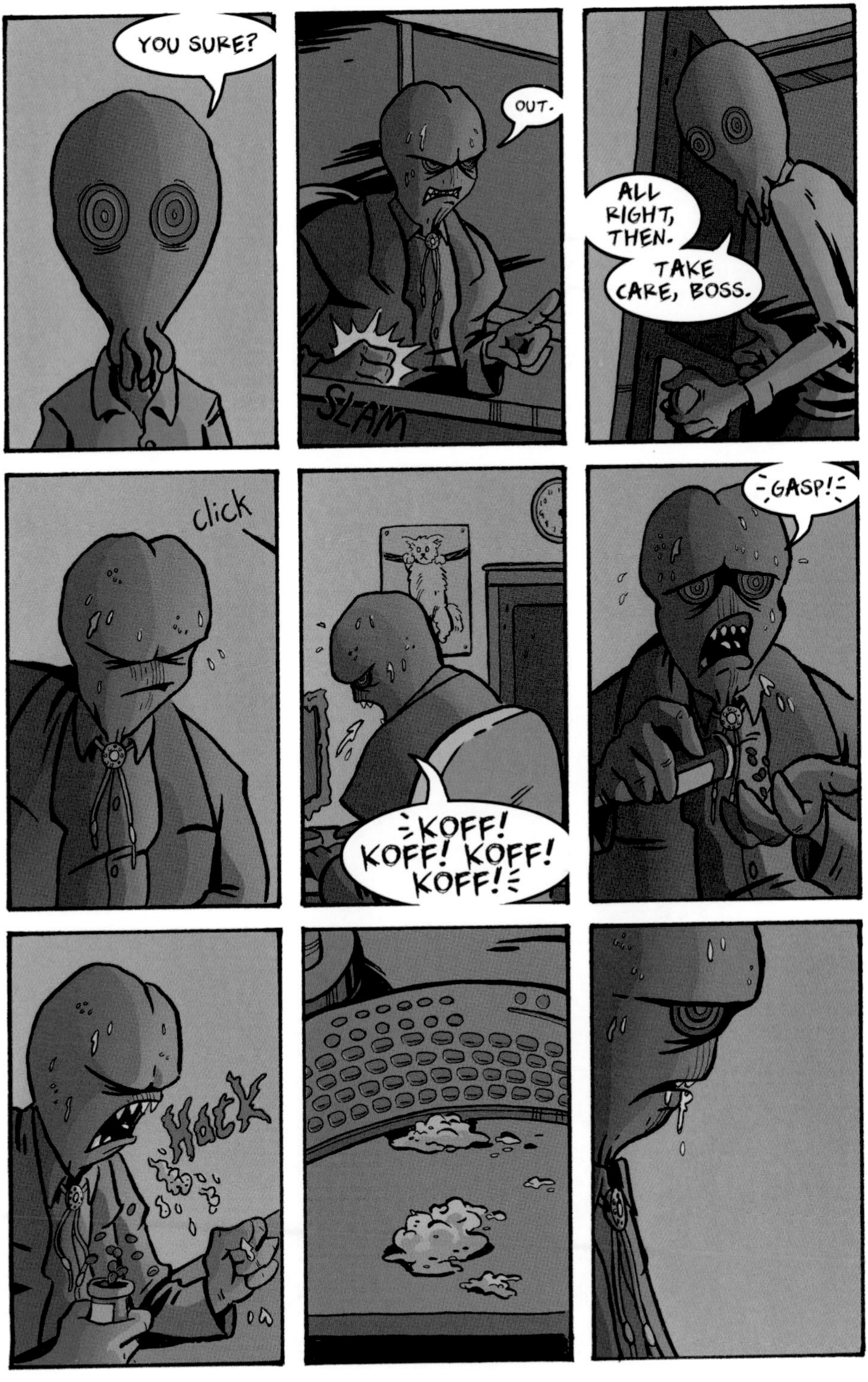
YOU SURE?
OUT.
SLAM
ALL RIGHT, THEN.
TAKE CARE, BOSS.
click
KOFF! KOFF! KOFF! KOFF!
GASP!
HACK

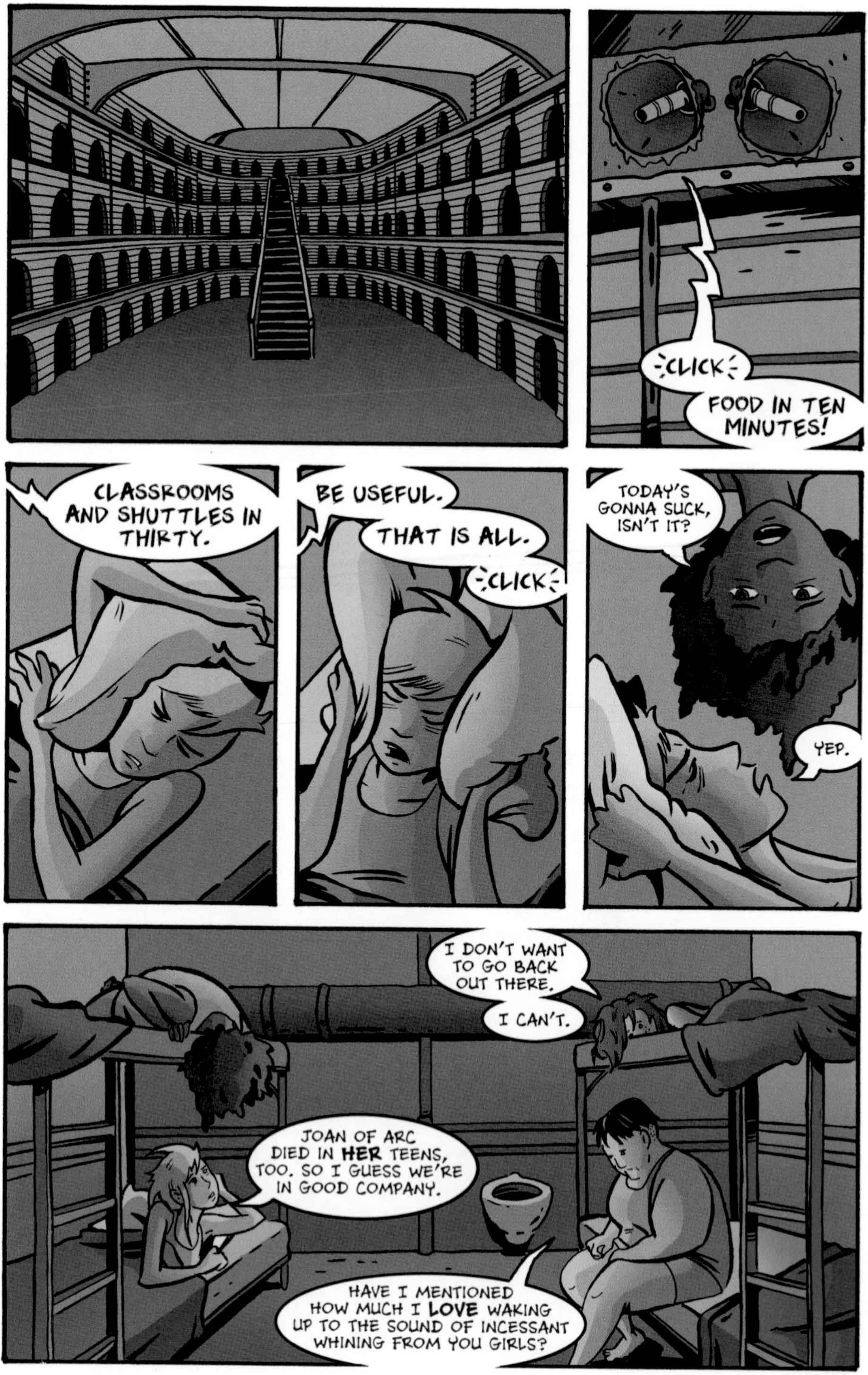
CLICK
FOOD IN TEN MINUTES!
CLASSROOMS AND SHUTTLES IN THIRTY.
BE USEFUL.
THAT IS ALL.
CLICK
TODAY'S GONNA SUCK, ISN'T IT?
YEP.
I DON'T WANT TO GO BACK OUT THERE.
I CAN'T.
JOAN OF ARC DIED IN HER TEENS, TOO. SO I GUESS WE'RE IN GOOD COMPANY.
HAVE I MENTIONED HOW MUCH I LOVE WAKING UP TO THE SOUND OF INCESSANT WHINING FROM YOU GIRLS?

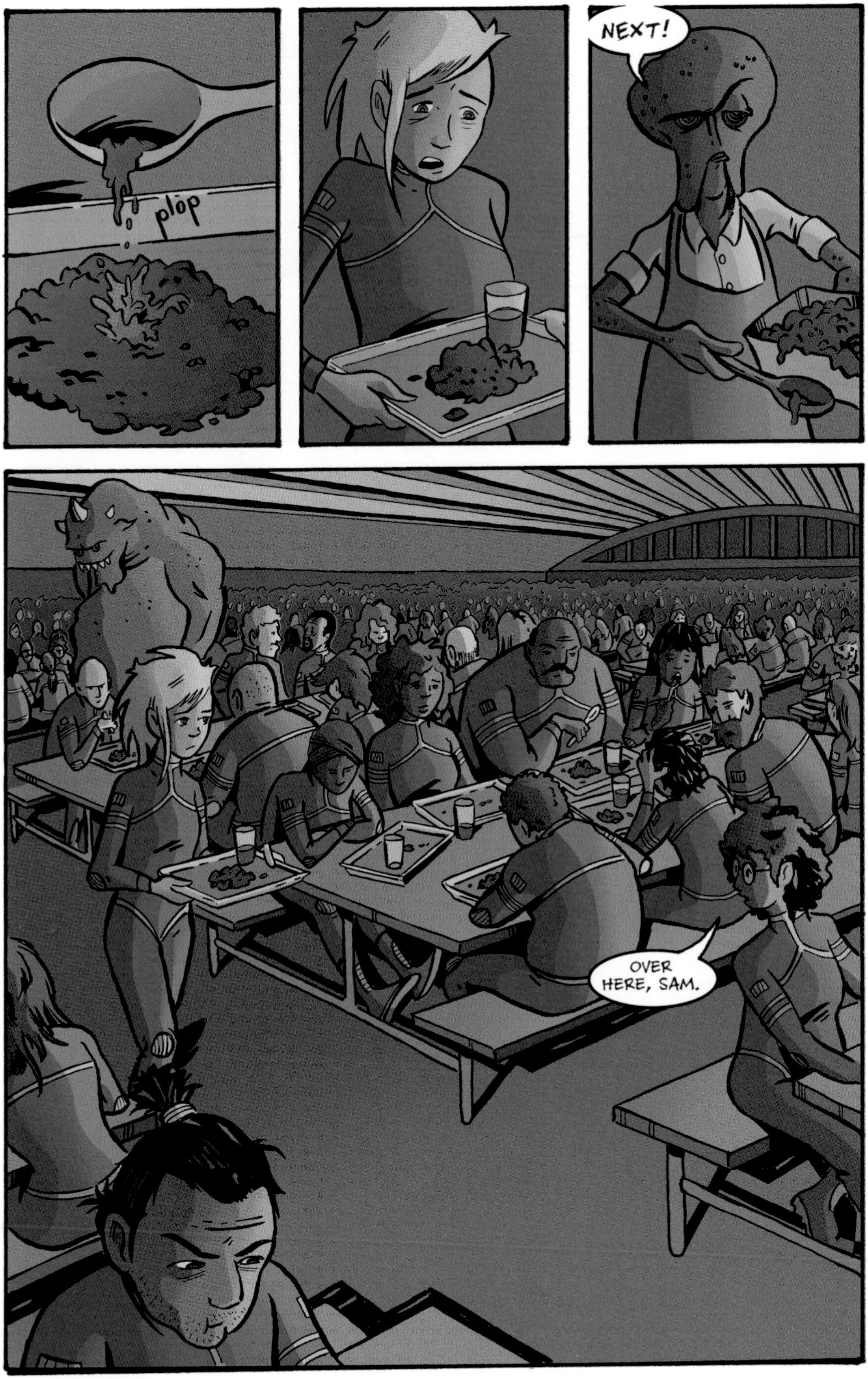
plop
NEXT!
OVER HERE, SAM.

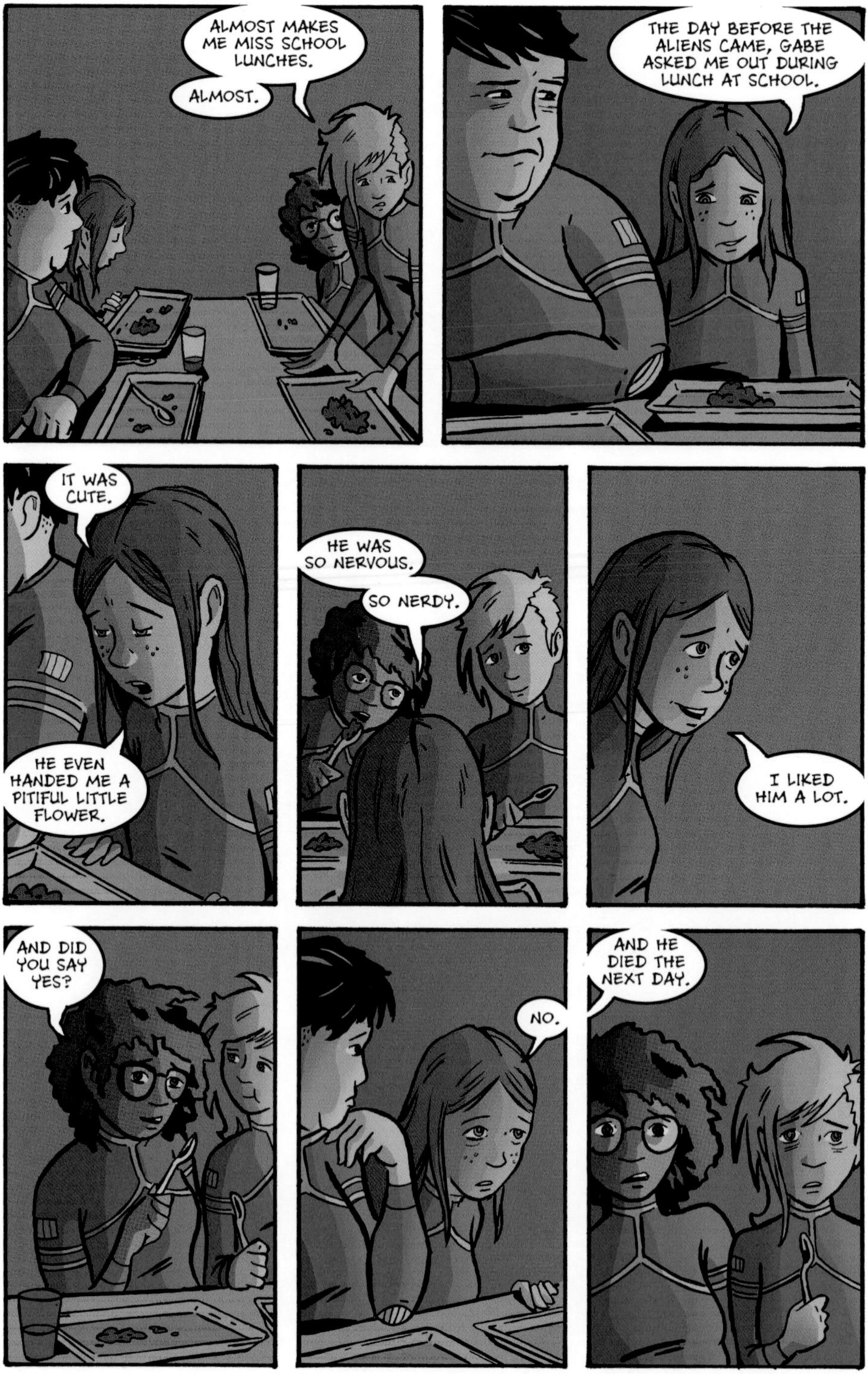
ALMOST MAKES ME MISS SCHOOL LUNCHES.
ALMOST.
THE DAY BEFORE THE ALIENS CAME, GABE ASKED ME OUT DURING LUNCH AT SCHOOL.
IT WAS CUTE.
HE EVEN HANDED ME A PITIFUL LITTLE FLOWER.
HE WAS SO NERVOUS.
SO NERDY.
I LIKED HIM A LOT.
AND DID YOU SAY YES?
NO.
AND HE DIED THE NEXT DAY.

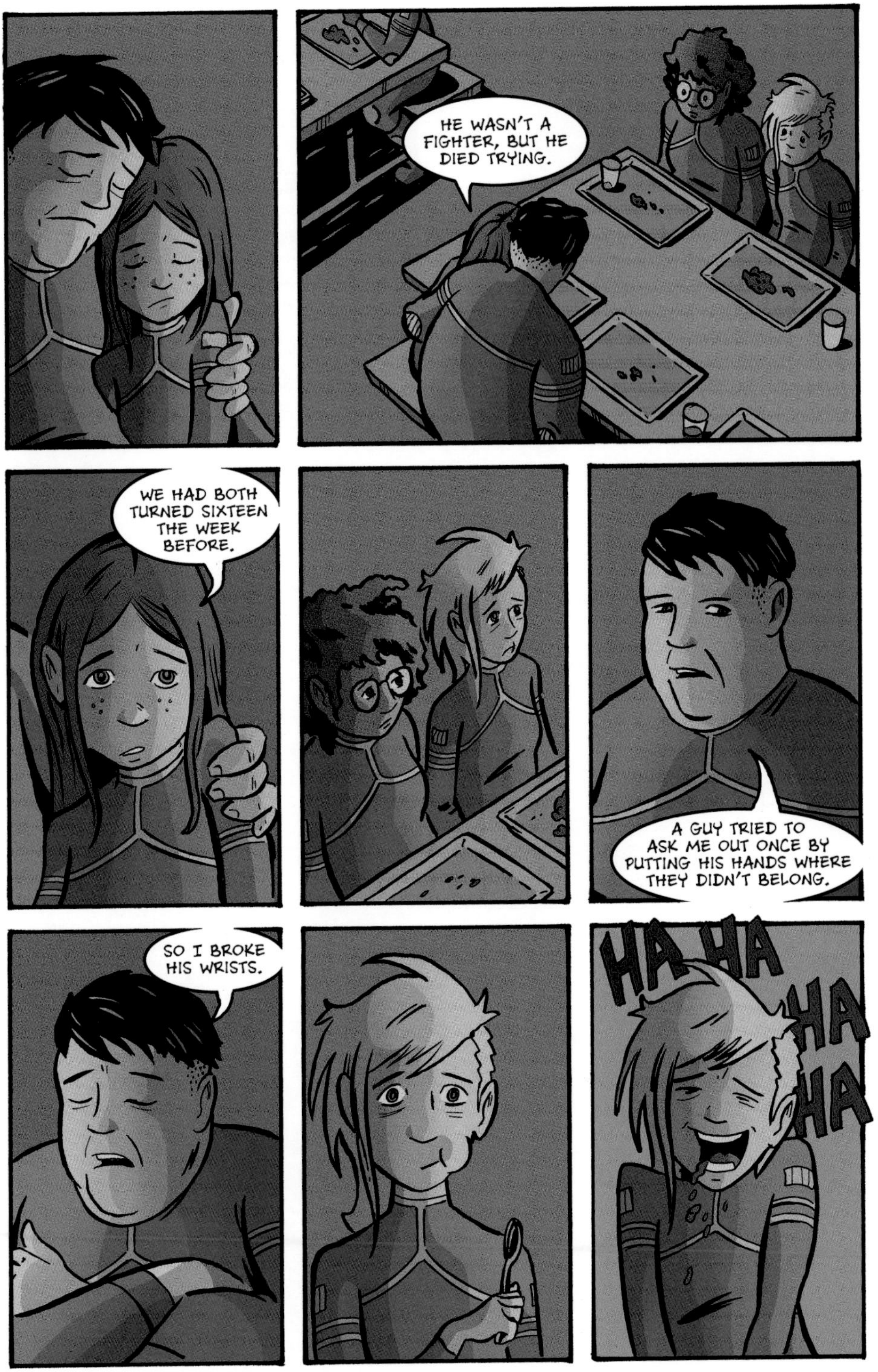
HE WASN'T A FIGHTER, BUT HE DIED TRYING.
WE HAD BOTH TURNED SIXTEEN THE WEEK BEFORE.
A GUY TRIED TO ASK ME OUT ONCE BY PUTTING HIS HANDS WHERE THEY DIDN'T BELONG.
SO I BROKE HIS WRISTS.
HA HA
HA
HA

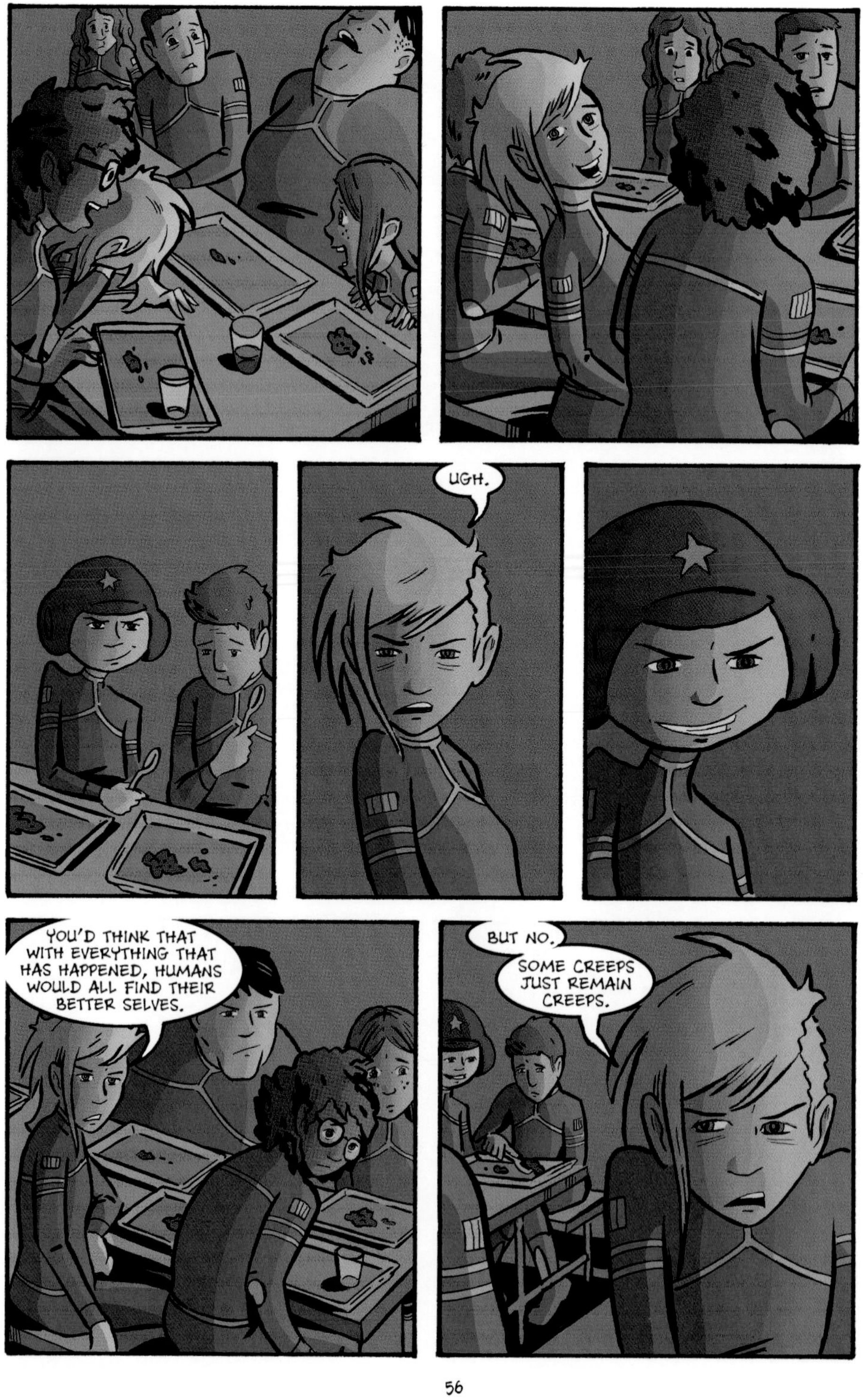
UGH.
YOU'D THINK THAT WITH EVERYTHING THAT HAS HAPPENED, HUMANS WOULD ALL FIND THEIR BETTER SELVES.
BUT NO.
SOME CREEPS JUST REMAIN CREEPS.

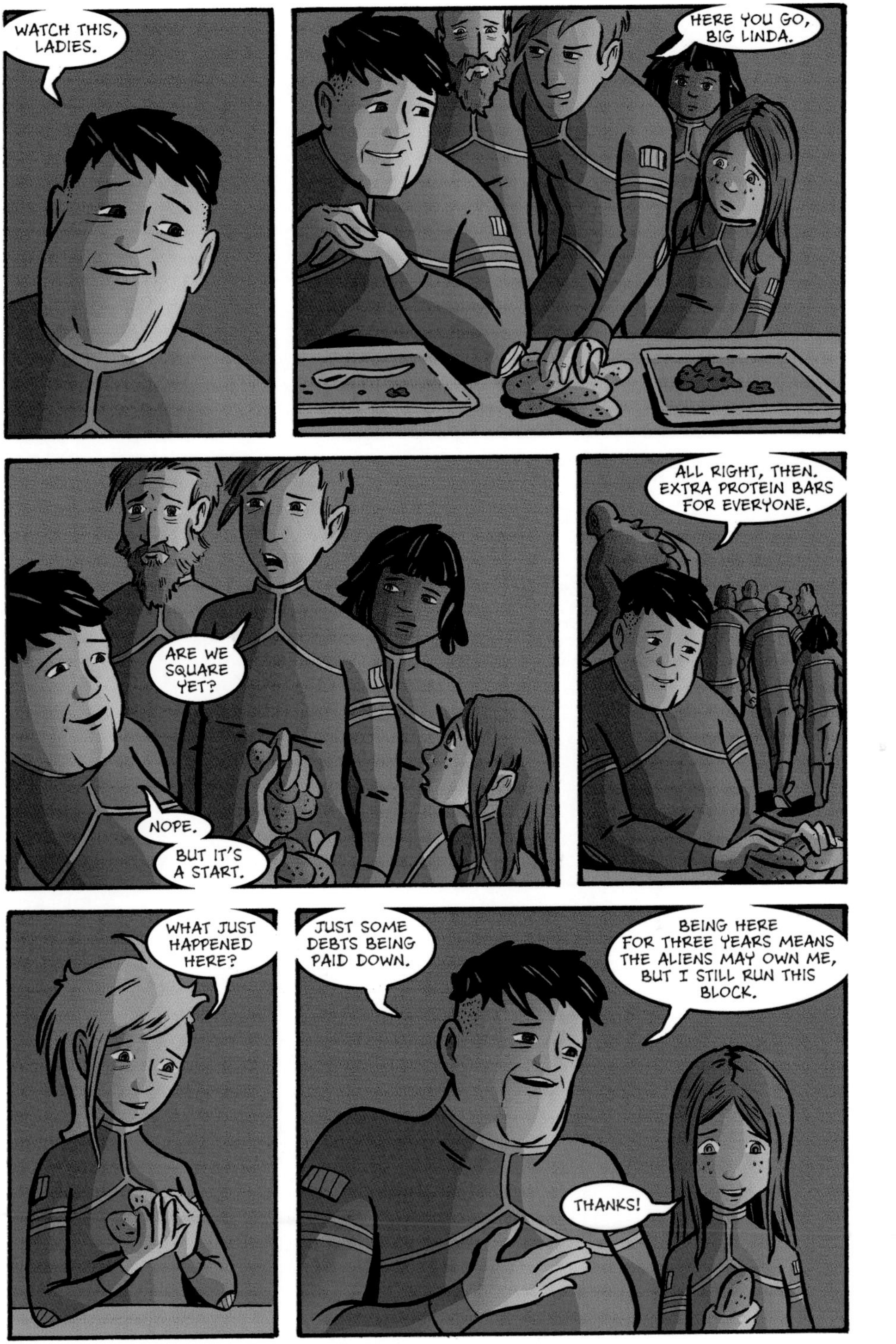
WATCH THIS, LADIES.
HERE YOU GO, BIG LINDA.
ARE WE SQUARE YET?
NOPE.
BUT IT'S A START.
ALL RIGHT, THEN. EXTRA PROTEIN BARS FOR EVERYONE.
WHAT JUST HAPPENED HERE?
JUST SOME DEBTS BEING PAID DOWN.
BEING HERE FOR THREE YEARS MEANS THE ALIENS MAY OWN ME, BUT I STILL RUN THIS BLOCK.
THANKS!

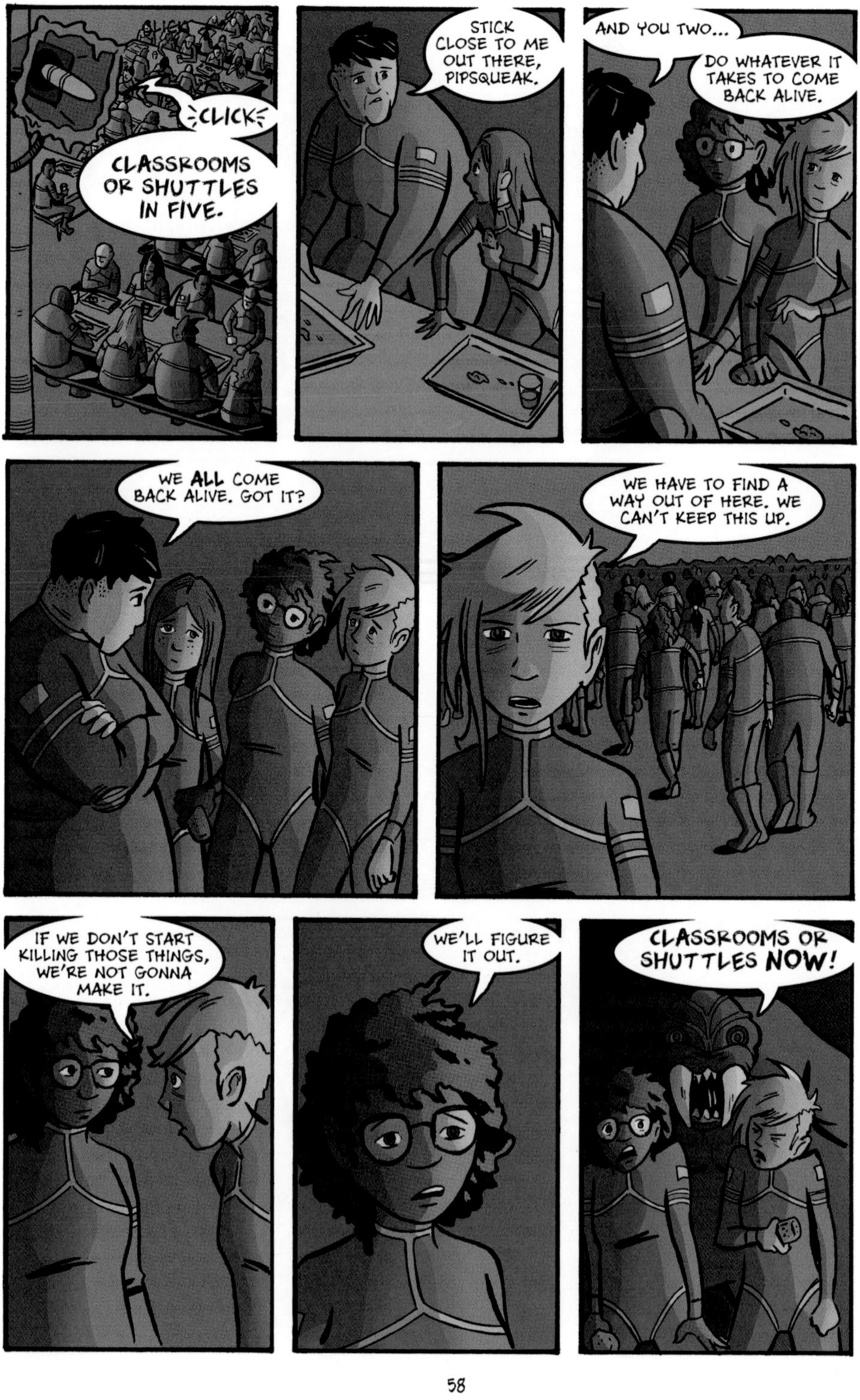
CLICK
CLICK
CLASSROOMS OR SHUTTLES IN FIVE.
STICK CLOSE TO ME OUT THERE, PIPSQUEAK.
AND YOU TWO...
DO WHATEVER IT TAKES TO COME BACK ALIVE.
WE **ALL** COME BACK ALIVE. GOT IT?
WE HAVE TO FIND A WAY OUT OF HERE. WE CAN'T KEEP THIS UP.
IF WE DON'T START KILLING THOSE THINGS, WE'RE NOT GONNA MAKE IT.
WE'LL FIGURE IT OUT.
CLASSROOMS OR SHUTTLES **NOW!**

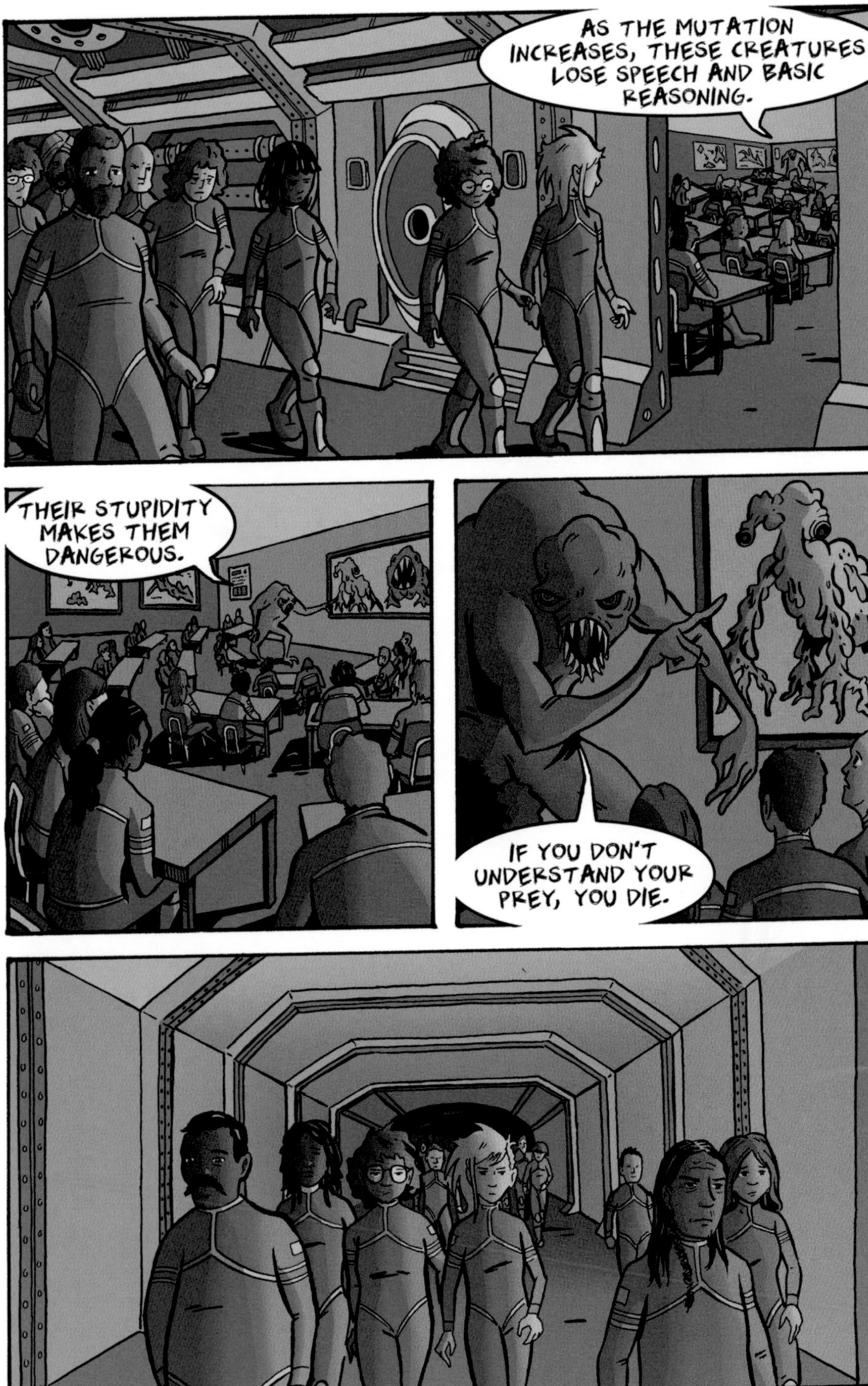
AS THE MUTATION INCREASES, THESE CREATURES LOSE SPEECH AND BASIC REASONING.
THEIR STUPIDITY MAKES THEM DANGEROUS.
IF YOU DON'T UNDERSTAND YOUR PREY, YOU DIE.

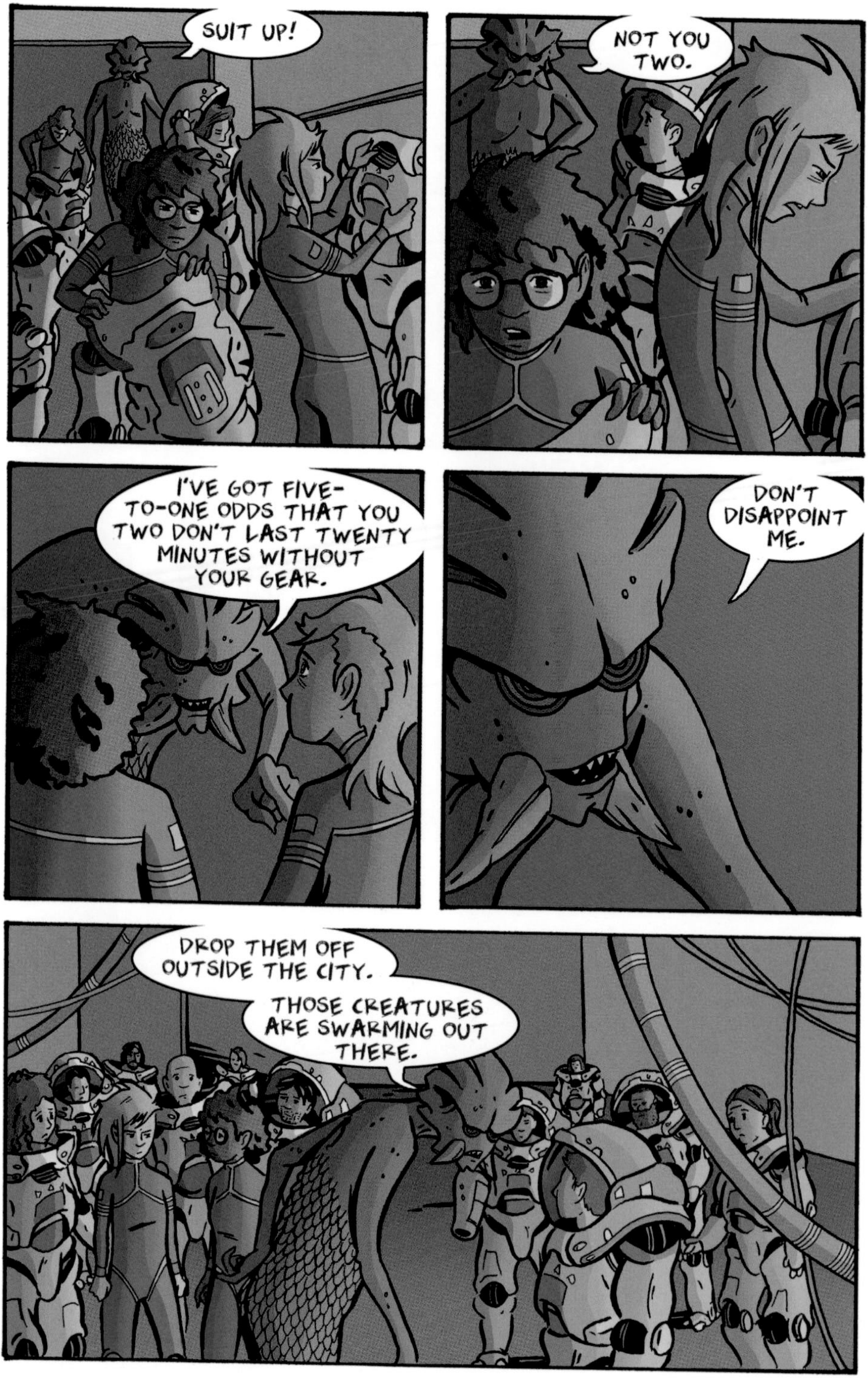
SUIT UP!
NOT YOU TWO.
I'VE GOT FIVE-TO-ONE ODDS THAT YOU TWO DON'T LAST TWENTY MINUTES WITHOUT YOUR GEAR.
DON'T DISAPPOINT ME.
DROP THEM OFF OUTSIDE THE CITY.
THOSE CREATURES ARE SWARMING OUT THERE.

YES, SIR.

I GUESS THIS IS WHERE YOU BOTH GET OFF.

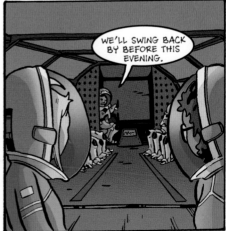

WE'LL SWING BACK BY BEFORE THIS EVENING.

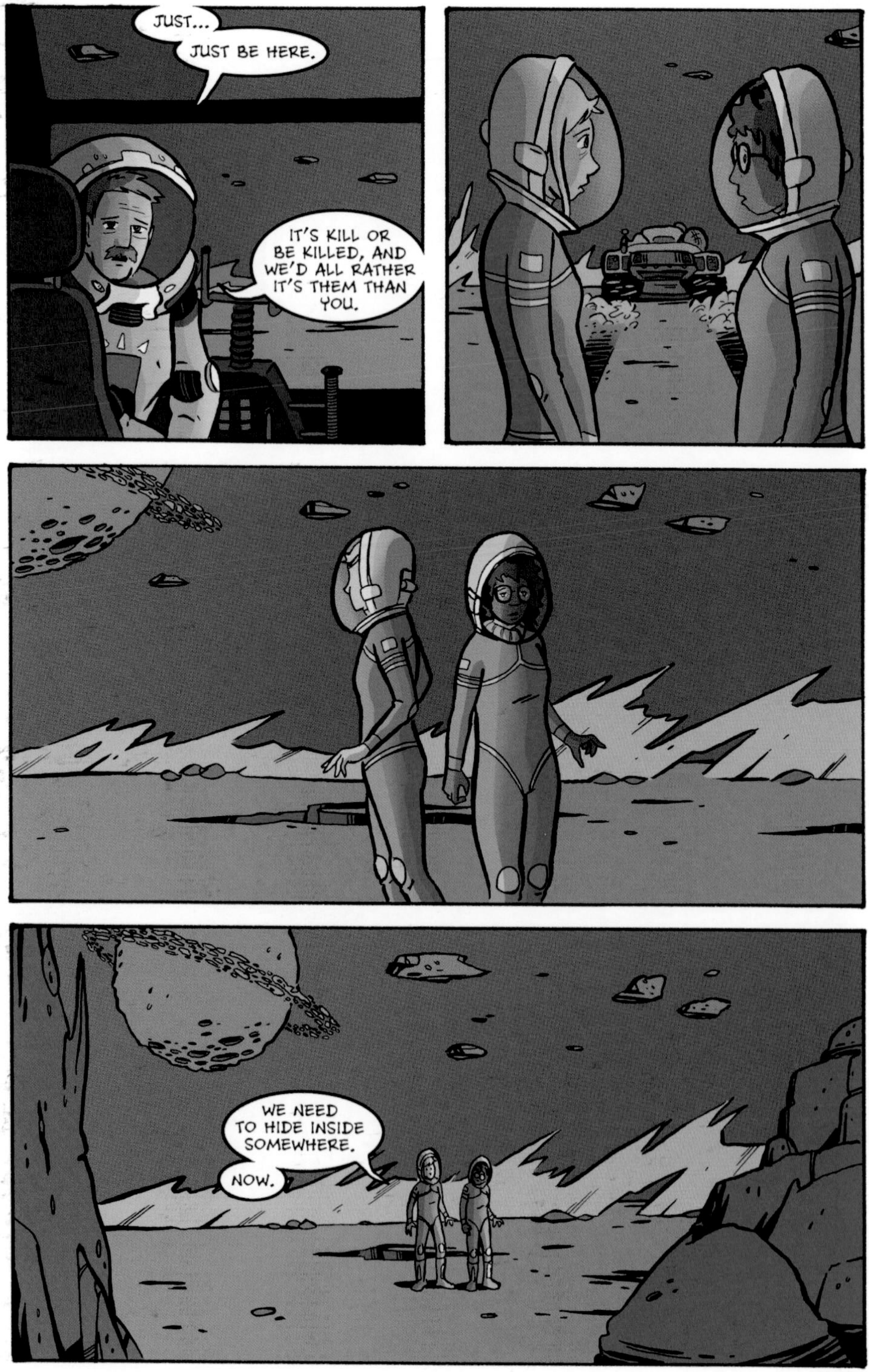
JUST...
JUST BE HERE.
IT'S KILL OR BE KILLED, AND WE'D ALL RATHER IT'S THEM THAN YOU.
WE NEED TO HIDE INSIDE SOMEWHERE.
NOW.

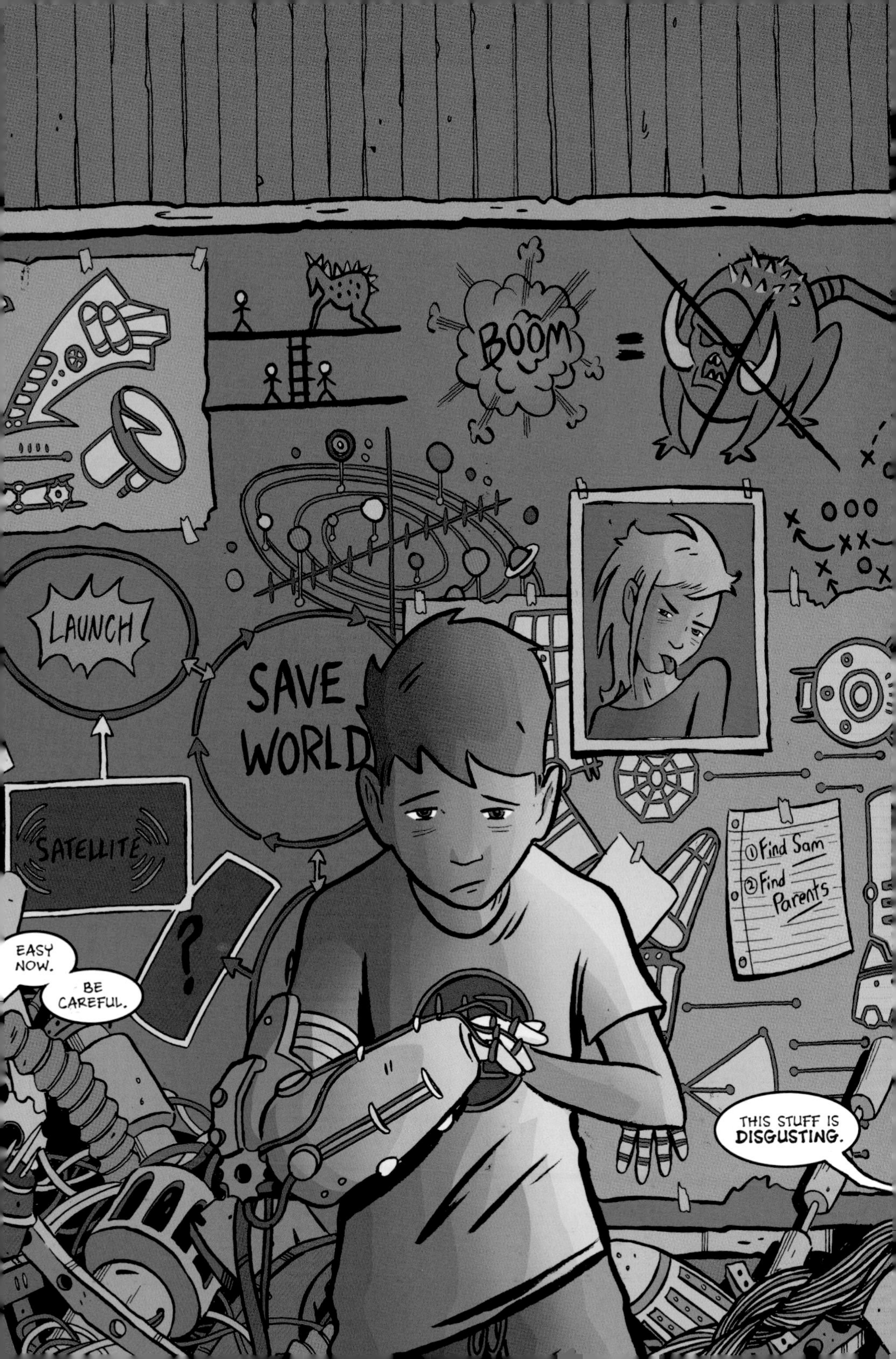
LAUNCH
SAVE WORLD
SATELLITE
?
BOOM
1 Find Sam
2 Find Parents
EASY NOW.
BE CAREFUL.
THIS STUFF IS **DISGUSTING.**

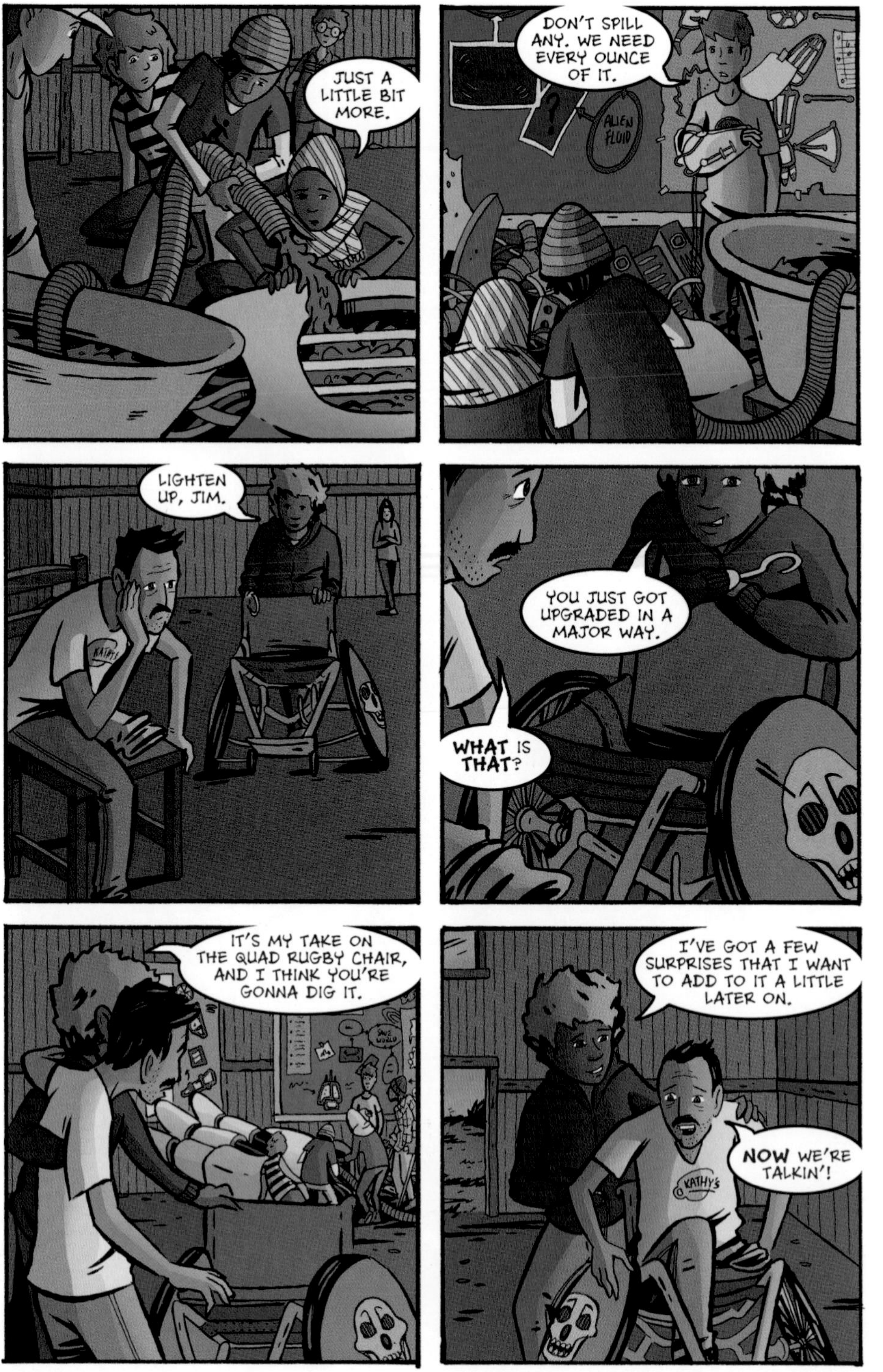
JUST A LITTLE BIT MORE.
DON'T SPILL ANY. WE NEED EVERY OUNCE OF IT.
ALIEN FLUID
LIGHTEN UP, JIM.
YOU JUST GOT UPGRADED IN A MAJOR WAY.
WHAT IS THAT?
IT'S MY TAKE ON THE QUAD RUGBY CHAIR, AND I THINK YOU'RE GONNA DIG IT.
I'VE GOT A FEW SURPRISES THAT I WANT TO ADD TO IT A LITTLE LATER ON.
NOW WE'RE TALKIN'!
KATHY'S

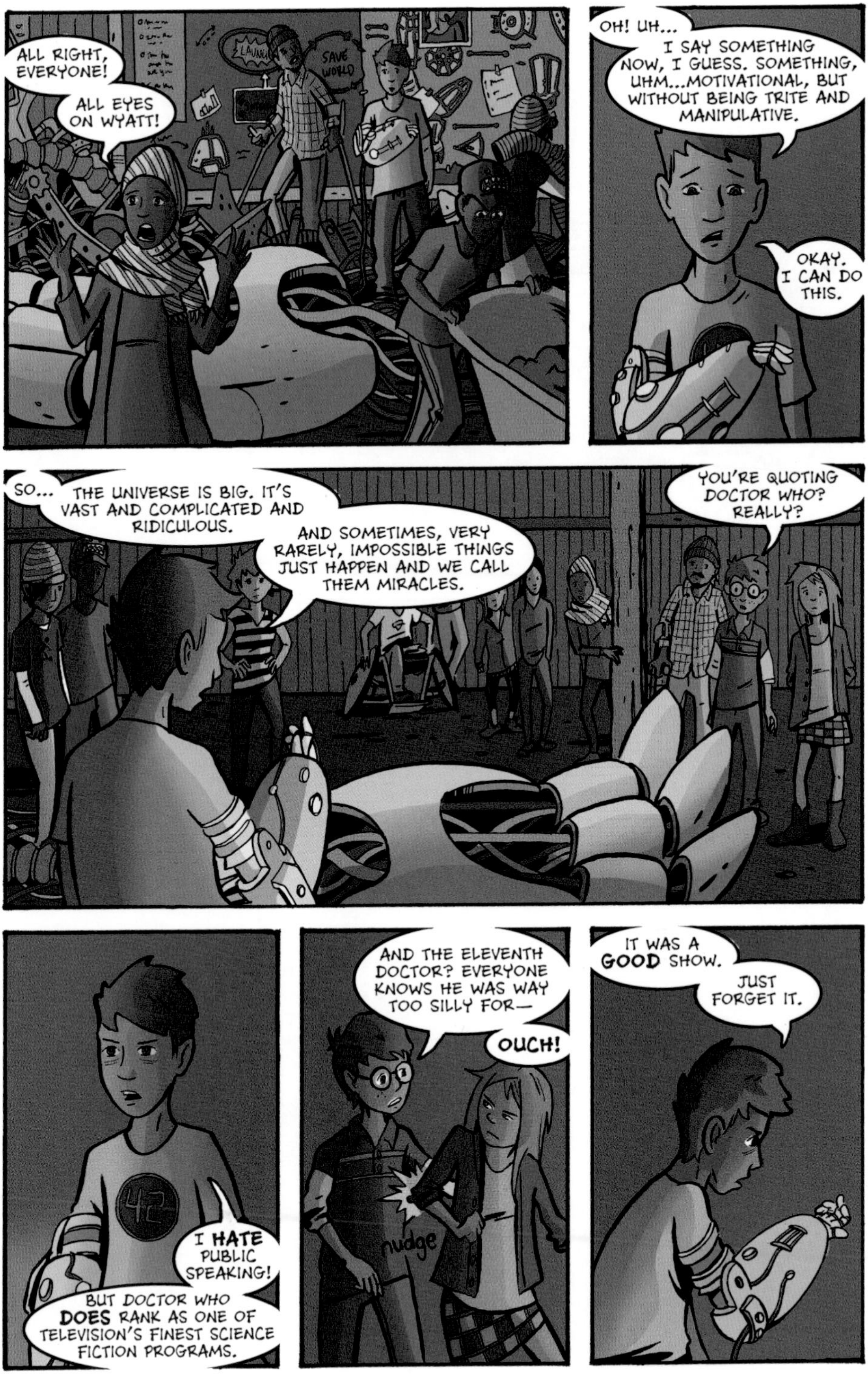
ALL RIGHT, EVERYONE!
ALL EYES ON WYATT!
OH! UH...
I SAY SOMETHING NOW, I GUESS. SOMETHING, UHM...MOTIVATIONAL, BUT WITHOUT BEING TRITE AND MANIPULATIVE.
OKAY. I CAN DO THIS.
SO...
THE UNIVERSE IS BIG. IT'S VAST AND COMPLICATED AND RIDICULOUS.
AND SOMETIMES, VERY RARELY, IMPOSSIBLE THINGS JUST HAPPEN AND WE CALL THEM MIRACLES.
YOU'RE QUOTING DOCTOR WHO? REALLY?
I **HATE** PUBLIC SPEAKING!
BUT DOCTOR WHO **DOES** RANK AS ONE OF TELEVISION'S FINEST SCIENCE FICTION PROGRAMS.
AND THE ELEVENTH DOCTOR? EVERYONE KNOWS HE WAS WAY TOO SILLY FOR—
OUCH!
nudge
IT WAS A **GOOD** SHOW.
JUST FORGET IT.

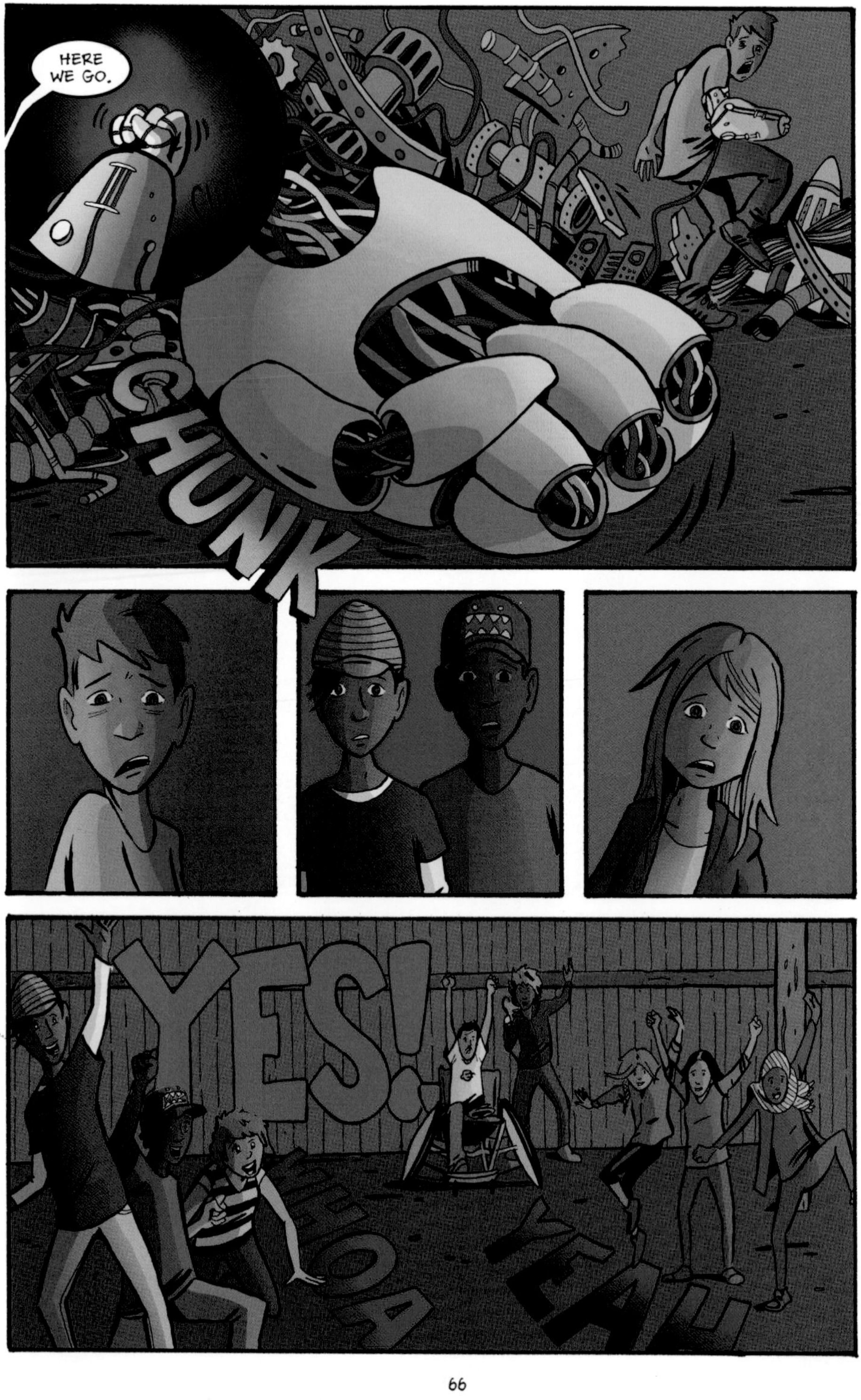
HERE WE GO.
CHUNK
YES!
WHOA
YEAH

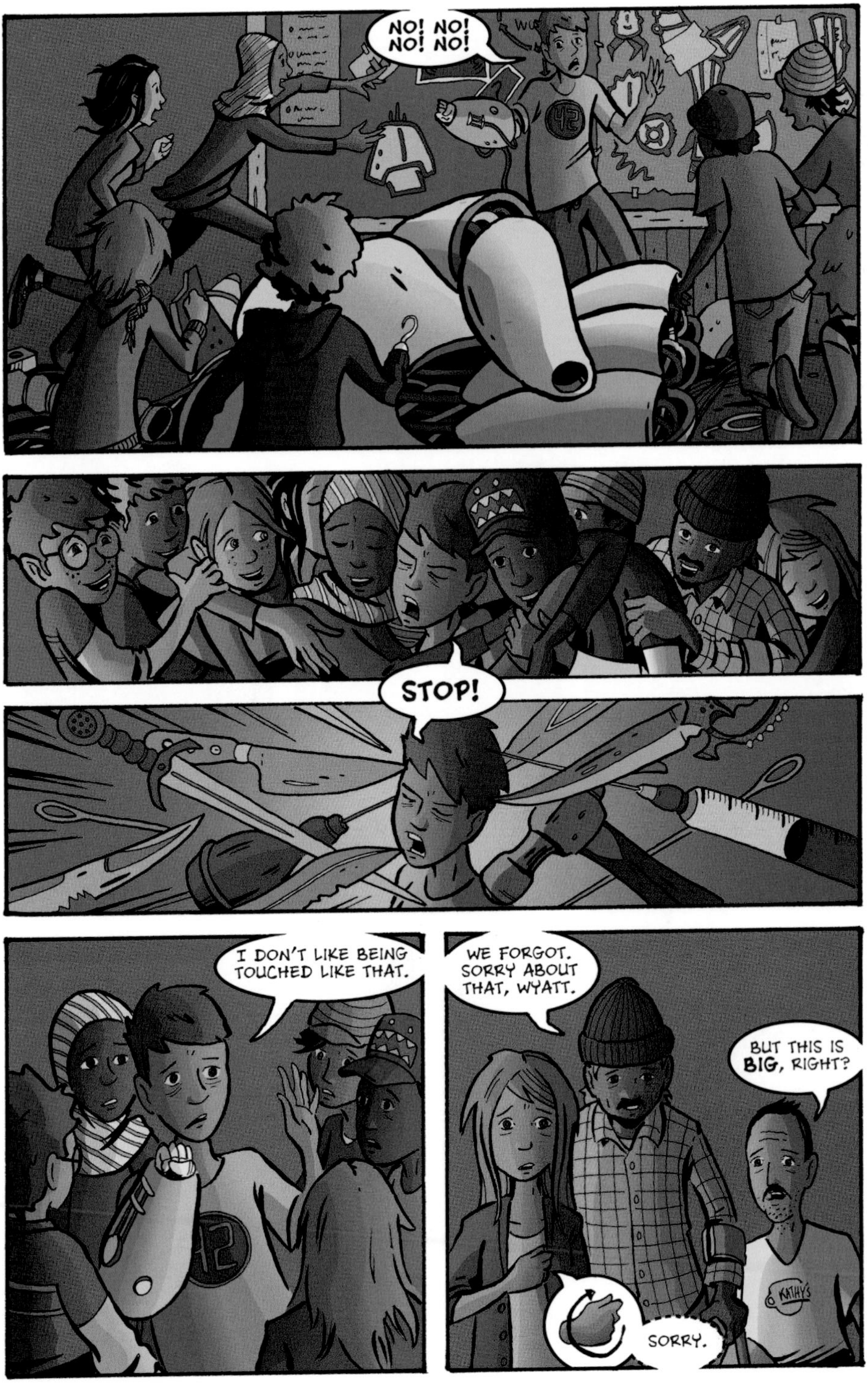
NO! NO!
NO! NO!
STOP!
I DON'T LIKE BEING TOUCHED LIKE THAT.
WE FORGOT. SORRY ABOUT THAT, WYATT.
BUT THIS IS BIG, RIGHT?
SORRY.
KATHY'S

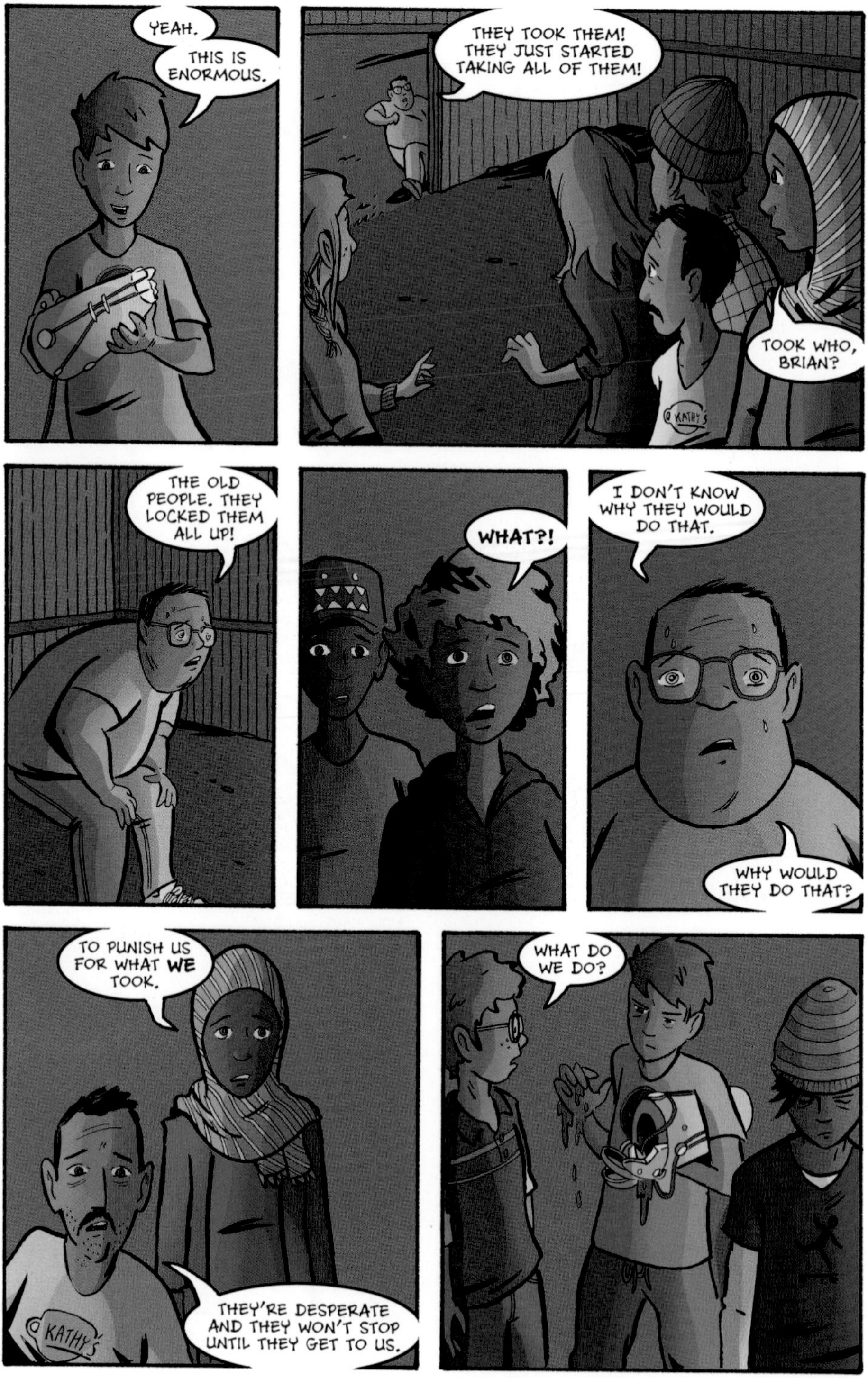
YEAH.
THIS IS ENORMOUS.
THEY TOOK THEM! THEY JUST STARTED TAKING ALL OF THEM!
TOOK WHO, BRIAN?
KATHY'S
THE OLD PEOPLE. THEY LOCKED THEM ALL UP!
WHAT?!
I DON'T KNOW WHY THEY WOULD DO THAT.
WHY WOULD THEY DO THAT?
TO PUNISH US FOR WHAT WE TOOK.
THEY'RE DESPERATE AND THEY WON'T STOP UNTIL THEY GET TO US.
KATHY'S
WHAT DO WE DO?

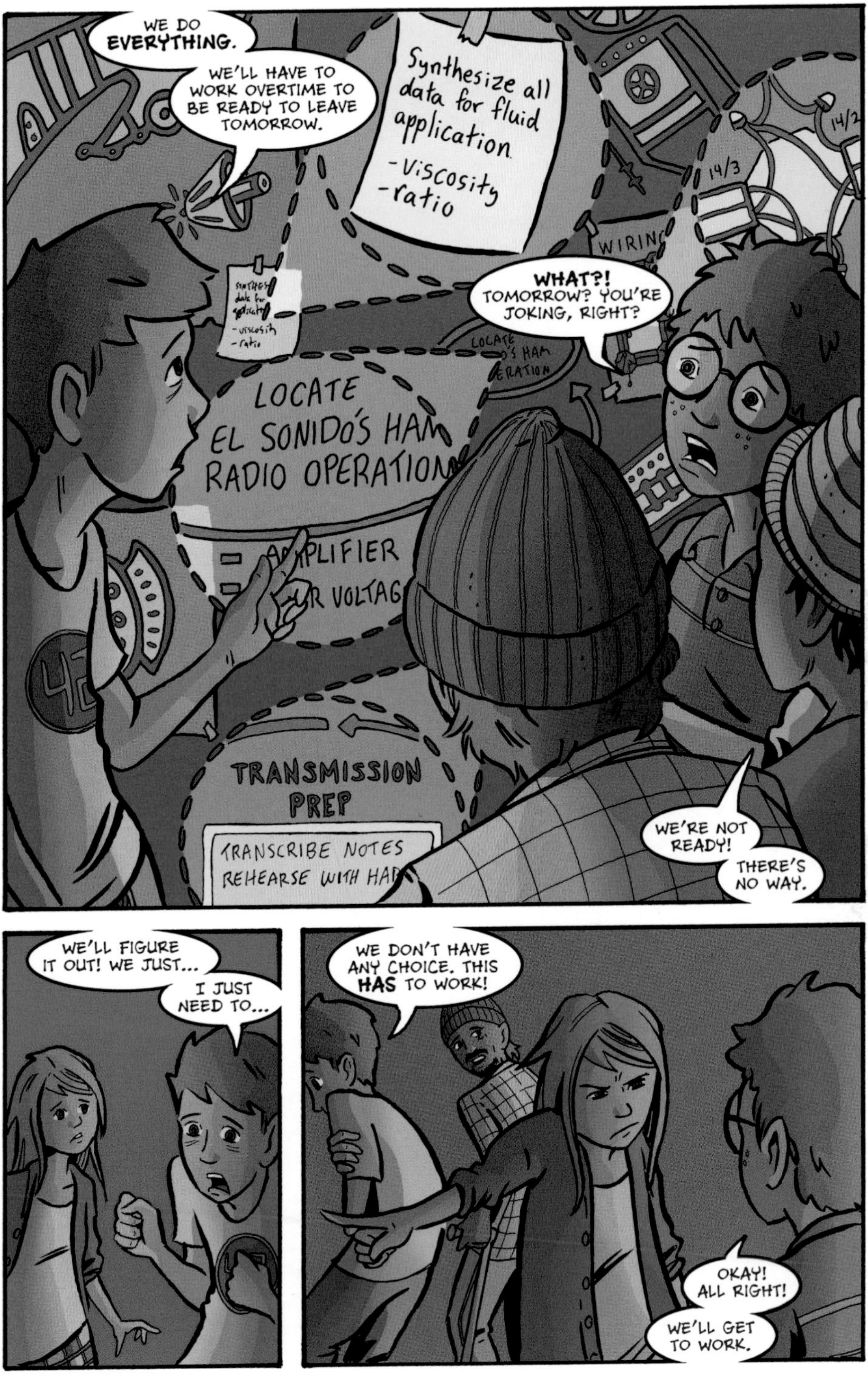
WE DO **EVERYTHING.**
WE'LL HAVE TO WORK OVERTIME TO BE READY TO LEAVE TOMORROW.
Synthesize all data for fluid application
-Viscosity
-ratio
14/2
14/3
WHAT?! TOMORROW? YOU'RE JOKING, RIGHT?
LOCATE
EL SONIDO'S HAM
RADIO OPERATION
TRANSMISSION PREP
TRANSCRIBE NOTES
WE'RE NOT READY!
THERE'S NO WAY.
WE'LL FIGURE IT OUT! WE JUST...
I JUST NEED TO...
WE DON'T HAVE ANY CHOICE. THIS **HAS** TO WORK!
OKAY! ALL RIGHT!
WE'LL GET TO WORK.

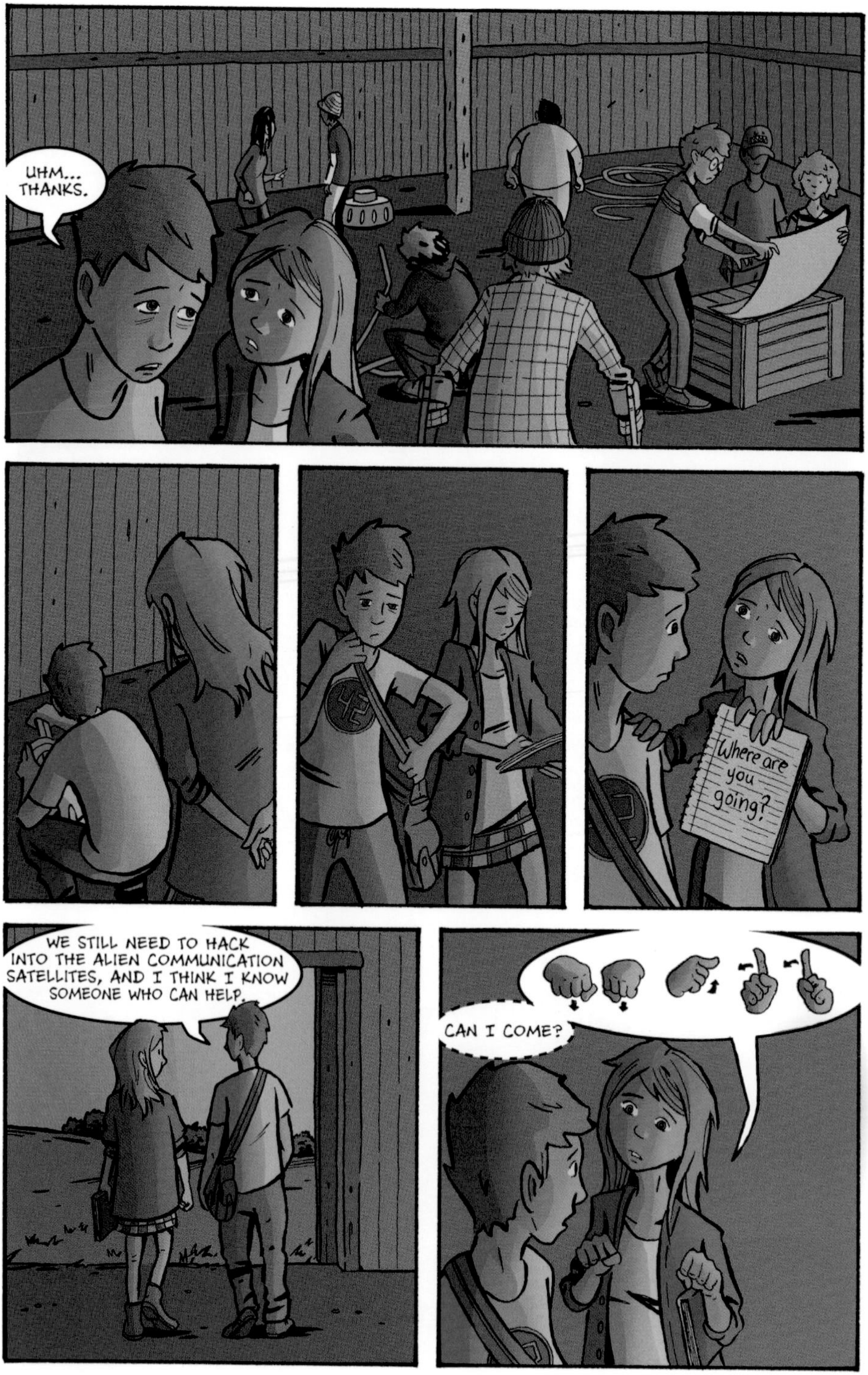
UHM... THANKS.
Where are you going?
WE STILL NEED TO HACK INTO THE ALIEN COMMUNICATION SATELLITES, AND I THINK I KNOW SOMEONE WHO CAN HELP.
CAN I COME?

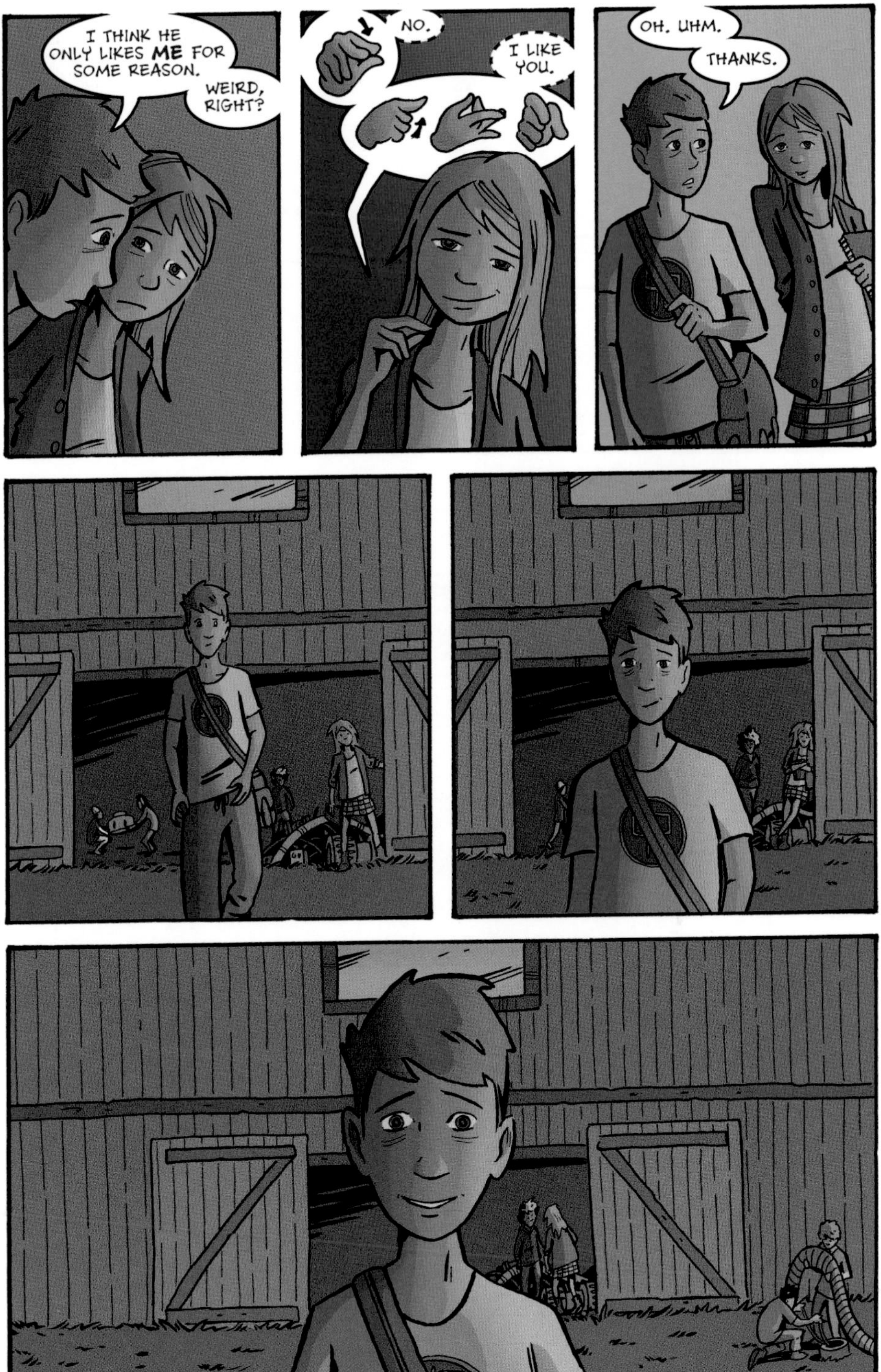
I THINK HE ONLY LIKES **ME** FOR SOME REASON.
WEIRD, RIGHT?
NO.
I LIKE YOU.
OH. UHM.
THANKS.

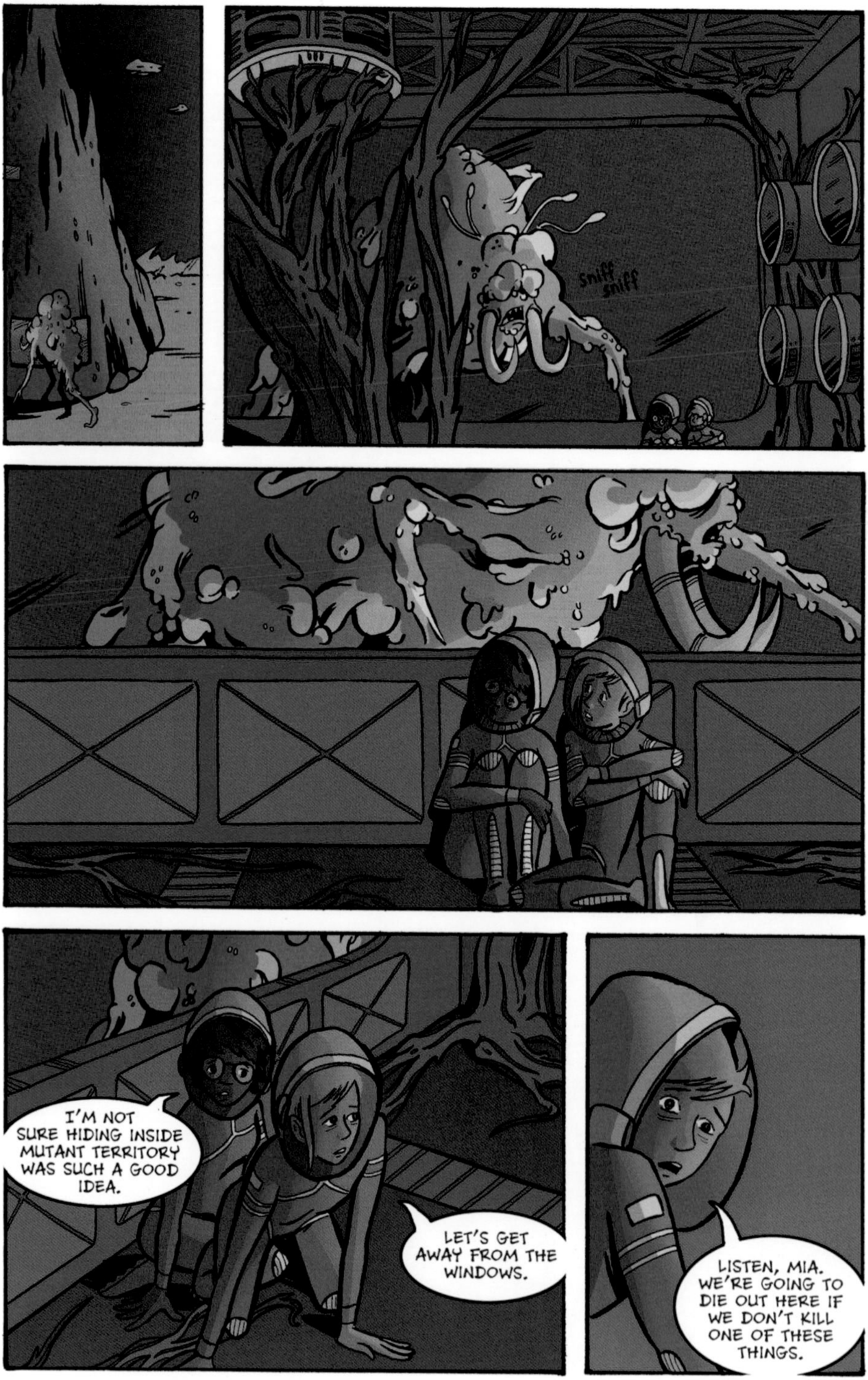
sniff sniff
I'M NOT SURE HIDING INSIDE MUTANT TERRITORY WAS SUCH A GOOD IDEA.
LET'S GET AWAY FROM THE WINDOWS.
LISTEN, MIA. WE'RE GOING TO DIE OUT HERE IF WE DON'T KILL ONE OF THESE THINGS.

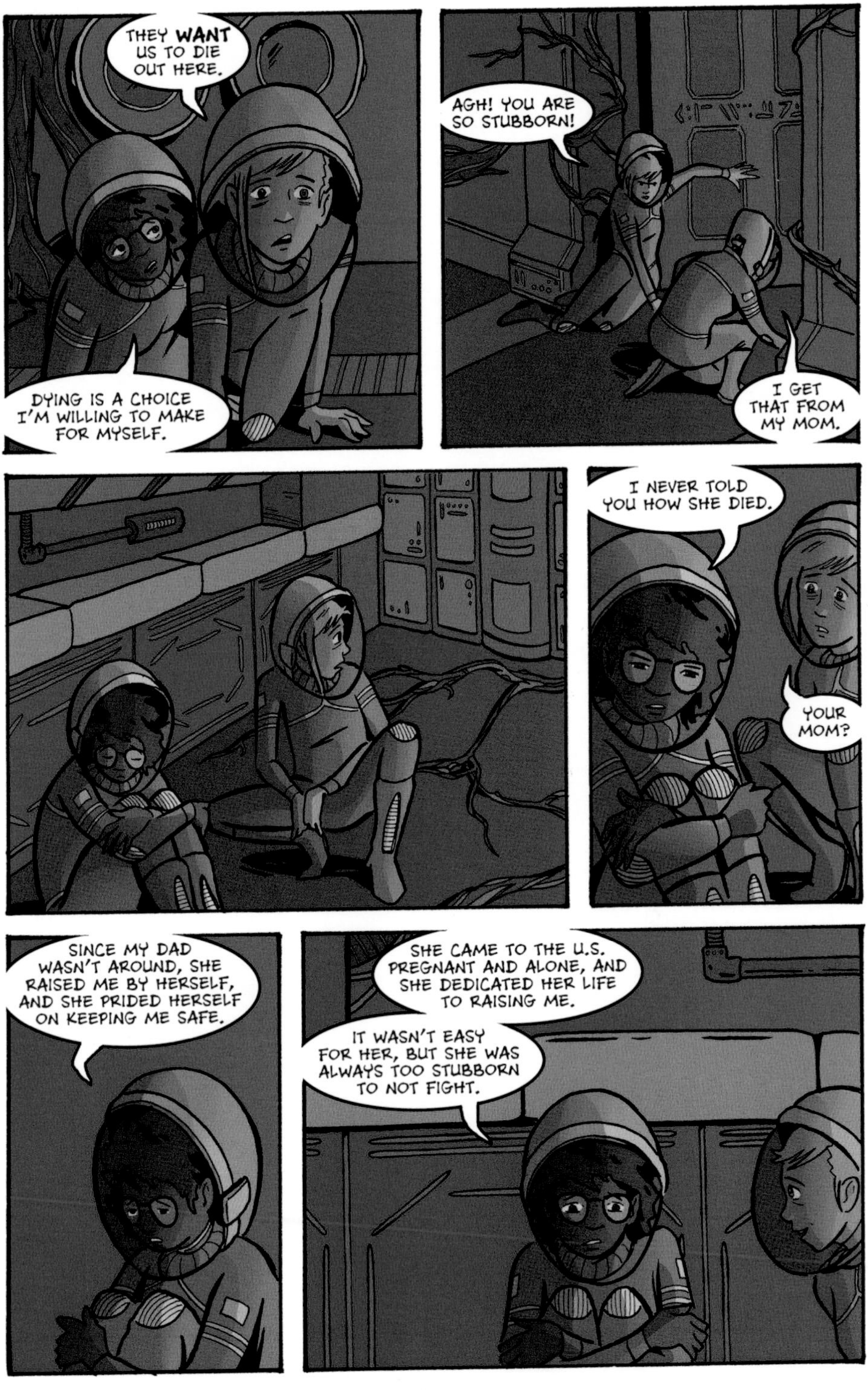

THEY WANT US TO DIE OUT HERE.
DYING IS A CHOICE I'M WILLING TO MAKE FOR MYSELF.
AGH! YOU ARE SO STUBBORN!
I GET THAT FROM MY MOM.
I NEVER TOLD YOU HOW SHE DIED.
YOUR MOM?
SINCE MY DAD WASN'T AROUND, SHE RAISED ME BY HERSELF, AND SHE PRIDED HERSELF ON KEEPING ME SAFE.
SHE CAME TO THE U.S. PREGNANT AND ALONE, AND SHE DEDICATED HER LIFE TO RAISING ME.
IT WASN'T EASY FOR HER, BUT SHE WAS ALWAYS TOO STUBBORN TO NOT FIGHT.

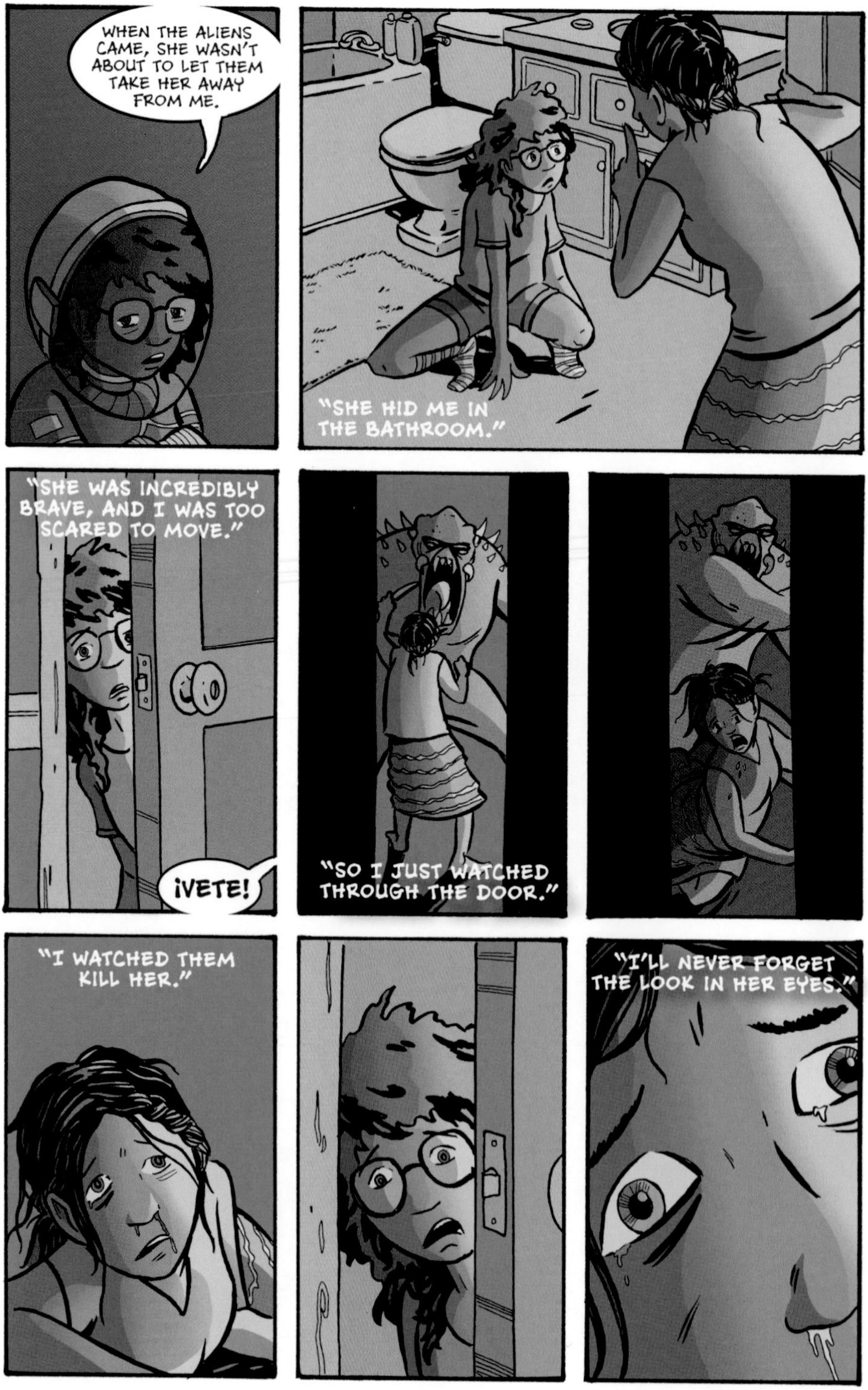
WHEN THE ALIENS CAME, SHE WASN'T ABOUT TO LET THEM TAKE HER AWAY FROM ME.
"SHE HID ME IN THE BATHROOM."
"SHE WAS INCREDIBLY BRAVE, AND I WAS TOO SCARED TO MOVE."
¡VETE!
"SO I JUST WATCHED THROUGH THE DOOR."
"I WATCHED THEM KILL HER."
"I'LL NEVER FORGET THE LOOK IN HER EYES."

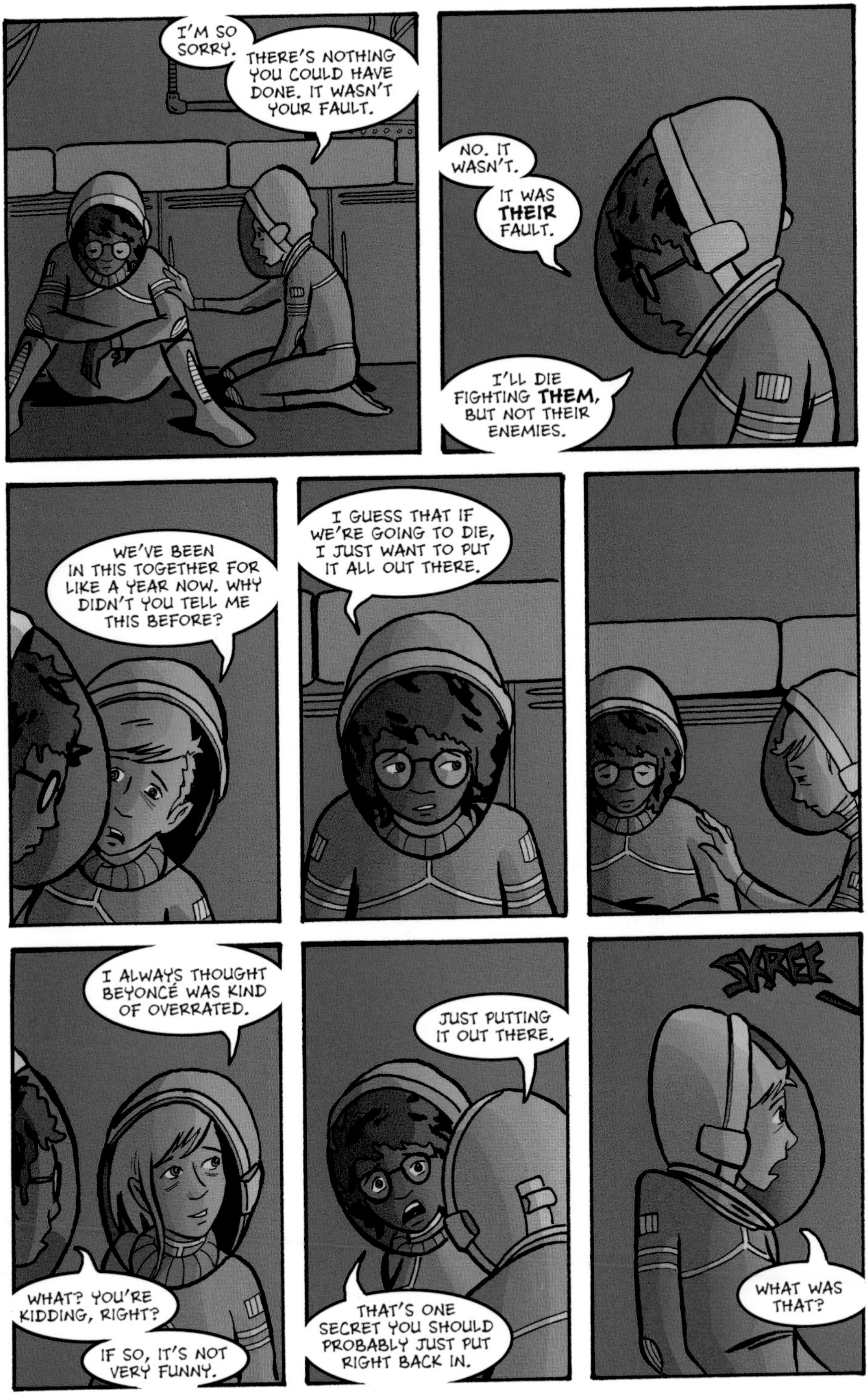
I'M SO SORRY.
THERE'S NOTHING YOU COULD HAVE DONE. IT WASN'T YOUR FAULT.
NO. IT WASN'T.
IT WAS **THEIR** FAULT.
I'LL DIE FIGHTING **THEM,** BUT NOT THEIR ENEMIES.
WE'VE BEEN IN THIS TOGETHER FOR LIKE A YEAR NOW. WHY DIDN'T YOU TELL ME THIS BEFORE?
I GUESS THAT IF WE'RE GOING TO DIE, I JUST WANT TO PUT IT ALL OUT THERE.
I ALWAYS THOUGHT BEYONCÉ WAS KIND OF OVERRATED.
WHAT? YOU'RE KIDDING, RIGHT?
IF SO, IT'S NOT VERY FUNNY.
JUST PUTTING IT OUT THERE.
THAT'S ONE SECRET YOU SHOULD PROBABLY JUST PUT RIGHT BACK IN.
SKREE
WHAT WAS THAT?

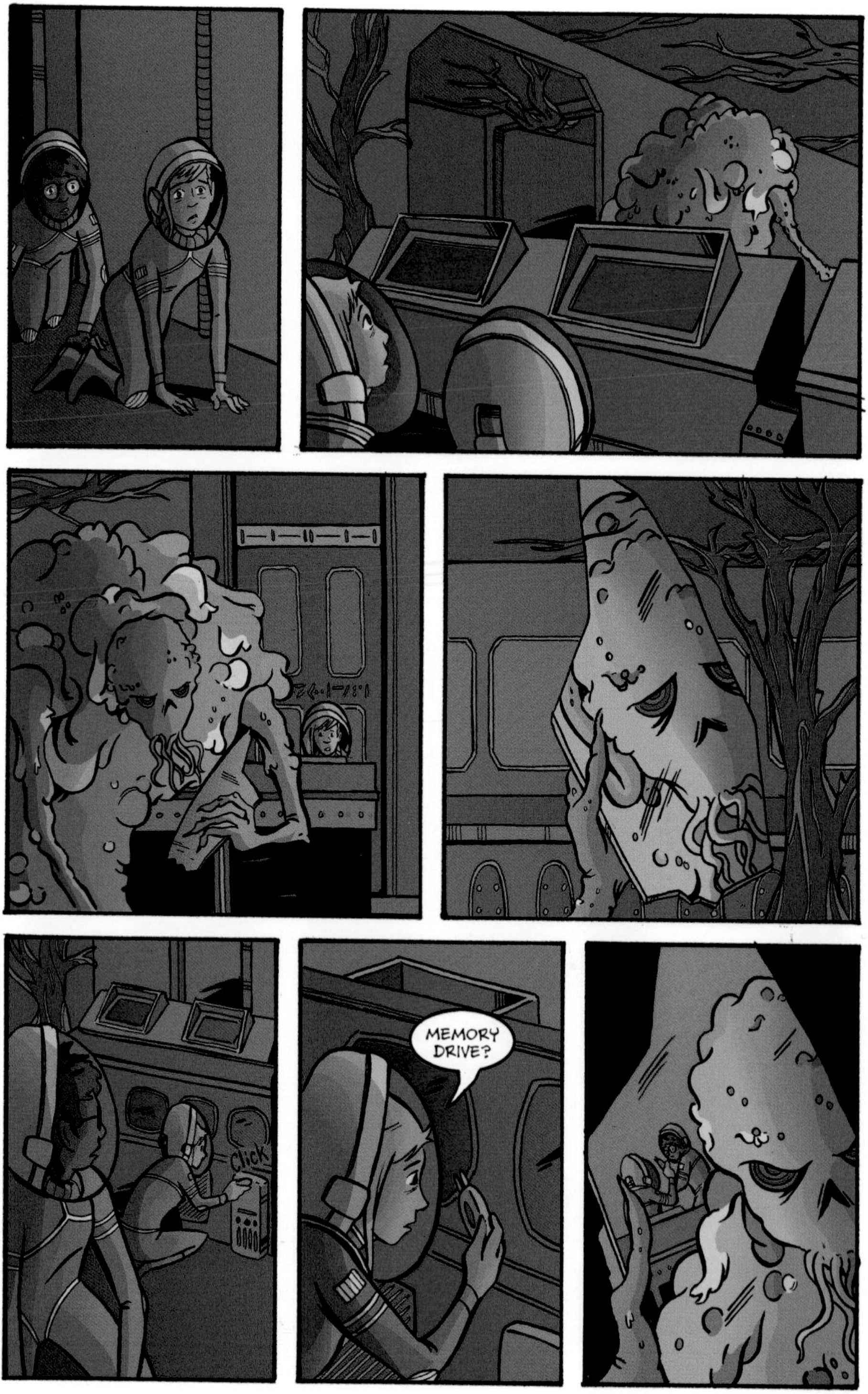
CLICK
MEMORY DRIVE?

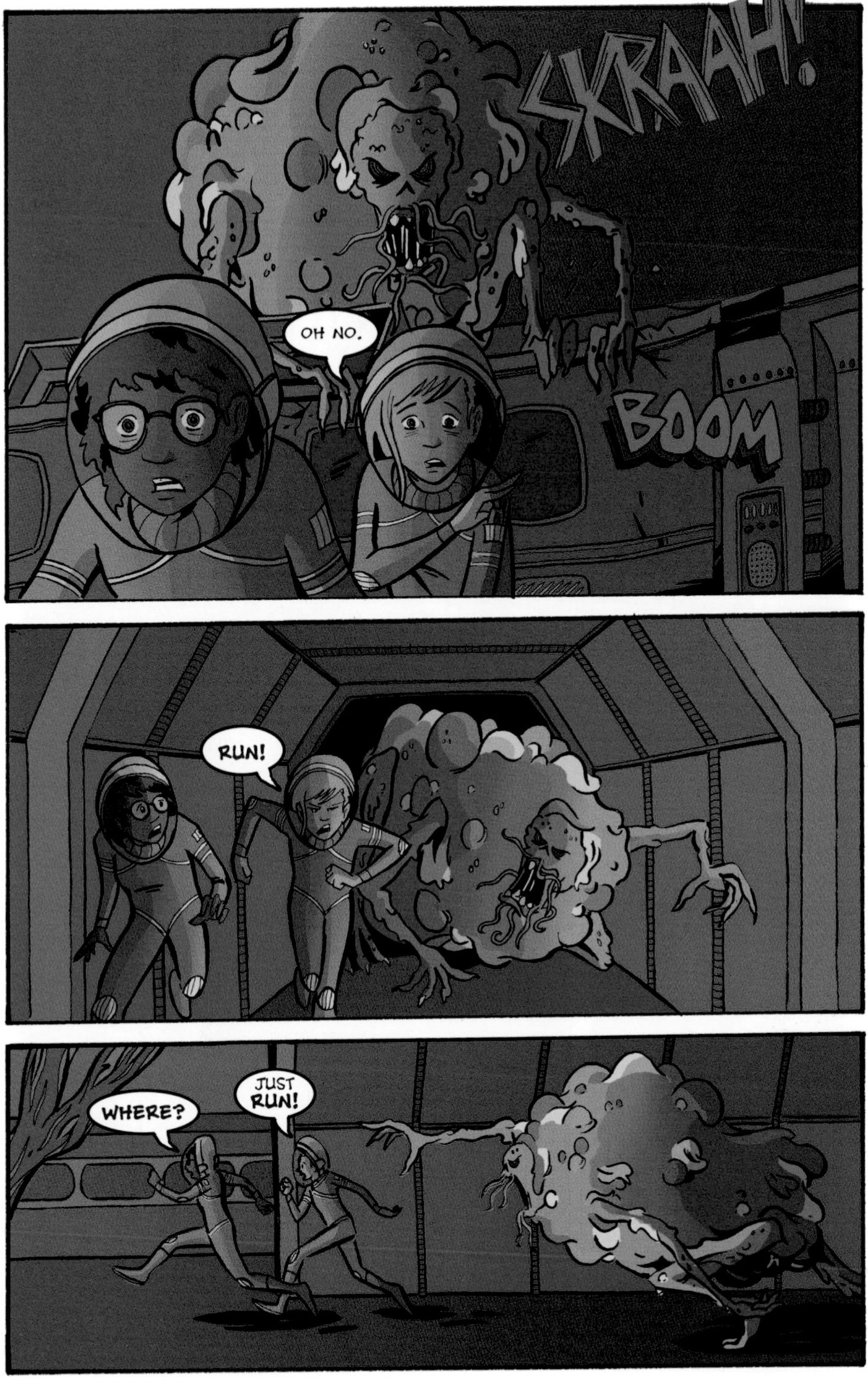
SKRAAH!
OH NO.
BOOM
RUN!
WHERE?
JUST RUN!

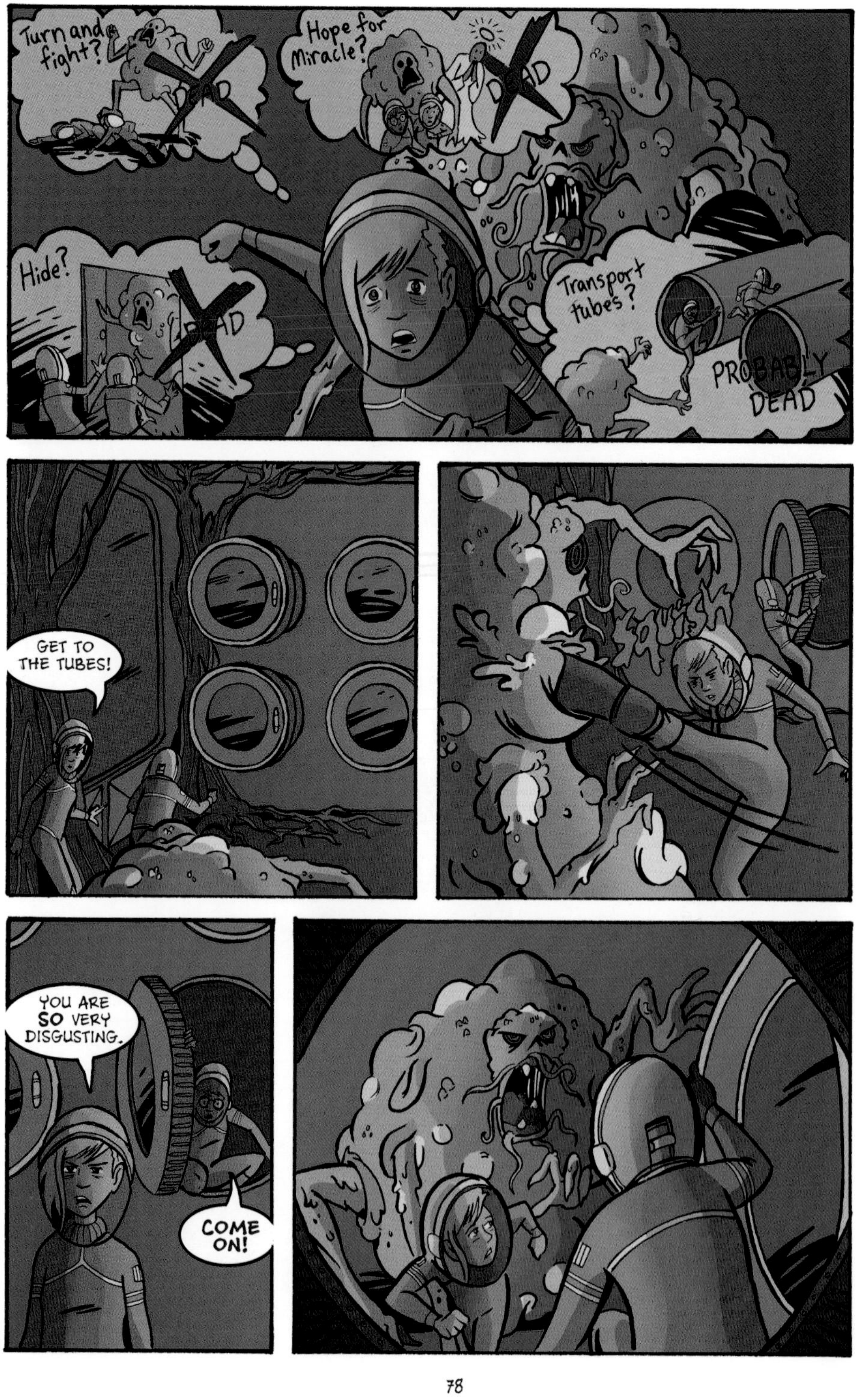
Turn and fight?
DEAD
Hope for Miracle?
DEAD
Hide?
DEAD
Transport tubes?
PROBABLY DEAD
GET TO THE TUBES!
YOU ARE **SO** VERY DISGUSTING.
COME ON!

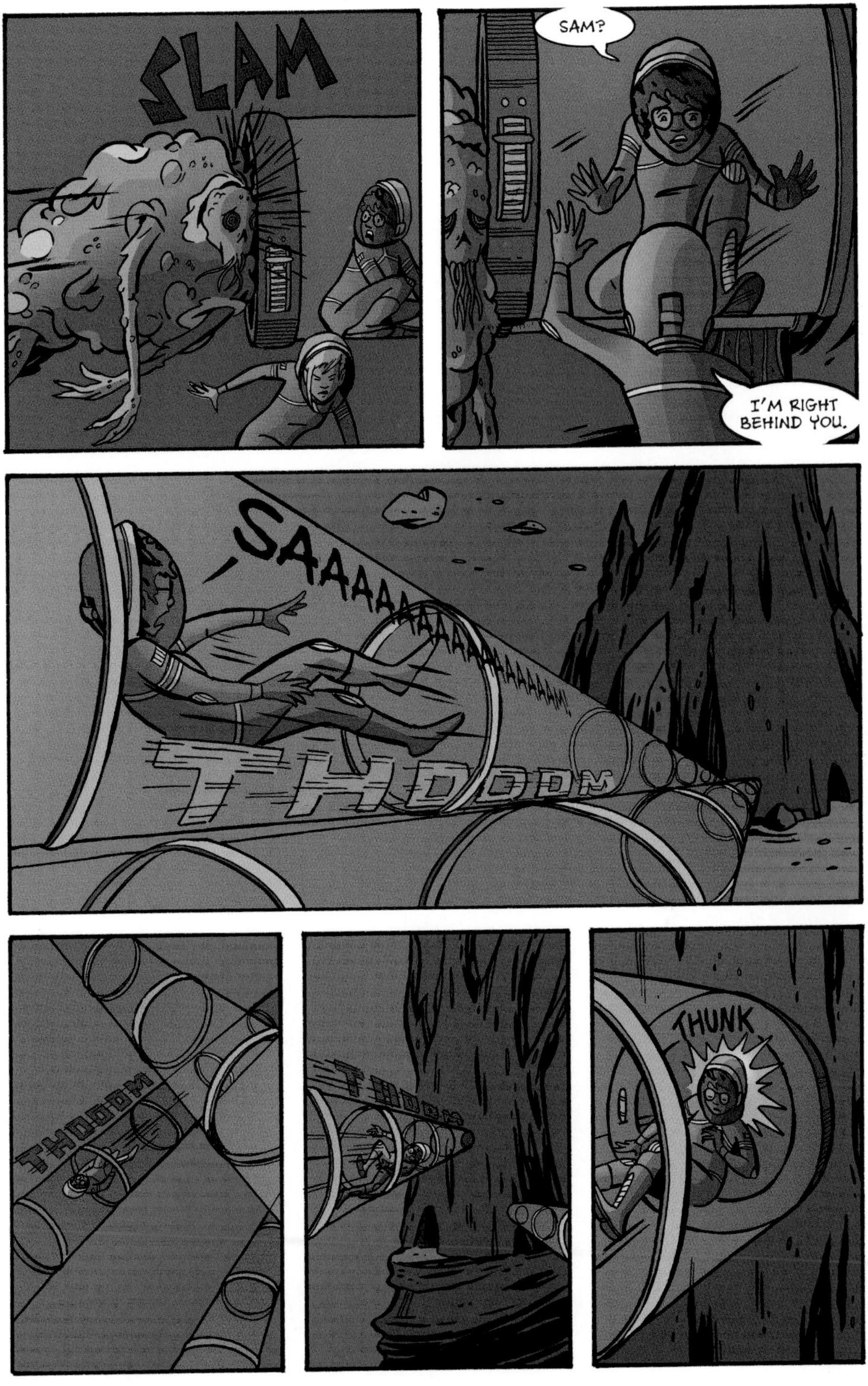
SLAM
SAM?
I'M RIGHT BEHIND YOU.
SAAAAAAAAAAAAAAAAAAAAM!
THDOOM
THDOOM
THDOOM
THUNK

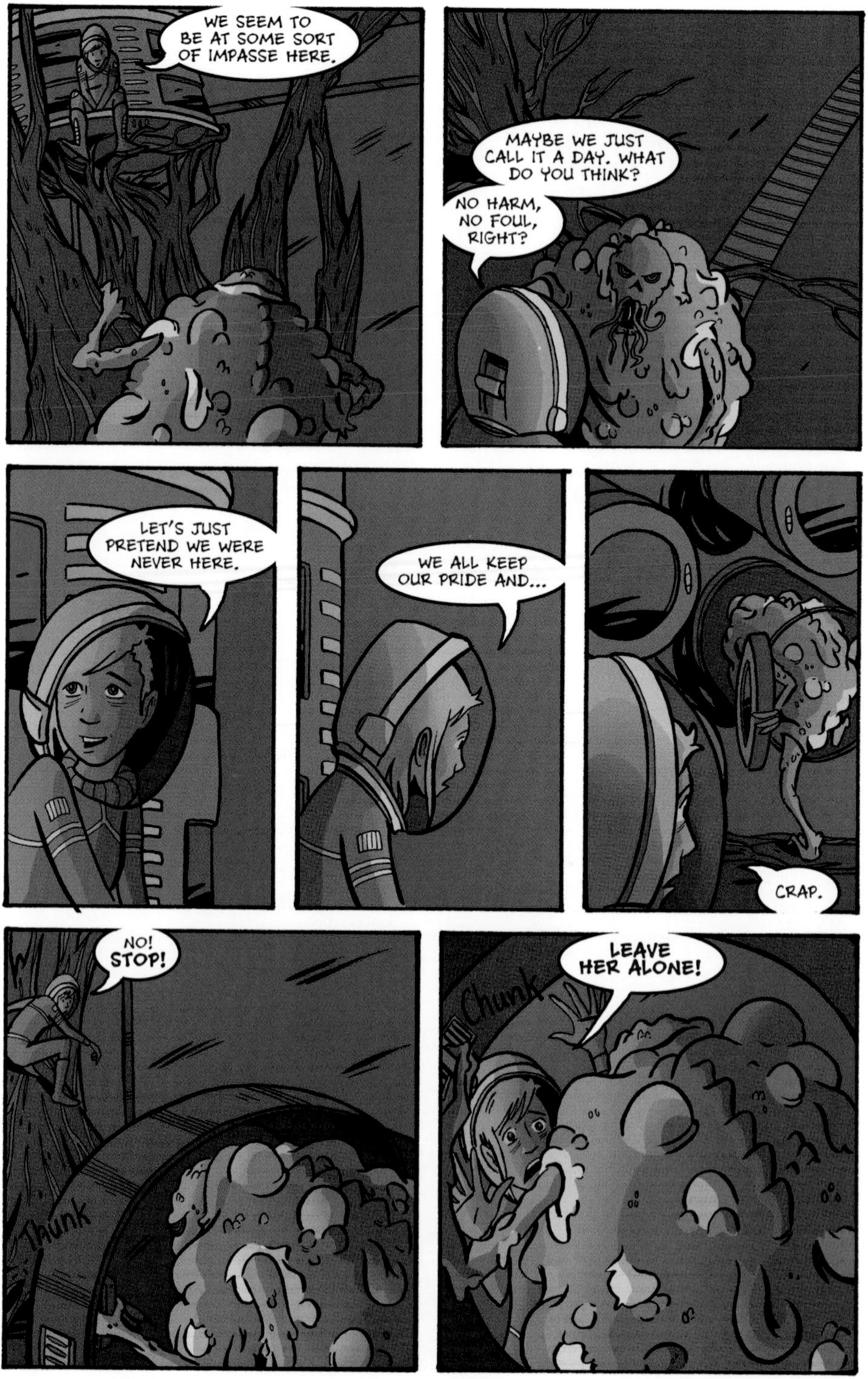
WE SEEM TO BE AT SOME SORT OF IMPASSE HERE.
MAYBE WE JUST CALL IT A DAY. WHAT DO YOU THINK?
NO HARM, NO FOUL, RIGHT?
LET'S JUST PRETEND WE WERE NEVER HERE.
WE ALL KEEP OUR PRIDE AND...
CRAP.
NO! STOP!
Thunk
LEAVE HER ALONE!
Chunk

THUNK
MIA.
THOOOM
RIP
THUMP

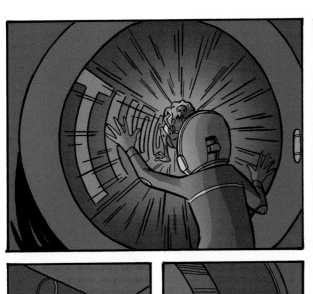

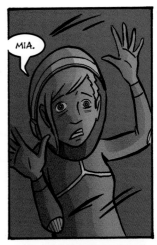

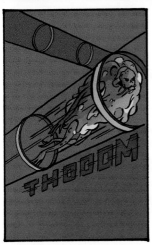

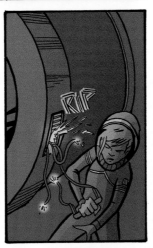

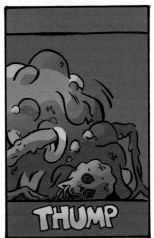

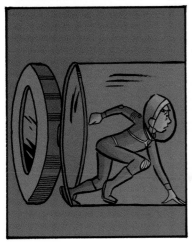

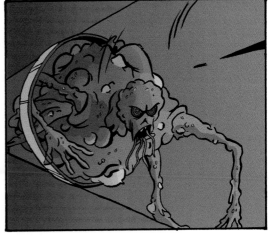

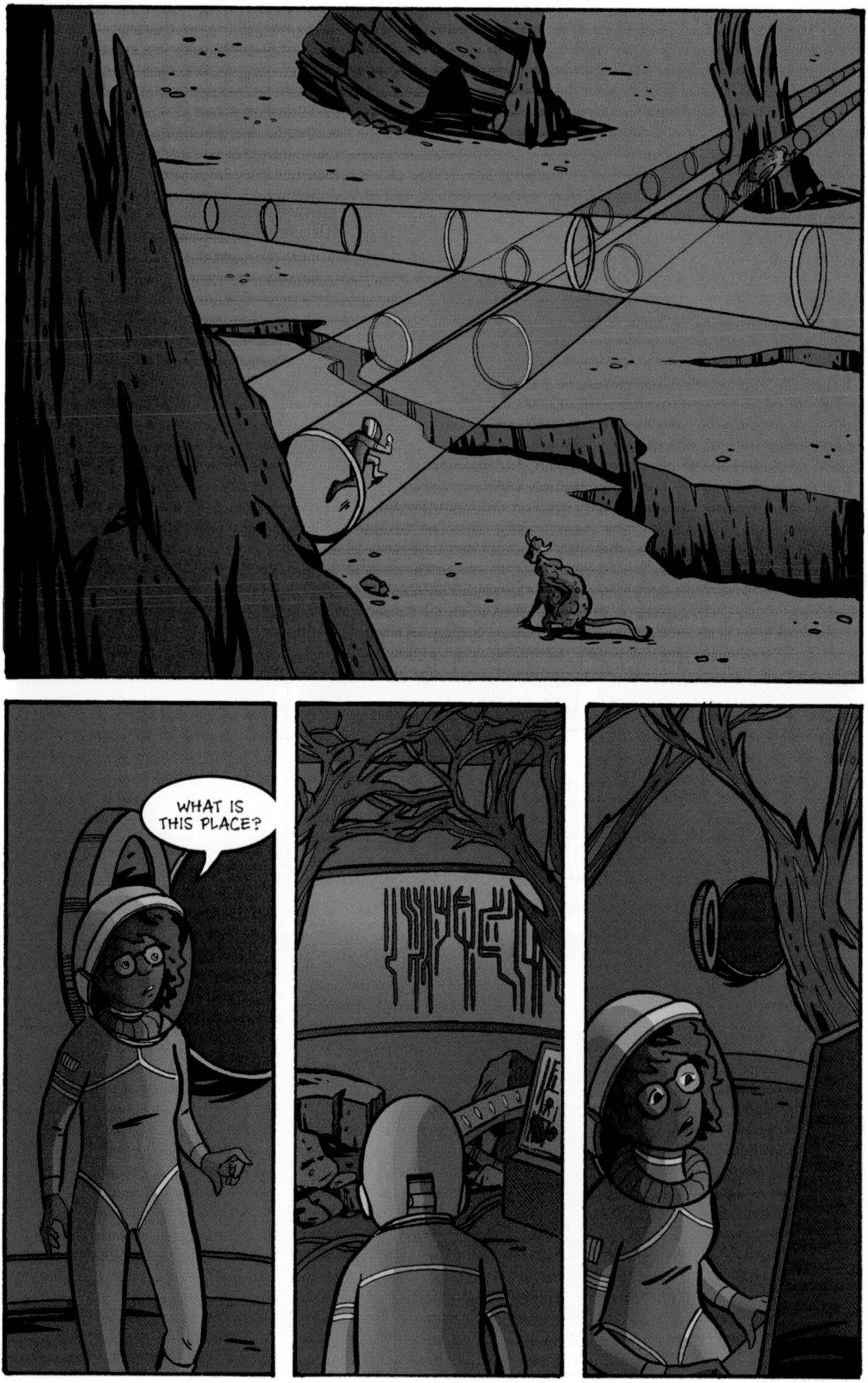
WHAT IS THIS PLACE?

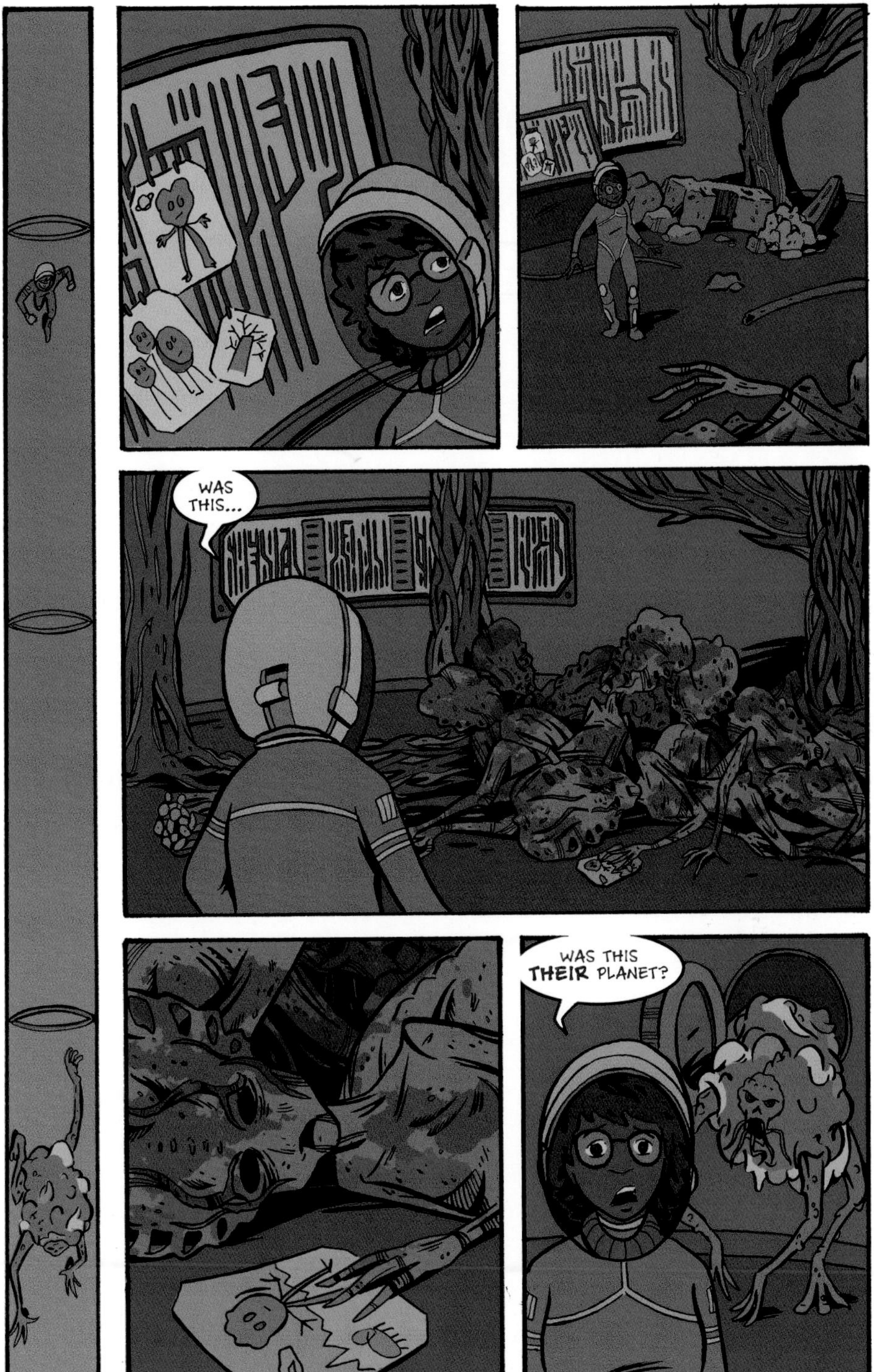
WAS THIS...
WAS THIS THEIR PLANET?

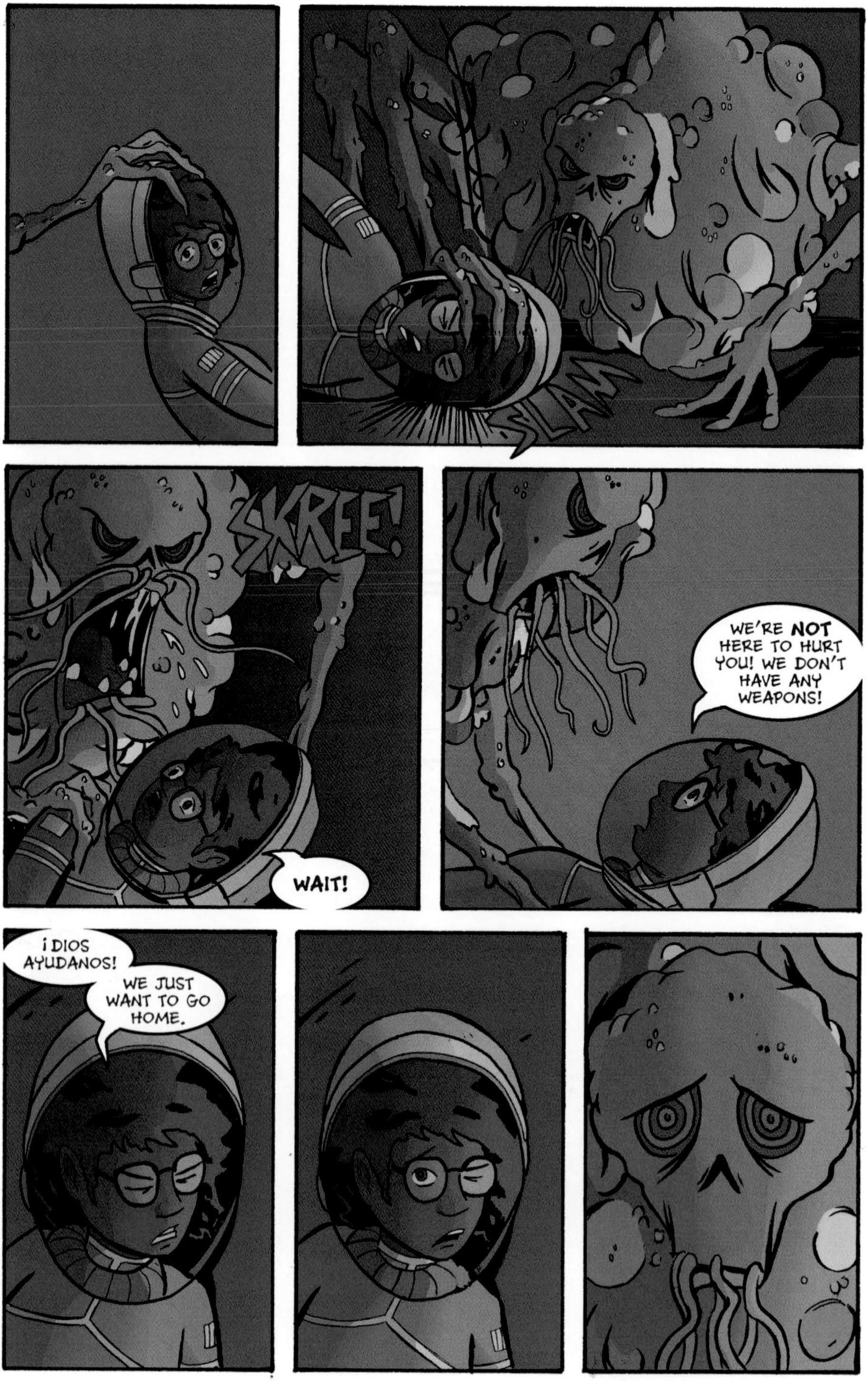
SLAM
SKREE!
WAIT!
WE'RE **NOT** HERE TO HURT YOU! WE DON'T HAVE ANY WEAPONS!
¡DIOS AYUDANOS!
WE JUST WANT TO GO HOME.

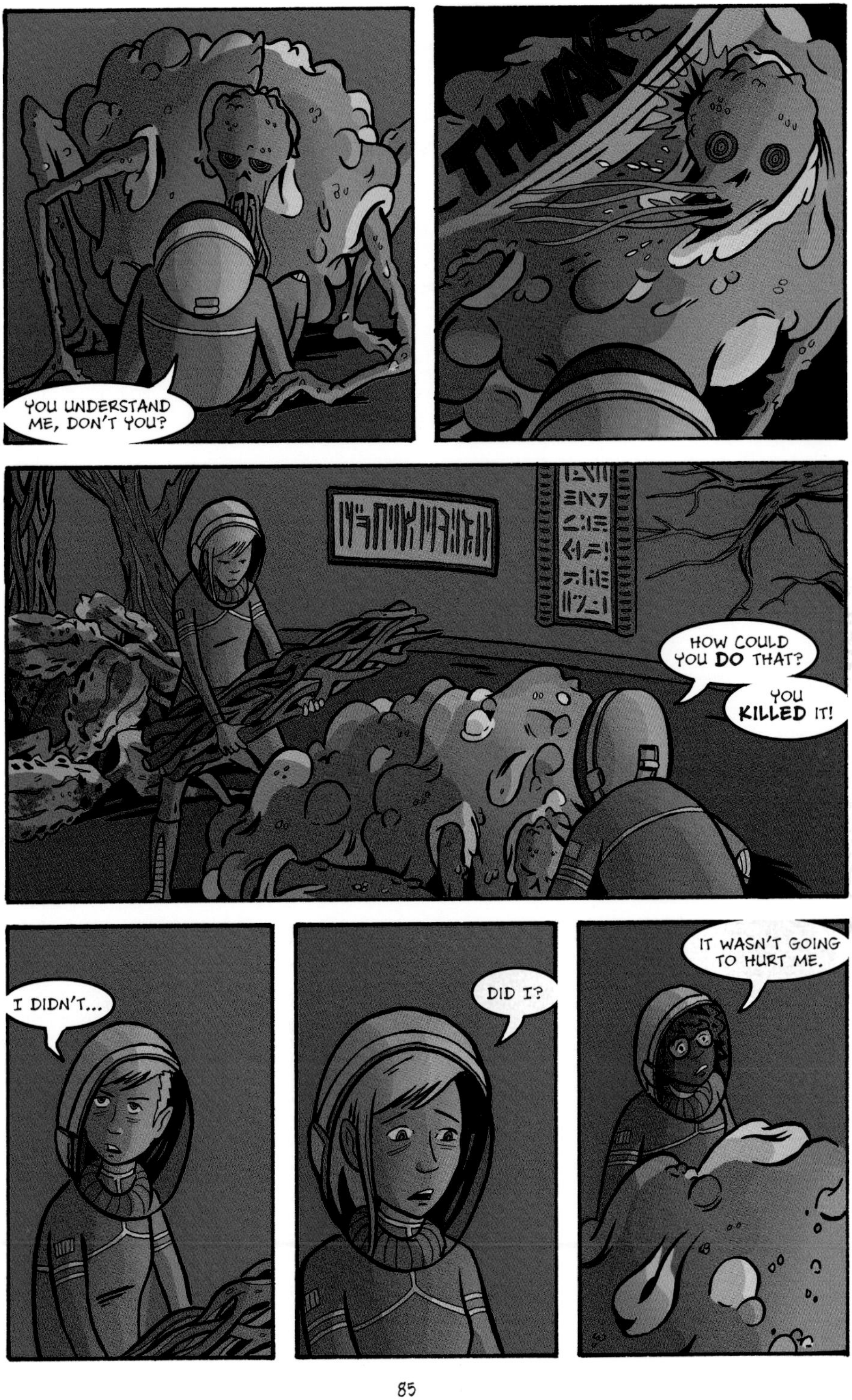
YOU UNDERSTAND ME, DON'T YOU?
THWAK
HOW COULD YOU DO THAT?
YOU KILLED IT!
I DIDN'T...
DID I?
IT WASN'T GOING TO HURT ME.

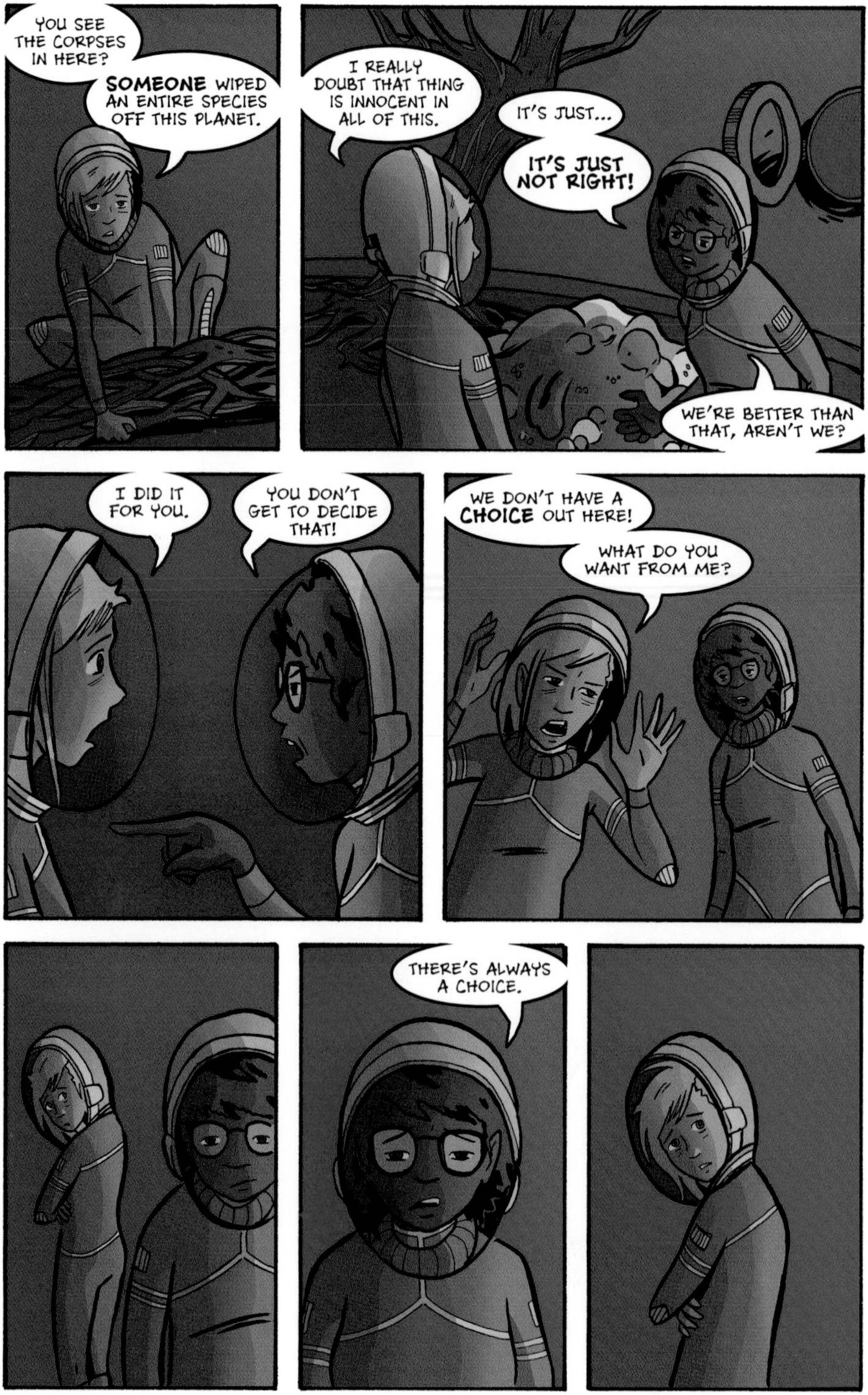

YOU SEE THE CORPSES IN HERE?
SOMEONE WIPED AN ENTIRE SPECIES OFF THIS PLANET.
I REALLY DOUBT THAT THING IS INNOCENT IN ALL OF THIS.
IT'S JUST...
IT'S JUST NOT RIGHT!
WE'RE BETTER THAN THAT, AREN'T WE?
I DID IT FOR YOU.
YOU DON'T GET TO DECIDE THAT!
WE DON'T HAVE A **CHOICE** OUT HERE!
WHAT DO YOU WANT FROM ME?
THERE'S ALWAYS A CHOICE.

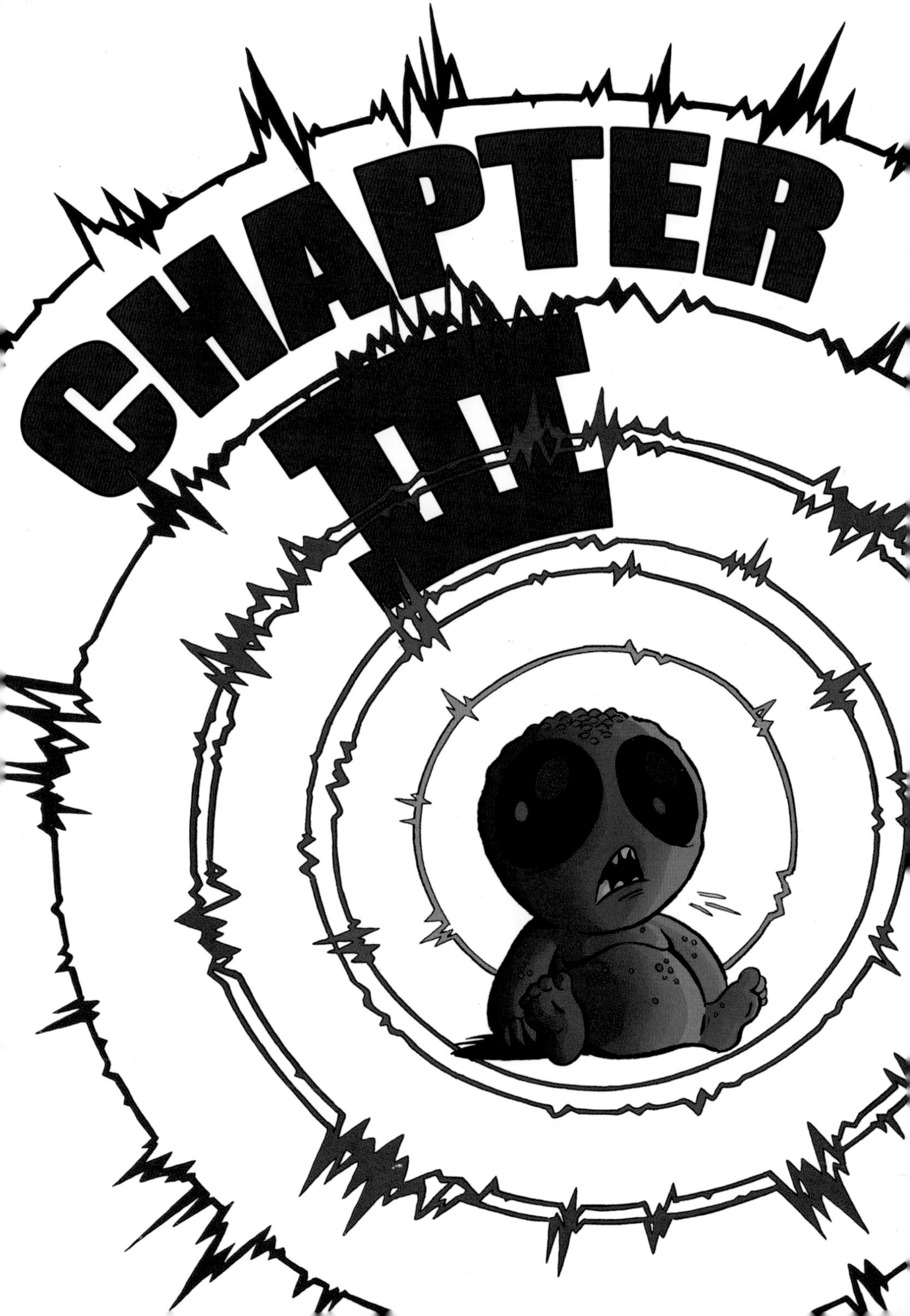
CHAPTER
III

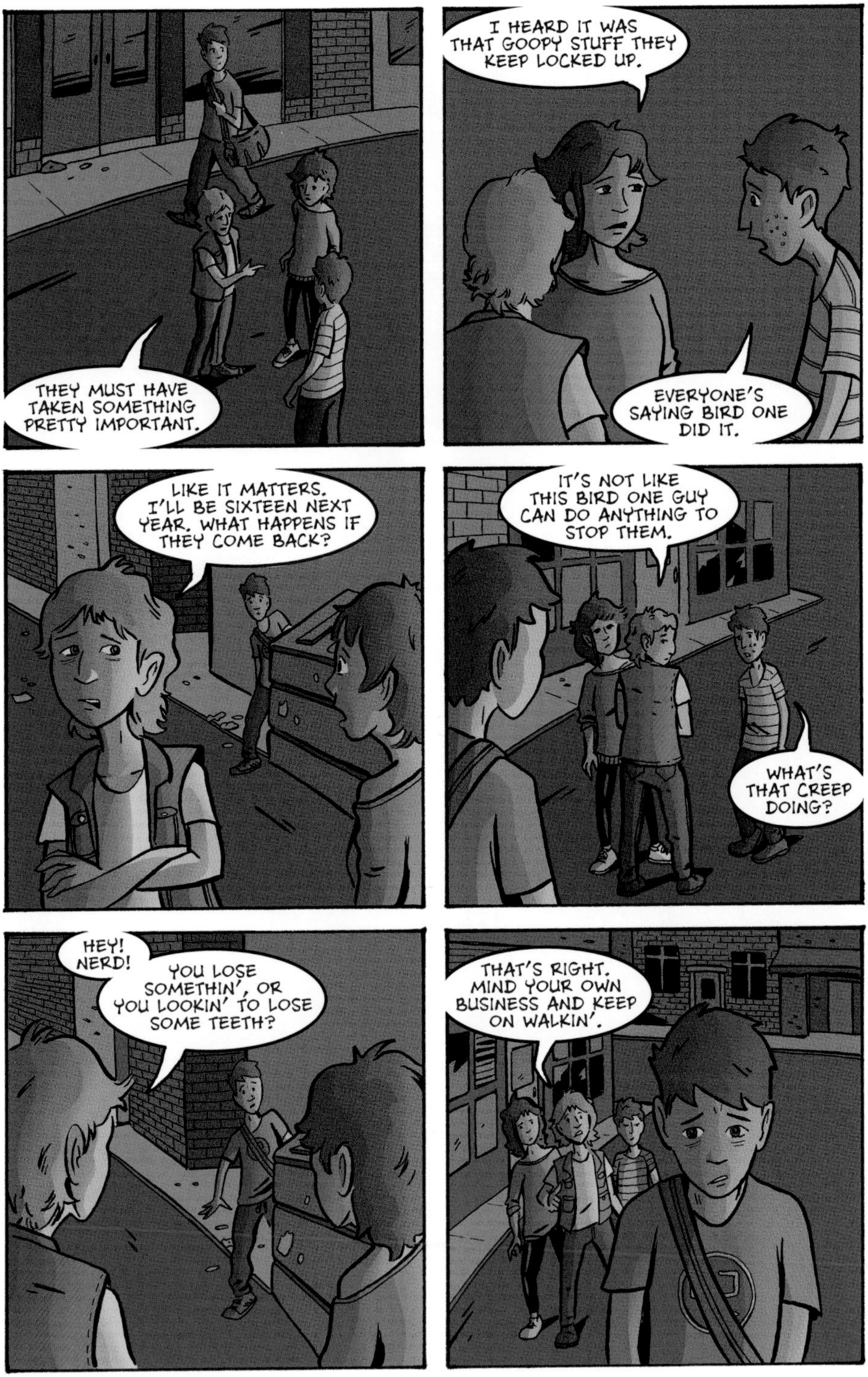
THEY MUST HAVE TAKEN SOMETHING PRETTY IMPORTANT.
I HEARD IT WAS THAT GOOPY STUFF THEY KEEP LOCKED UP.
EVERYONE'S SAYING BIRD ONE DID IT.
LIKE IT MATTERS. I'LL BE SIXTEEN NEXT YEAR. WHAT HAPPENS IF THEY COME BACK?
IT'S NOT LIKE THIS BIRD ONE GUY CAN DO ANYTHING TO STOP THEM.
WHAT'S THAT CREEP DOING?
HEY! NERD!
YOU LOSE SOMETHIN', OR YOU LOOKIN' TO LOSE SOME TEETH?
THAT'S RIGHT. MIND YOUR OWN BUSINESS AND KEEP ON WALKIN'.

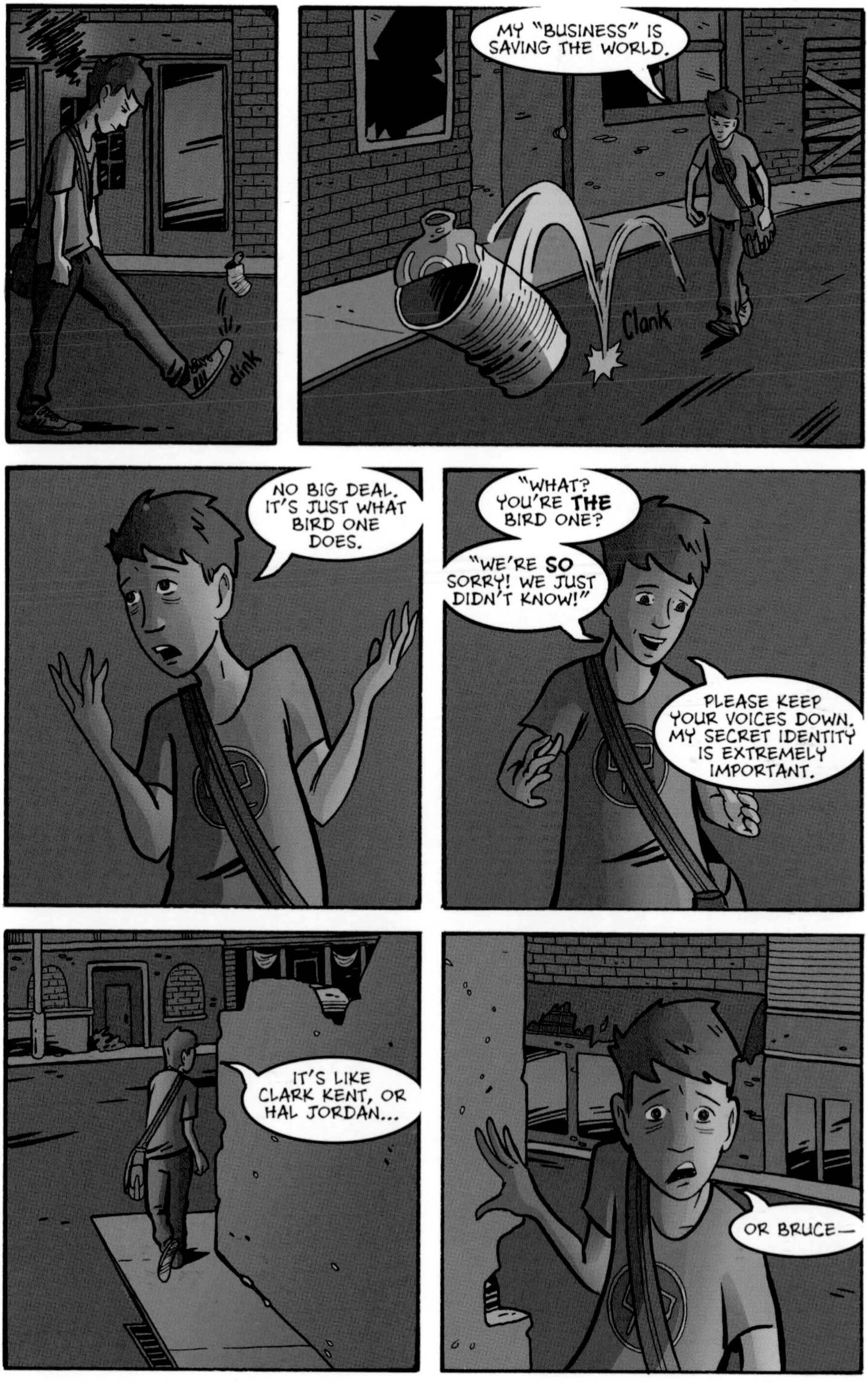
dink
MY "BUSINESS" IS SAVING THE WORLD.
Clank
NO BIG DEAL. IT'S JUST WHAT BIRD ONE DOES.
"WHAT? YOU'RE THE BIRD ONE?
"WE'RE SO SORRY! WE JUST DIDN'T KNOW!"
PLEASE KEEP YOUR VOICES DOWN. MY SECRET IDENTITY IS EXTREMELY IMPORTANT.
IT'S LIKE CLARK KENT, OR HAL JORDAN...
OR BRUCE—

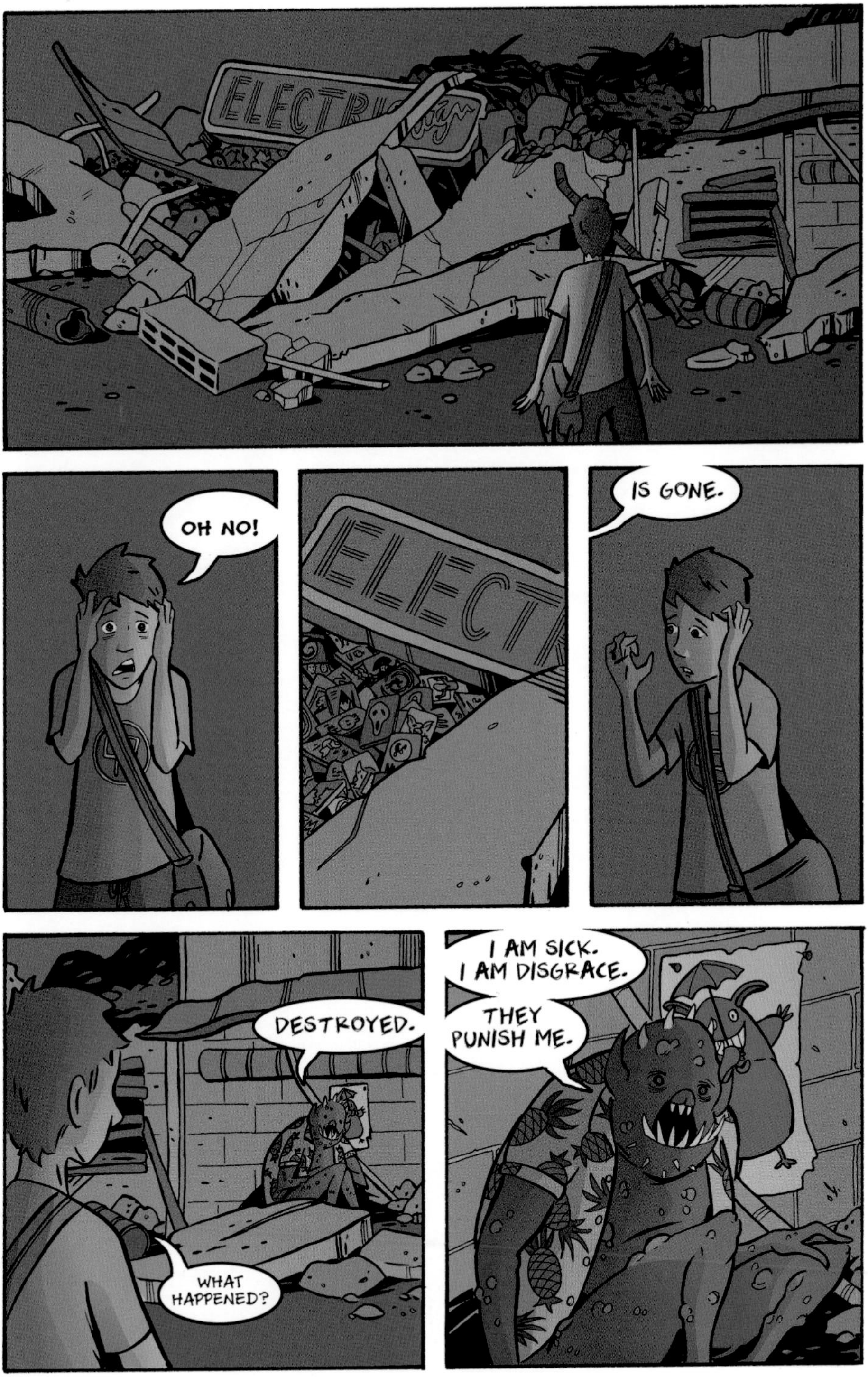
ELECTRI
ELECTR
OH NO!
IS GONE.
WHAT HAPPENED?
DESTROYED.
I AM SICK. I AM DISGRACE.
THEY PUNISH ME.

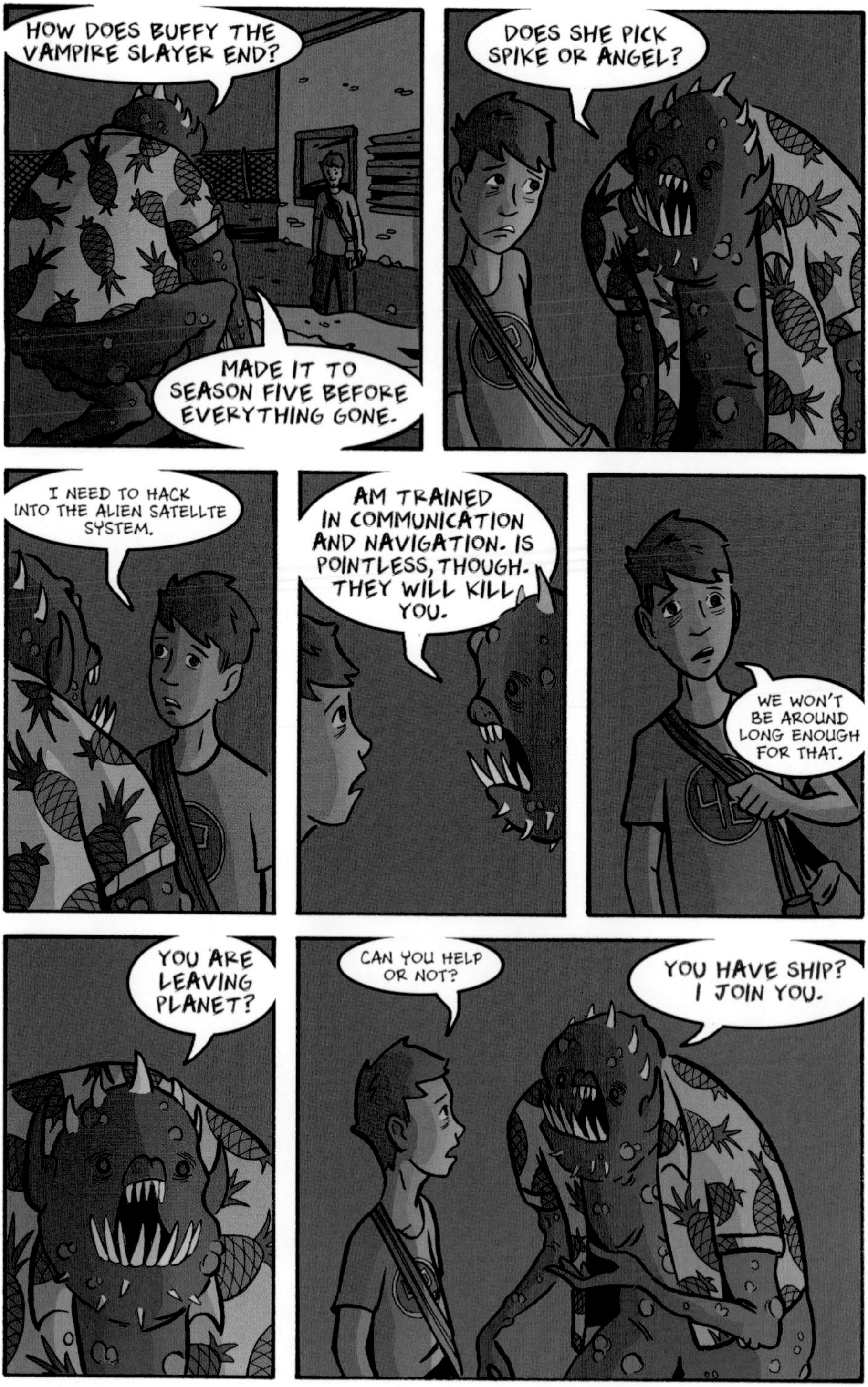
HOW DOES BUFFY THE VAMPIRE SLAYER END?
MADE IT TO SEASON FIVE BEFORE EVERYTHING GONE.
DOES SHE PICK SPIKE OR ANGEL?
I NEED TO HACK INTO THE ALIEN SATELLTE SYSTEM.
AM TRAINED IN COMMUNICATION AND NAVIGATION. IS POINTLESS, THOUGH. THEY WILL KILL YOU.
WE WON'T BE AROUND LONG ENOUGH FOR THAT.
YOU ARE LEAVING PLANET?
CAN YOU HELP OR NOT?
YOU HAVE SHIP? I JOIN YOU.

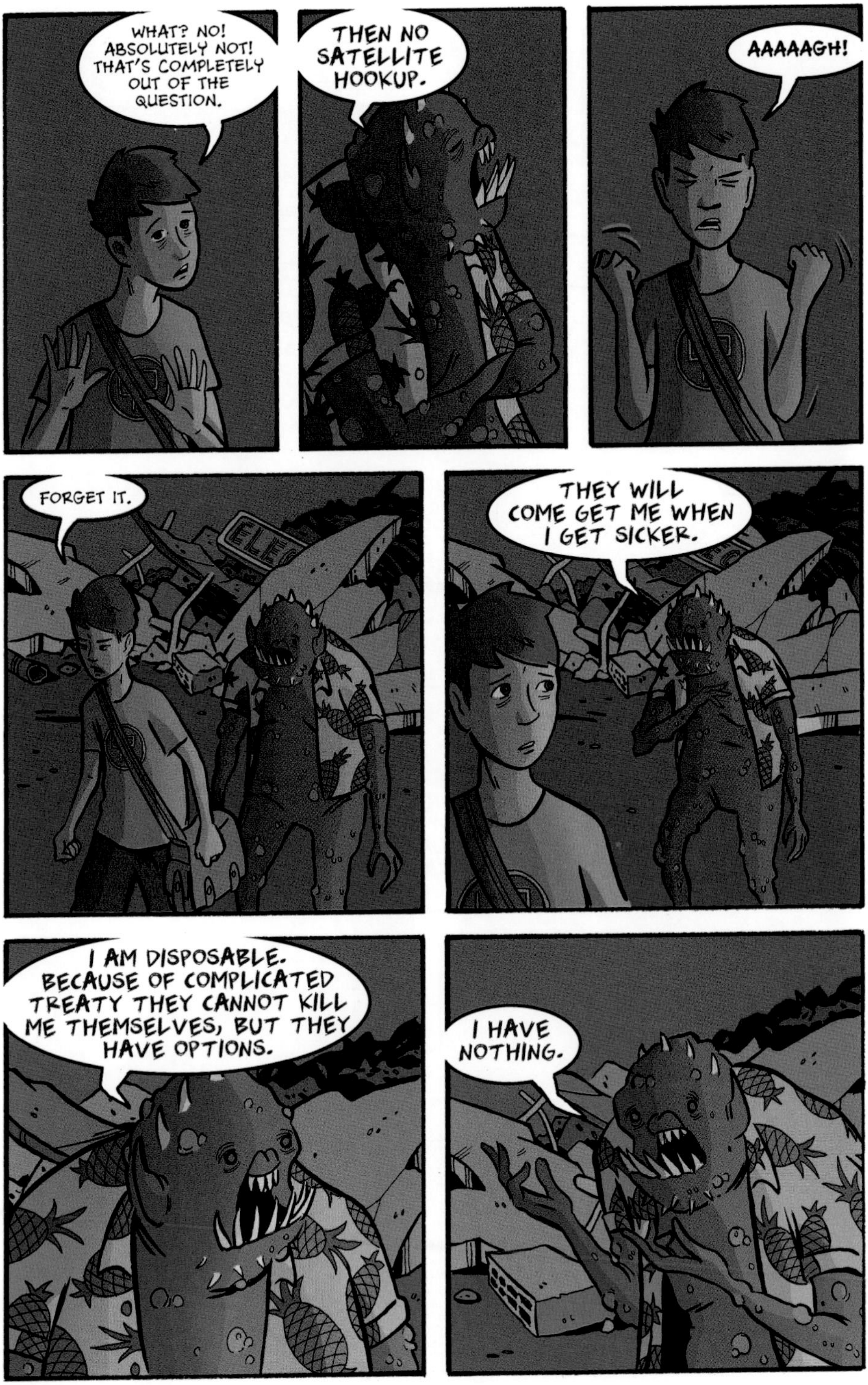
WHAT? NO! ABSOLUTELY NOT! THAT'S COMPLETELY OUT OF THE QUESTION.
THEN NO SATELLITE HOOKUP.
AAAAAGH!
FORGET IT.
THEY WILL COME GET ME WHEN I GET SICKER.
I AM DISPOSABLE. BECAUSE OF COMPLICATED TREATY THEY CANNOT KILL ME THEMSELVES, BUT THEY HAVE OPTIONS.
I HAVE NOTHING.

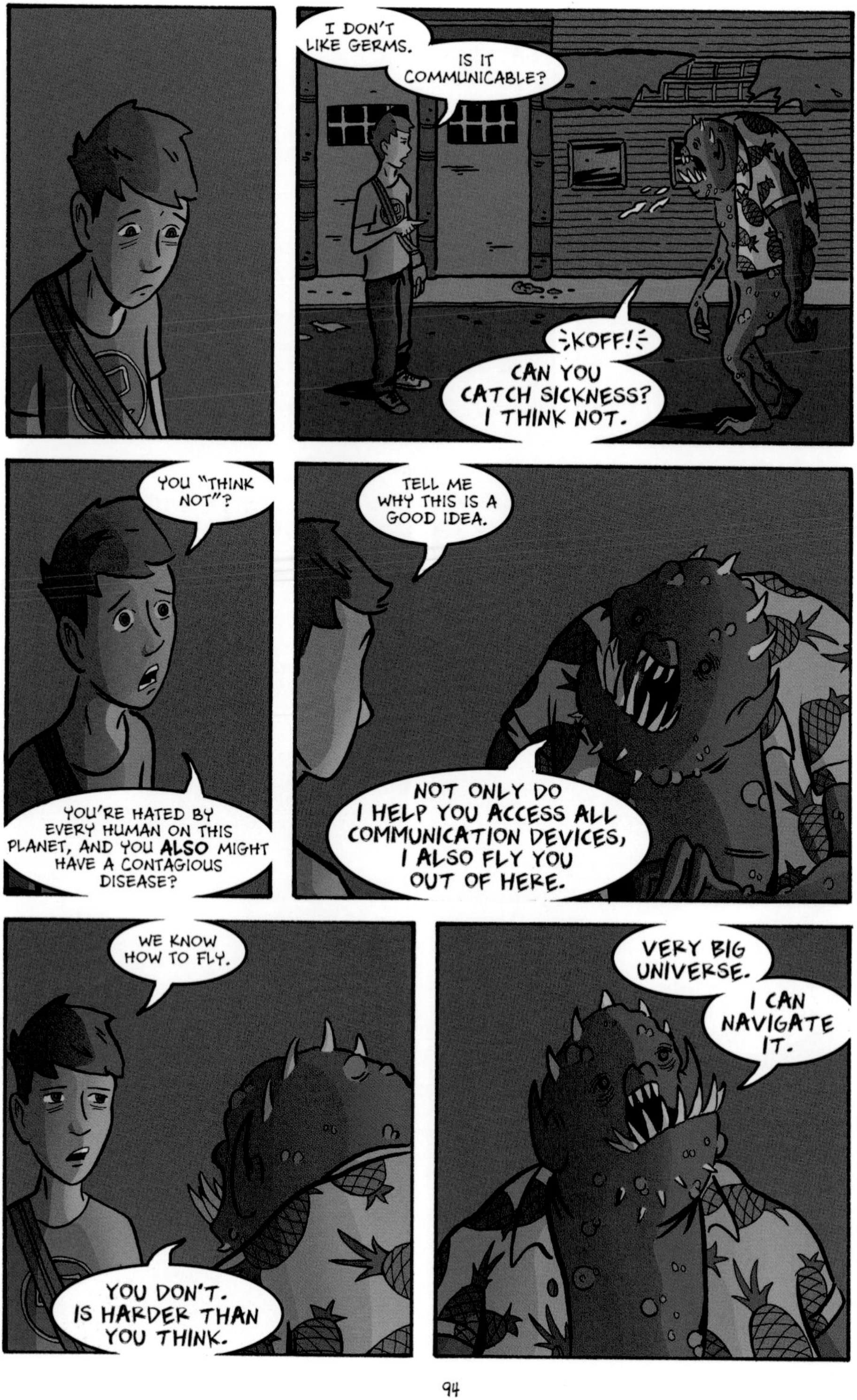
I DON'T LIKE GERMS.
IS IT COMMUNICABLE?
KOFF!
CAN YOU CATCH SICKNESS? I THINK NOT.
YOU "THINK NOT"?
YOU'RE HATED BY EVERY HUMAN ON THIS PLANET, AND YOU ALSO MIGHT HAVE A CONTAGIOUS DISEASE?
TELL ME WHY THIS IS A GOOD IDEA.
NOT ONLY DO I HELP YOU ACCESS ALL COMMUNICATION DEVICES, I ALSO FLY YOU OUT OF HERE.
WE KNOW HOW TO FLY.
YOU DON'T. IS HARDER THAN YOU THINK.
VERY BIG UNIVERSE.
I CAN NAVIGATE IT.

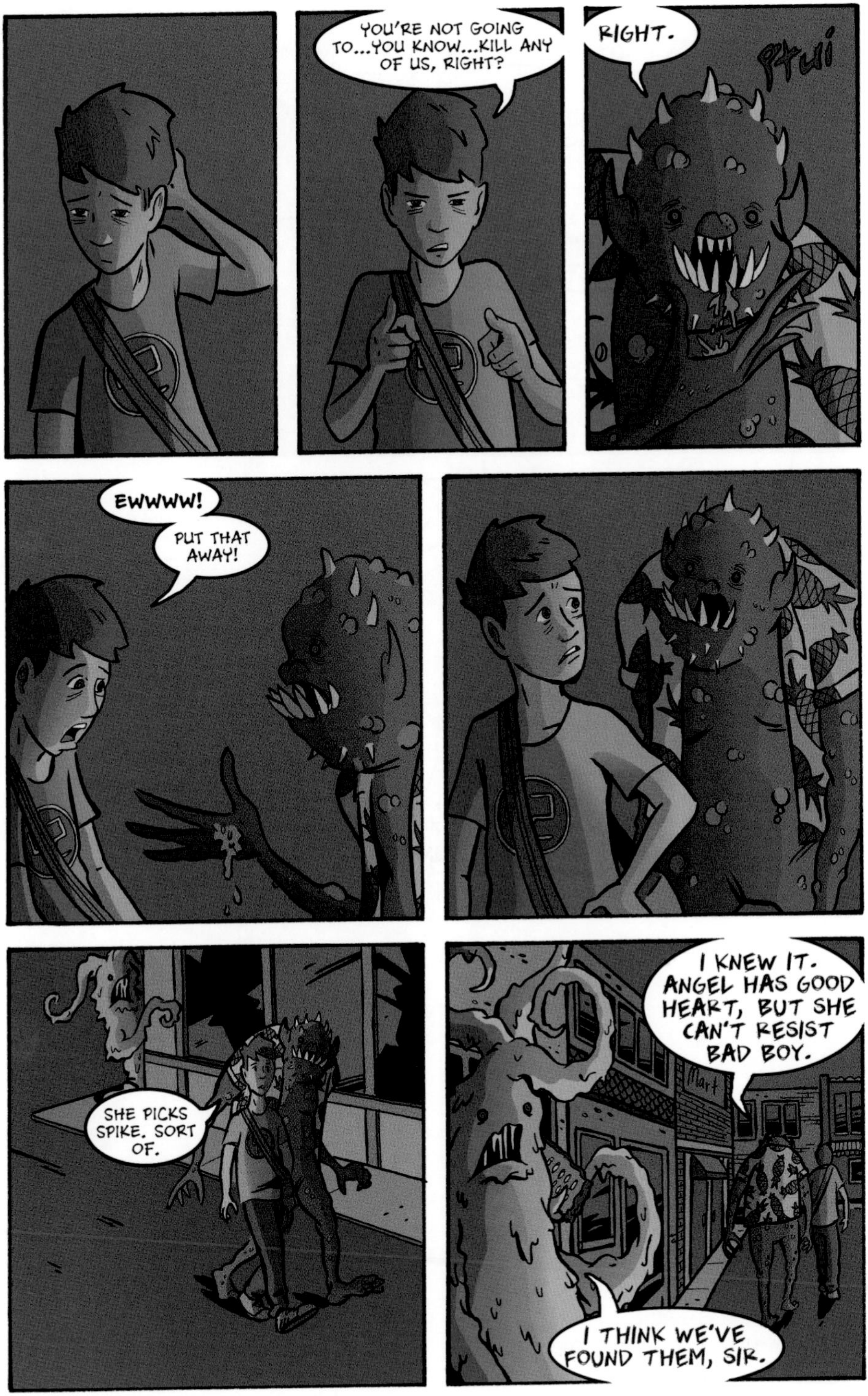
YOU'RE NOT GOING TO...YOU KNOW...KILL ANY OF US, RIGHT?
RIGHT.
PTUI
EWWWW!
PUT THAT AWAY!
SHE PICKS SPIKE. SORT OF.
I KNEW IT. ANGEL HAS GOOD HEART, BUT SHE CAN'T RESIST BAD BOY.
I THINK WE'VE FOUND THEM, SIR.

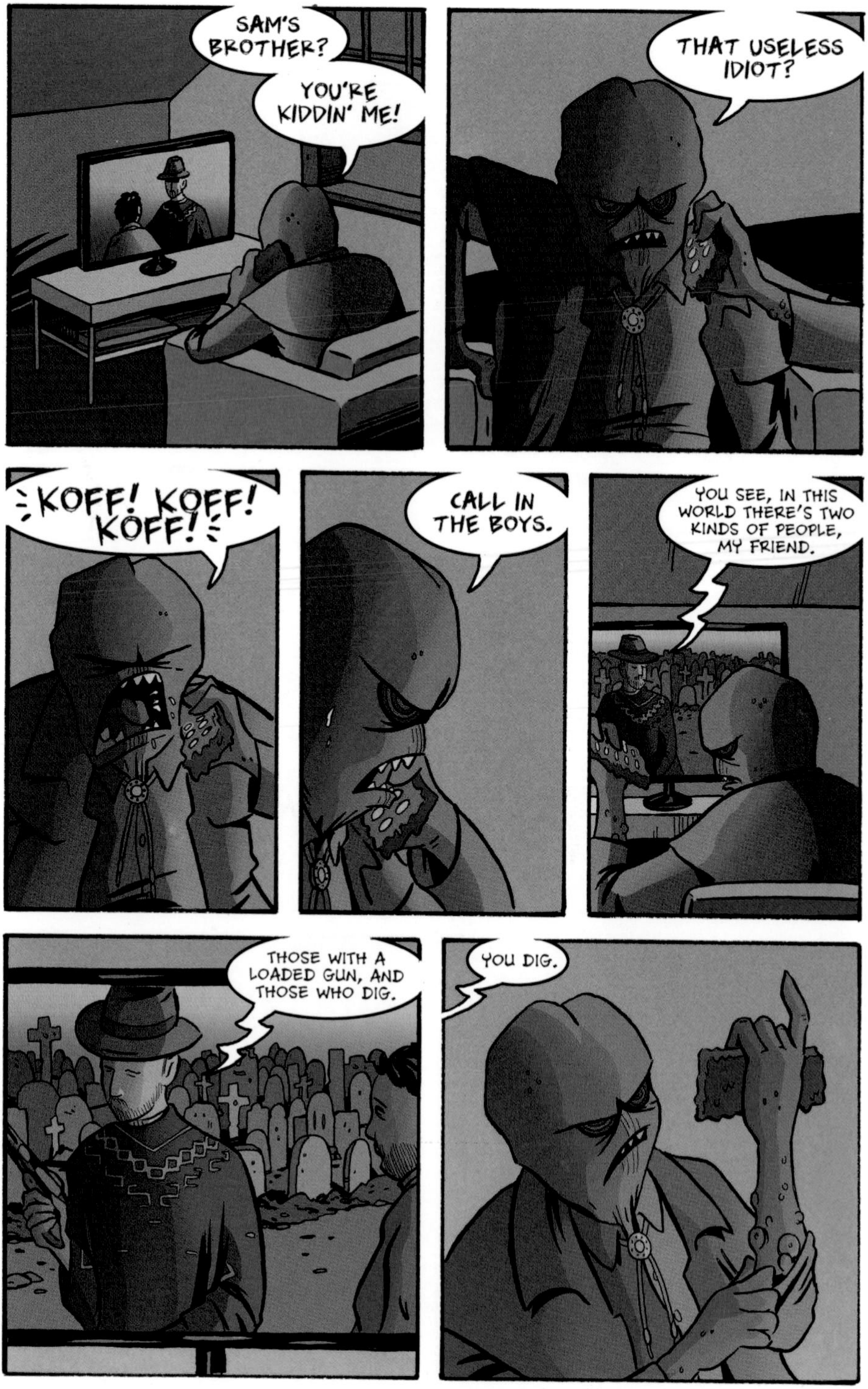
SAM'S BROTHER?
YOU'RE KIDDIN' ME!
THAT USELESS IDIOT?
KOFF! KOFF! KOFF!
CALL IN THE BOYS.
YOU SEE, IN THIS WORLD THERE'S TWO KINDS OF PEOPLE, MY FRIEND.
THOSE WITH A LOADED GUN, AND THOSE WHO DIG.
YOU DIG.

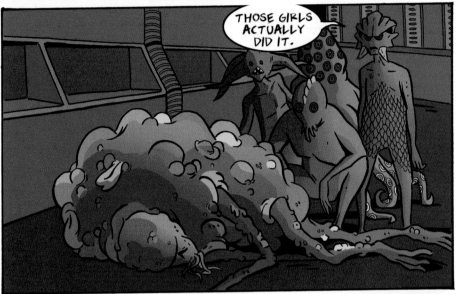

THOSE GIRLS
ACTUALLY
DID IT.

I HAVEN'T SEEN
ONE UP CLOSE IN
A LONG TIME.

YOU OWE ME
THIRTY RATIONS!

HA!

SEND THEM OUT
TOMORROW. I WANT
THEM DEAD.

EYES
FORWARD,
LINDA.

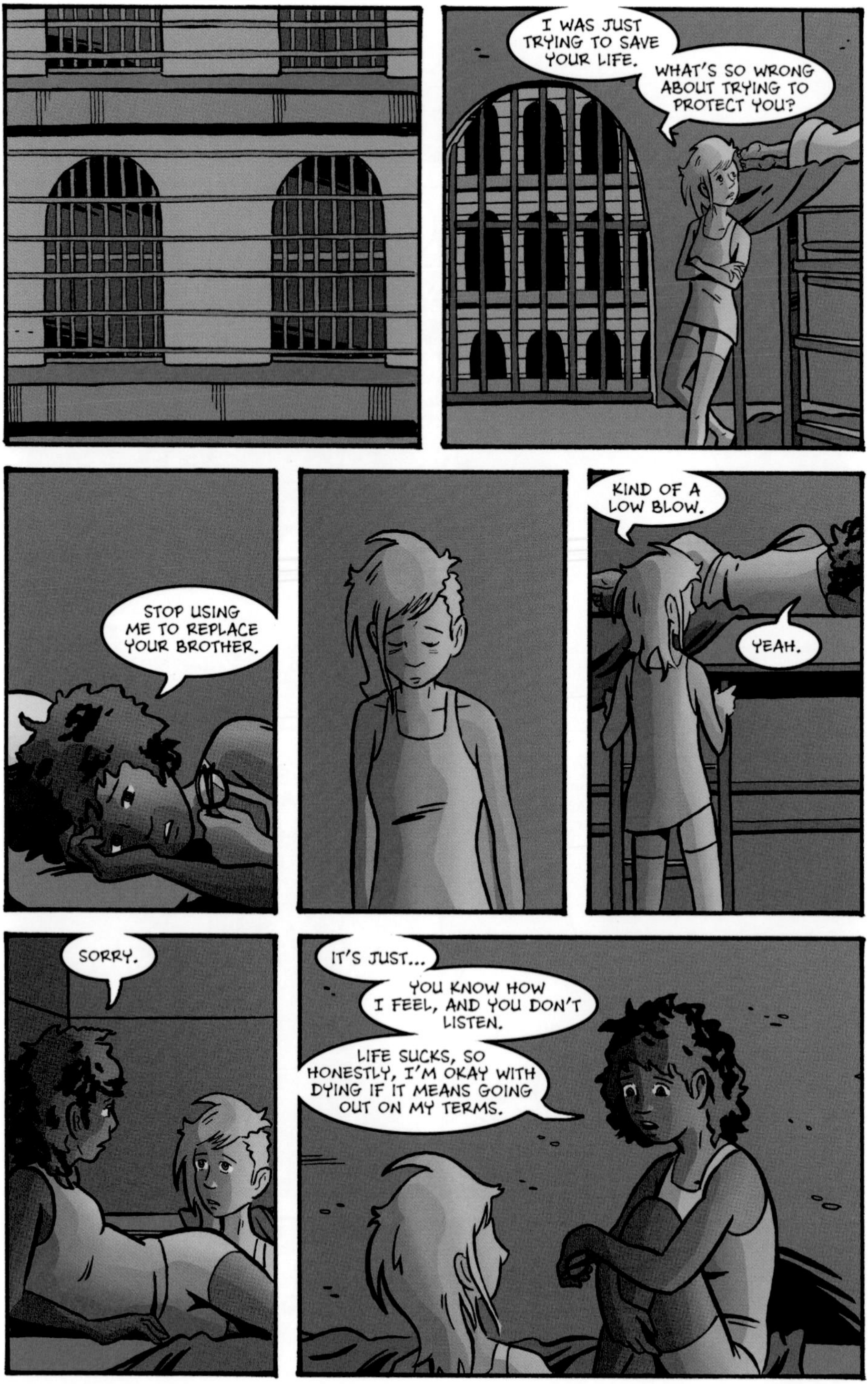
I WAS JUST TRYING TO SAVE YOUR LIFE.
WHAT'S SO WRONG ABOUT TRYING TO PROTECT YOU?
STOP USING ME TO REPLACE YOUR BROTHER.
KIND OF A LOW BLOW.
YEAH.
SORRY.
IT'S JUST...
YOU KNOW HOW I FEEL, AND YOU DON'T LISTEN.
LIFE SUCKS, SO HONESTLY, I'M OKAY WITH DYING IF IT MEANS GOING OUT ON MY TERMS.

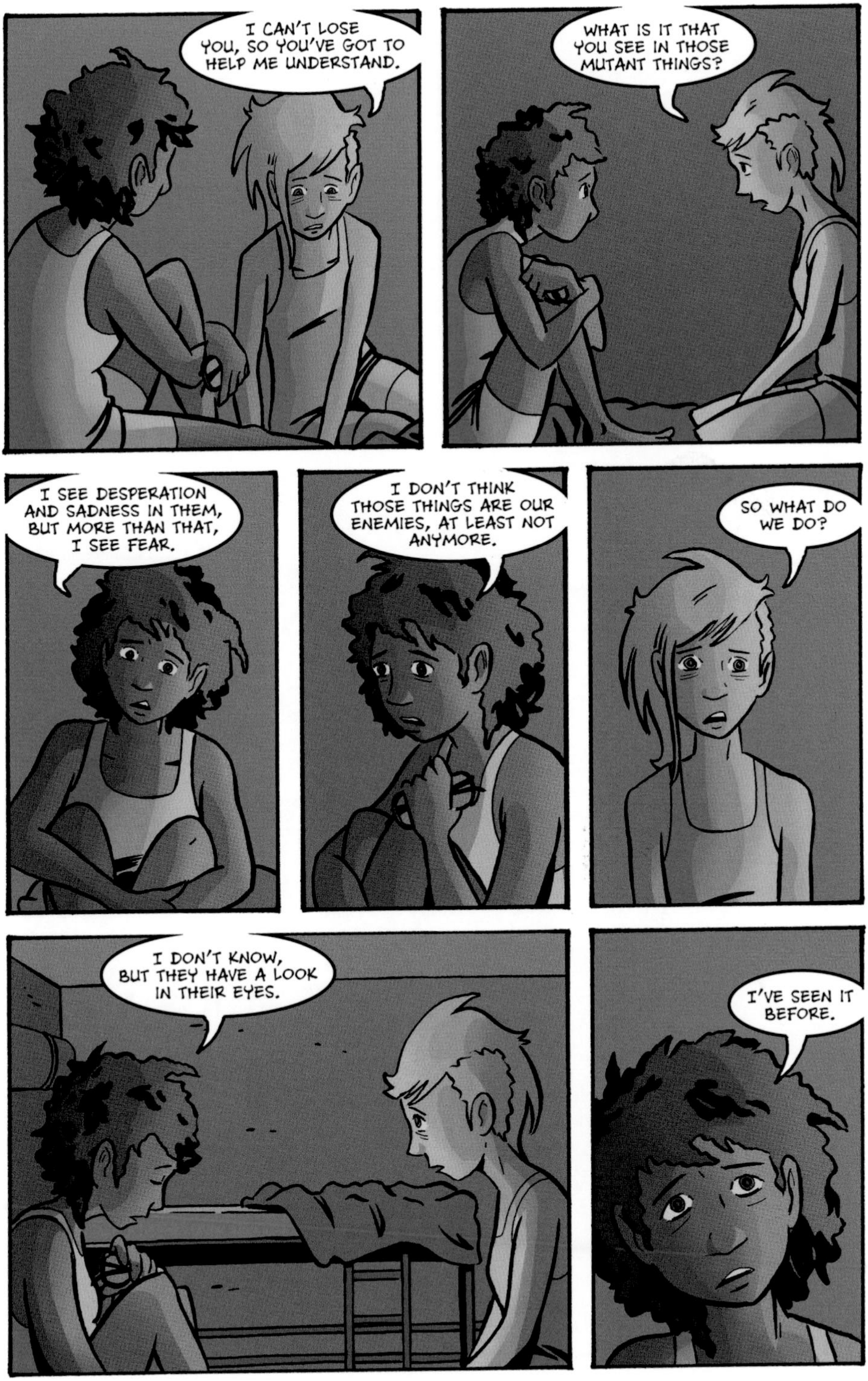

I CAN'T LOSE YOU, SO YOU'VE GOT TO HELP ME UNDERSTAND.
WHAT IS IT THAT YOU SEE IN THOSE MUTANT THINGS?
I SEE DESPERATION AND SADNESS IN THEM, BUT MORE THAN THAT, I SEE FEAR.
I DON'T THINK THOSE THINGS ARE OUR ENEMIES, AT LEAST NOT ANYMORE.
SO WHAT DO WE DO?
I DON'T KNOW, BUT THEY HAVE A LOOK IN THEIR EYES.
I'VE SEEN IT BEFORE.

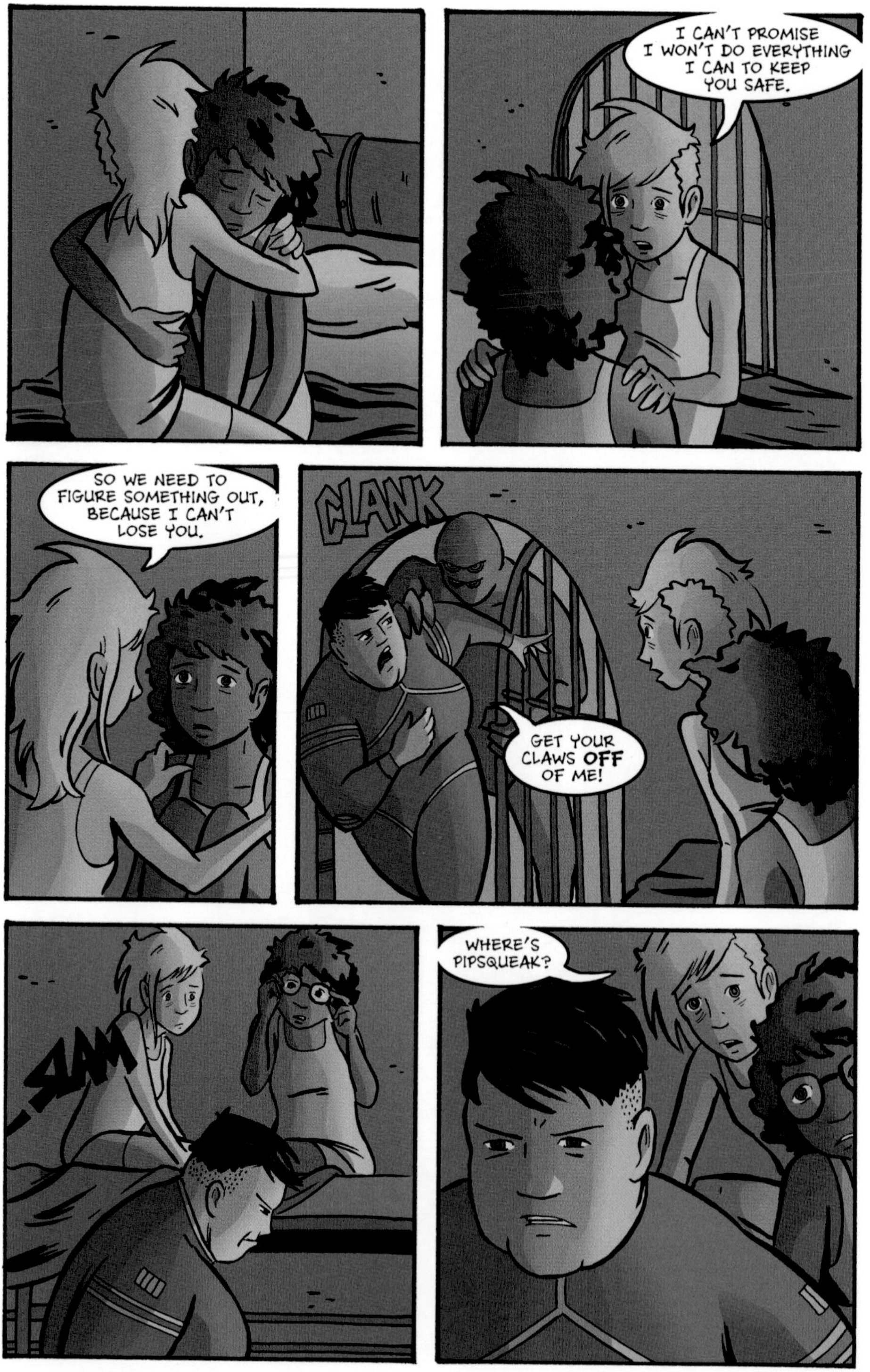
I CAN'T PROMISE I WON'T DO EVERYTHING I CAN TO KEEP YOU SAFE.
SO WE NEED TO FIGURE SOMETHING OUT, BECAUSE I CAN'T LOSE YOU.
CLANK
GET YOUR CLAWS **OFF** OF ME!
SLAM
WHERE'S PIPSQUEAK?

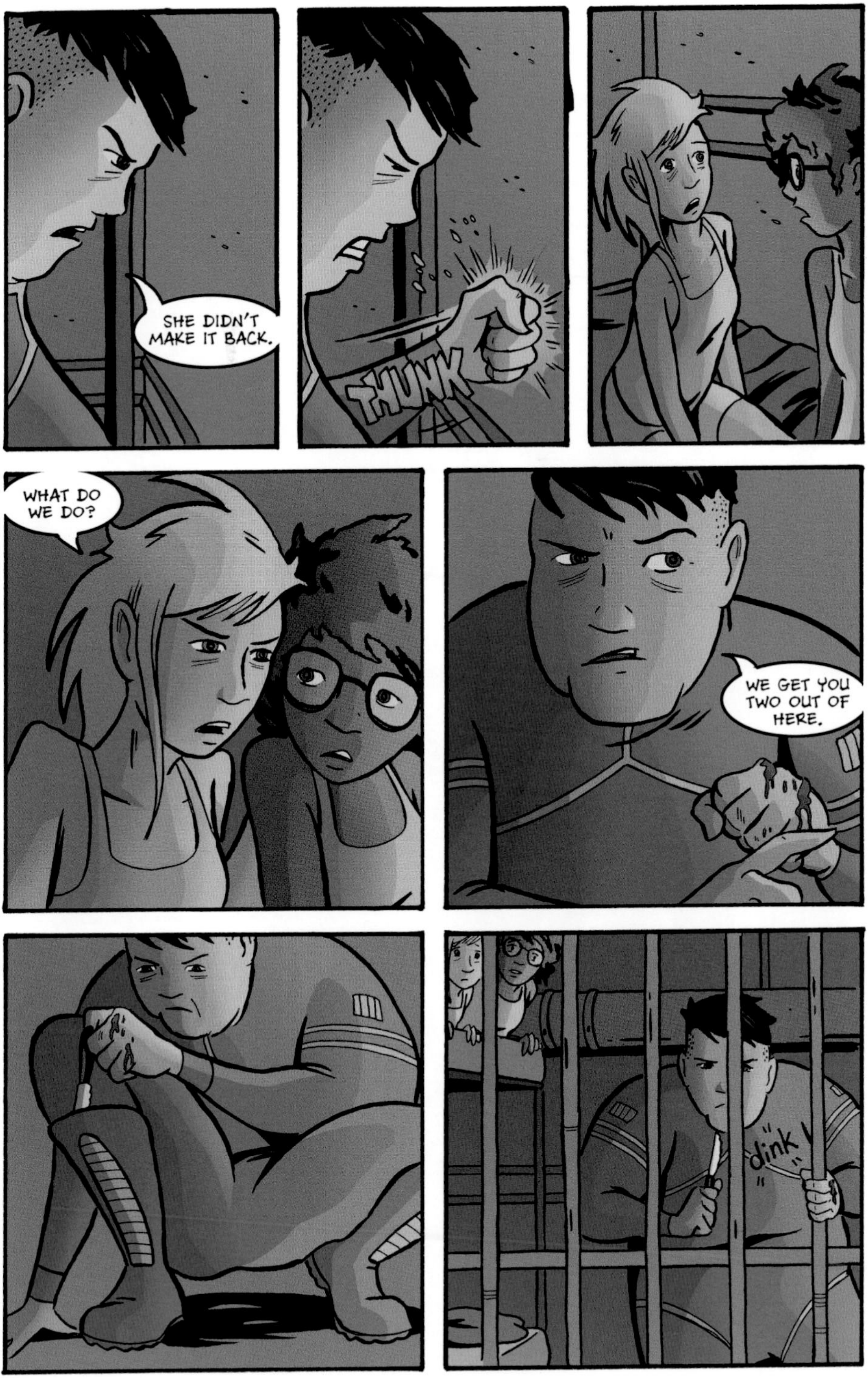
SHE DIDN'T MAKE IT BACK.
THUNK
WHAT DO WE DO?
WE GET YOU TWO OUT OF HERE.
dink

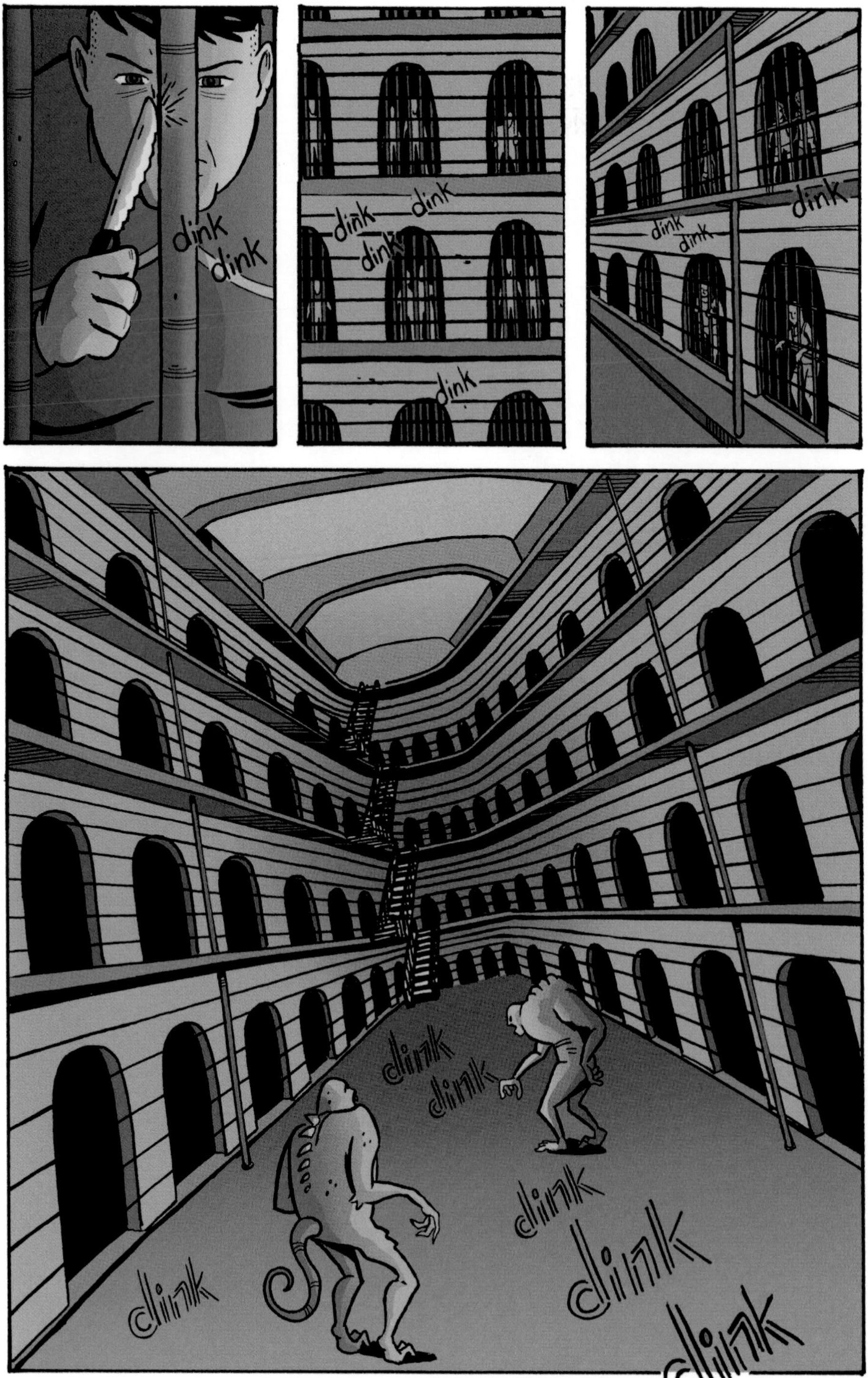
dink
dink
dink
dink
dink
dink
dink
dink
dink
dink
dink
dink
dink
dink
dink
dink

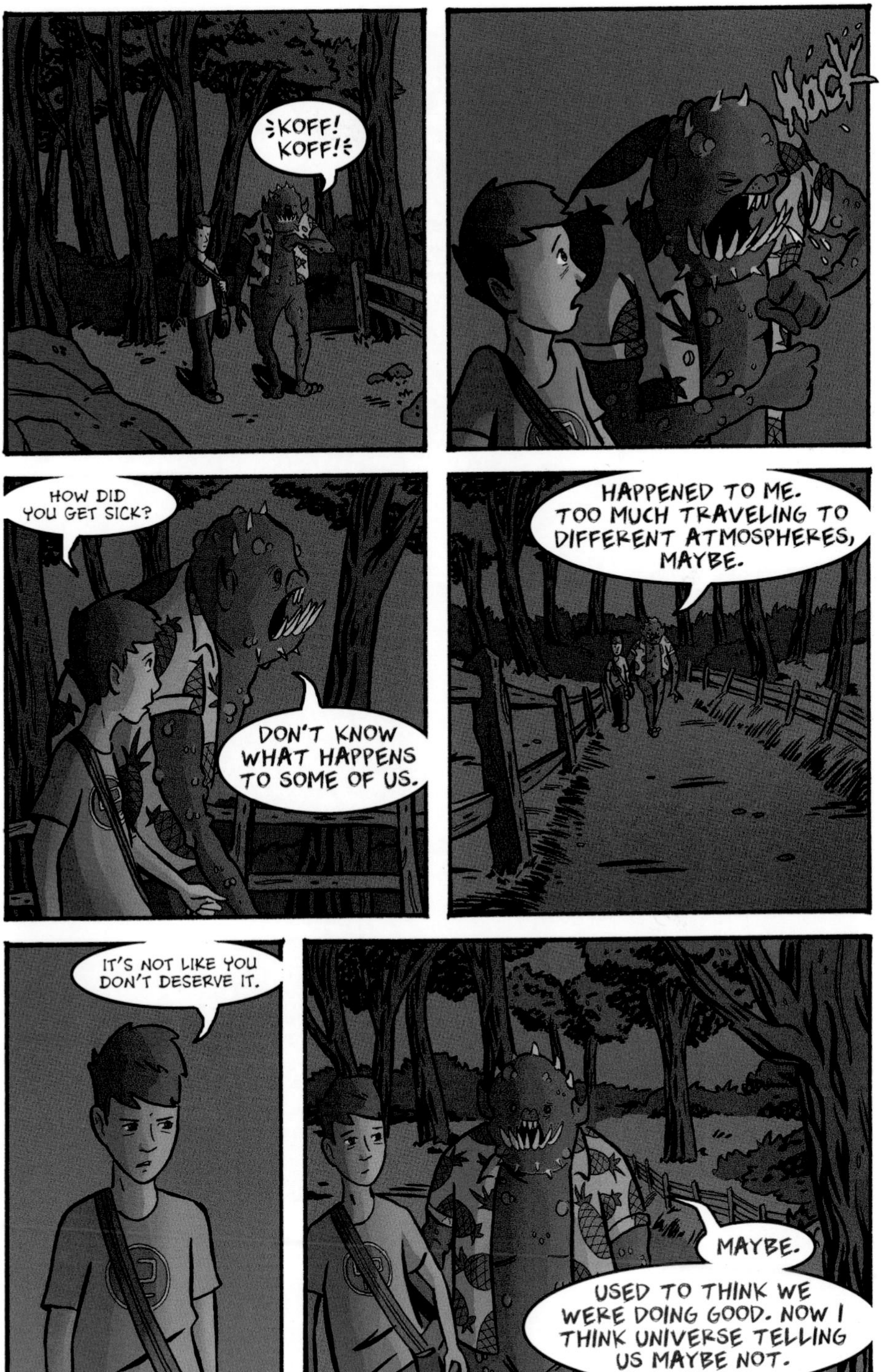
KOFF! KOFF!
HACK
HOW DID YOU GET SICK?
DON'T KNOW WHAT HAPPENS TO SOME OF US.
HAPPENED TO ME. TOO MUCH TRAVELING TO DIFFERENT ATMOSPHERES, MAYBE.
IT'S NOT LIKE YOU DON'T DESERVE IT.
MAYBE.
USED TO THINK WE WERE DOING GOOD. NOW I THINK UNIVERSE TELLING US MAYBE NOT.

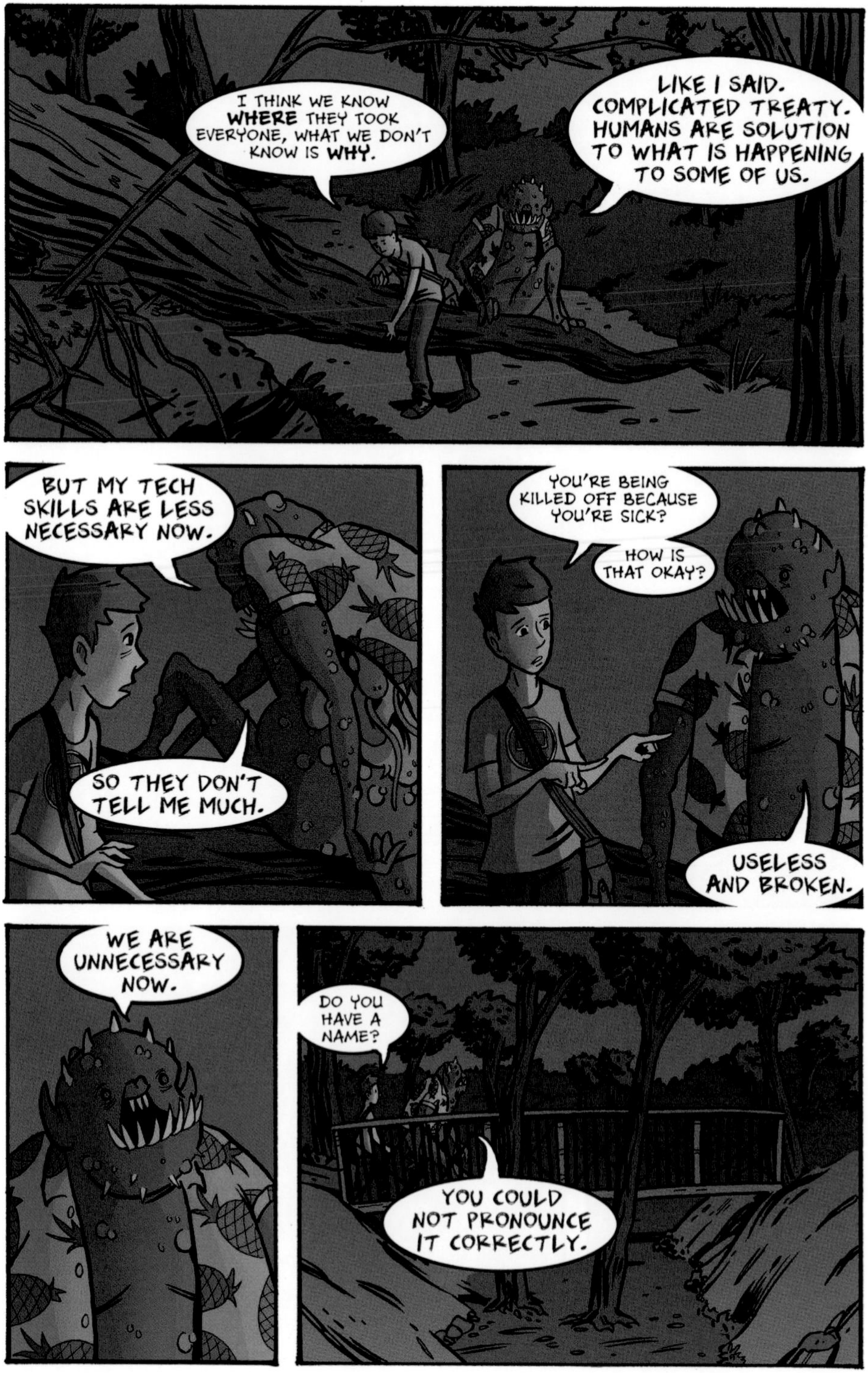
I THINK WE KNOW WHERE THEY TOOK EVERYONE, WHAT WE DON'T KNOW IS WHY.
LIKE I SAID. COMPLICATED TREATY. HUMANS ARE SOLUTION TO WHAT IS HAPPENING TO SOME OF US.
BUT MY TECH SKILLS ARE LESS NECESSARY NOW.
SO THEY DON'T TELL ME MUCH.
YOU'RE BEING KILLED OFF BECAUSE YOU'RE SICK?
HOW IS THAT OKAY?
USELESS AND BROKEN.
WE ARE UNNECESSARY NOW.
DO YOU HAVE A NAME?
YOU COULD NOT PRONOUNCE IT CORRECTLY.

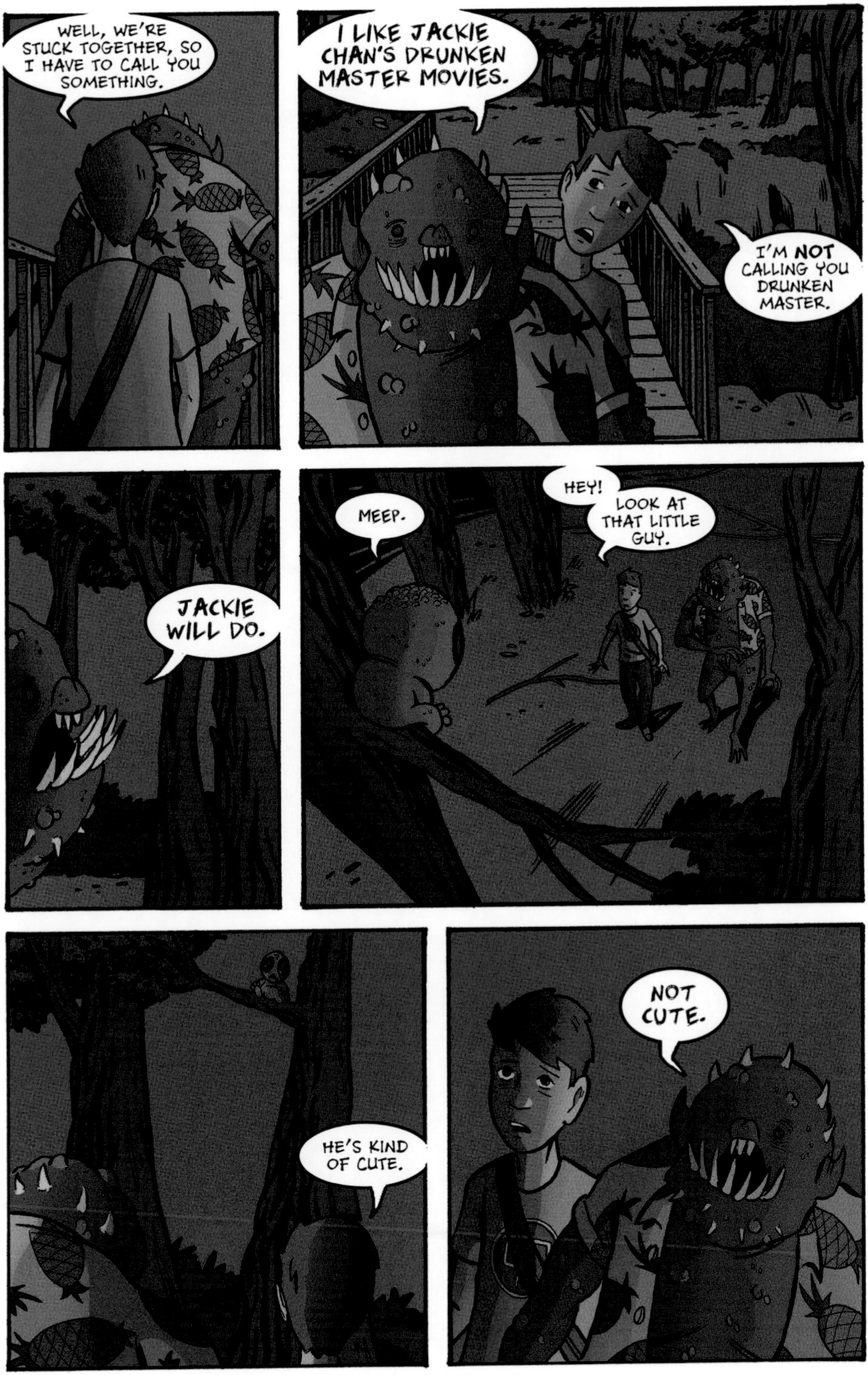
WELL, WE'RE STUCK TOGETHER, SO I HAVE TO CALL YOU SOMETHING.
I LIKE JACKIE CHAN'S DRUNKEN MASTER MOVIES.
I'M NOT CALLING YOU DRUNKEN MASTER.
JACKIE WILL DO.
MEEP.
HEY! LOOK AT THAT LITTLE GUY.
HE'S KIND OF CUTE.
NOT CUTE.

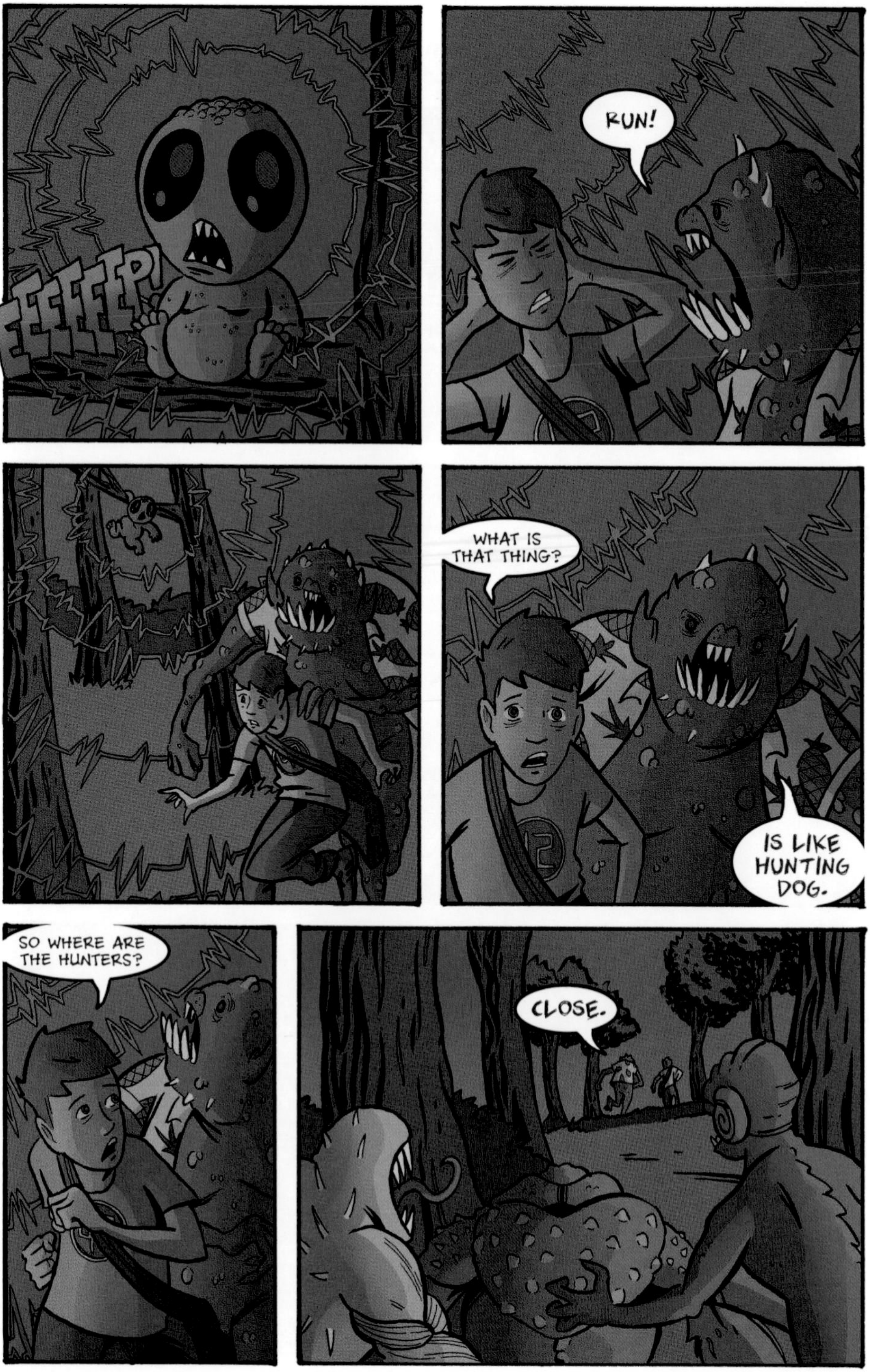
EEEEEEP!
RUN!
WHAT IS THAT THING?
IS LIKE HUNTING DOG.
SO WHERE ARE THE HUNTERS?
CLOSE.

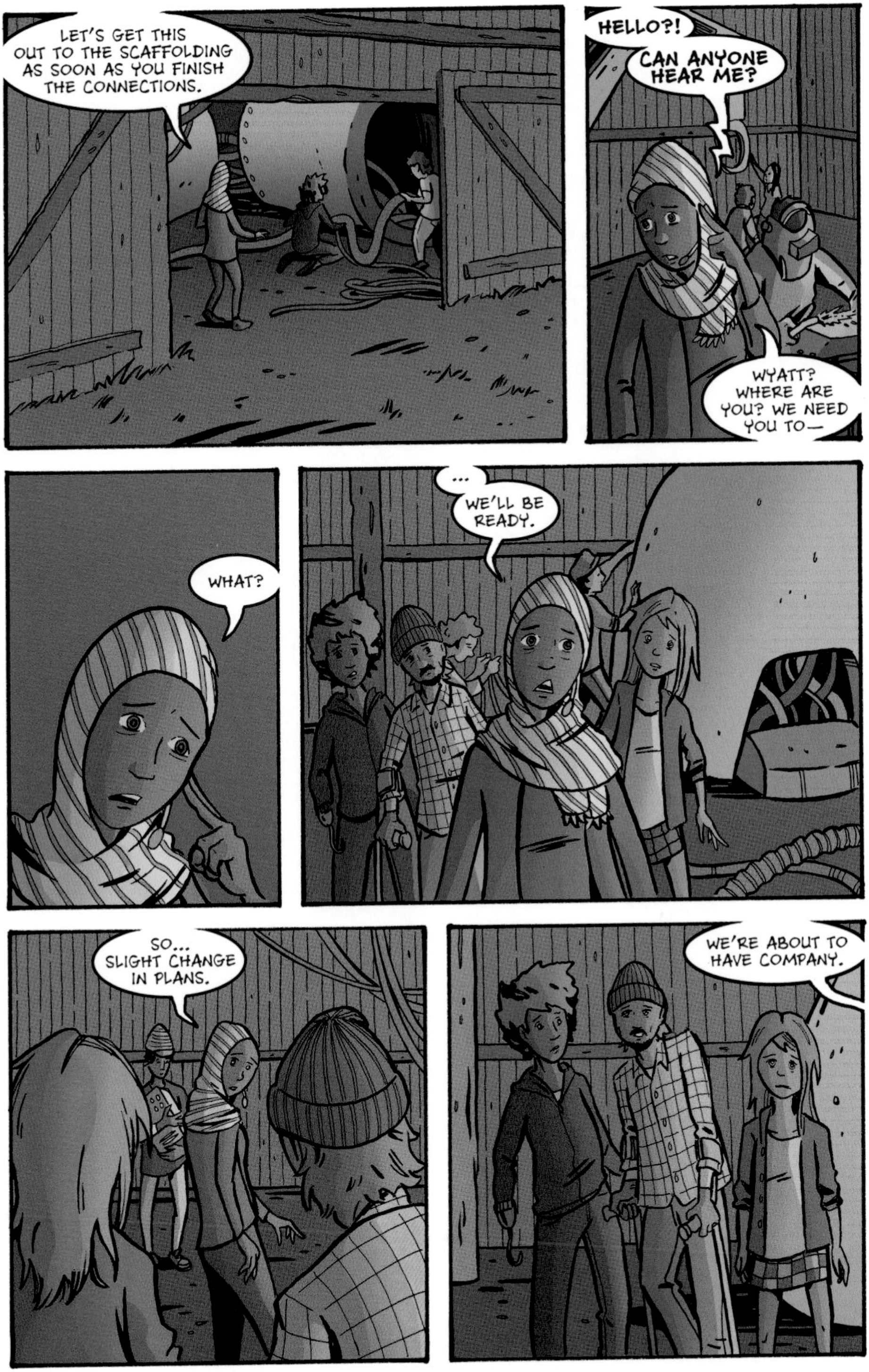
LET'S GET THIS OUT TO THE SCAFFOLDING AS SOON AS YOU FINISH THE CONNECTIONS.
HELLO?!
CAN ANYONE HEAR ME?
WYATT? WHERE ARE YOU? WE NEED YOU TO—
WHAT?
...
WE'LL BE READY.
SO... SLIGHT CHANGE IN PLANS.
WE'RE ABOUT TO HAVE COMPANY.

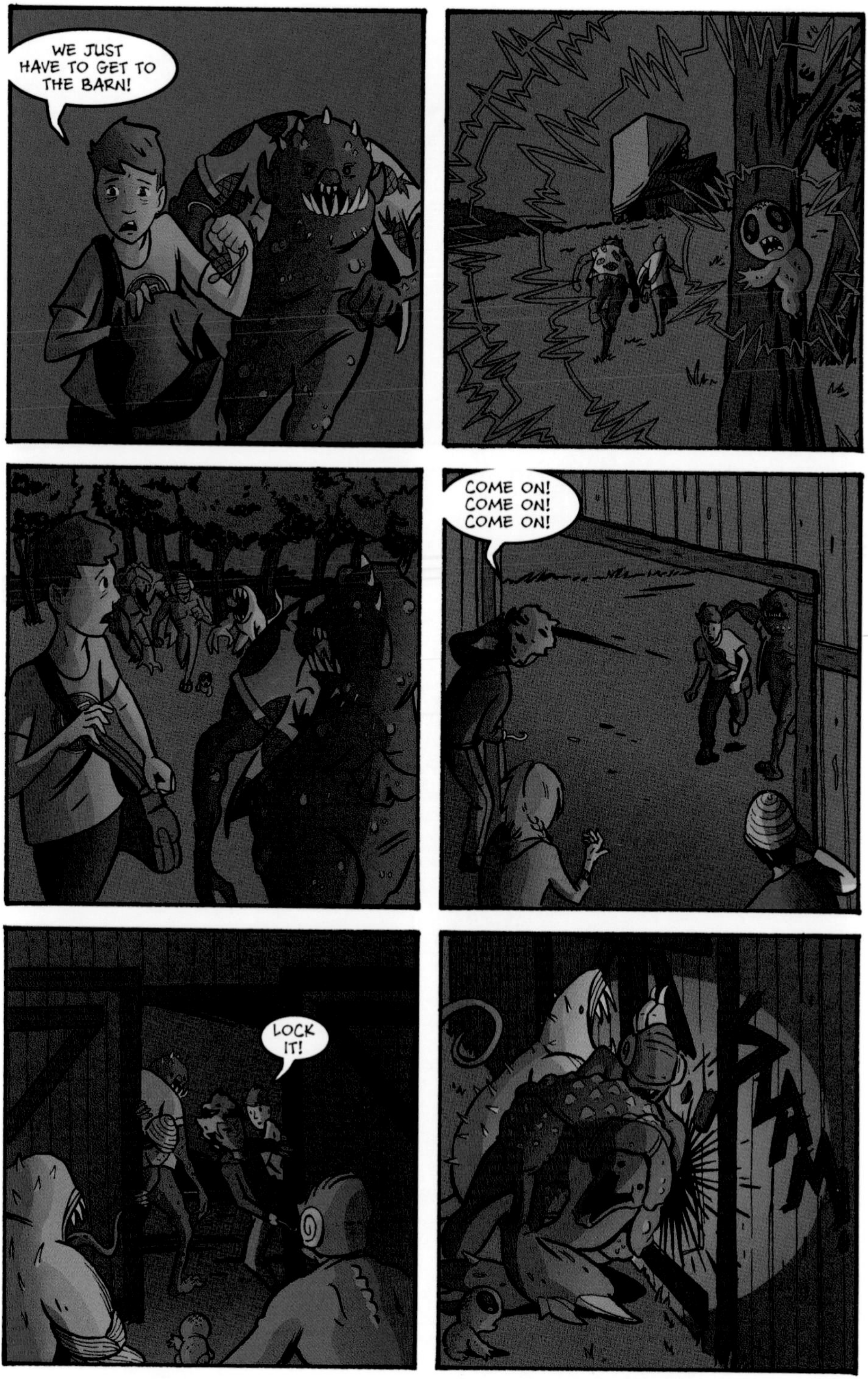
WE JUST HAVE TO GET TO THE BARN!
COME ON! COME ON! COME ON!
LOCK IT!

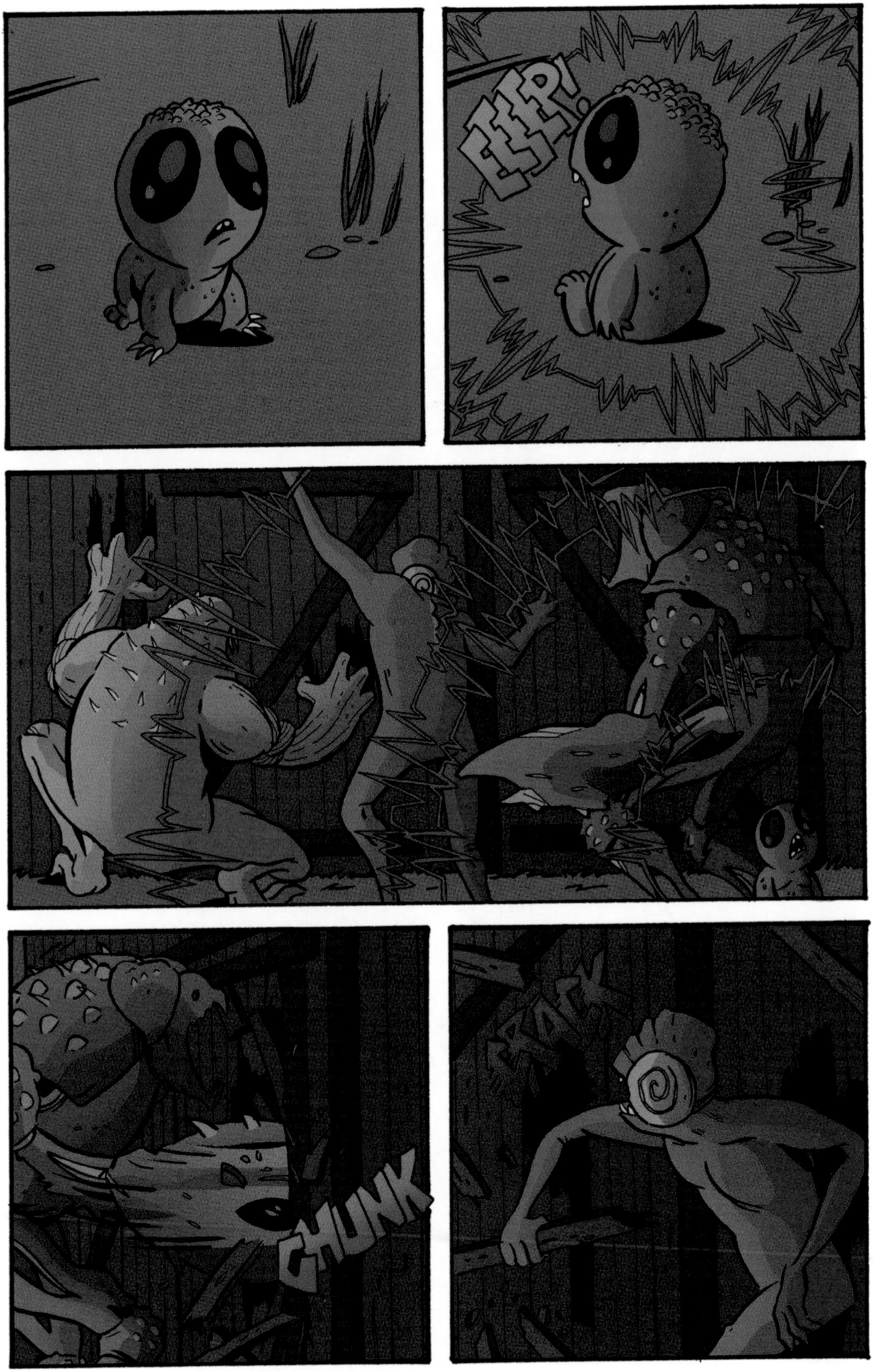
EEEP!
CHUNK
CRACK

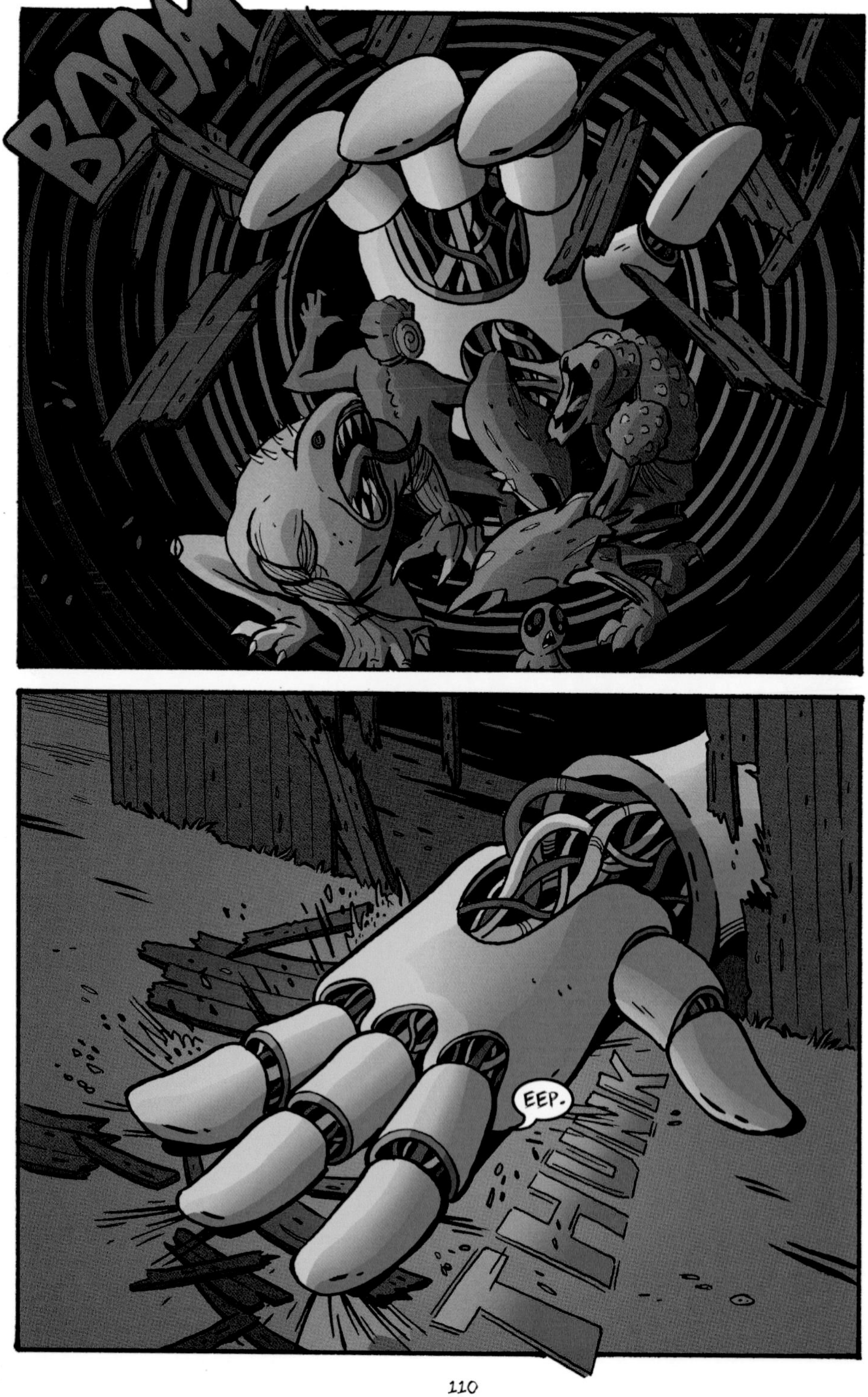
BOOM
EEP.
THUNK

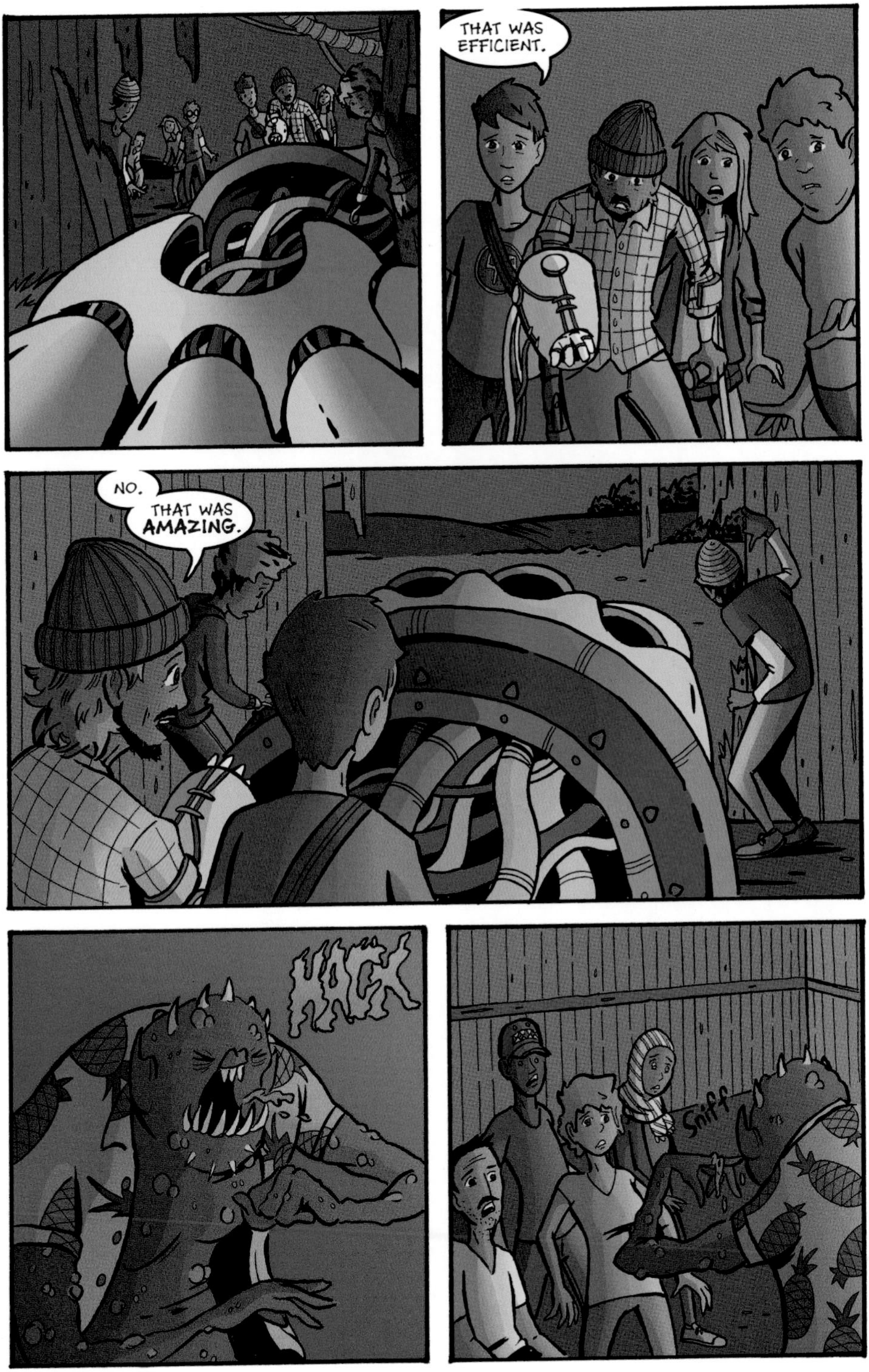
THAT WAS EFFICIENT.
NO.
THAT WAS AMAZING.
HACK
Sniff

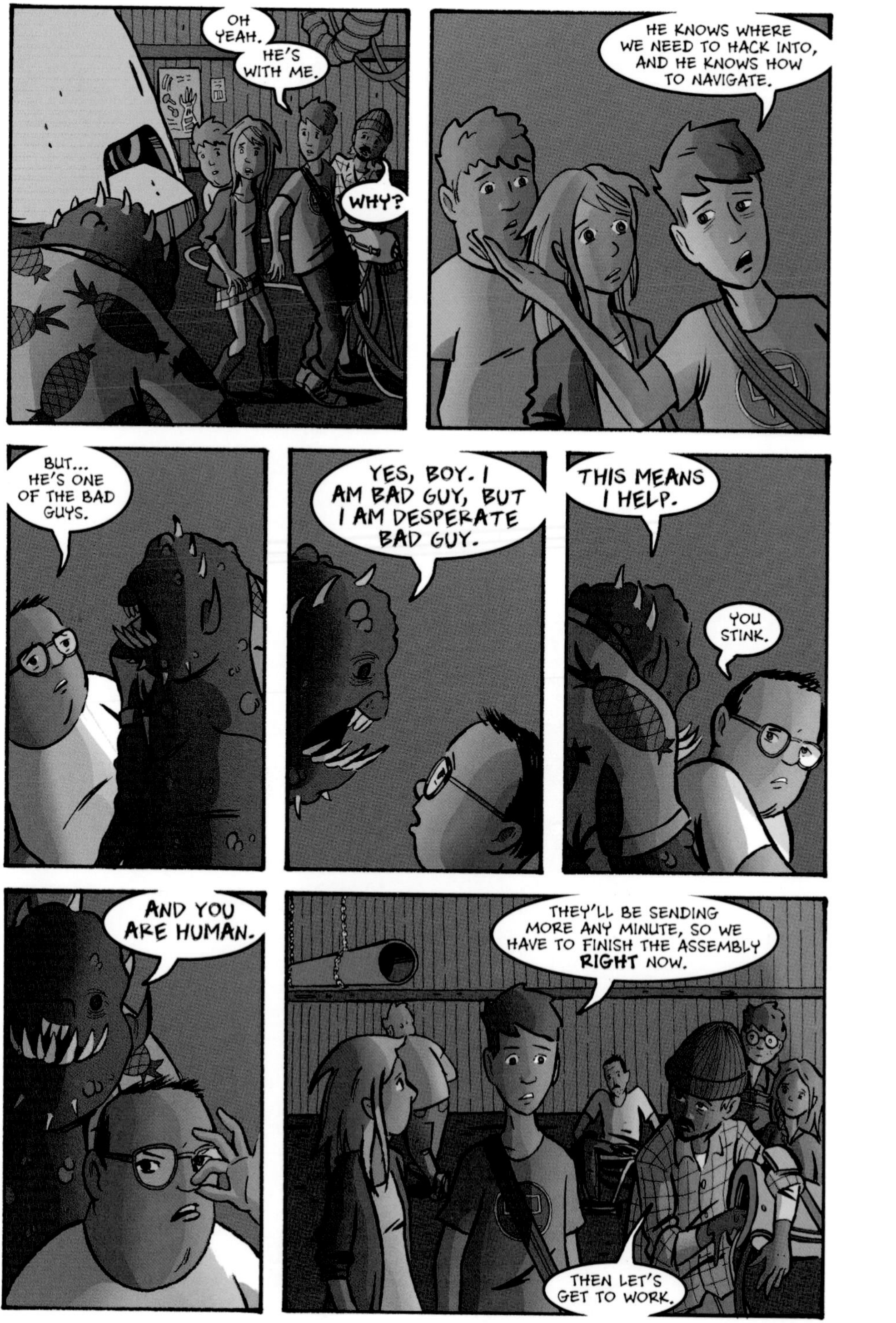
OH YEAH.
HE'S WITH ME.
WHY?
HE KNOWS WHERE WE NEED TO HACK INTO, AND HE KNOWS HOW TO NAVIGATE.
BUT... HE'S ONE OF THE BAD GUYS.
YES, BOY. I AM BAD GUY, BUT I AM DESPERATE BAD GUY.
THIS MEANS I HELP.
YOU STINK.
AND YOU ARE HUMAN.
THEY'LL BE SENDING MORE ANY MINUTE, SO WE HAVE TO FINISH THE ASSEMBLY RIGHT NOW.
THEN LET'S GET TO WORK.

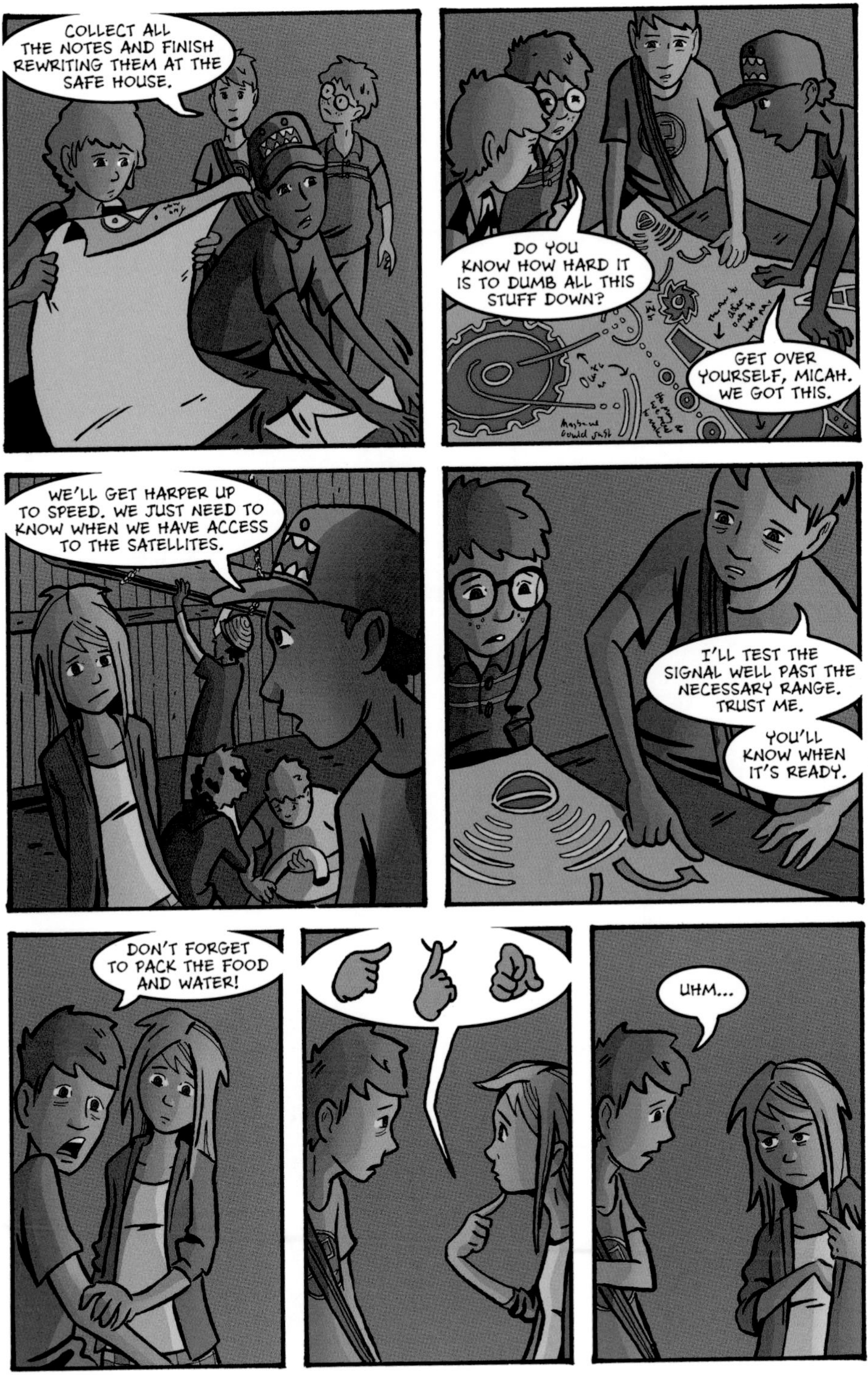
COLLECT ALL THE NOTES AND FINISH REWRITING THEM AT THE SAFE HOUSE.
DO YOU KNOW HOW HARD IT IS TO DUMB ALL THIS STUFF DOWN?
GET OVER YOURSELF, MICAH. WE GOT THIS.
WE'LL GET HARPER UP TO SPEED. WE JUST NEED TO KNOW WHEN WE HAVE ACCESS TO THE SATELLITES.
I'LL TEST THE SIGNAL WELL PAST THE NECESSARY RANGE. TRUST ME.
YOU'LL KNOW WHEN IT'S READY.
DON'T FORGET TO PACK THE FOOD AND WATER!
UHM...

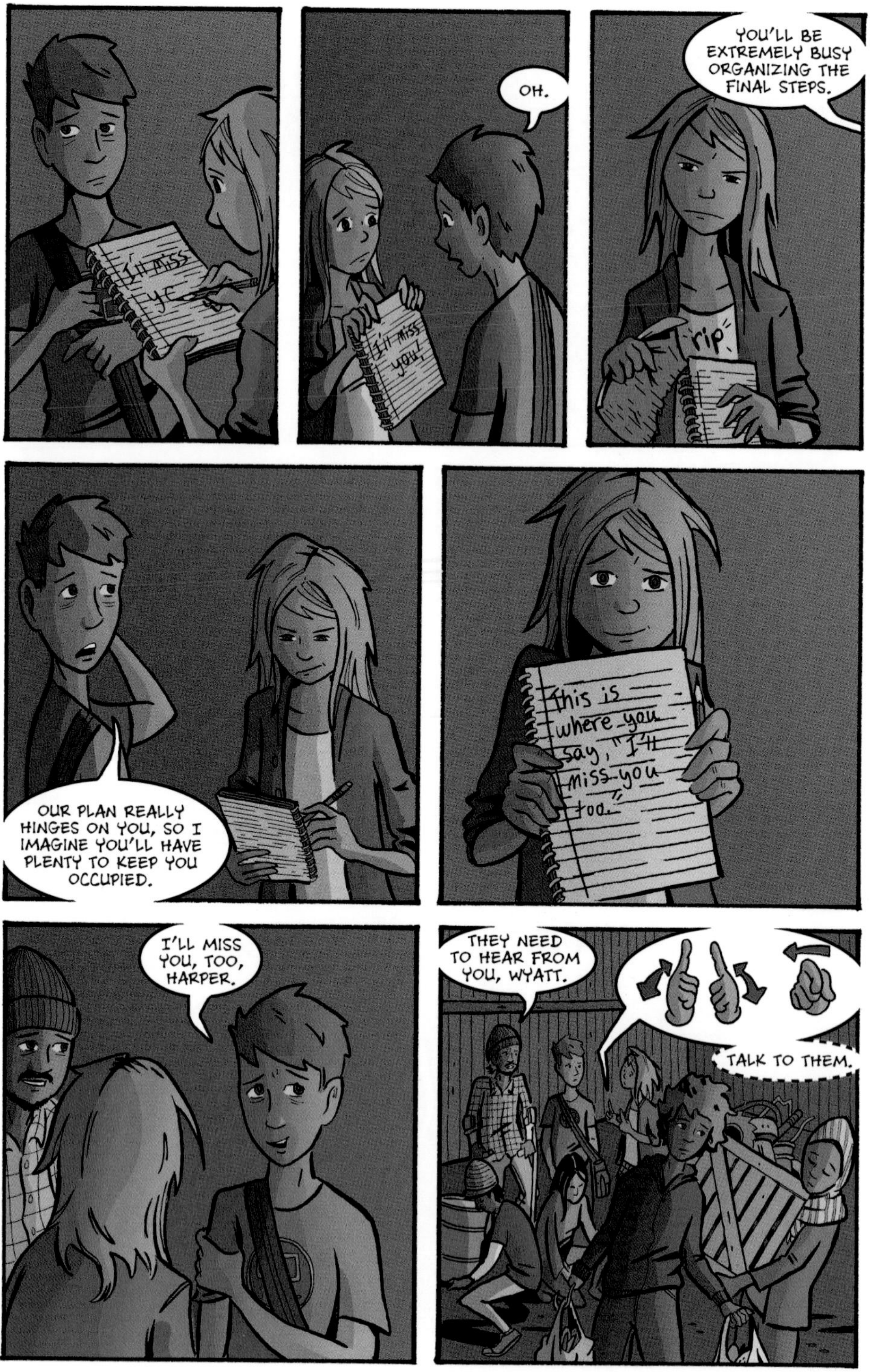
I'll miss
yo
OH.
I'll miss you!
YOU'LL BE EXTREMELY BUSY ORGANIZING THE FINAL STEPS.
rip
OUR PLAN REALLY HINGES ON YOU, SO I IMAGINE YOU'LL HAVE PLENTY TO KEEP YOU OCCUPIED.
this is where you say, "I'll miss you too."
I'LL MISS YOU, TOO, HARPER.
THEY NEED TO HEAR FROM YOU, WYATT.
TALK TO THEM.

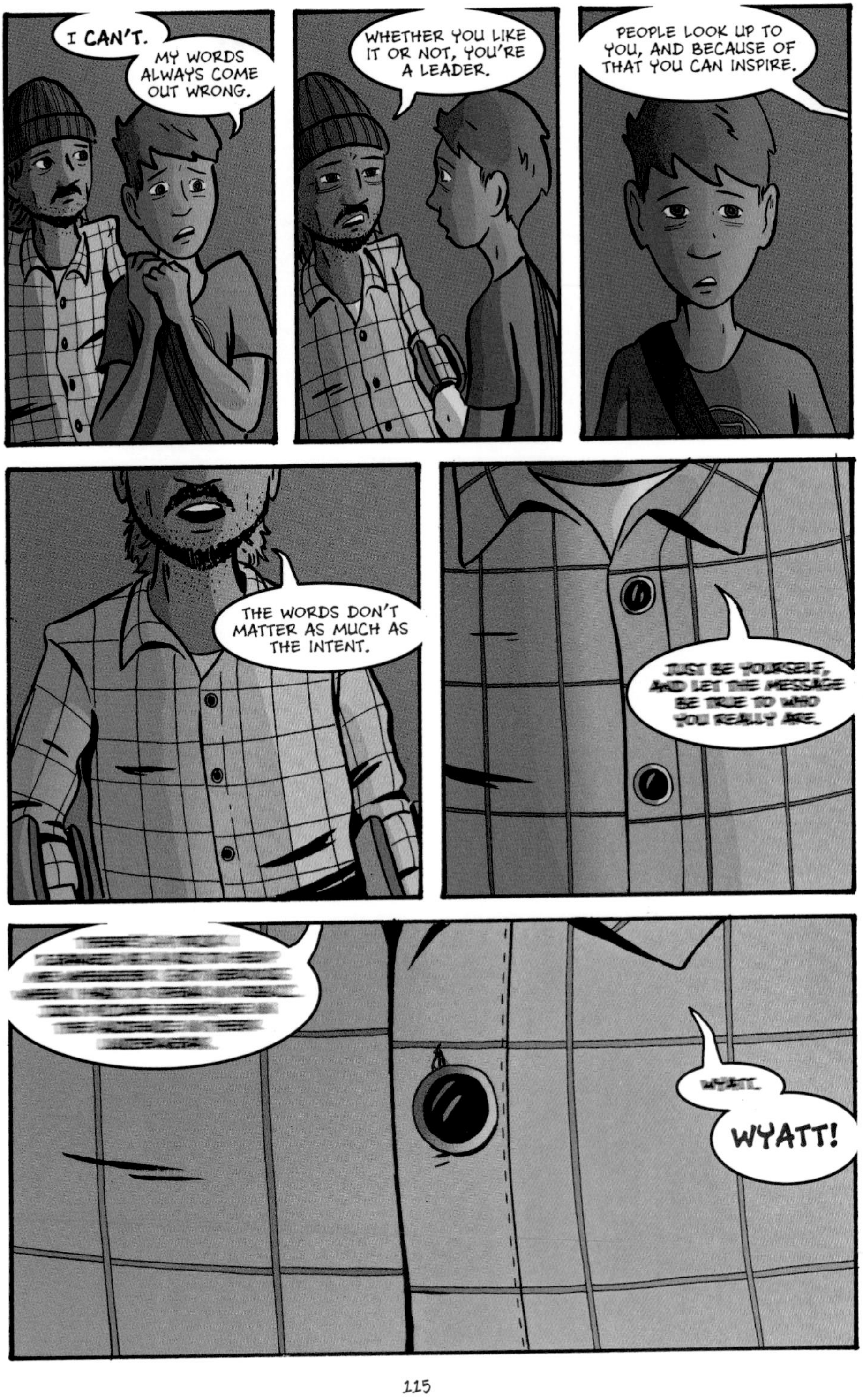
I CAN'T.
MY WORDS ALWAYS COME OUT WRONG.
WHETHER YOU LIKE IT OR NOT, YOU'RE A LEADER.
PEOPLE LOOK UP TO YOU, AND BECAUSE OF THAT YOU CAN INSPIRE.
THE WORDS DON'T MATTER AS MUCH AS THE INTENT.
JUST BE YOURSELF, AND LET THE MESSAGE BE TRUE TO WHO YOU REALLY ARE.
WYATT.
WYATT!

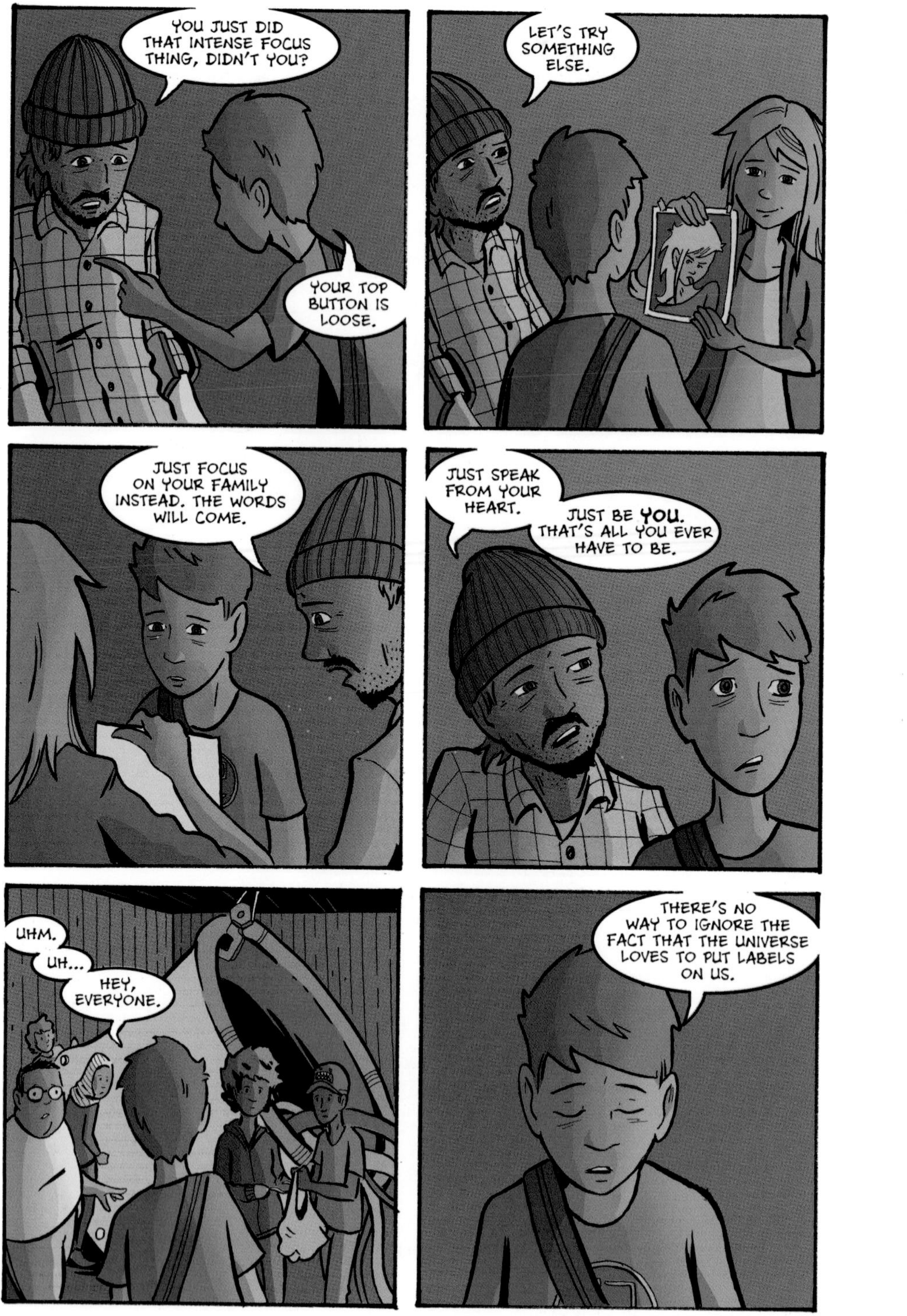
YOU JUST DID THAT INTENSE FOCUS THING, DIDN'T YOU?
YOUR TOP BUTTON IS LOOSE.
LET'S TRY SOMETHING ELSE.
JUST FOCUS ON YOUR FAMILY INSTEAD. THE WORDS WILL COME.
JUST SPEAK FROM YOUR HEART.
JUST BE YOU. THAT'S ALL YOU EVER HAVE TO BE.
UHM.
UH...
HEY, EVERYONE.
THERE'S NO WAY TO IGNORE THE FACT THAT THE UNIVERSE LOVES TO PUT LABELS ON US.

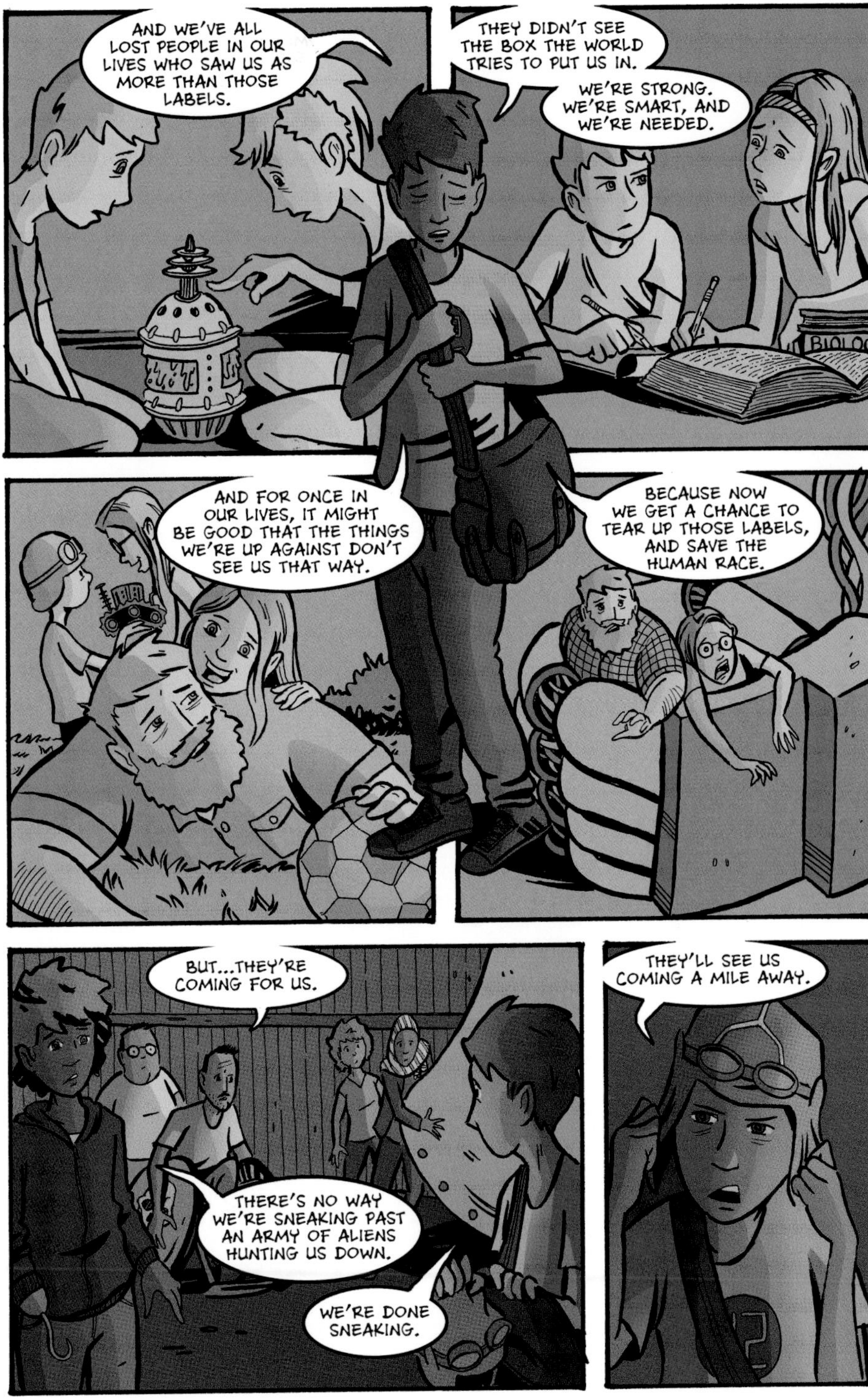
AND WE'VE ALL LOST PEOPLE IN OUR LIVES WHO SAW US AS MORE THAN THOSE LABELS.
THEY DIDN'T SEE THE BOX THE WORLD TRIES TO PUT US IN.
WE'RE STRONG. WE'RE SMART, AND WE'RE NEEDED.
BIOLOG
AND FOR ONCE IN OUR LIVES, IT MIGHT BE GOOD THAT THE THINGS WE'RE UP AGAINST DON'T SEE US THAT WAY.
BECAUSE NOW WE GET A CHANCE TO TEAR UP THOSE LABELS, AND SAVE THE HUMAN RACE.
BUT...THEY'RE COMING FOR US.
THERE'S NO WAY WE'RE SNEAKING PAST AN ARMY OF ALIENS HUNTING US DOWN.
WE'RE DONE SNEAKING.
THEY'LL SEE US COMING A MILE AWAY.

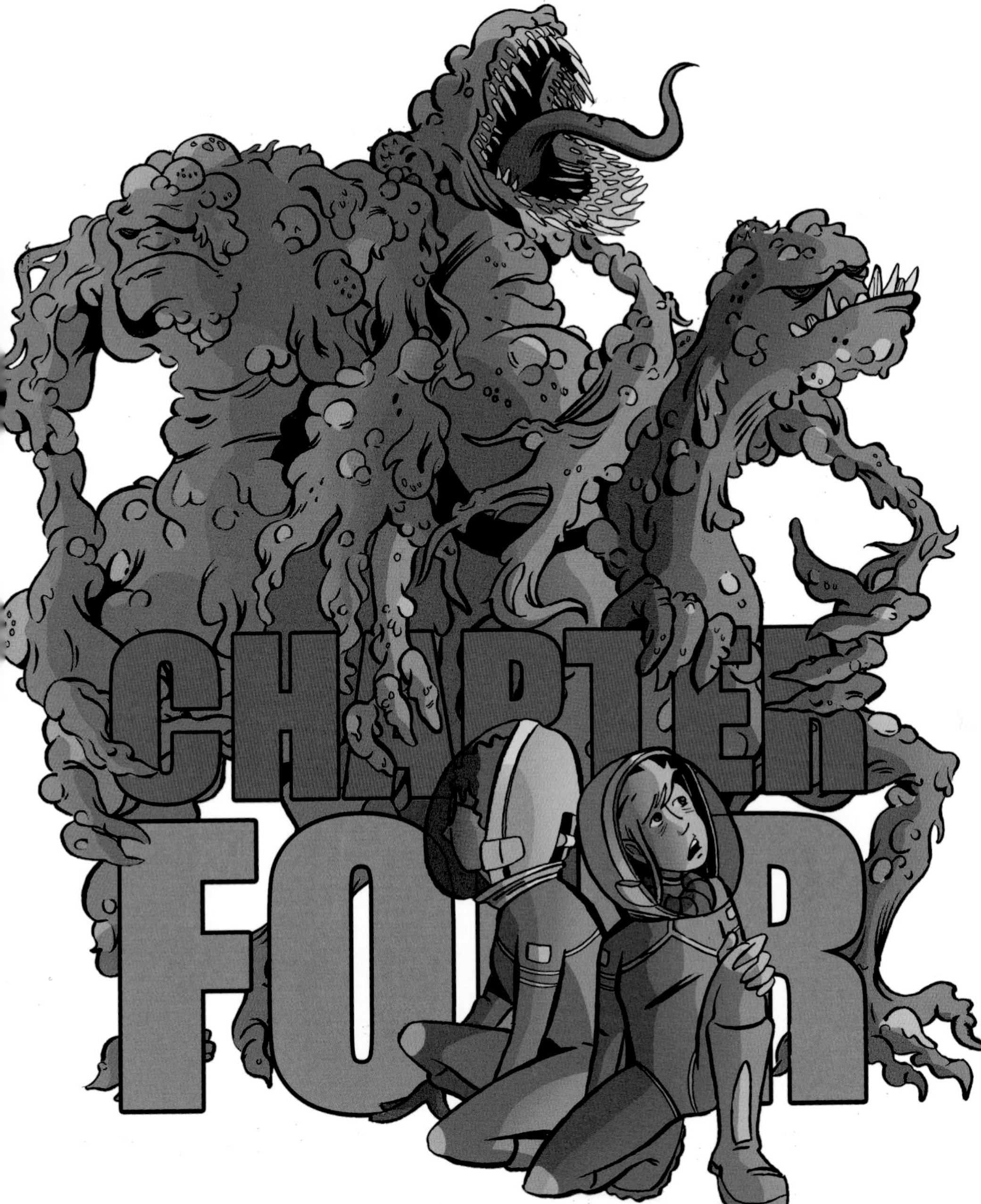
CHAPTER
FOUR

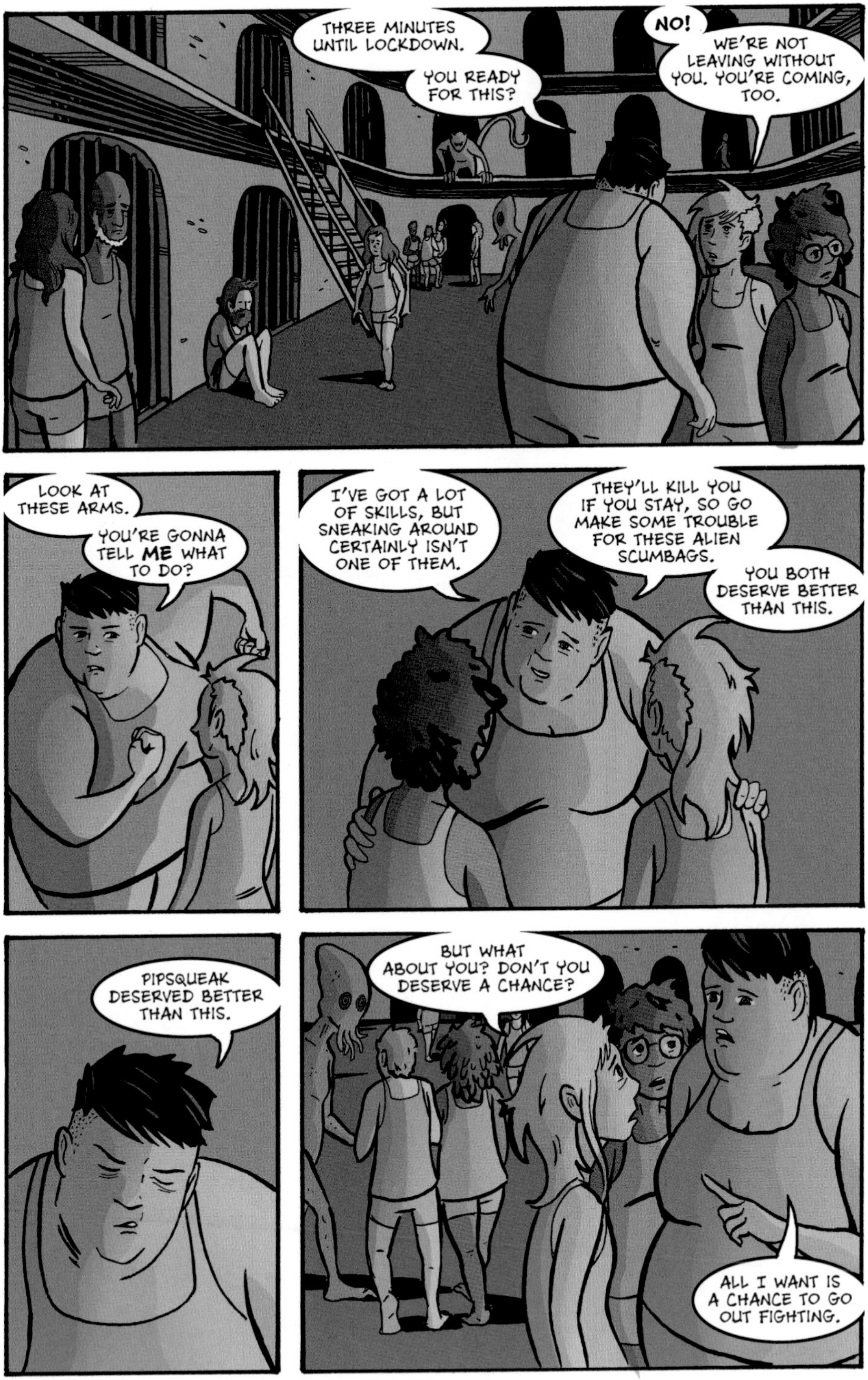
THREE MINUTES UNTIL LOCKDOWN.
YOU READY FOR THIS?
NO!
WE'RE NOT LEAVING WITHOUT YOU. YOU'RE COMING, TOO.
LOOK AT THESE ARMS.
YOU'RE GONNA TELL ME WHAT TO DO?
I'VE GOT A LOT OF SKILLS, BUT SNEAKING AROUND CERTAINLY ISN'T ONE OF THEM.
THEY'LL KILL YOU IF YOU STAY, SO GO MAKE SOME TROUBLE FOR THESE ALIEN SCUMBAGS.
YOU BOTH DESERVE BETTER THAN THIS.
PIPSQUEAK DESERVED BETTER THAN THIS.
BUT WHAT ABOUT YOU? DON'T YOU DESERVE A CHANCE?
ALL I WANT IS A CHANCE TO GO OUT FIGHTING.

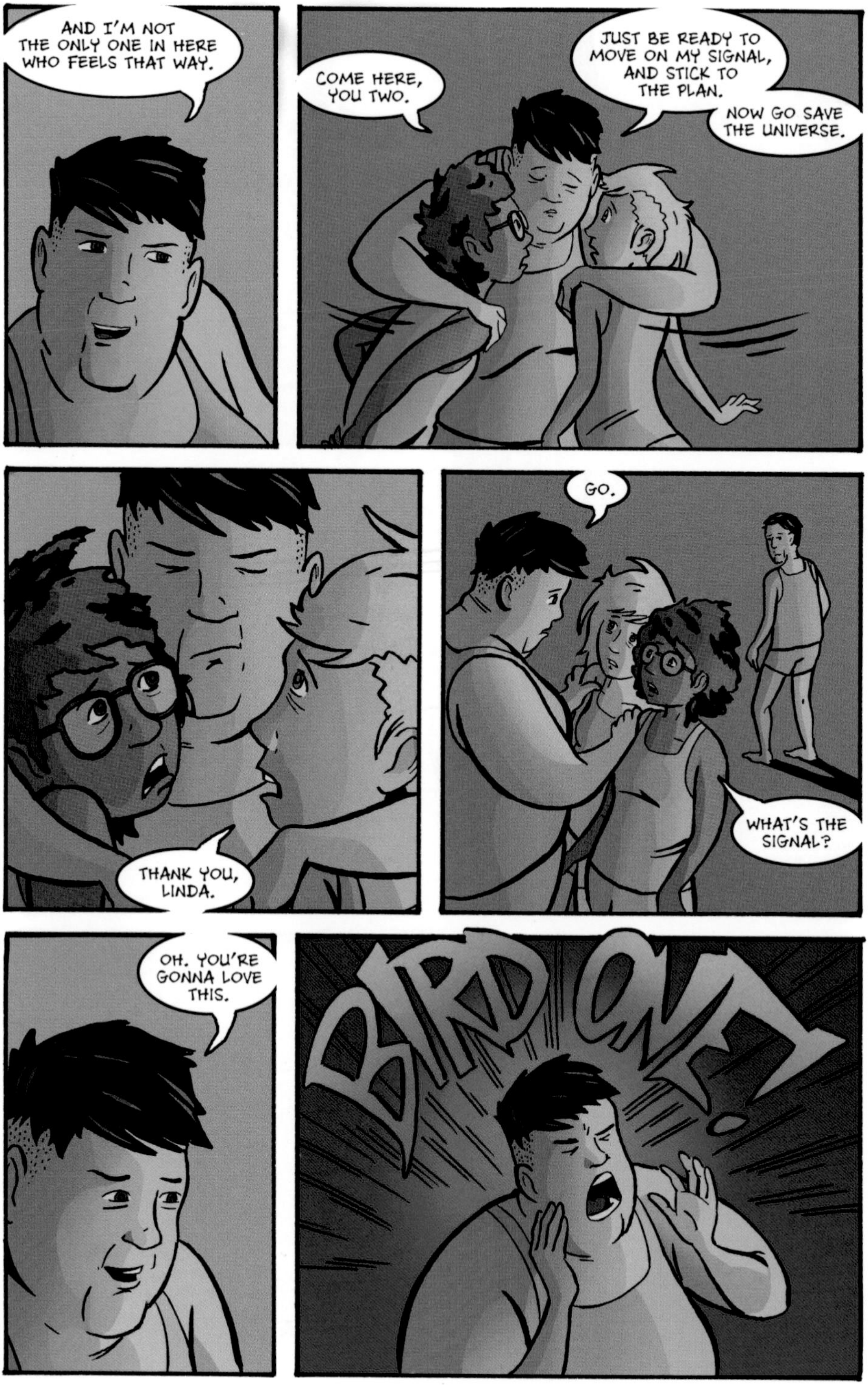
AND I'M NOT THE ONLY ONE IN HERE WHO FEELS THAT WAY.
COME HERE, YOU TWO.
JUST BE READY TO MOVE ON MY SIGNAL, AND STICK TO THE PLAN.
NOW GO SAVE THE UNIVERSE.
THANK YOU, LINDA.
GO.
WHAT'S THE SIGNAL?
OH. YOU'RE GONNA LOVE THIS.
BIRD ON!

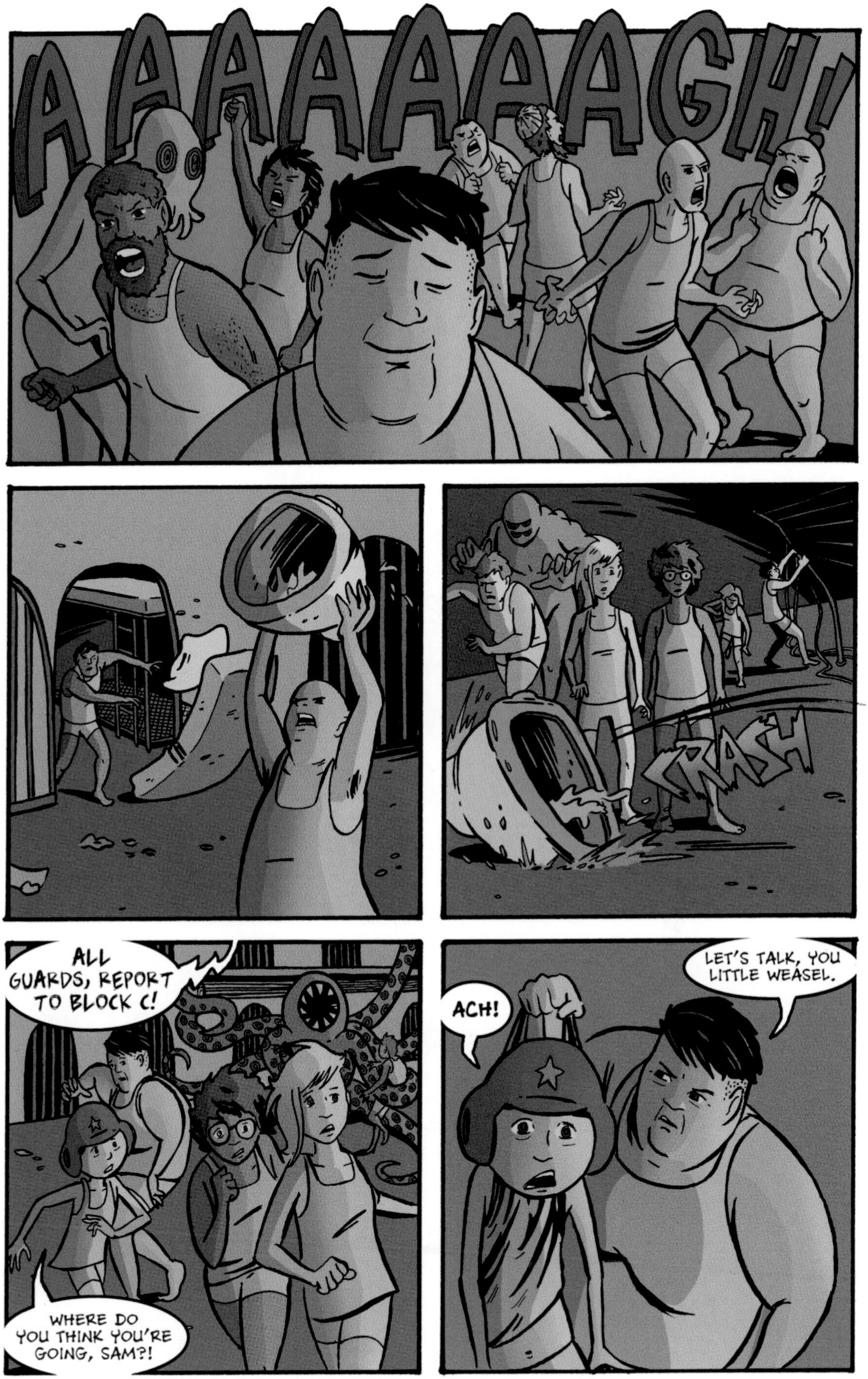
AAAAAAAAGH!
CRASH
ALL GUARDS, REPORT TO BLOCK C!
WHERE DO YOU THINK YOU'RE GOING, SAM?!
ACH!
LET'S TALK, YOU LITTLE WEASEL.

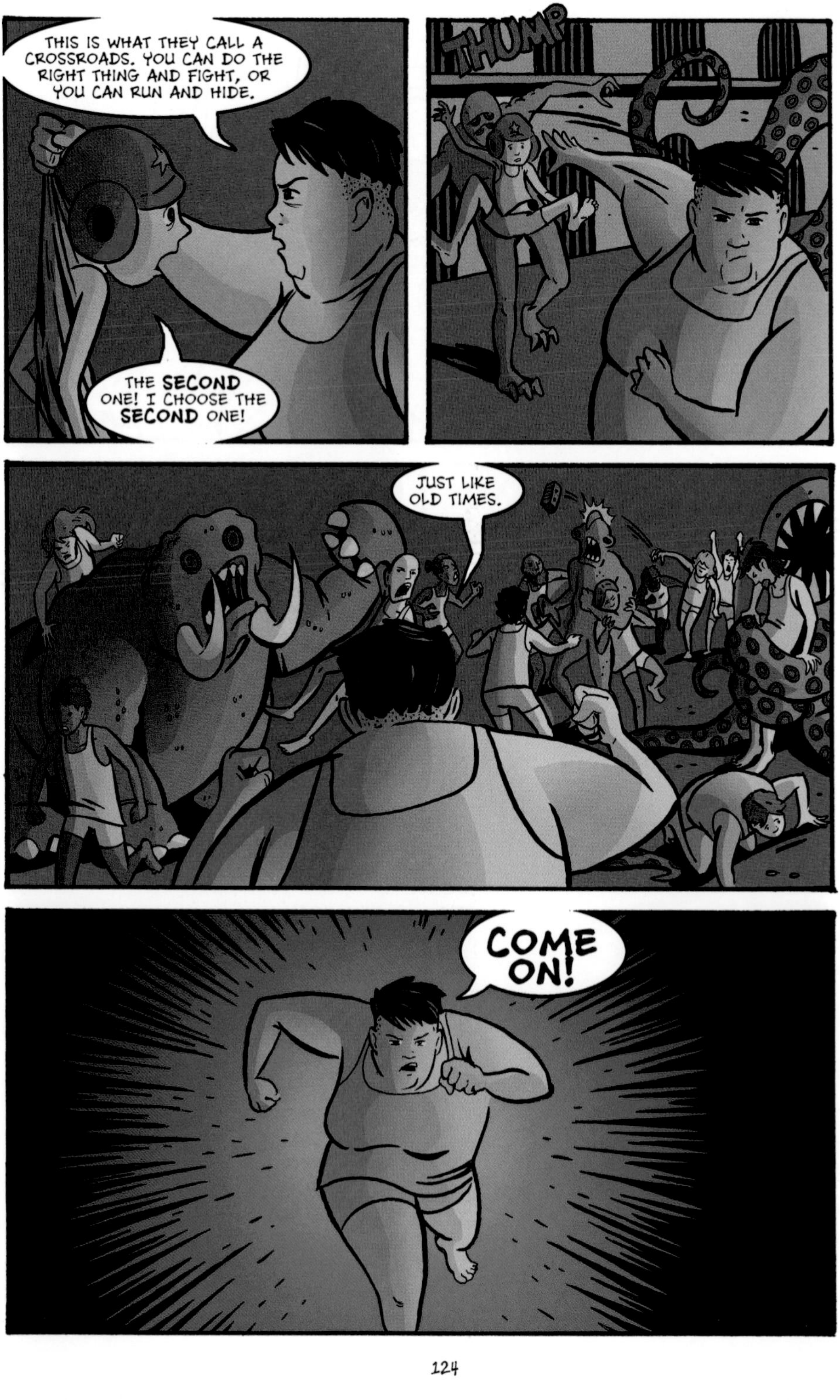
THIS IS WHAT THEY CALL A CROSSROADS. YOU CAN DO THE RIGHT THING AND FIGHT, OR YOU CAN RUN AND HIDE.
THE **SECOND** ONE! I CHOOSE THE **SECOND** ONE!
THUMP
JUST LIKE OLD TIMES.
COME ON!

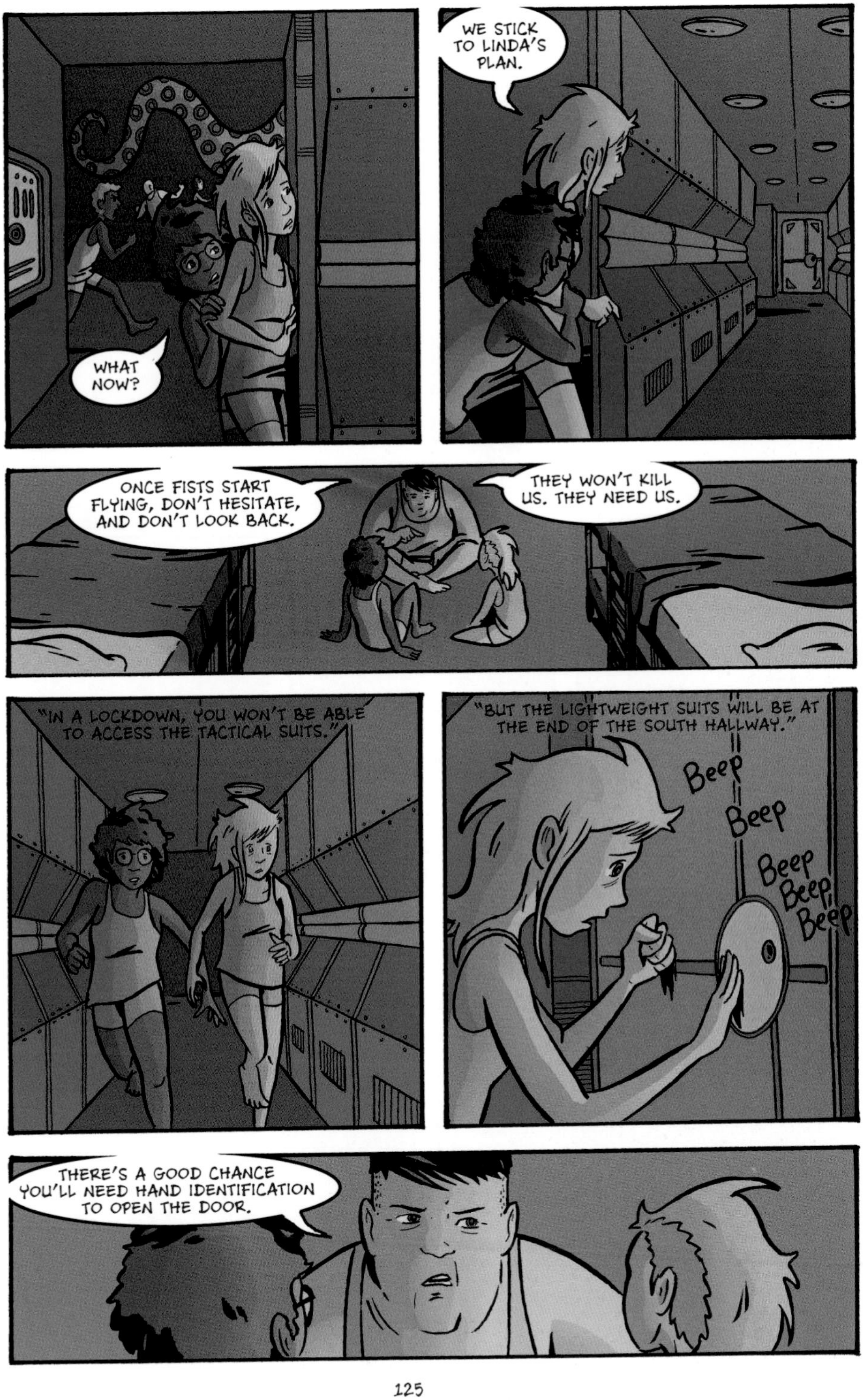
WHAT NOW?
WE STICK TO LINDA'S PLAN.
ONCE FISTS START FLYING, DON'T HESITATE, AND DON'T LOOK BACK.
THEY WON'T KILL US. THEY NEED US.
"IN A LOCKDOWN, YOU WON'T BE ABLE TO ACCESS THE TACTICAL SUITS."
"BUT THE LIGHTWEIGHT SUITS WILL BE AT THE END OF THE SOUTH HALLWAY."
Beep
Beep
Beep
Beep
Beep
THERE'S A GOOD CHANCE YOU'LL NEED HAND IDENTIFICATION TO OPEN THE DOOR.

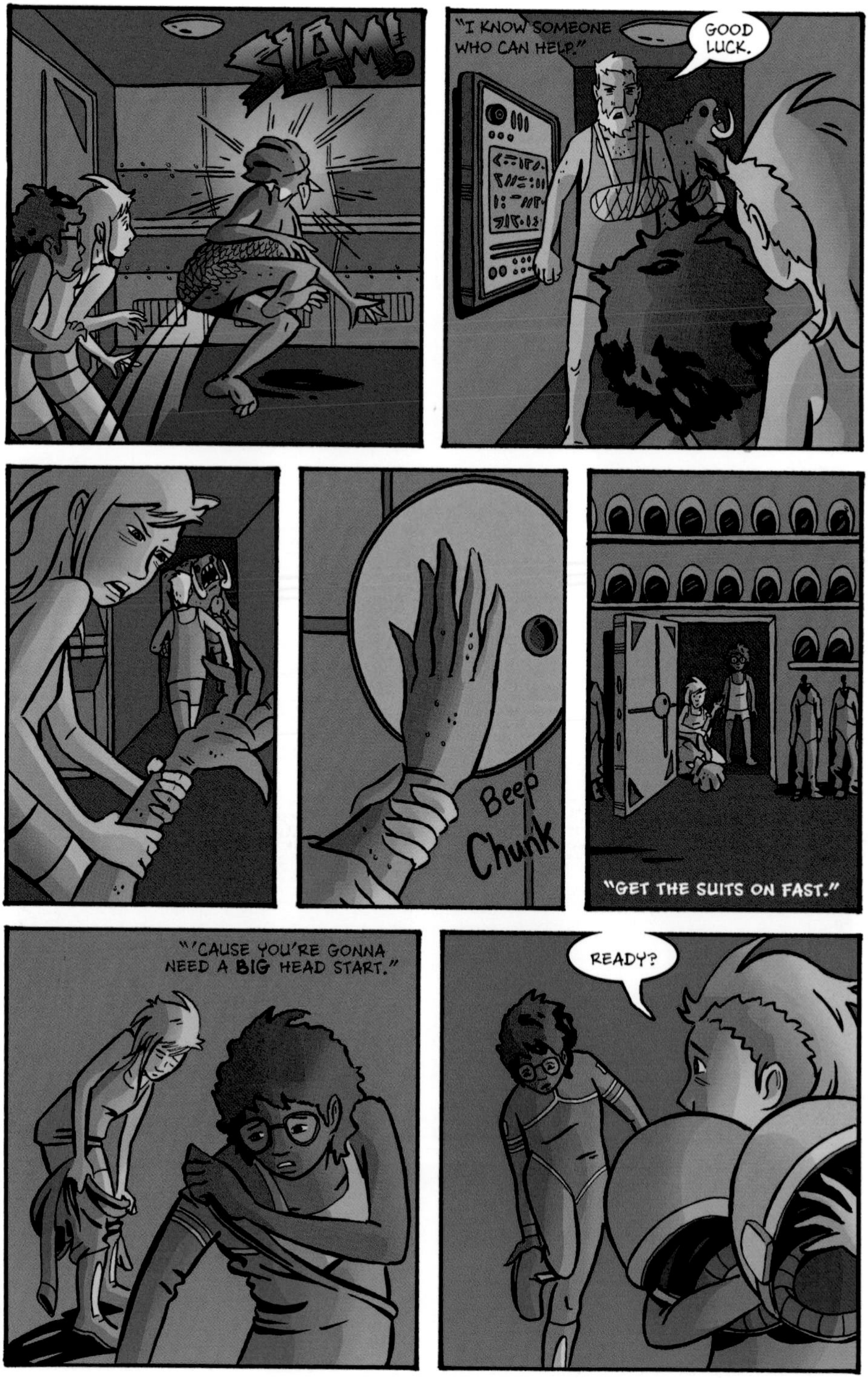
SLAM!
"I KNOW SOMEONE WHO CAN HELP."
GOOD LUCK.
Beep
Chunk
"GET THE SUITS ON FAST."
"'CAUSE YOU'RE GONNA NEED A BIG HEAD START."
READY?

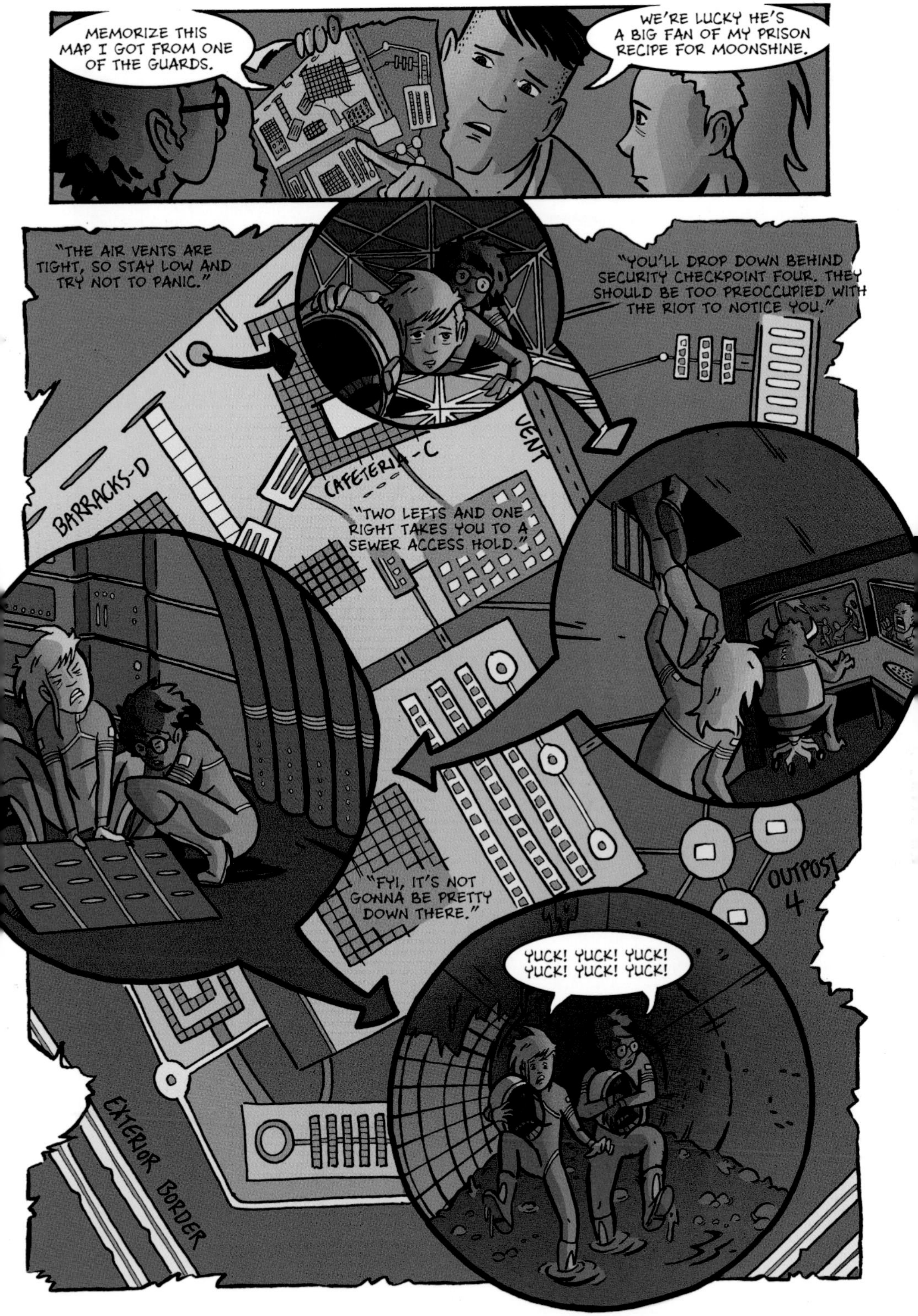
MEMORIZE THIS MAP I GOT FROM ONE OF THE GUARDS.
WE'RE LUCKY HE'S A BIG FAN OF MY PRISON RECIPE FOR MOONSHINE.
"THE AIR VENTS ARE TIGHT, SO STAY LOW AND TRY NOT TO PANIC."
"YOU'LL DROP DOWN BEHIND SECURITY CHECKPOINT FOUR. THEY SHOULD BE TOO PREOCCUPIED WITH THE RIOT TO NOTICE YOU."
VENT
CAFETERIA-C
BARRACKS-D
"TWO LEFTS AND ONE RIGHT TAKES YOU TO A SEWER ACCESS HOLD."
"FYI, IT'S NOT GONNA BE PRETTY DOWN THERE."
OUTPOST 4
YUCK! YUCK! YUCK! YUCK! YUCK! YUCK!
EXTERIOR BORDER

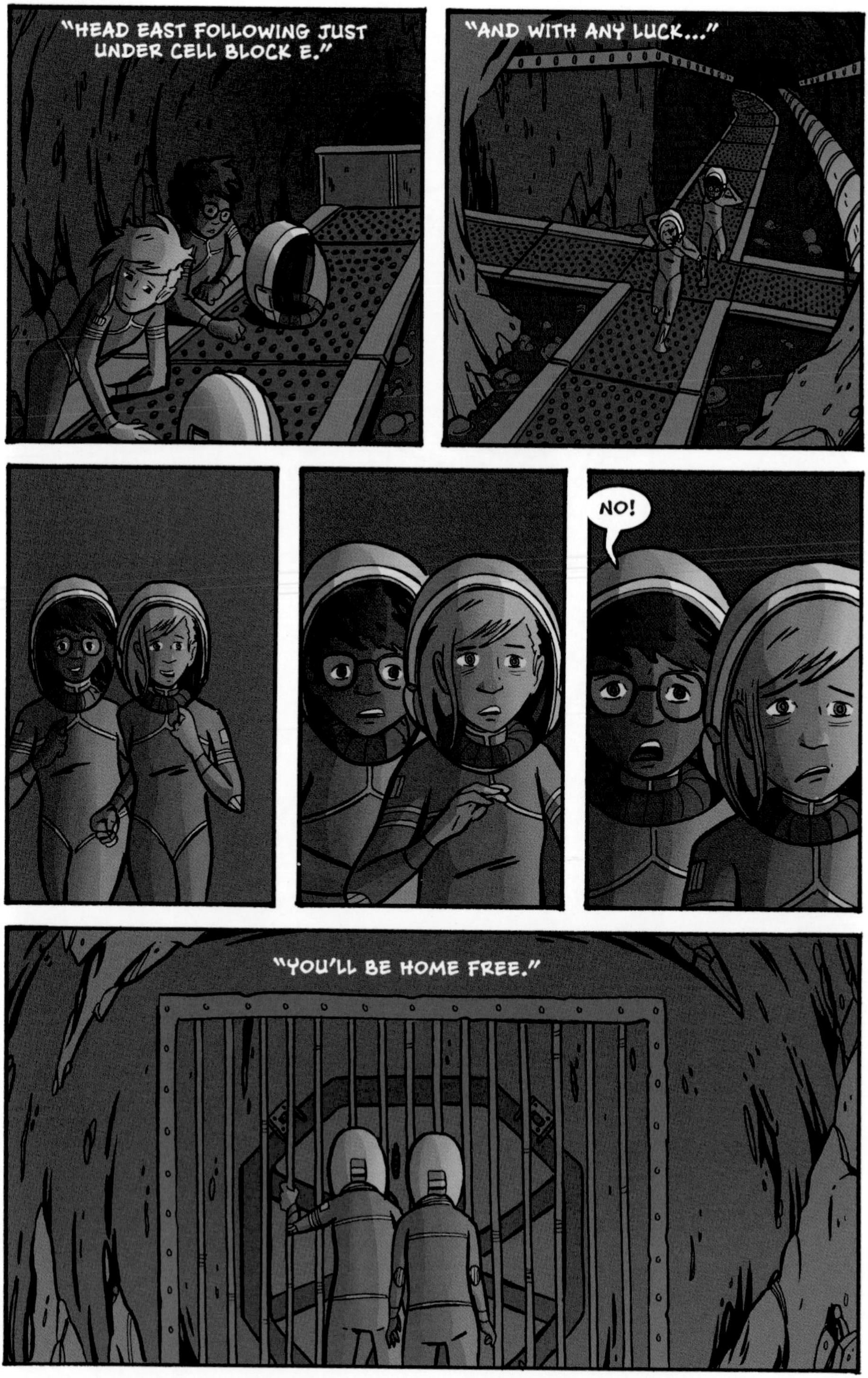
"HEAD EAST FOLLOWING JUST UNDER CELL BLOCK E."
"AND WITH ANY LUCK..."
NO!
"YOU'LL BE HOME FREE."

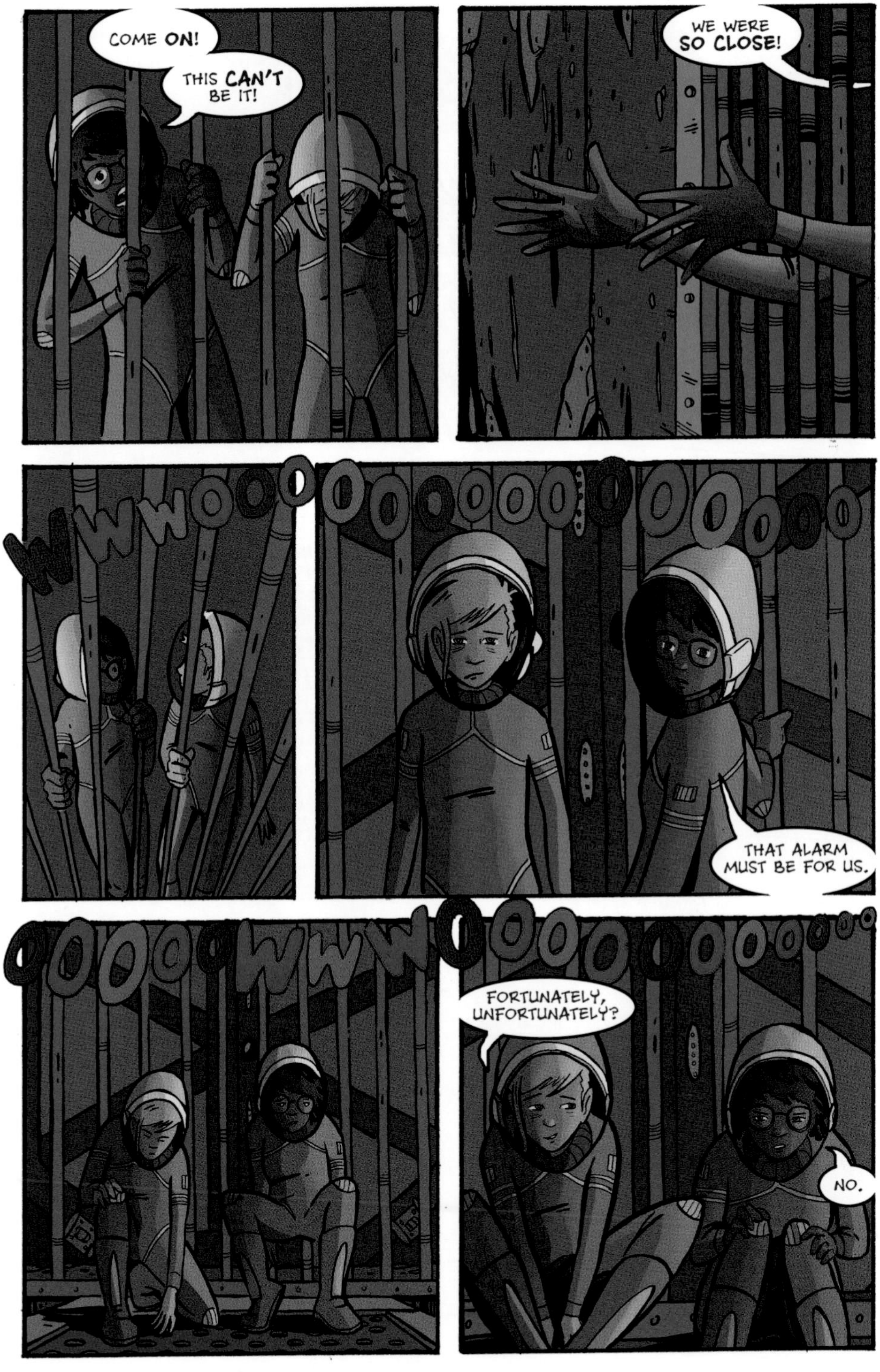
COME ON!
THIS CAN'T BE IT!
WE WERE SO CLOSE!
WWWOOOOOOOOOOOOOOOOO
THAT ALARM MUST BE FOR US.
OOOOOWWWWOOOOOOOOOOO
FORTUNATELY, UNFORTUNATELY?
NO.

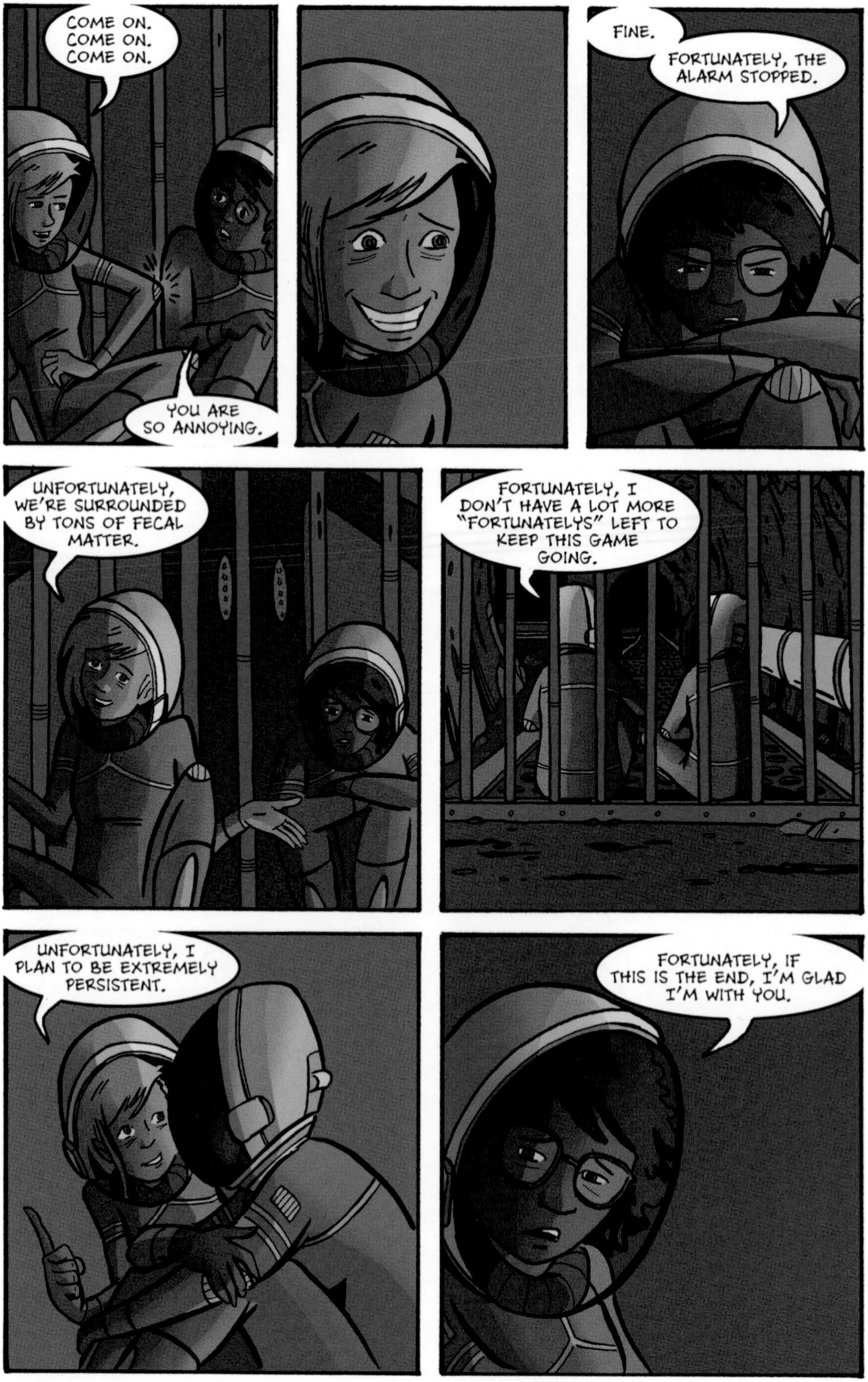
COME ON. COME ON. COME ON.
YOU ARE SO ANNOYING.
FINE.
FORTUNATELY, THE ALARM STOPPED.
UNFORTUNATELY, WE'RE SURROUNDED BY TONS OF FECAL MATTER.
FORTUNATELY, I DON'T HAVE A LOT MORE "FORTUNATELYS" LEFT TO KEEP THIS GAME GOING.
UNFORTUNATELY, I PLAN TO BE EXTREMELY PERSISTENT.
FORTUNATELY, IF THIS IS THE END, I'M GLAD I'M WITH YOU.

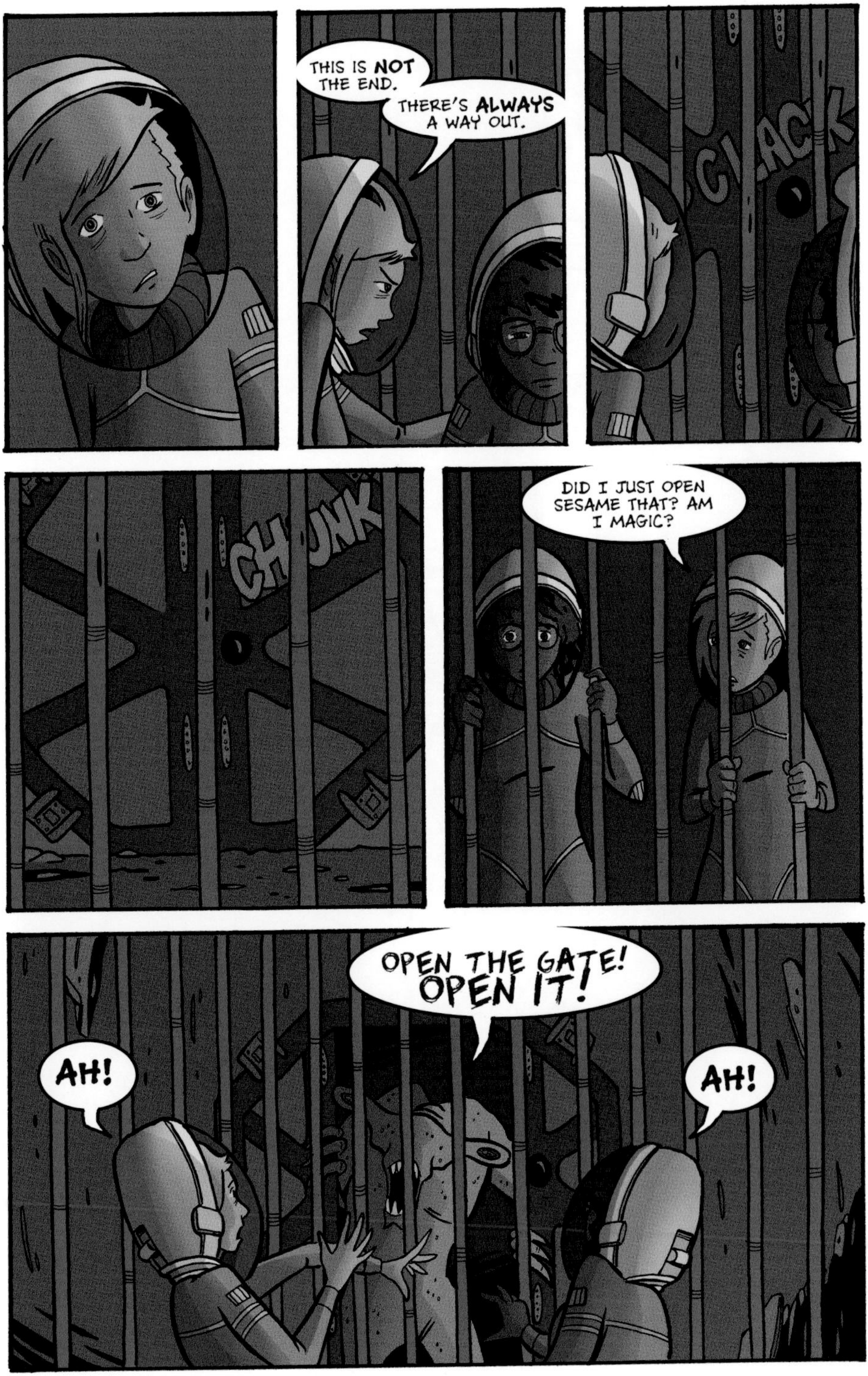
THIS IS NOT THE END.
THERE'S ALWAYS A WAY OUT.
CLACK
CHUNK
DID I JUST OPEN SESAME THAT? AM I MAGIC?
OPEN THE GATE! OPEN IT!
AH!
AH!

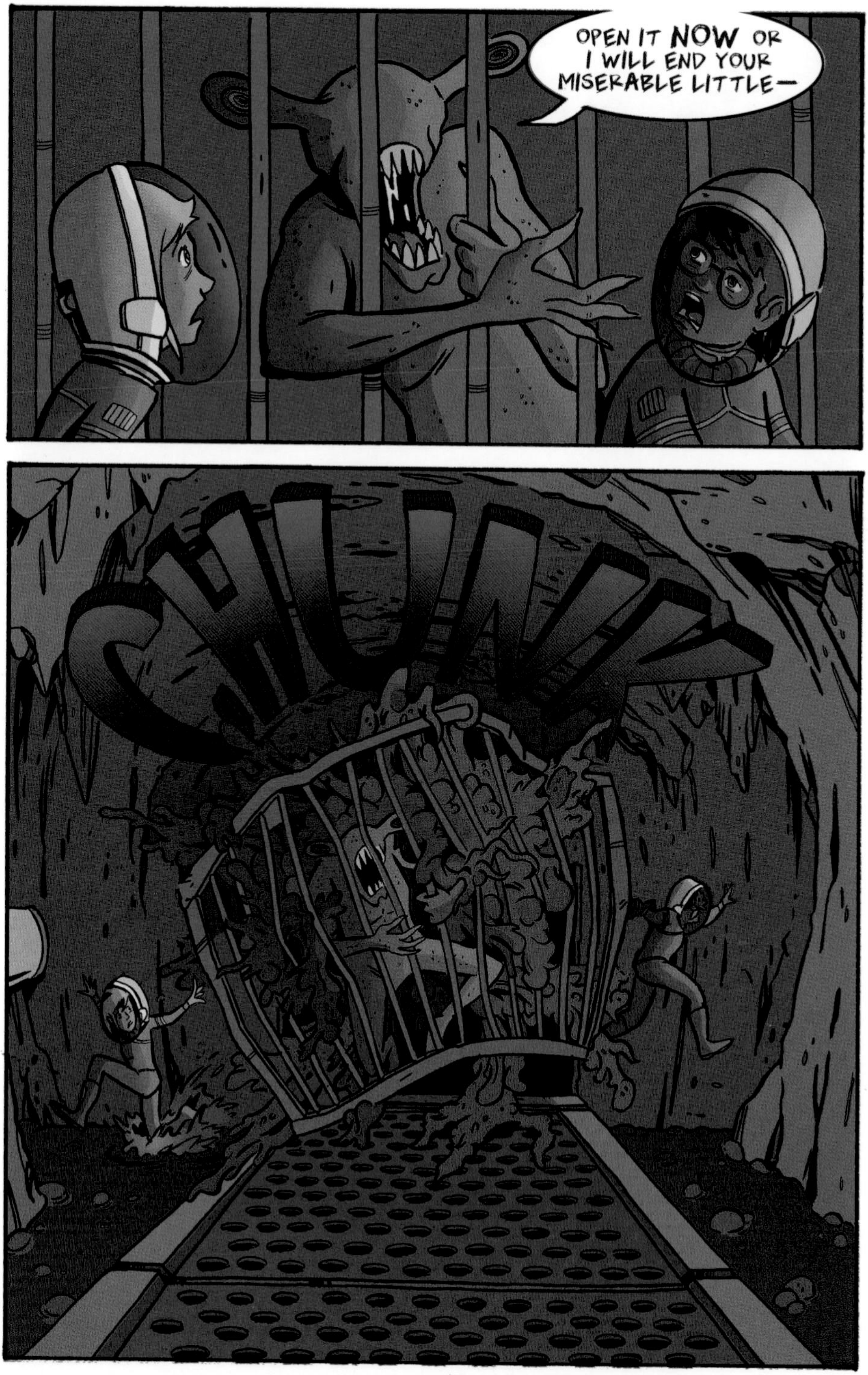
OPEN IT NOW OR I WILL END YOUR MISERABLE LITTLE—
CHUNK

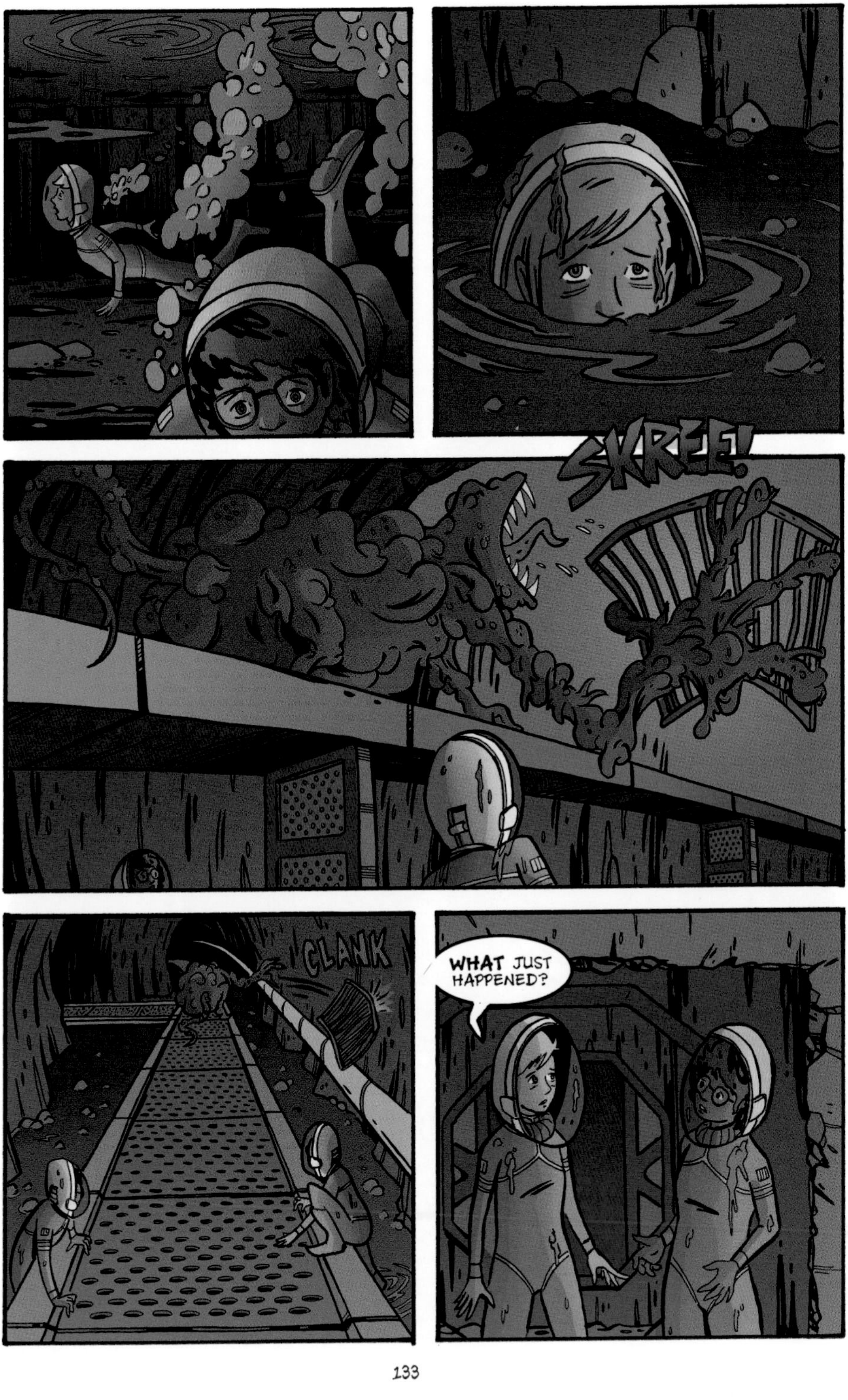
SKREE!
CLANK
WHAT JUST HAPPENED?

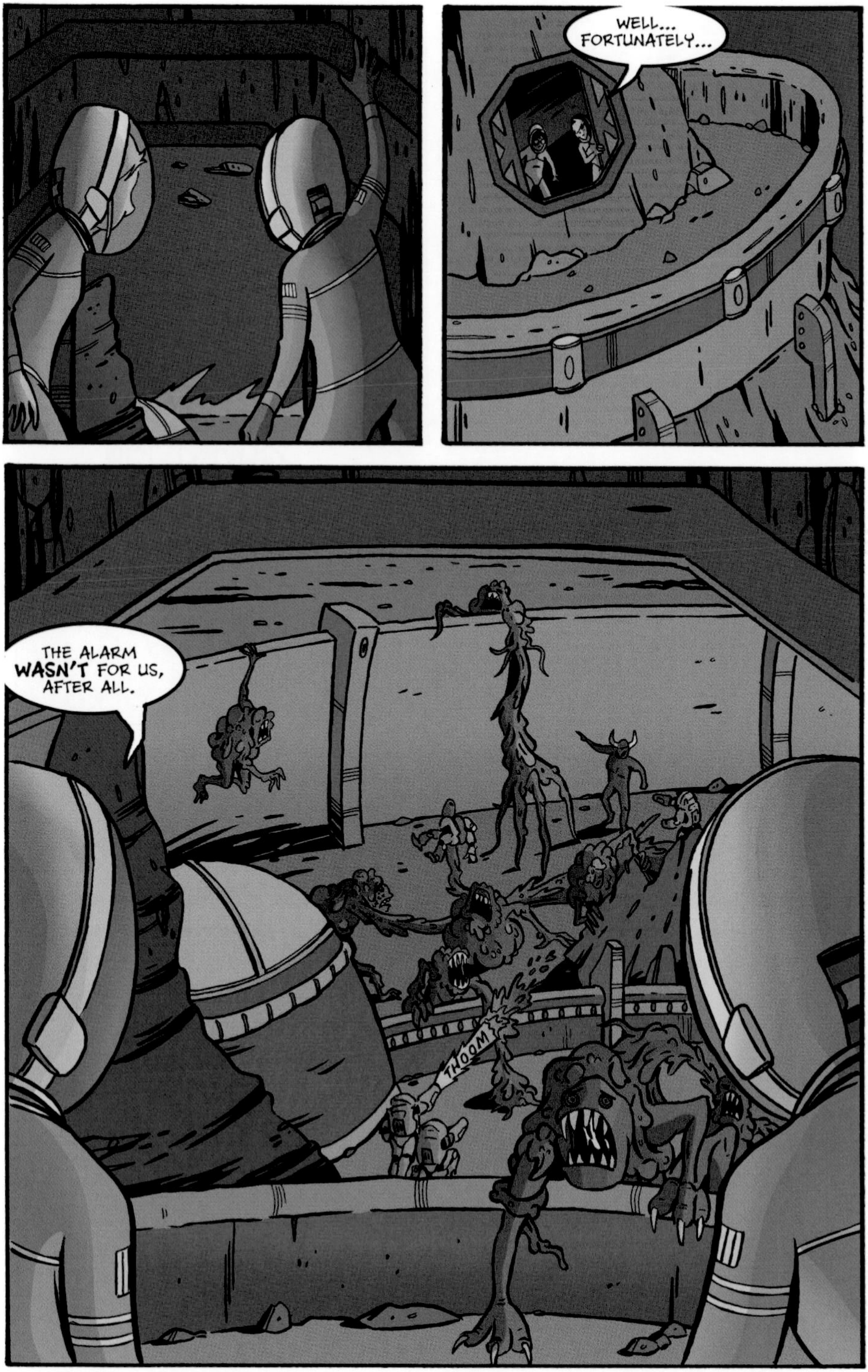
WELL... FORTUNATELY...
THE ALARM **WASN'T** FOR US, AFTER ALL.
THOOM

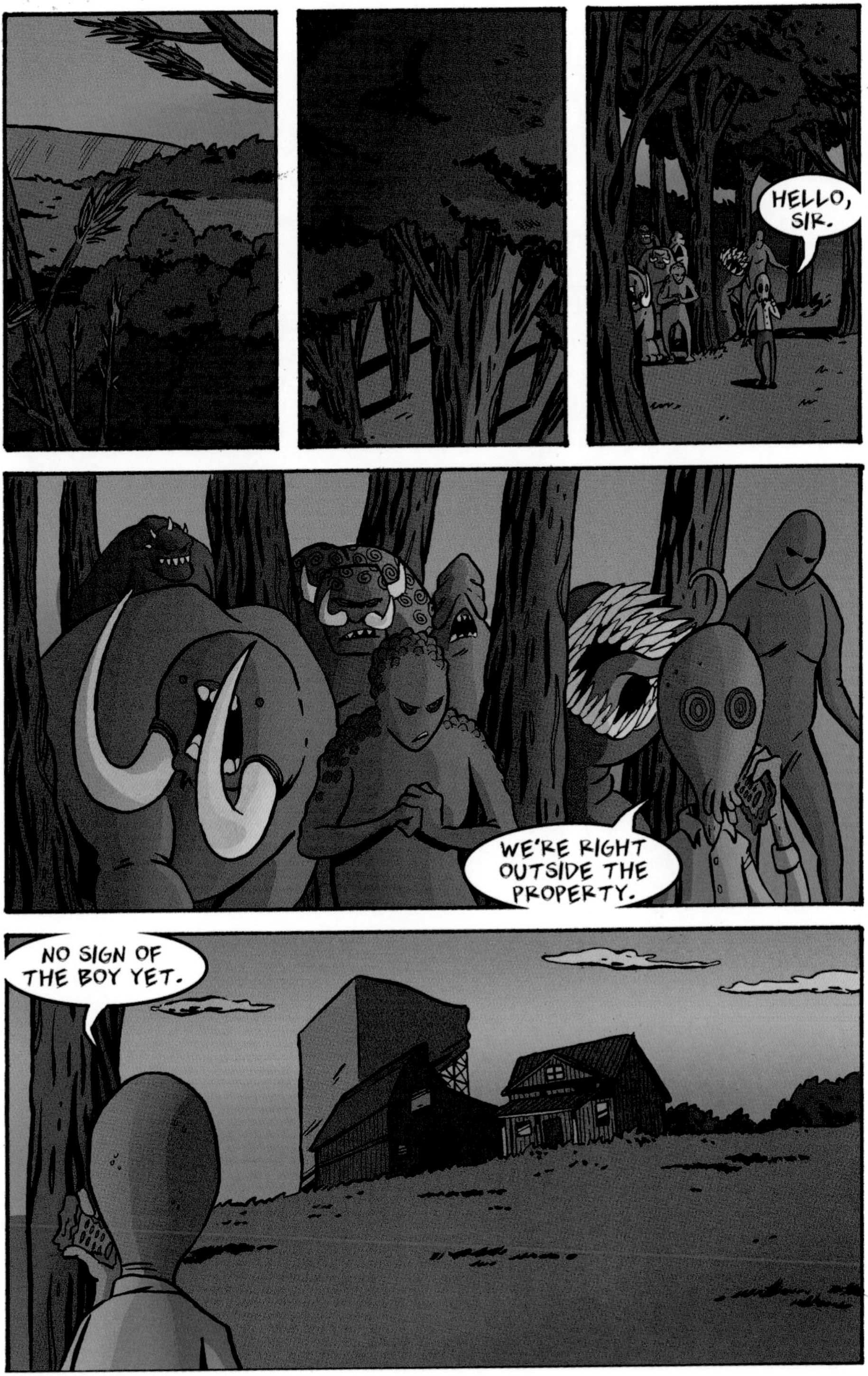
HELLO, SIR.
WE'RE RIGHT OUTSIDE THE PROPERTY.
NO SIGN OF THE BOY YET.

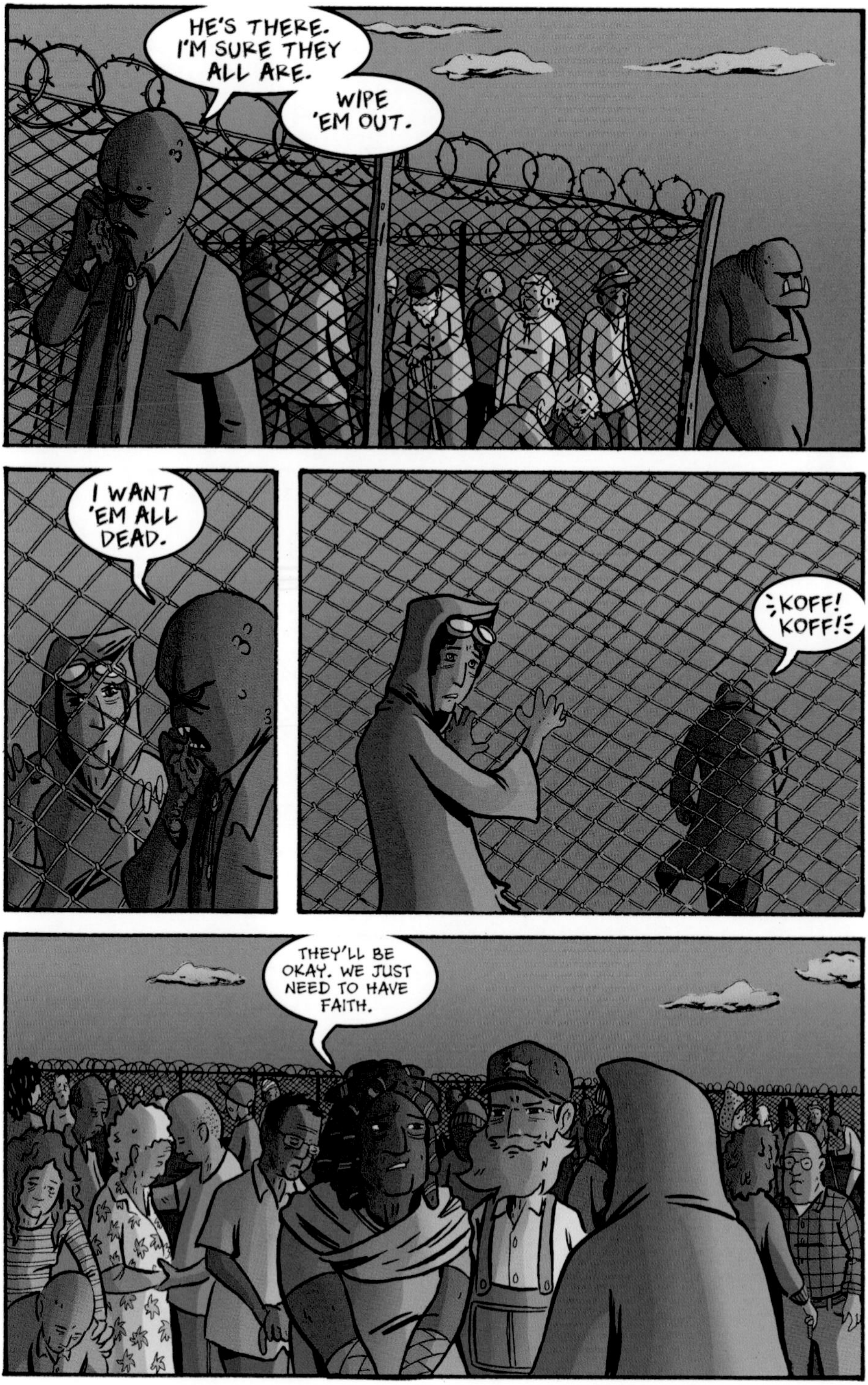
HE'S THERE. I'M SURE THEY ALL ARE.
WIPE 'EM OUT.
I WANT 'EM ALL DEAD.
KOFF! KOFF!
THEY'LL BE OKAY. WE JUST NEED TO HAVE FAITH.

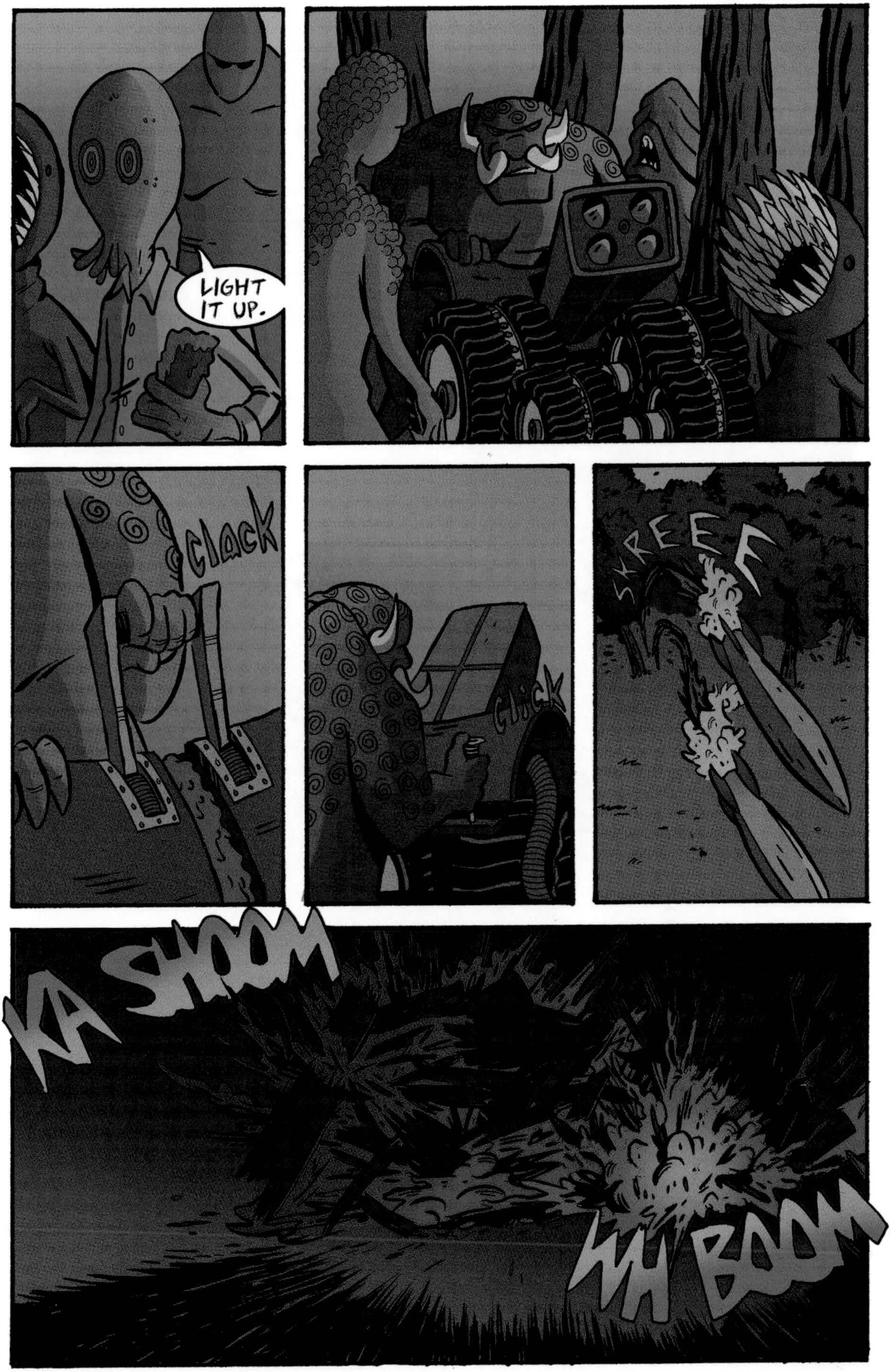
LIGHT IT UP.
CLACK
CLICK
SKREEE
KA SHOOM
KA BOOM

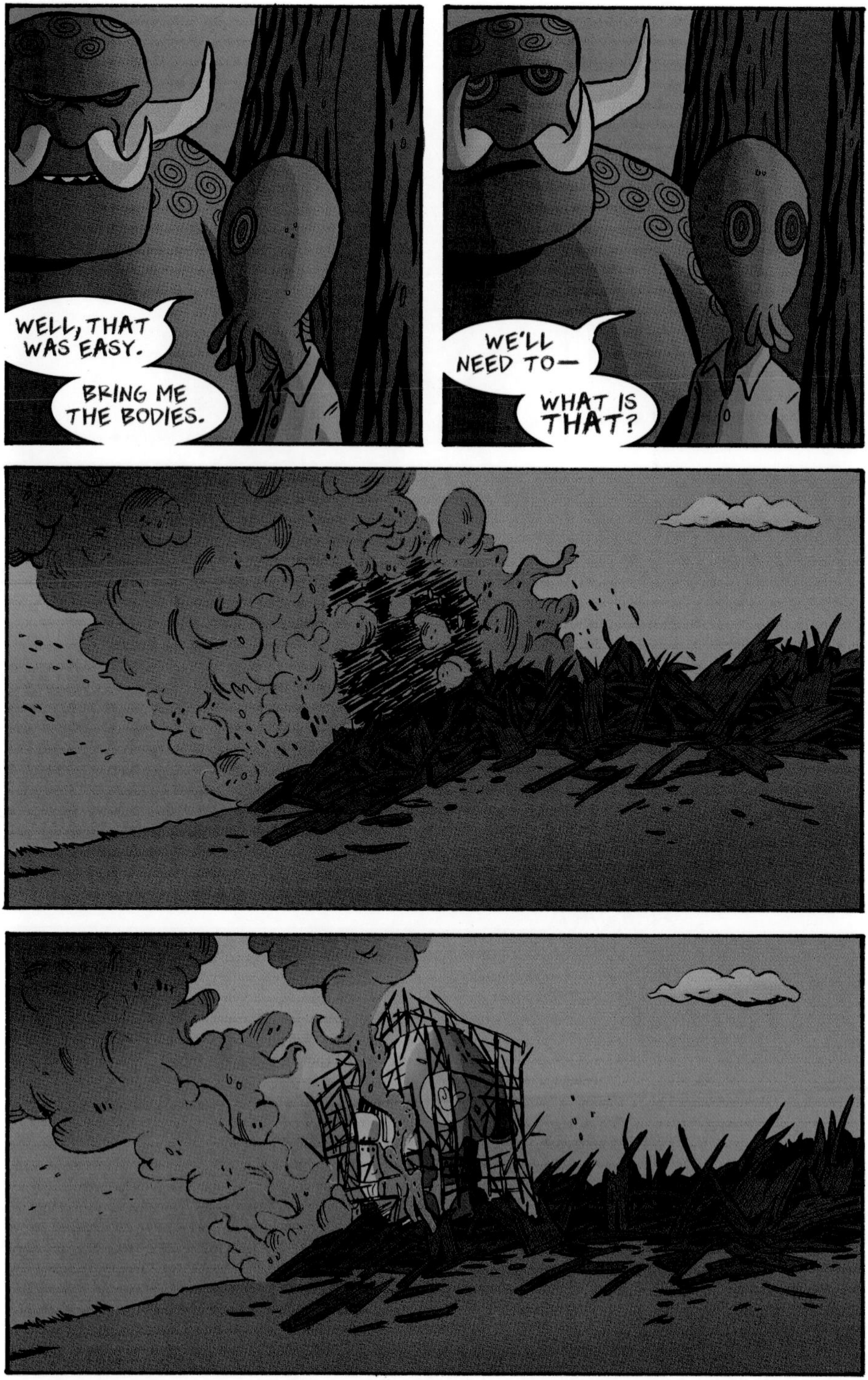
WELL, THAT WAS EASY.
BRING ME THE BODIES.
WE'LL NEED TO—
WHAT IS THAT?

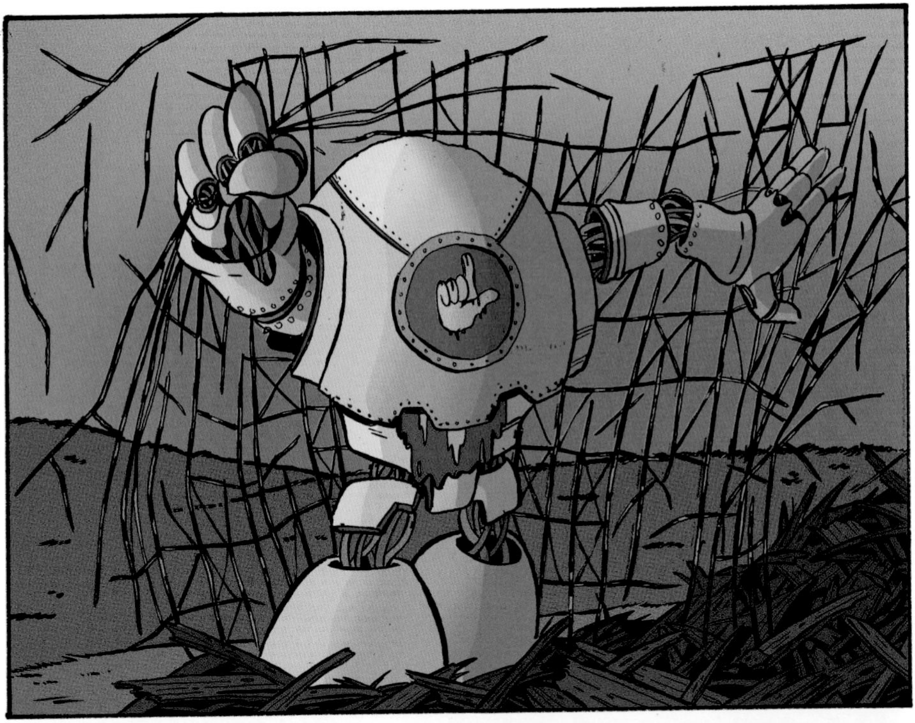

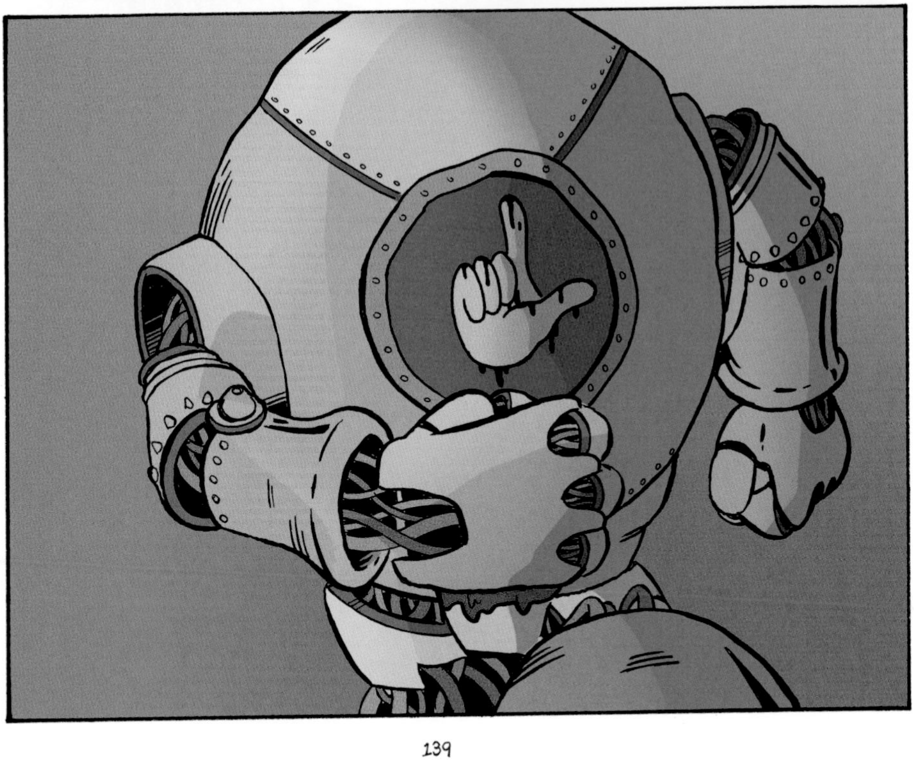

OH, COME ON.
WHACK

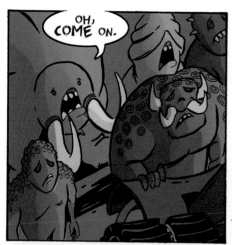

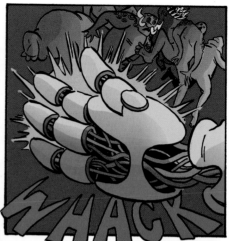

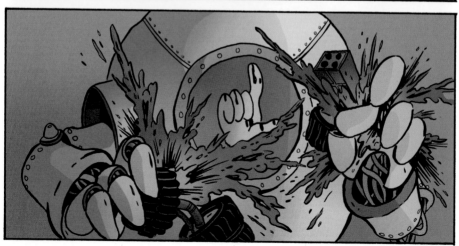

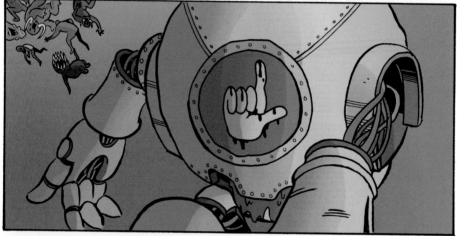

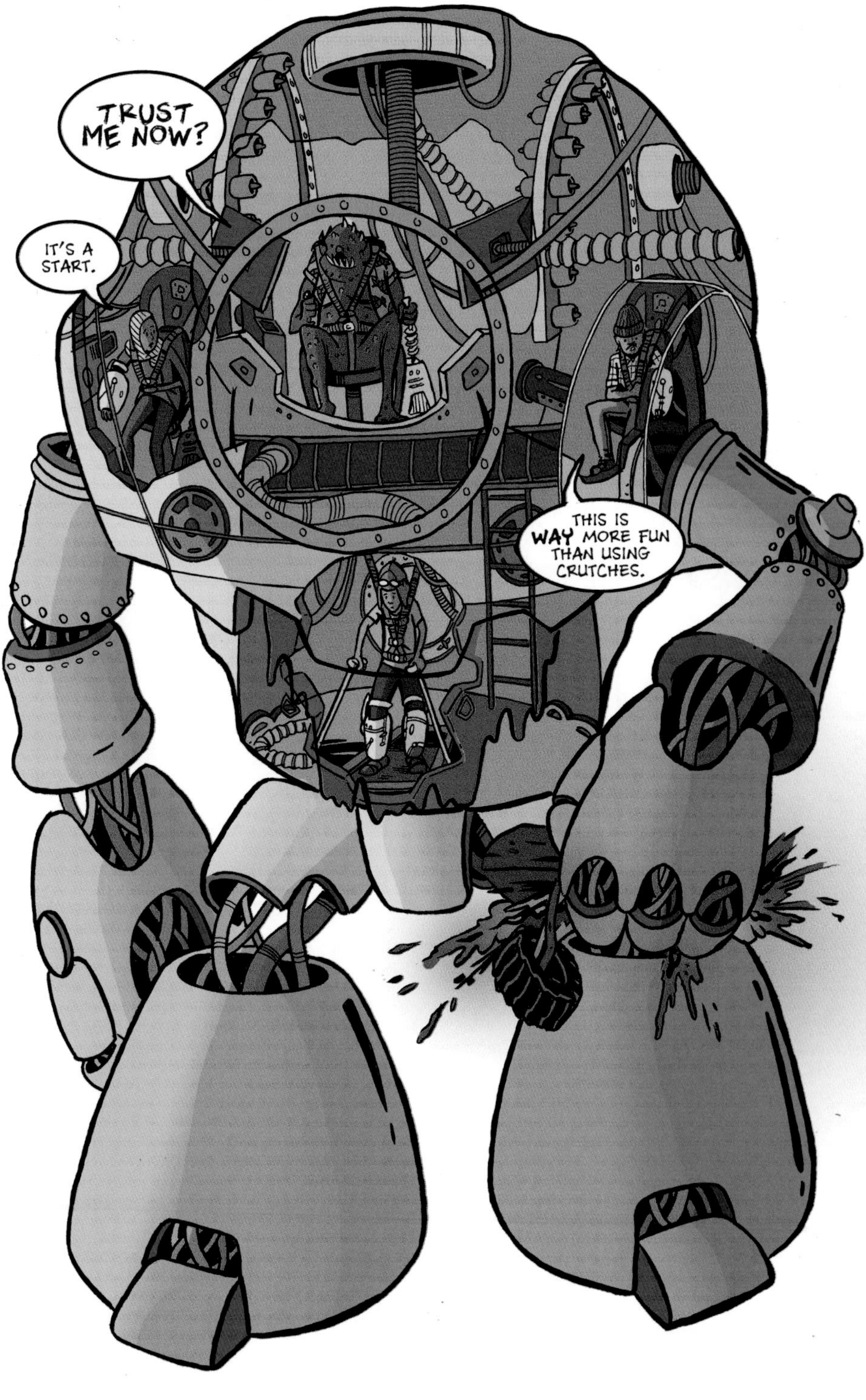
TRUST ME NOW?
IT'S A START.
THIS IS WAY MORE FUN THAN USING CRUTCHES.

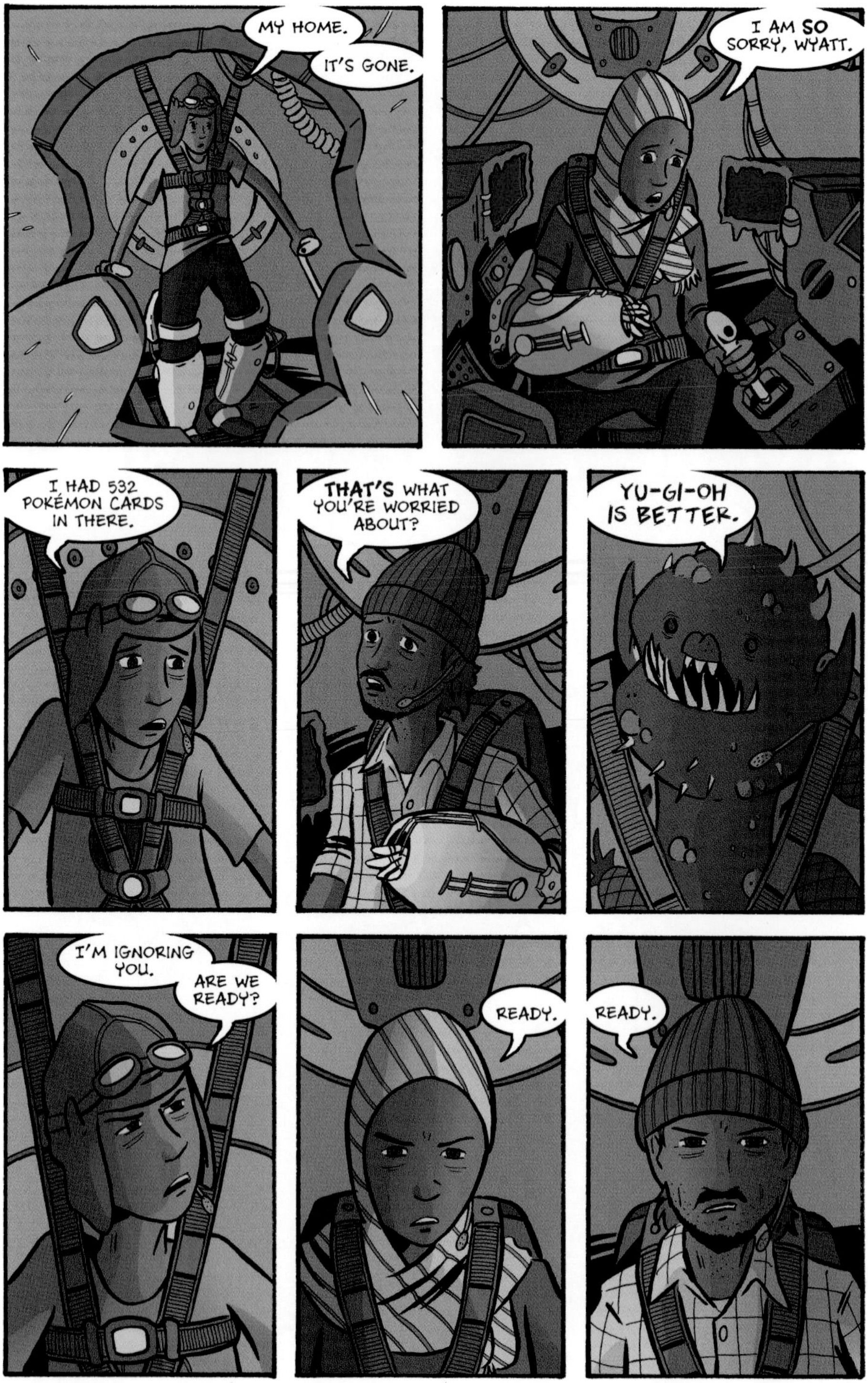

MY HOME.
IT'S GONE.
I AM SO SORRY, WYATT.
I HAD 532 POKÉMON CARDS IN THERE.
THAT'S WHAT YOU'RE WORRIED ABOUT?
YU-GI-OH IS BETTER.
I'M IGNORING YOU.
ARE WE READY?
READY.
READY.

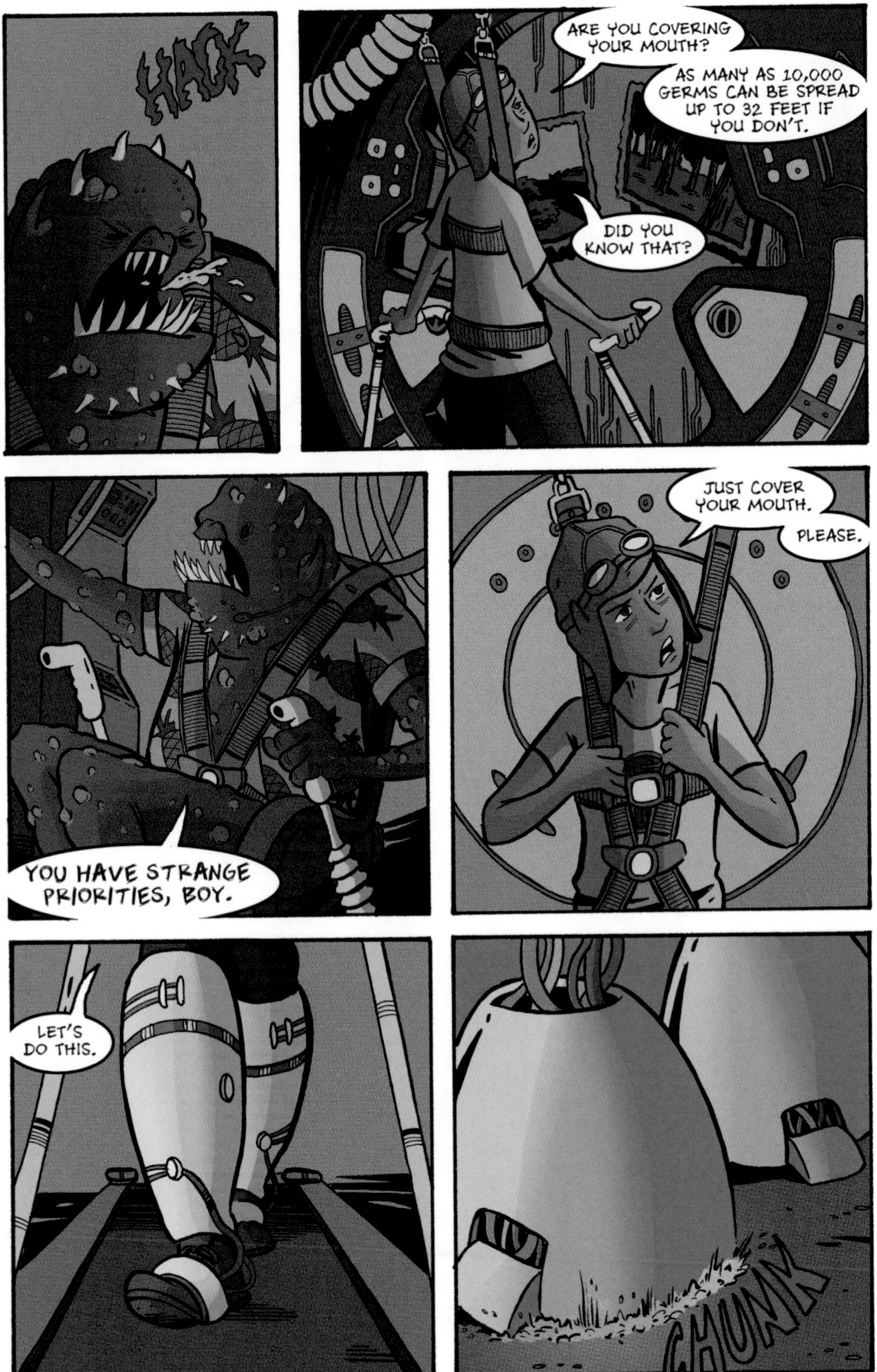
HACK
ARE YOU COVERING YOUR MOUTH?
AS MANY AS 10,000 GERMS CAN BE SPREAD UP TO 32 FEET IF YOU DON'T.
DID YOU KNOW THAT?
YOU HAVE STRANGE PRIORITIES, BOY.
JUST COVER YOUR MOUTH.
PLEASE.
LET'S DO THIS.
CHUNK

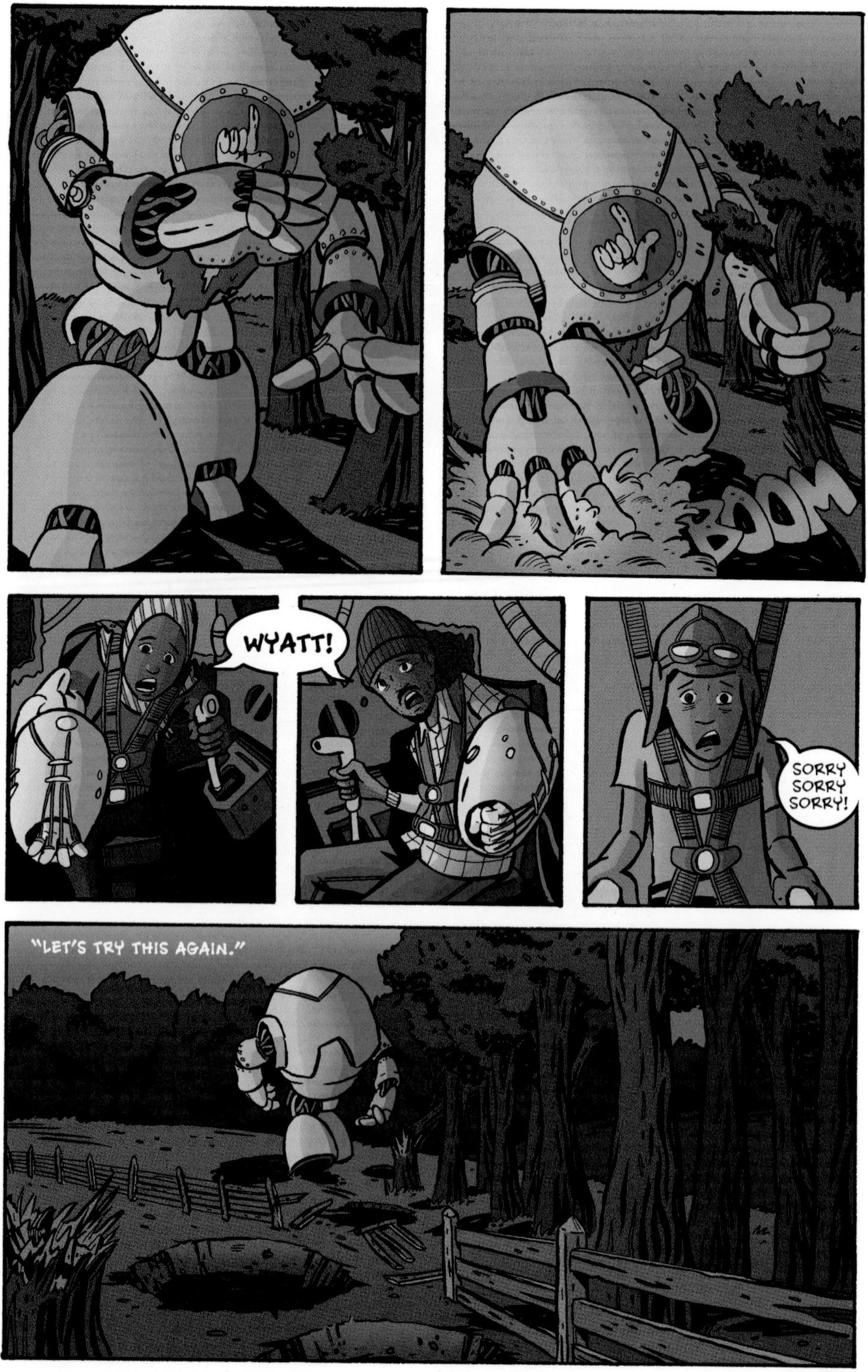
BOOM
WYATT!
SORRY SORRY SORRY!
"LET'S TRY THIS AGAIN."

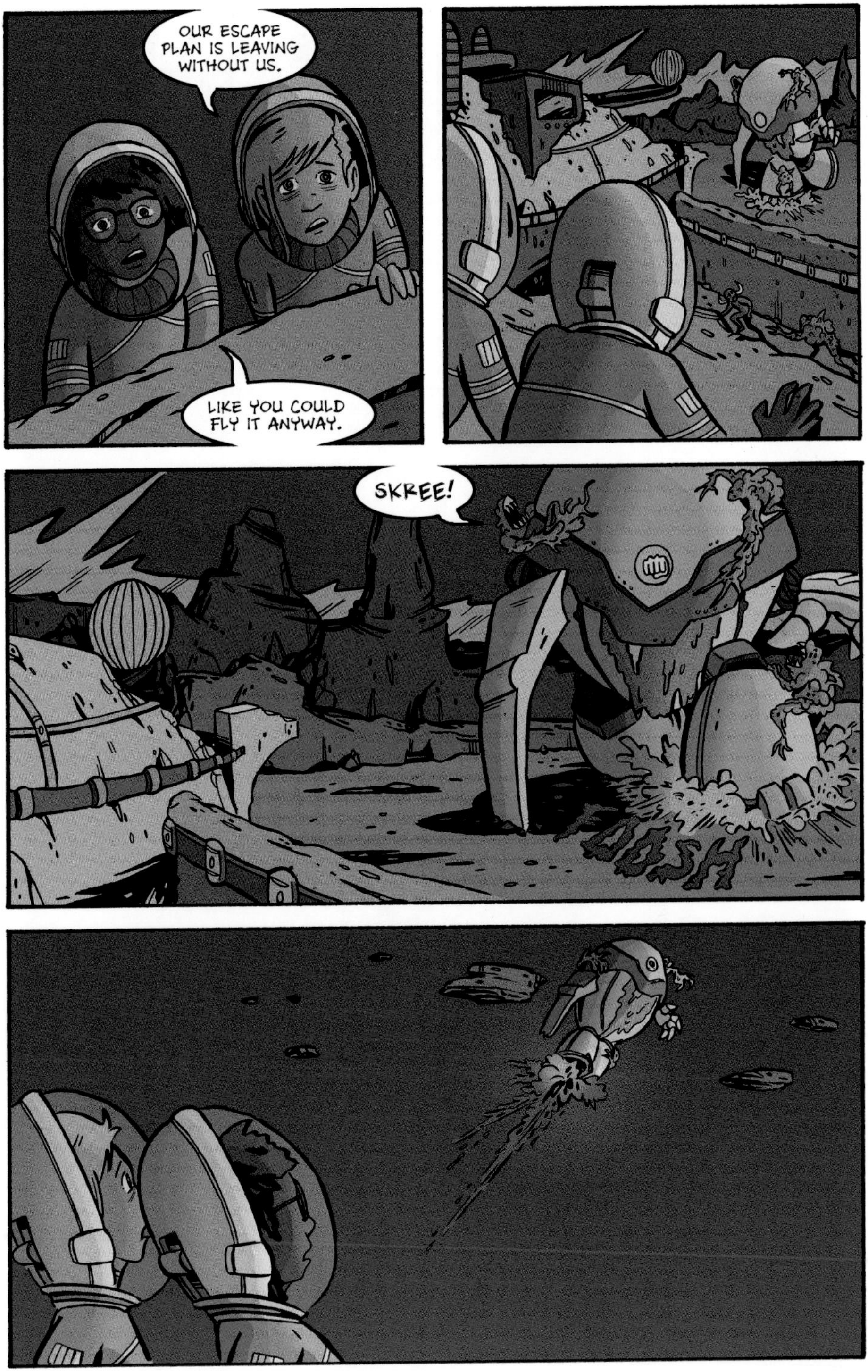
OUR ESCAPE PLAN IS LEAVING WITHOUT US.
LIKE YOU COULD FLY IT ANYWAY.
SKREE!

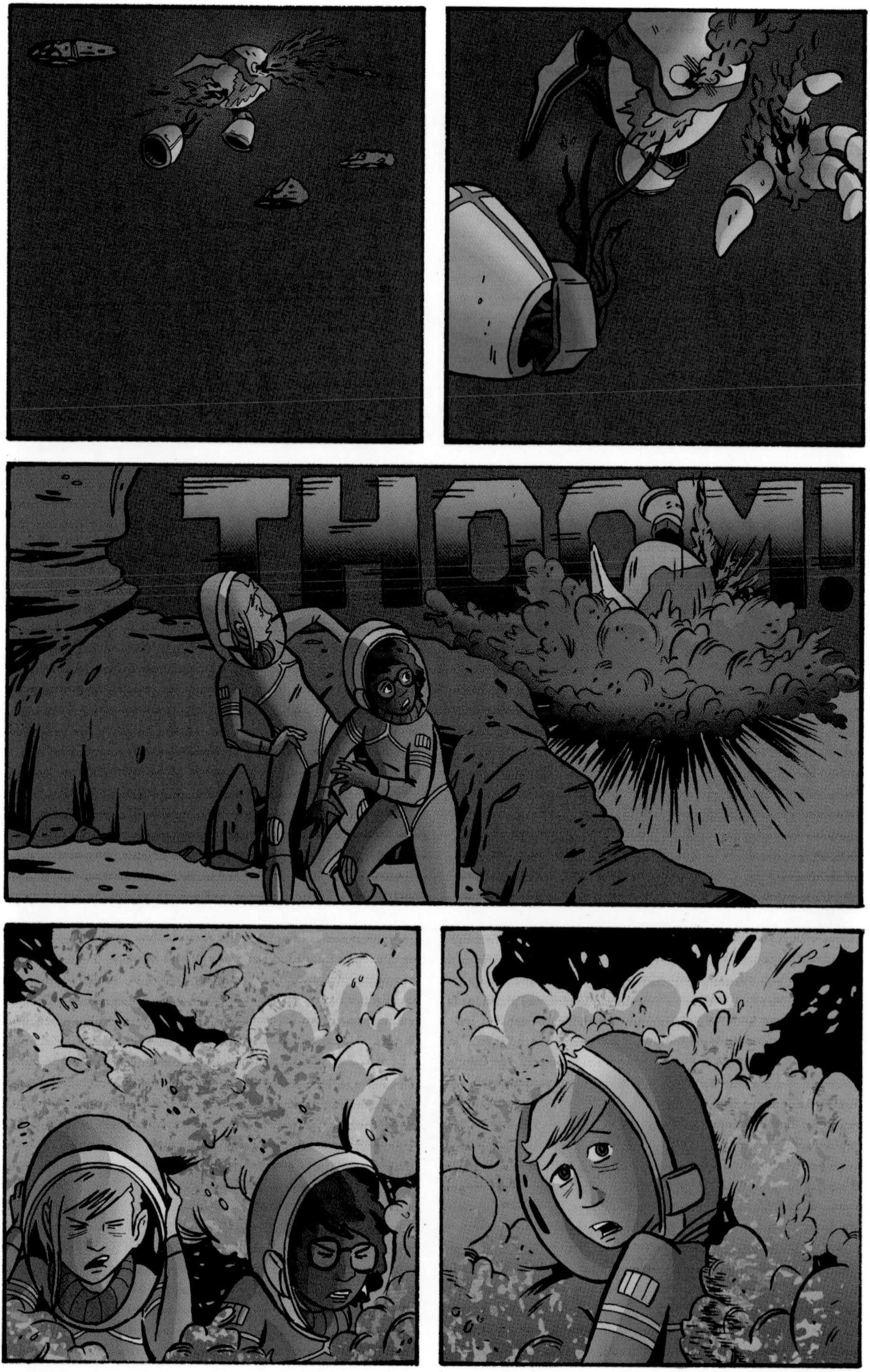
THOOM!

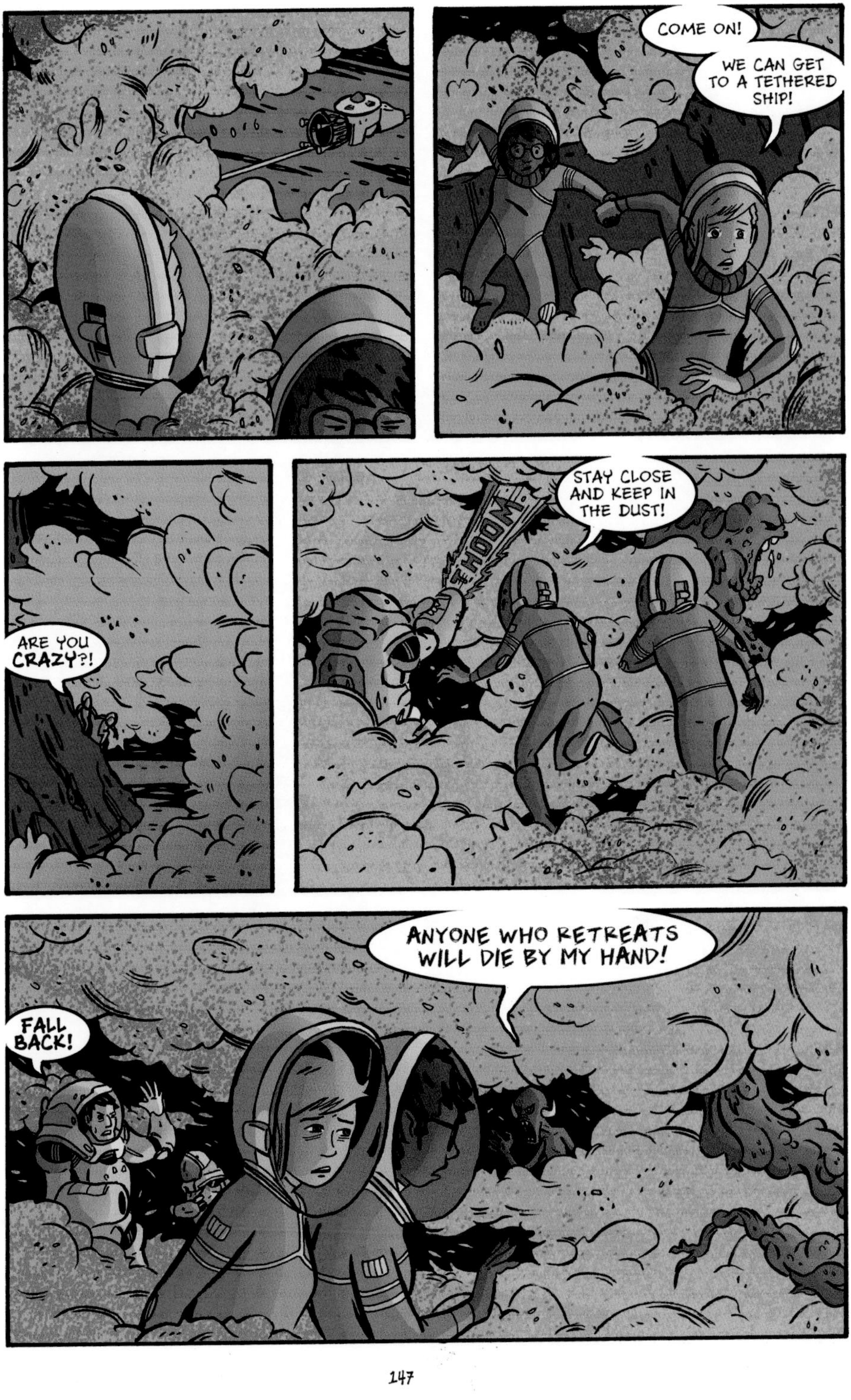
COME ON!
WE CAN GET TO A TETHERED SHIP!
ARE YOU CRAZY?!
STAY CLOSE AND KEEP IN THE DUST!
FWOOSH
ANYONE WHO RETREATS WILL DIE BY MY HAND!
FALL BACK!

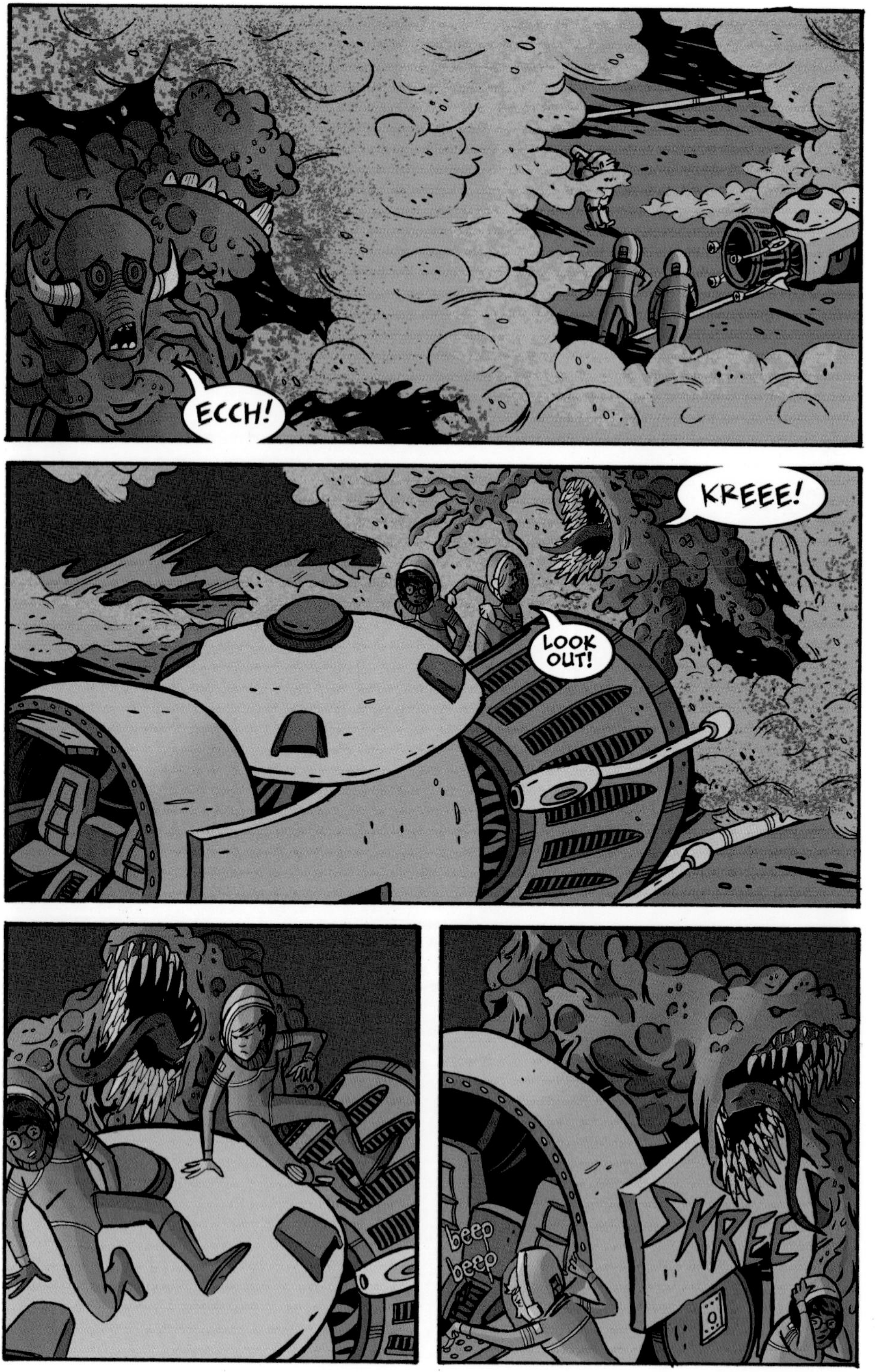
ECCH!
KREEE!
LOOK OUT!
beep beep
SKREE

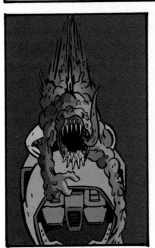

NEW PLAN?

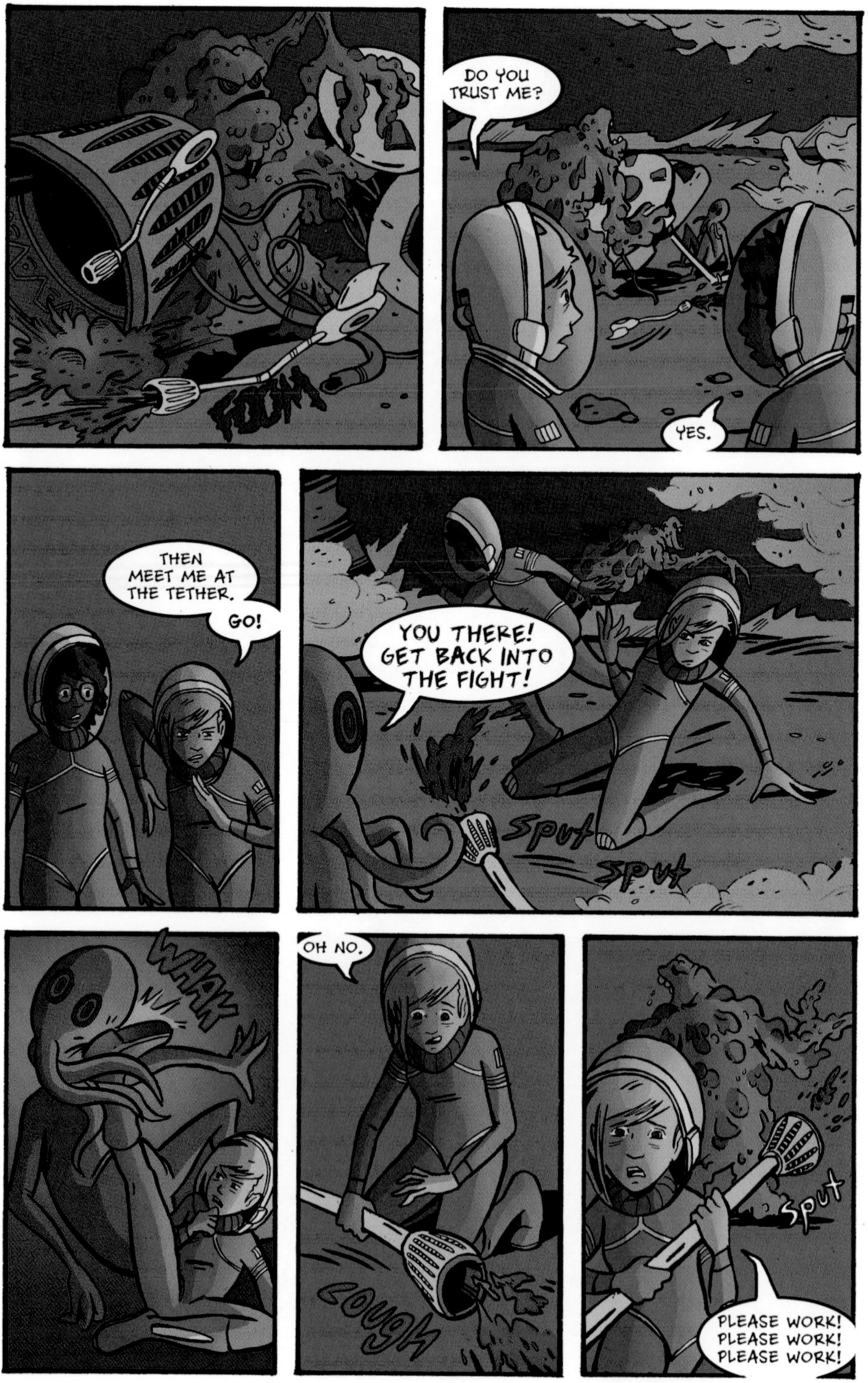
FOOM
DO YOU TRUST ME?
YES.
THEN MEET ME AT THE TETHER.
GO!
YOU THERE! GET BACK INTO THE FIGHT!
SPUT
SPUT
WHAK
OH NO.
COUGH
SPUT
PLEASE WORK! PLEASE WORK! PLEASE WORK!

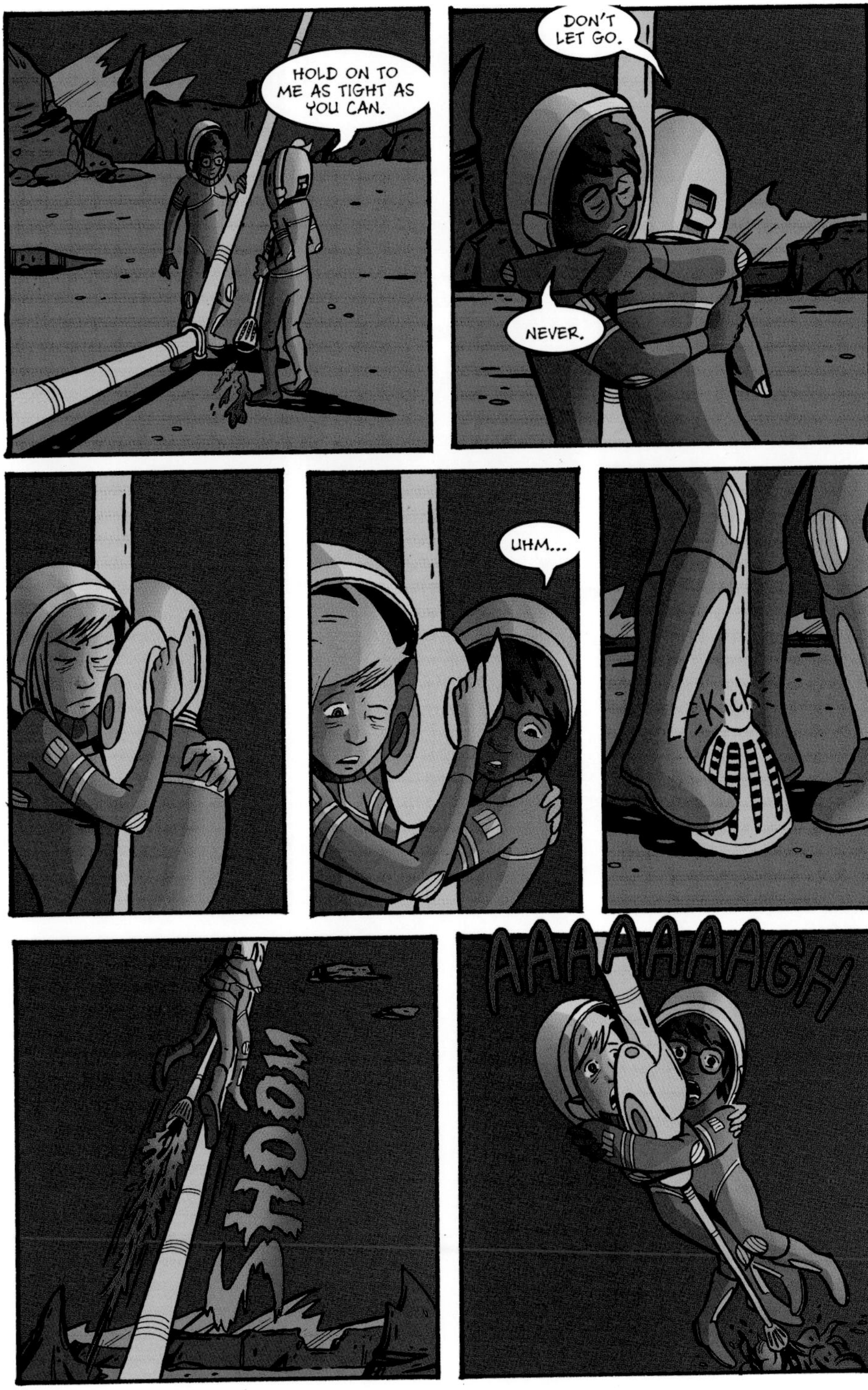
HOLD ON TO ME AS TIGHT AS YOU CAN.
DON'T LET GO.
NEVER.
UHM...
KICK
WHOOSH
AAAAAAAAGH

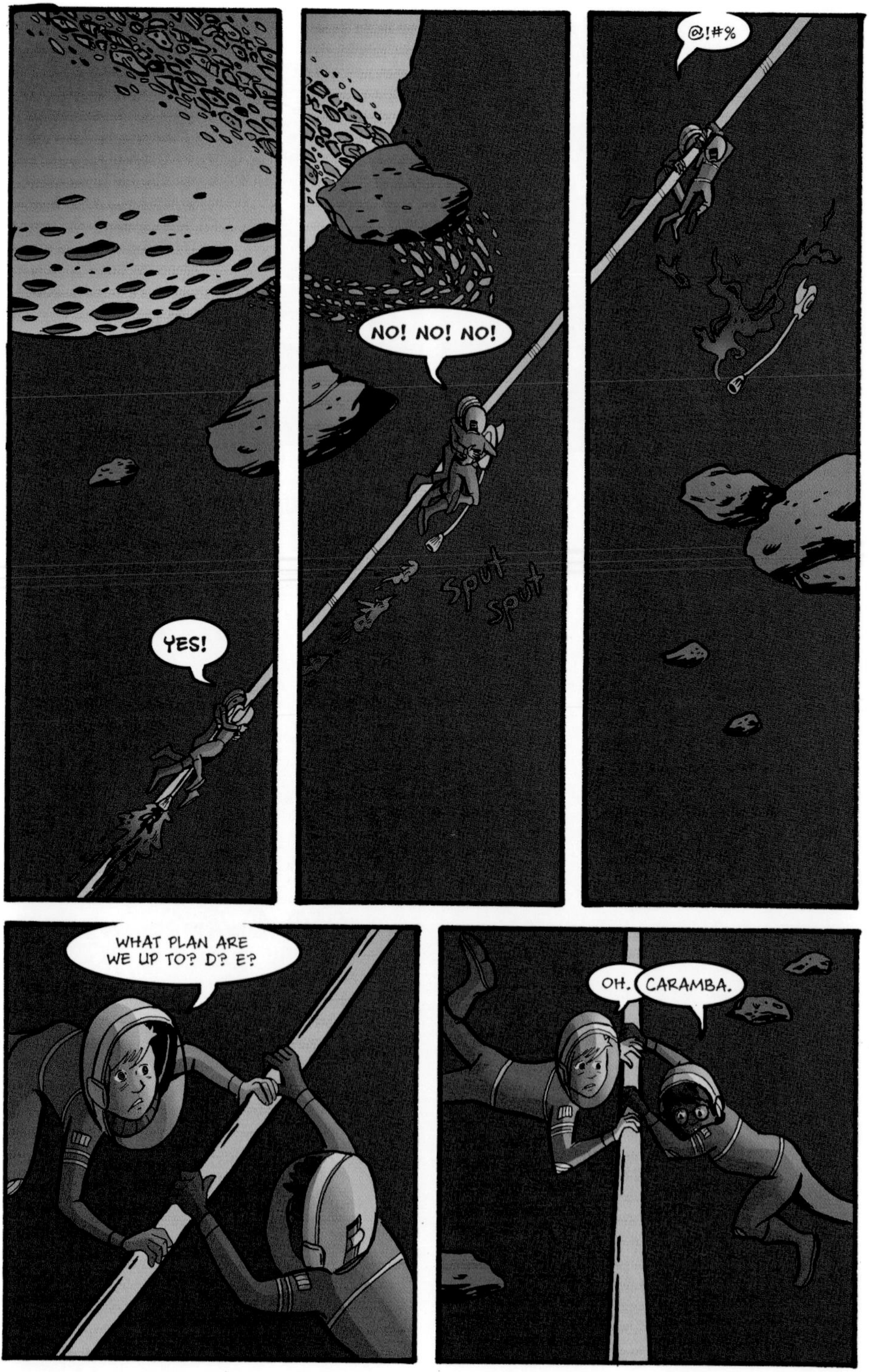

YES!
NO! NO! NO!
SPUT SPUT
@!#%
WHAT PLAN ARE WE UP TO? D? E?
OH.
CARAMBA.

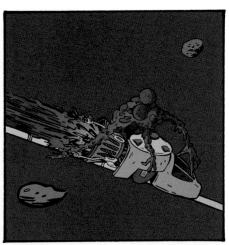

I'M GONNA MAKE IT! I'M GONNA MAKE IT!

PSHHHH

AAAGH!

VRRRRRR

dink

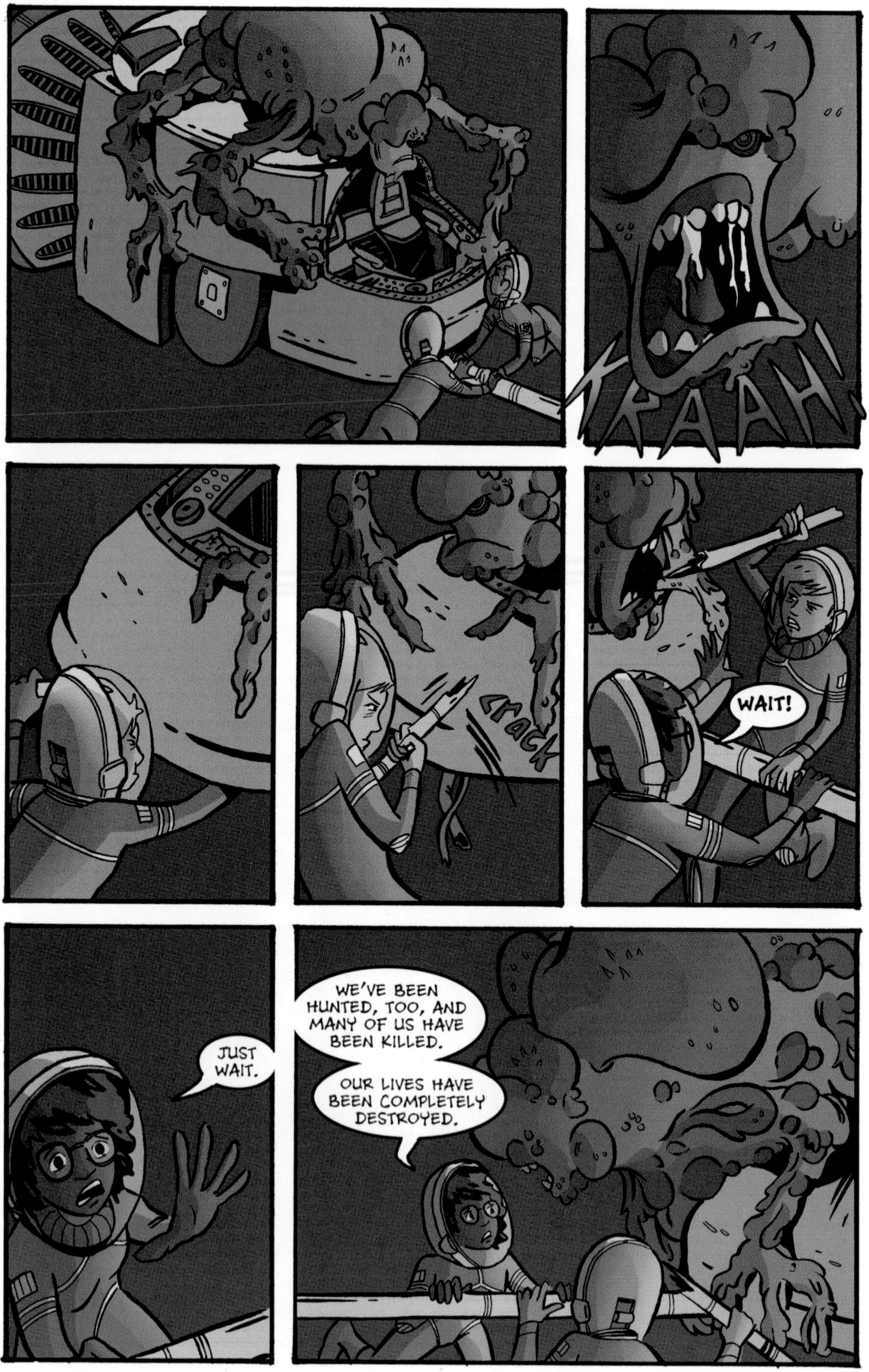
KRAAH!
CRACK
WAIT!
JUST WAIT.
WE'VE BEEN HUNTED, TOO, AND MANY OF US HAVE BEEN KILLED.
OUR LIVES HAVE BEEN COMPLETELY DESTROYED.

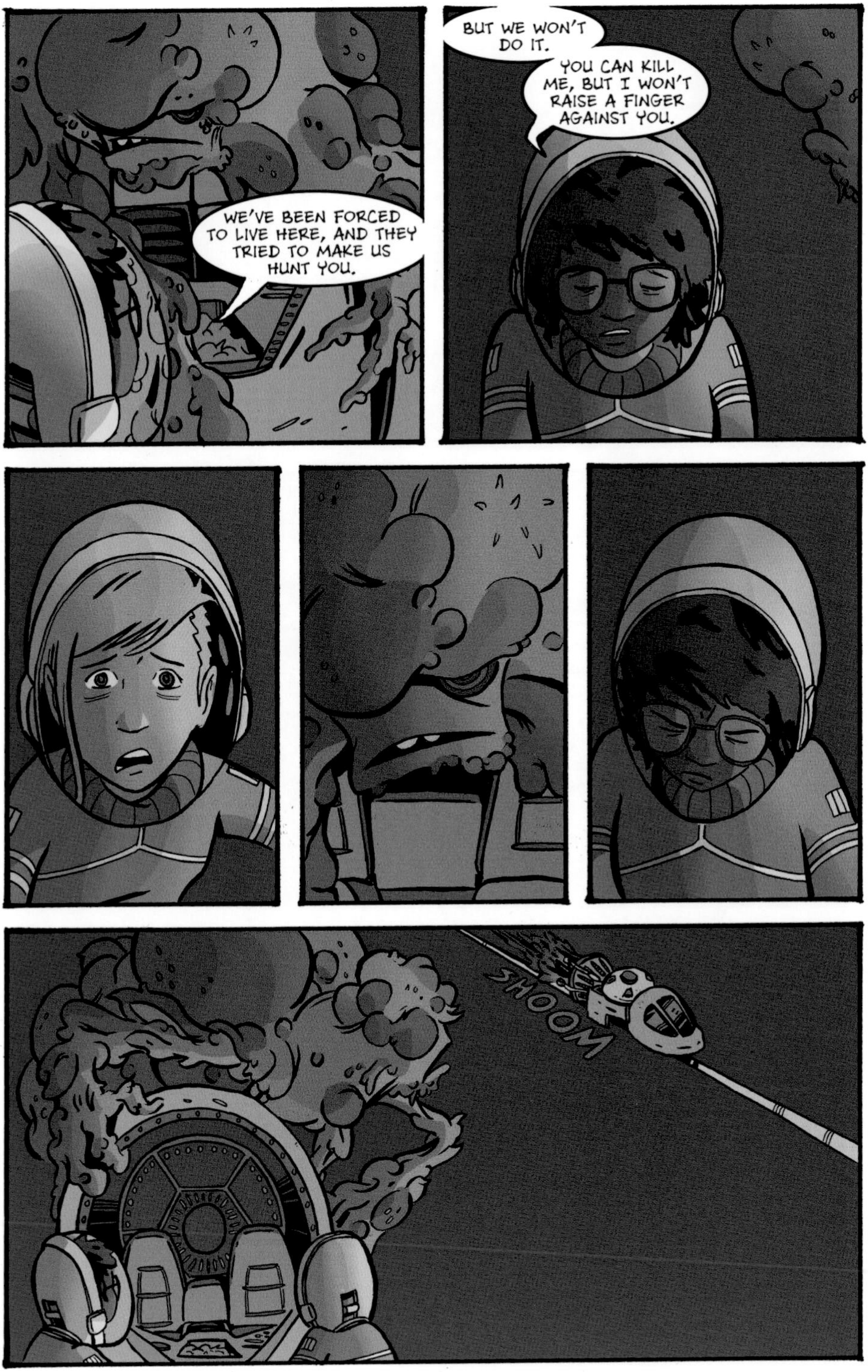
WE'VE BEEN FORCED TO LIVE HERE, AND THEY TRIED TO MAKE US HUNT YOU.
BUT WE WON'T DO IT.
YOU CAN KILL ME, BUT I WON'T RAISE A FINGER AGAINST YOU.
SHOOM

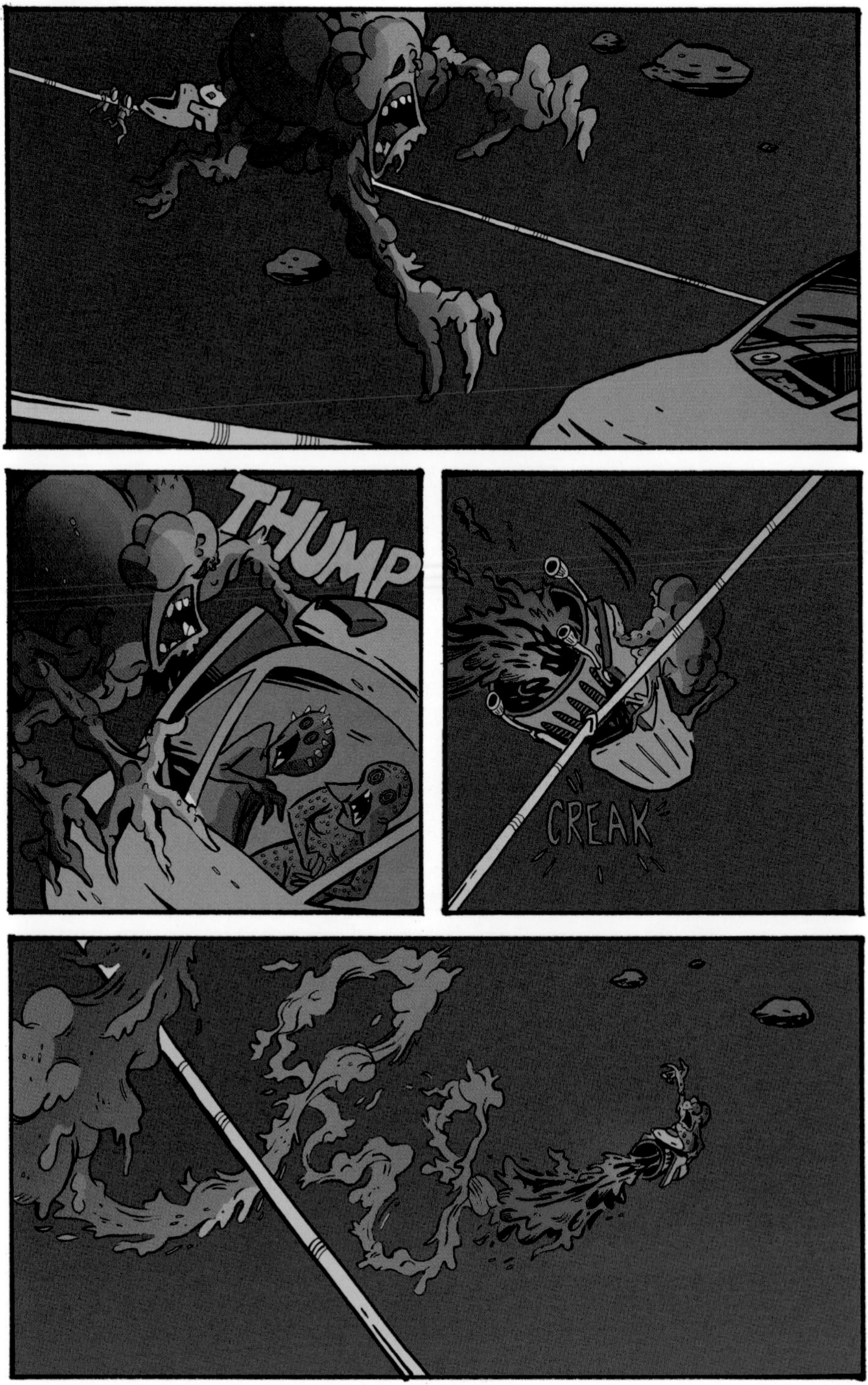
THUMP
CREAK

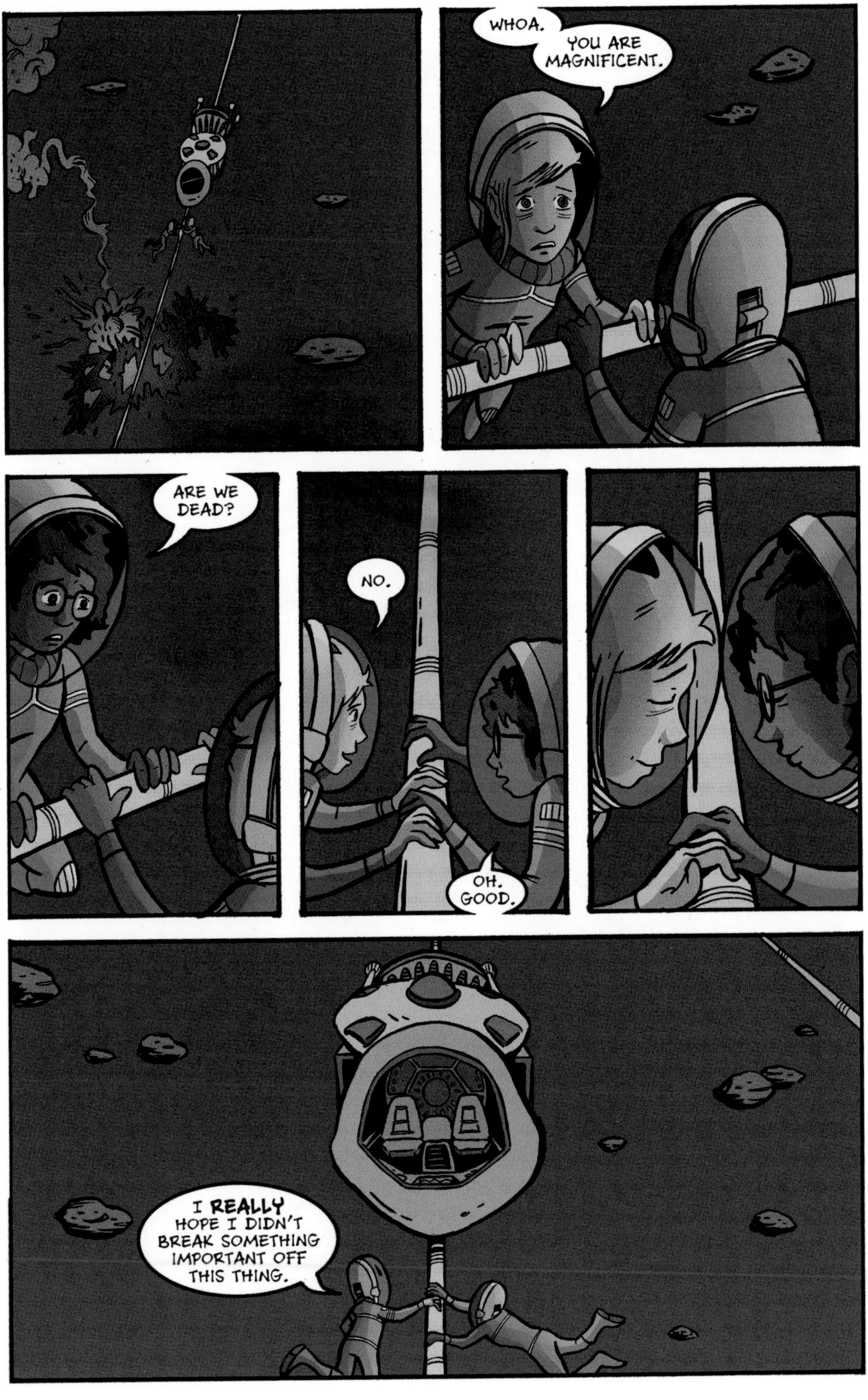
WHOA.
YOU ARE MAGNIFICENT.
ARE WE DEAD?
NO.
OH. GOOD.
I REALLY HOPE I DIDN'T BREAK SOMETHING IMPORTANT OFF THIS THING.

CHAPTER 5

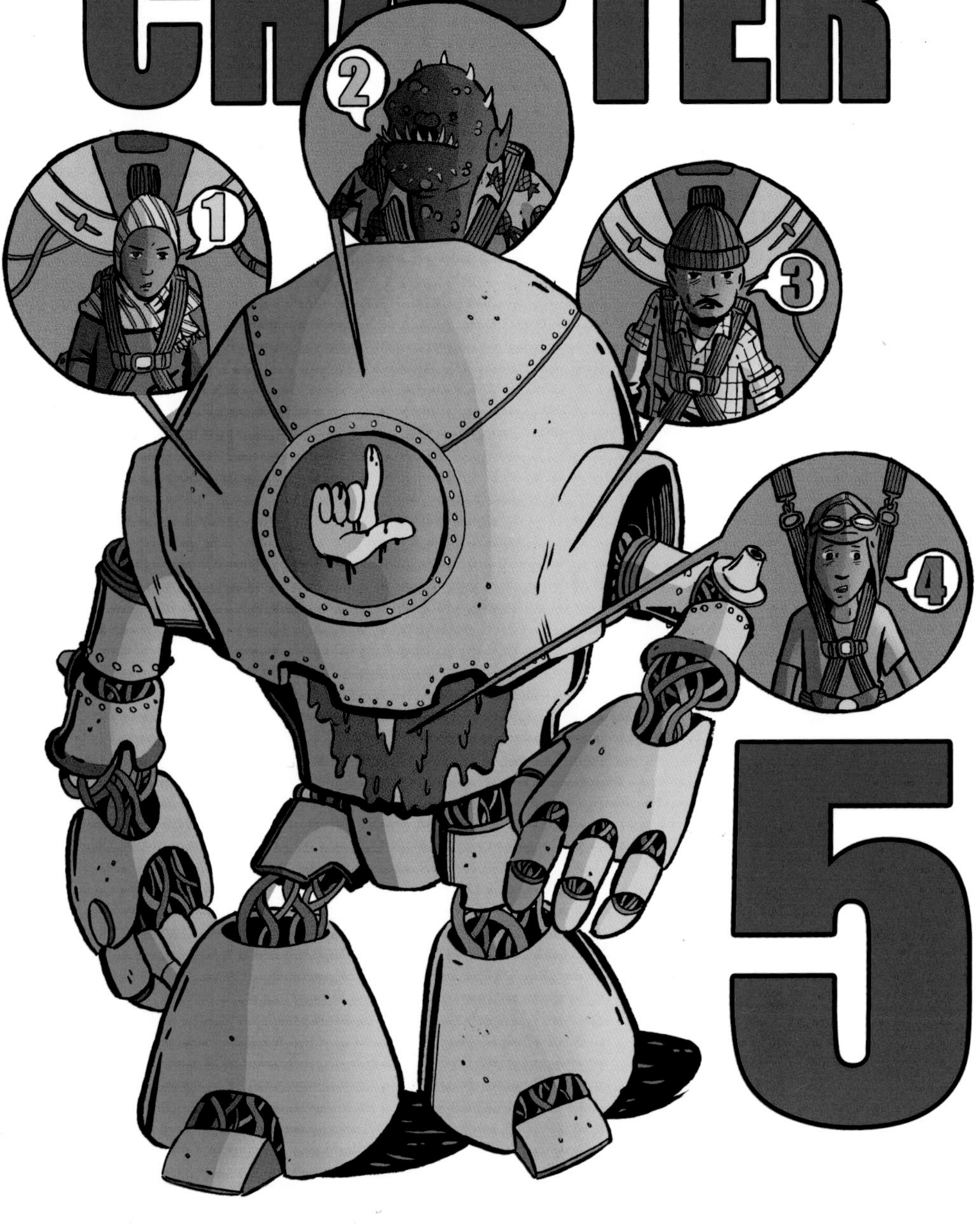
1
2
3
4

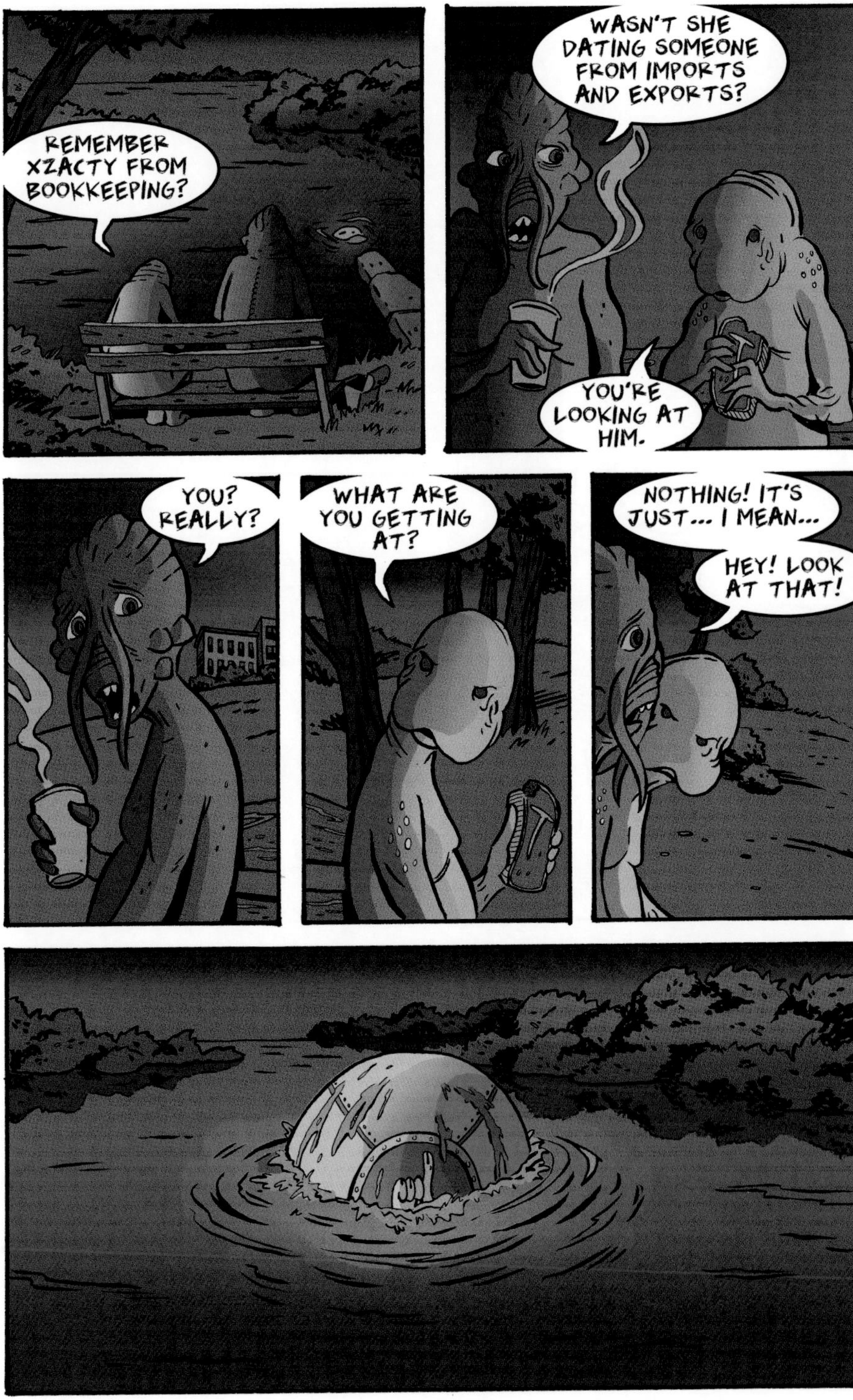
REMEMBER XZACTY FROM BOOKKEEPING?
WASN'T SHE DATING SOMEONE FROM IMPORTS AND EXPORTS?
YOU'RE LOOKING AT HIM.
YOU? REALLY?
WHAT ARE YOU GETTING AT?
NOTHING! IT'S JUST... I MEAN...
HEY! LOOK AT THAT!

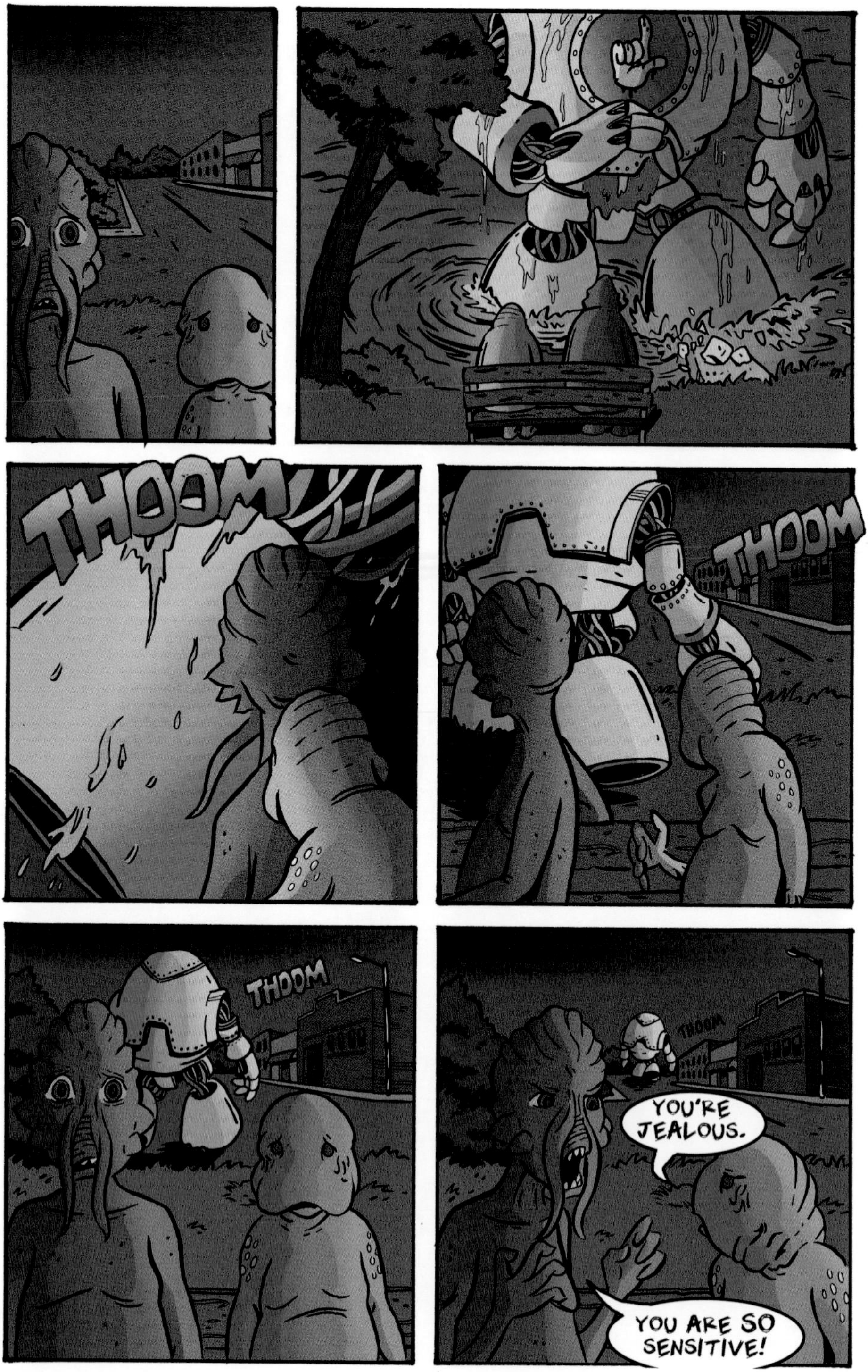
THOOM
THOOM
THOOM
THOOM
YOU'RE JEALOUS.
YOU ARE SO SENSITIVE!

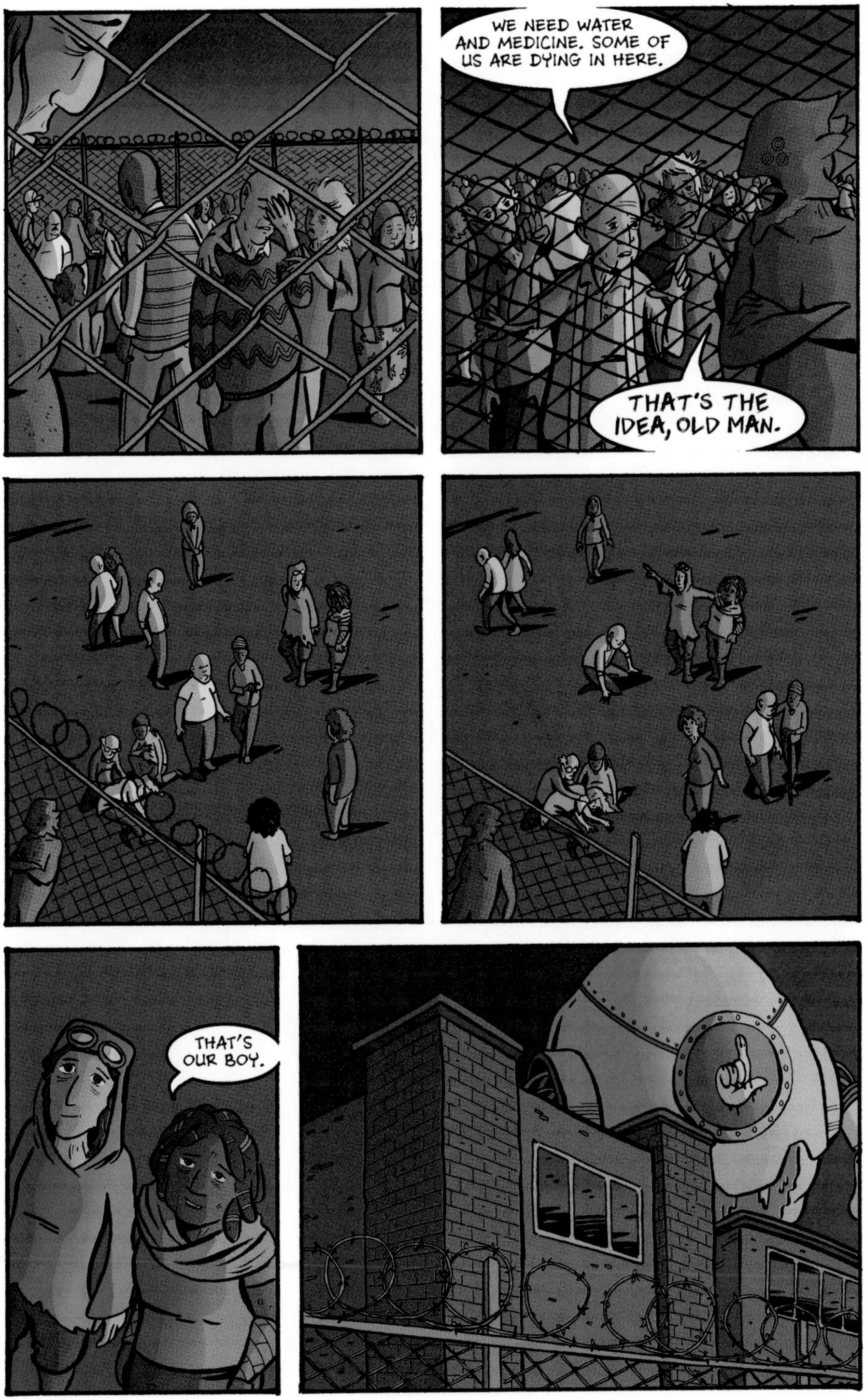
WE NEED WATER AND MEDICINE. SOME OF US ARE DYING IN HERE.
THAT'S THE IDEA, OLD MAN.
THAT'S OUR BOY.

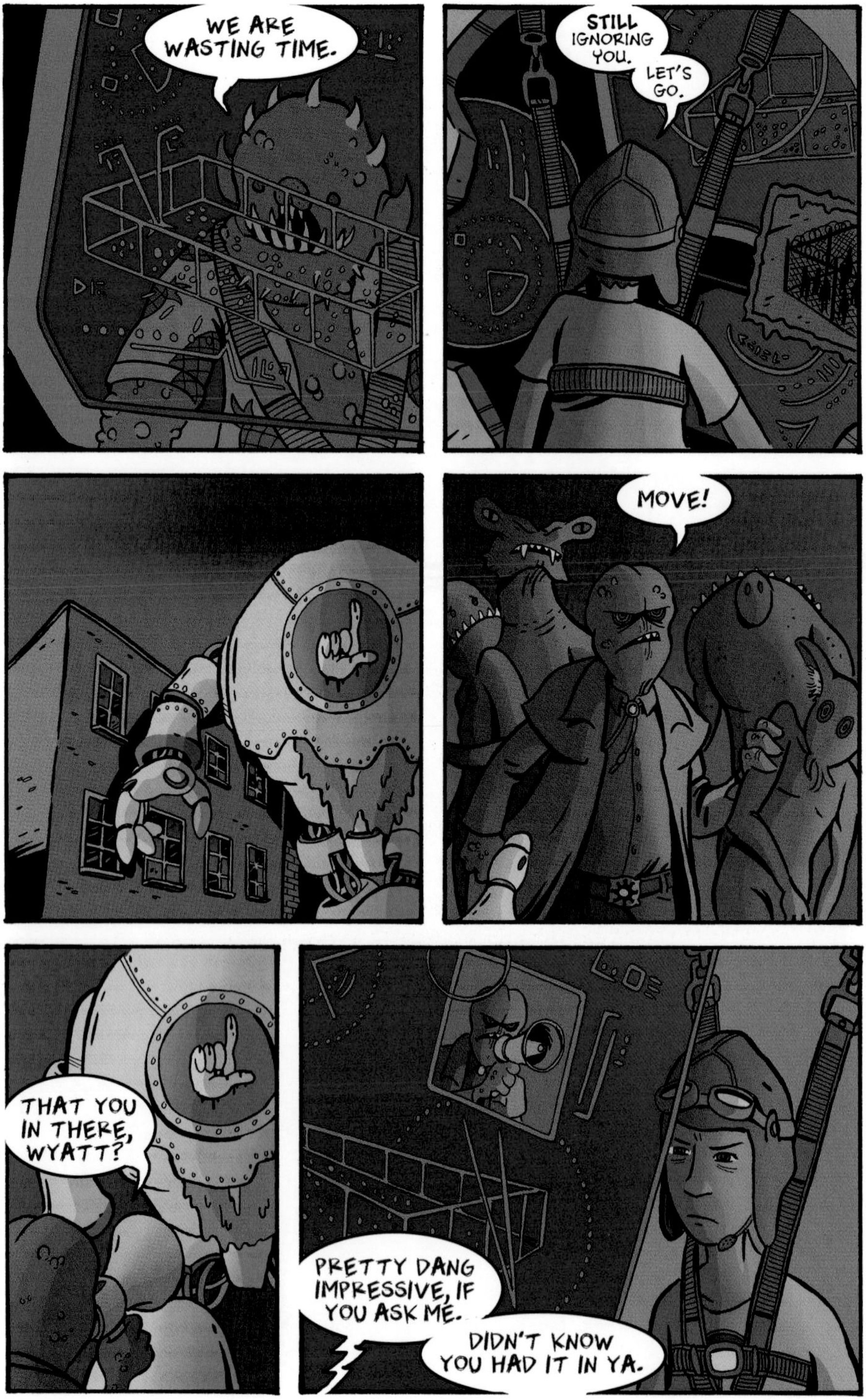
WE ARE WASTING TIME.
STILL IGNORING YOU.
LET'S GO.
MOVE!
THAT YOU IN THERE, WYATT?
PRETTY DANG IMPRESSIVE, IF YOU ASK ME.
DIDN'T KNOW YOU HAD IT IN YA.

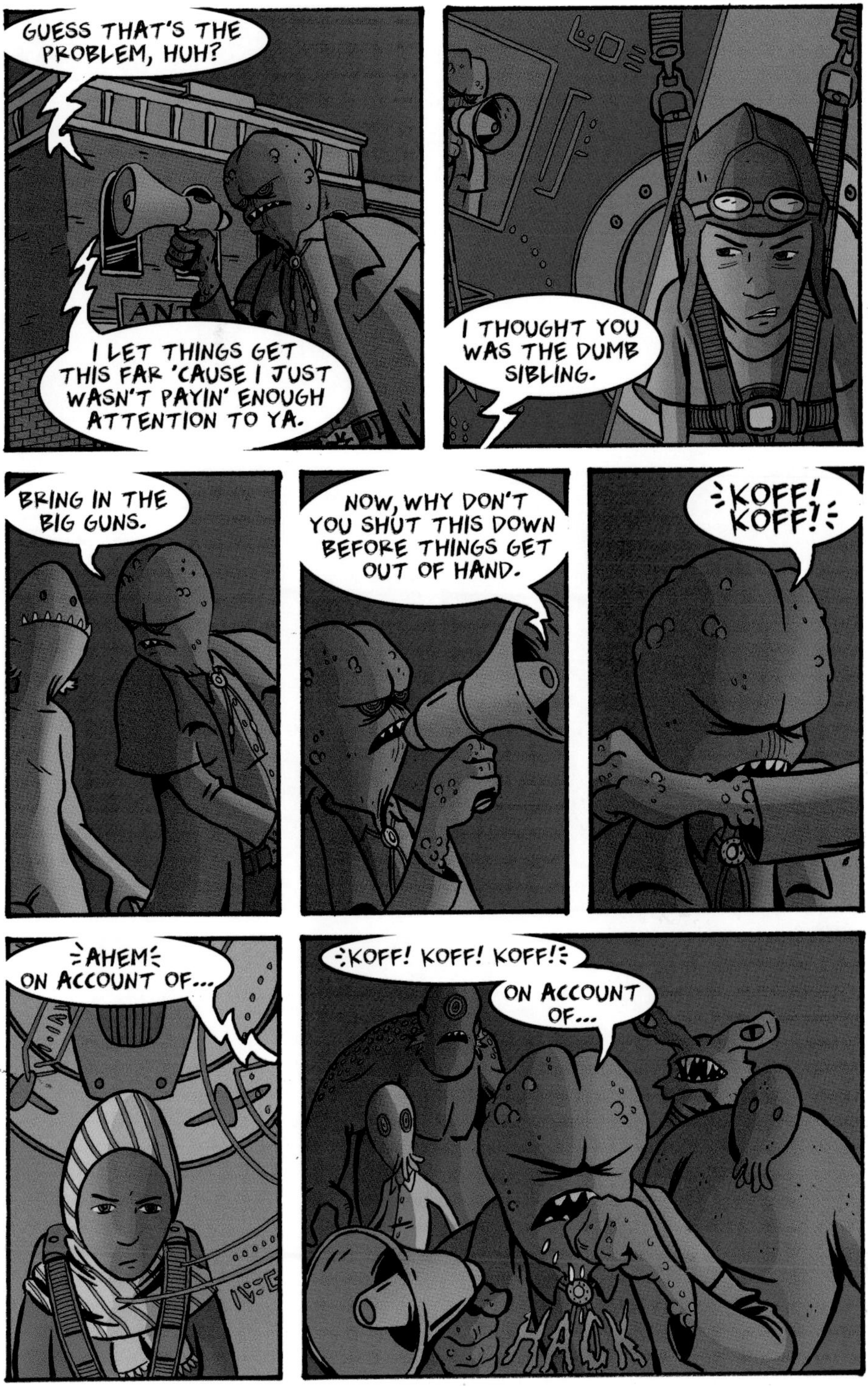
GUESS THAT'S THE PROBLEM, HUH?
I LET THINGS GET THIS FAR 'CAUSE I JUST WASN'T PAYIN' ENOUGH ATTENTION TO YA.
I THOUGHT YOU WAS THE DUMB SIBLING.
BRING IN THE BIG GUNS.
NOW, WHY DON'T YOU SHUT THIS DOWN BEFORE THINGS GET OUT OF HAND.
KOFF! KOFF!
AHEM
ON ACCOUNT OF...
KOFF! KOFF! KOFF!
ON ACCOUNT OF...
HACK

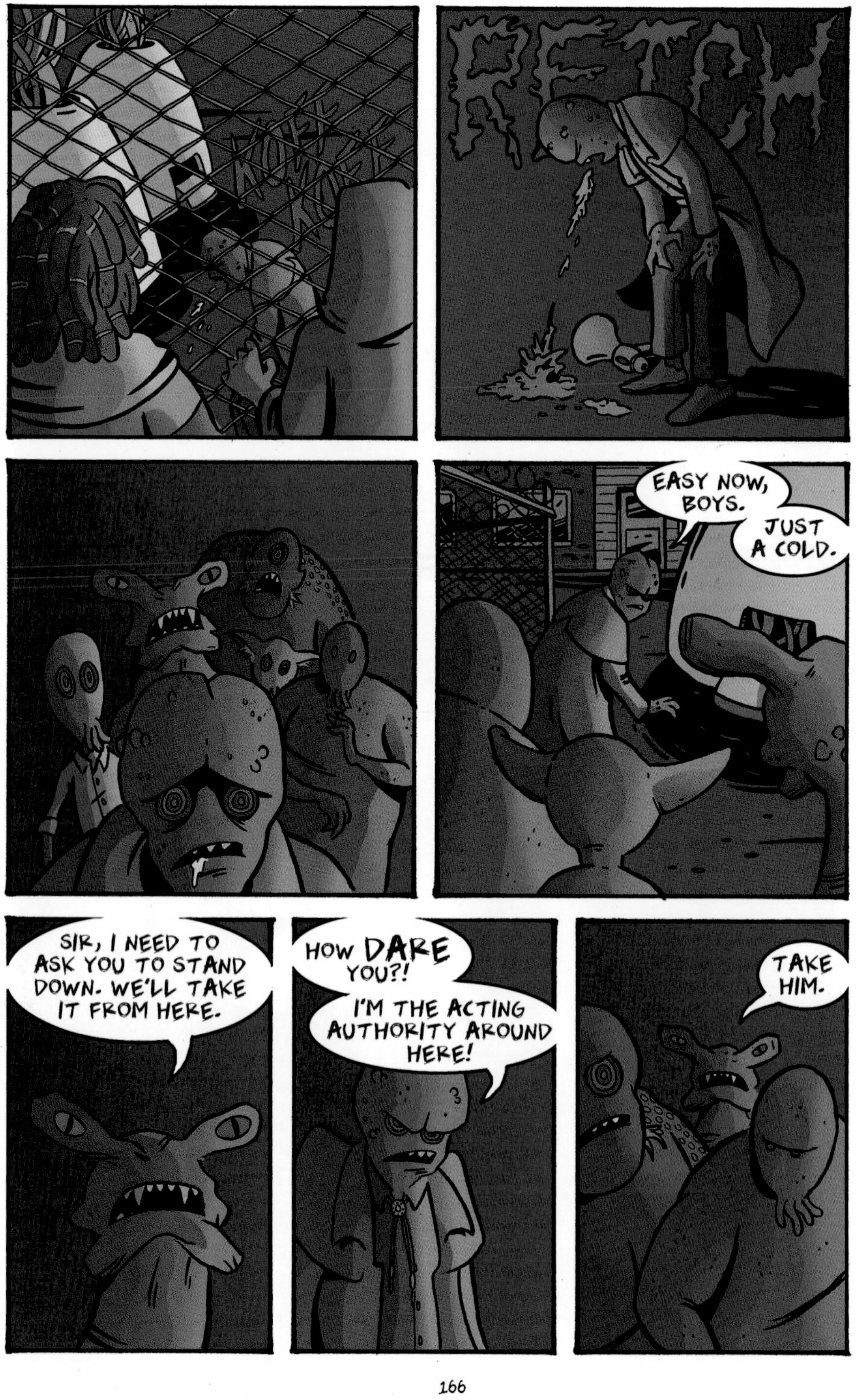
KOFF
RETCH
EASY NOW, BOYS.
JUST A COLD.
SIR, I NEED TO ASK YOU TO STAND DOWN. WE'LL TAKE IT FROM HERE.
HOW DARE YOU?!
I'M THE ACTING AUTHORITY AROUND HERE!
TAKE HIM.

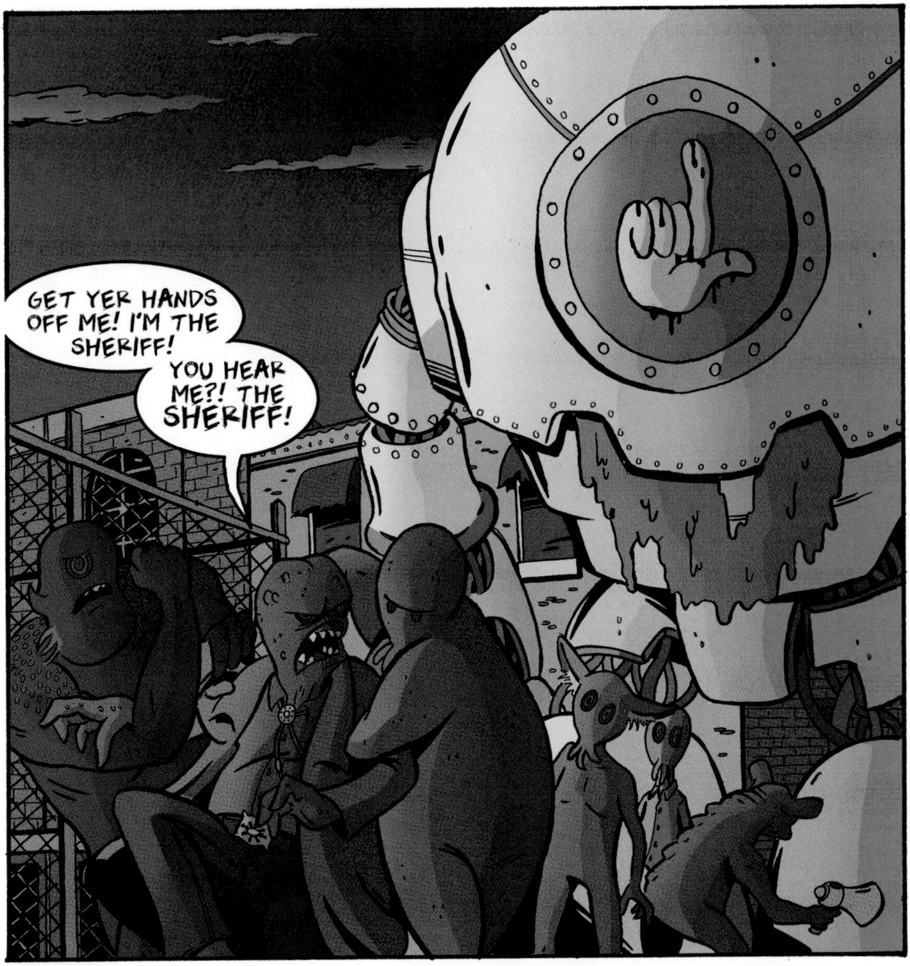
GET YER HANDS OFF ME! I'M THE SHERIFF!
YOU HEAR ME?! THE SHERIFF!

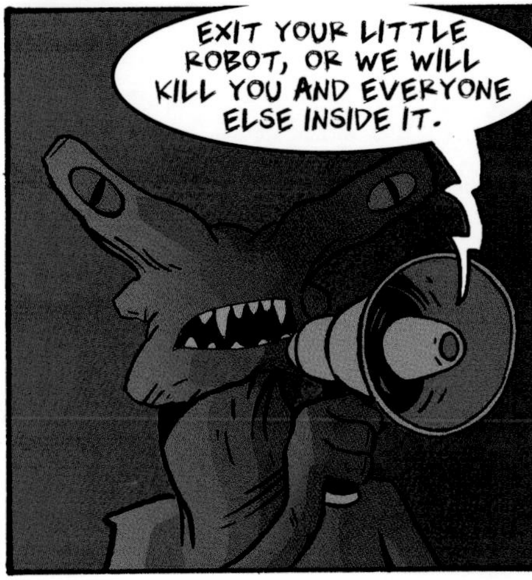
EXIT YOUR LITTLE ROBOT, OR WE WILL KILL YOU AND EVERYONE ELSE INSIDE IT.

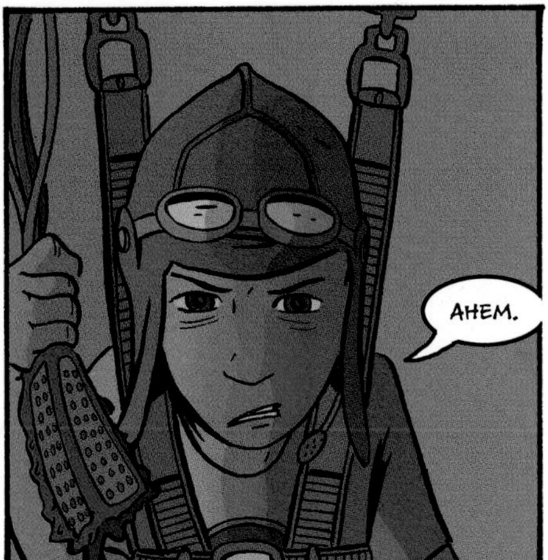
AHEM.

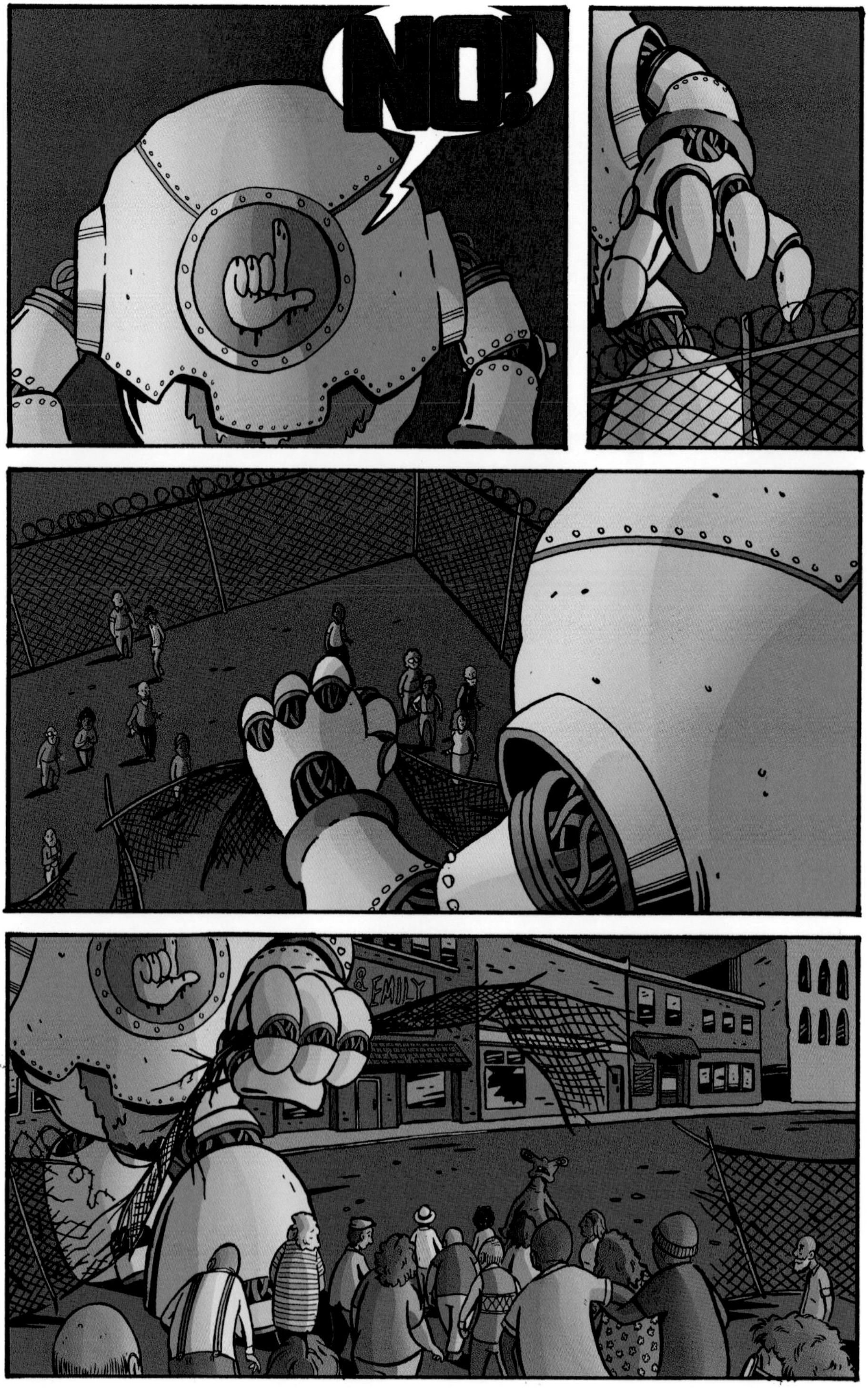
NO!
& EMILY

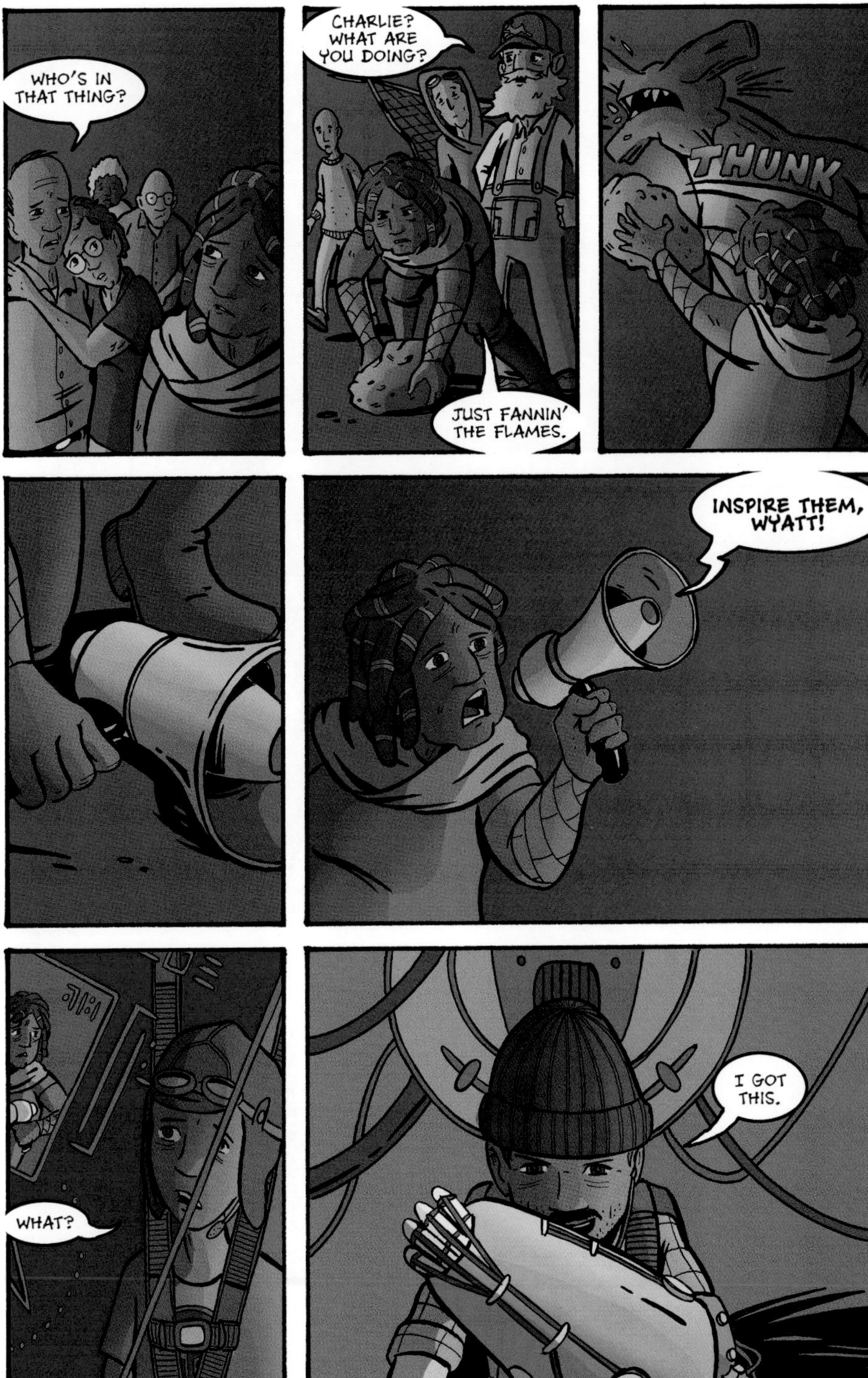
WHO'S IN THAT THING?
CHARLIE? WHAT ARE YOU DOING?
JUST FANNIN' THE FLAMES.
THUNK
INSPIRE THEM, WYATT!
WHAT?
I GOT THIS.

BIRD
ONE

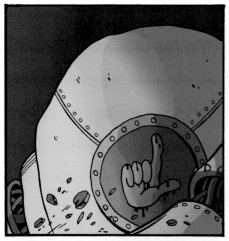

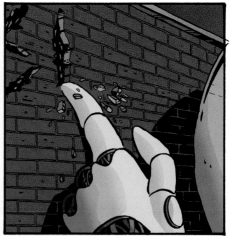

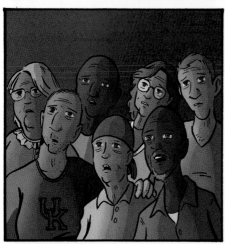

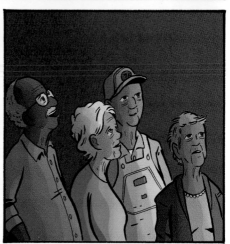

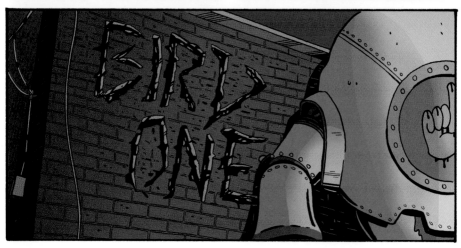

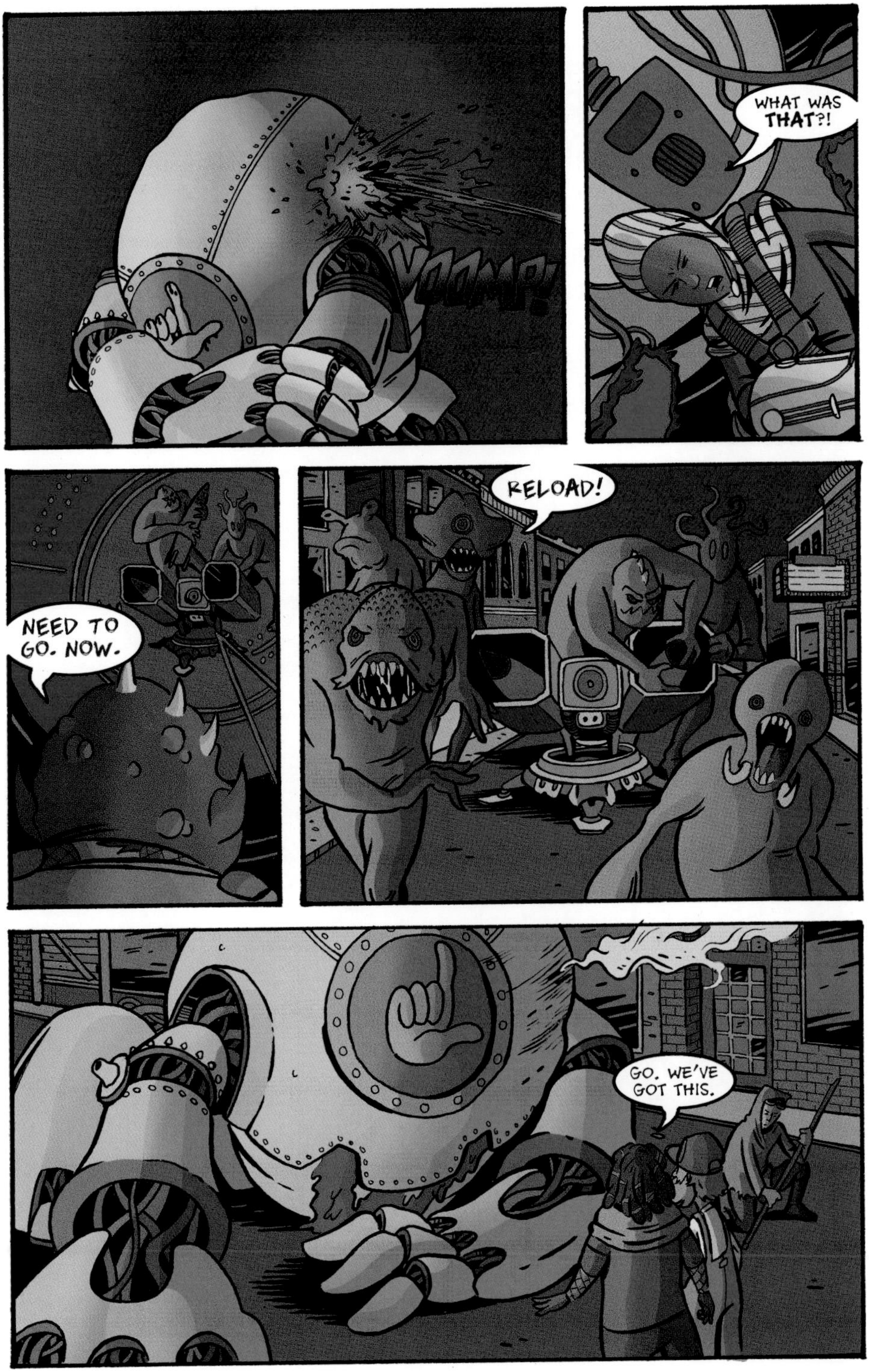
VOOMP!
WHAT WAS THAT?!
NEED TO GO. NOW.
RELOAD!
GO. WE'VE GOT THIS.

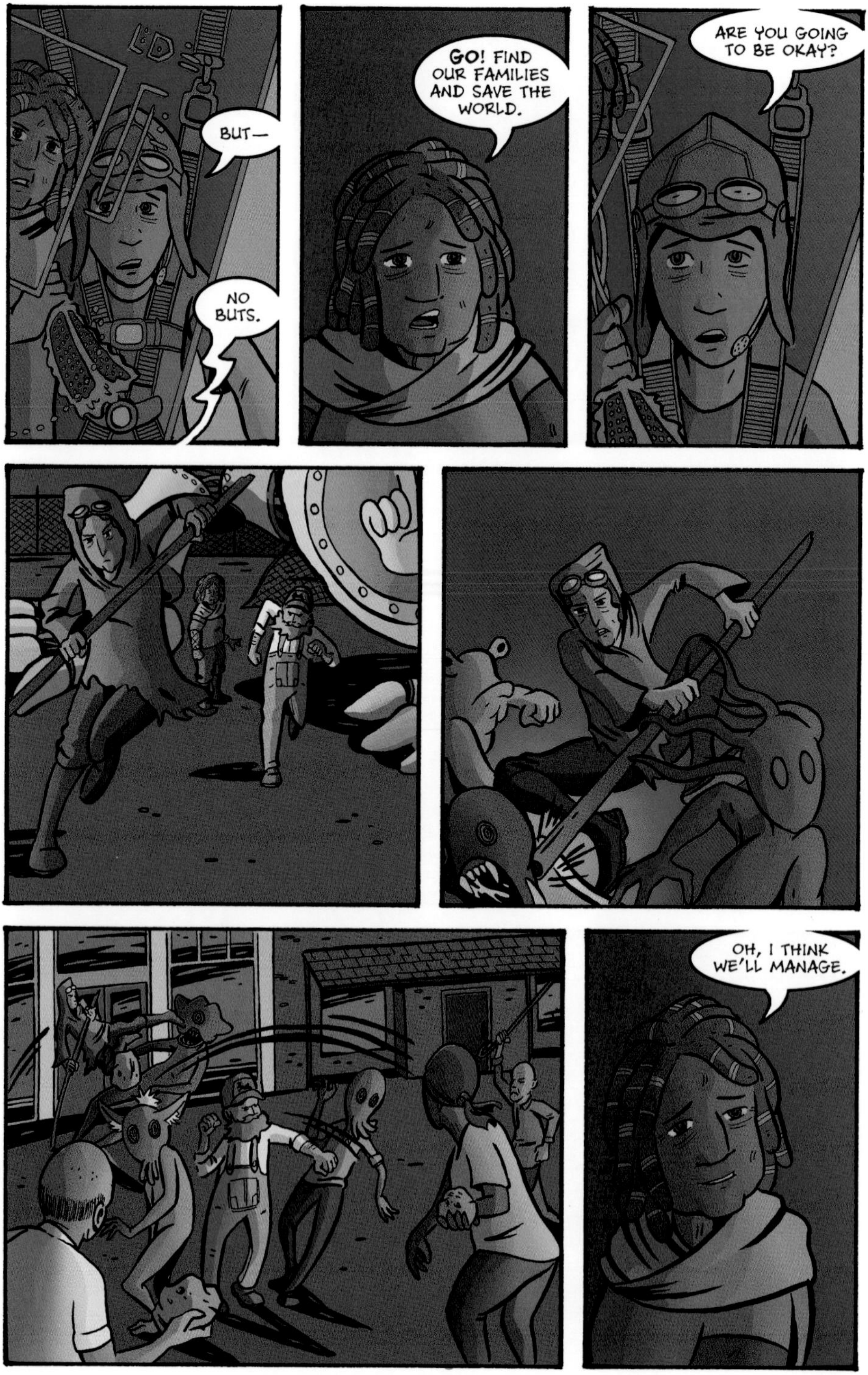
BUT—
NO BUTS.
GO! FIND OUR FAMILIES AND SAVE THE WORLD.
ARE YOU GOING TO BE OKAY?
OH, I THINK WE'LL MANAGE.

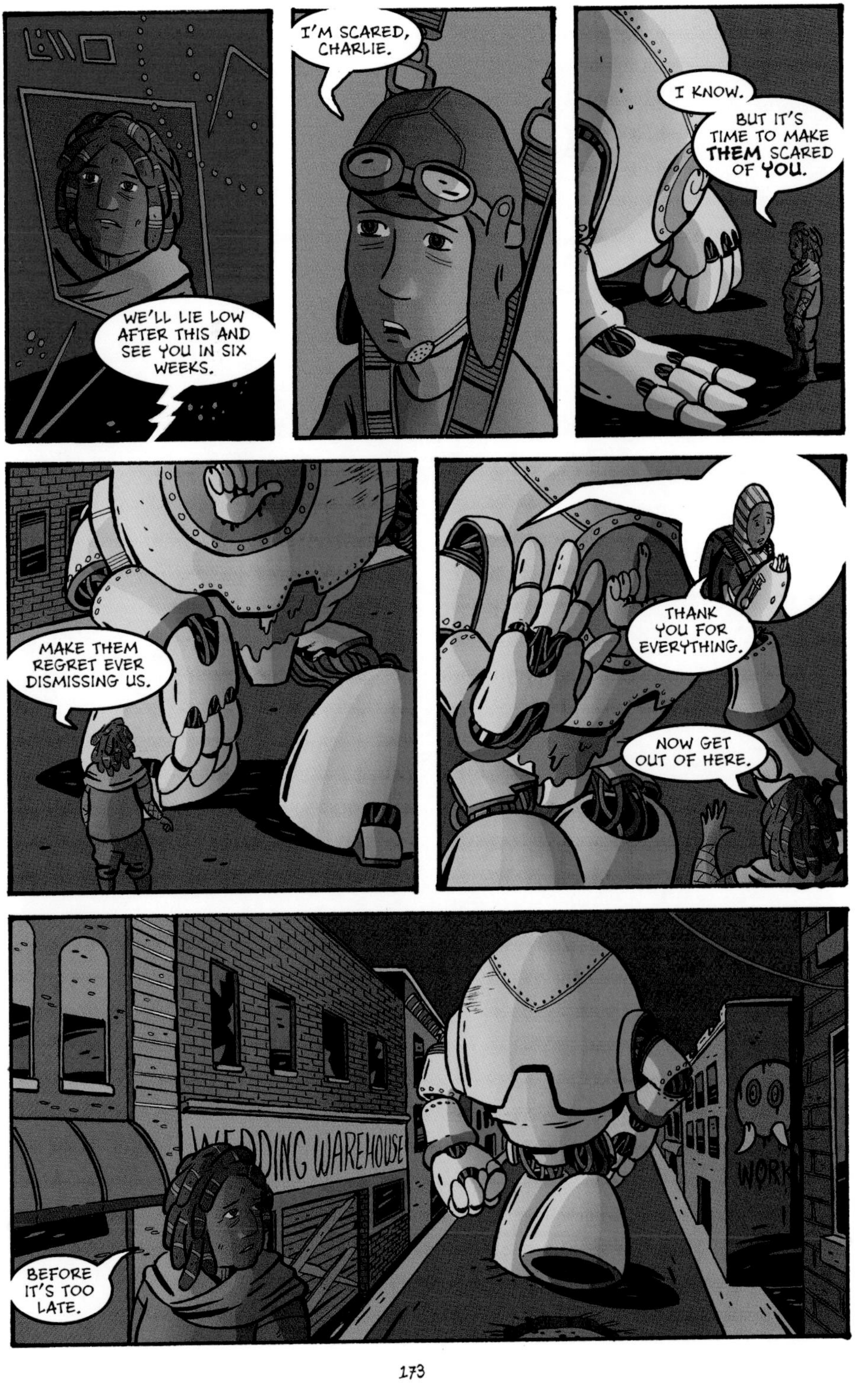
WE'LL LIE LOW AFTER THIS AND SEE YOU IN SIX WEEKS.
I'M SCARED, CHARLIE.
I KNOW.
BUT IT'S TIME TO MAKE **THEM** SCARED OF **YOU**.
MAKE THEM REGRET EVER DISMISSING US.
THANK YOU FOR EVERYTHING.
NOW GET OUT OF HERE.
WEDDING WAREHOUSE
WORK
BEFORE IT'S TOO LATE.

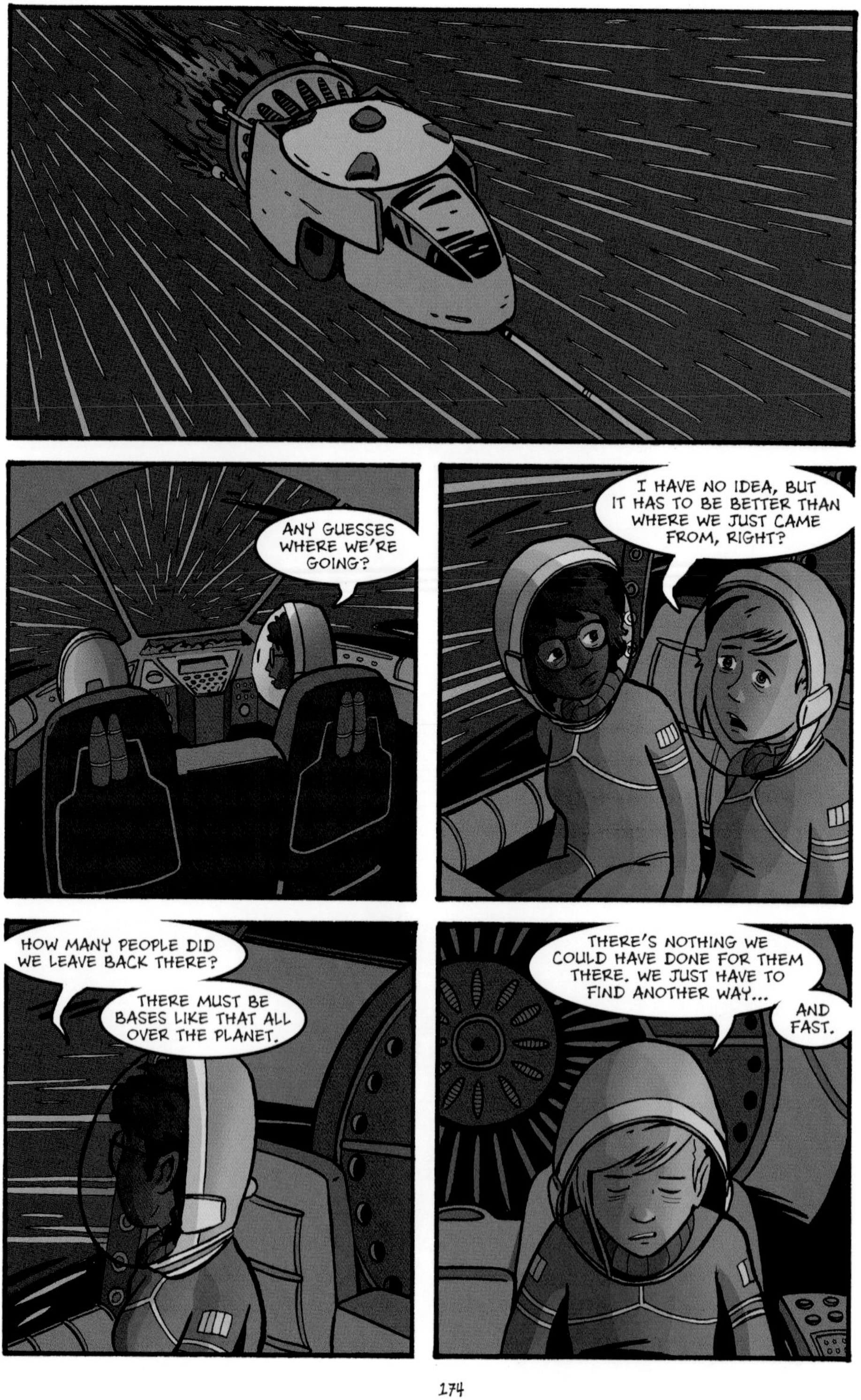
ANY GUESSES WHERE WE'RE GOING?
I HAVE NO IDEA, BUT IT HAS TO BE BETTER THAN WHERE WE JUST CAME FROM, RIGHT?
HOW MANY PEOPLE DID WE LEAVE BACK THERE?
THERE MUST BE BASES LIKE THAT ALL OVER THE PLANET.
THERE'S NOTHING WE COULD HAVE DONE FOR THEM THERE. WE JUST HAVE TO FIND ANOTHER WAY...
AND FAST.

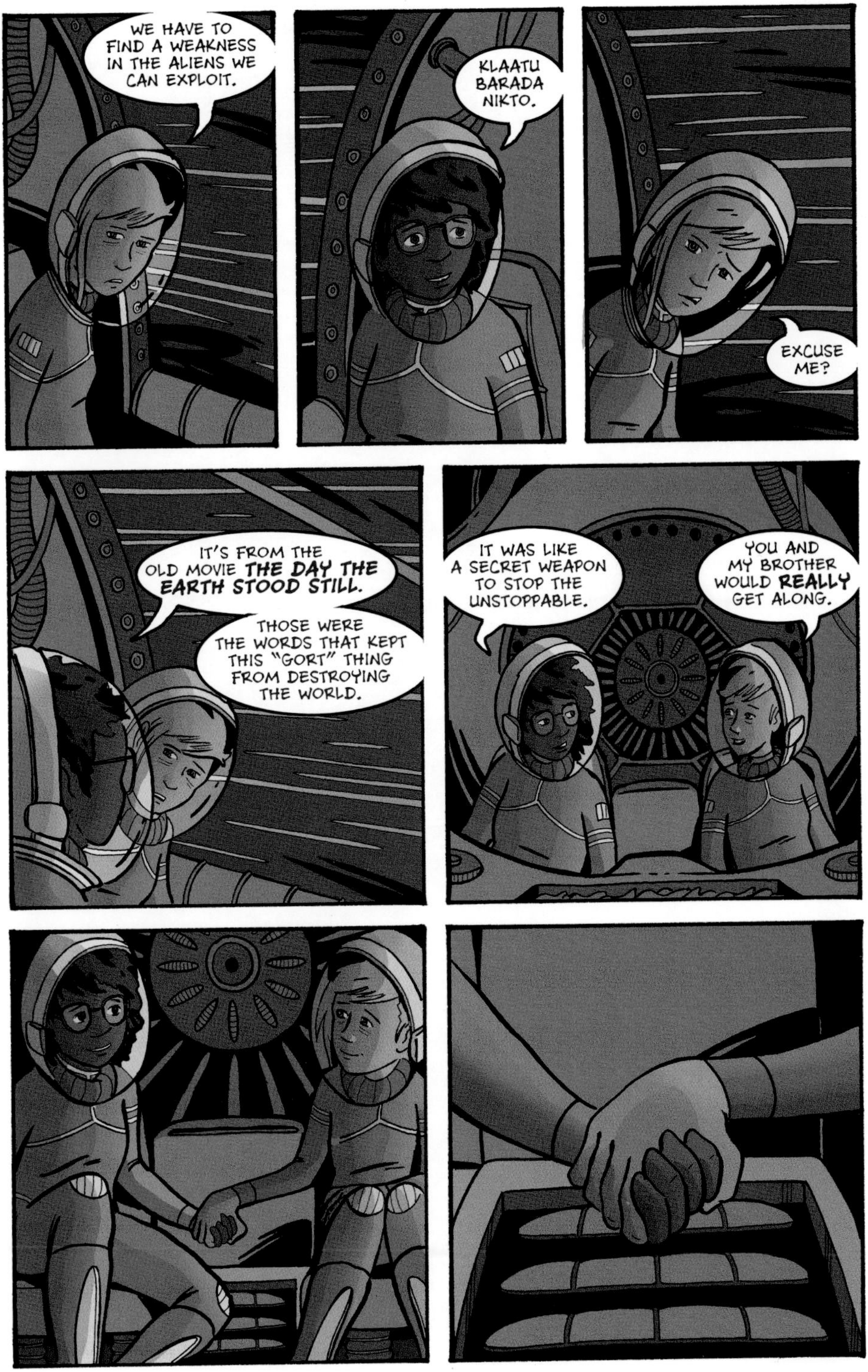
WE HAVE TO FIND A WEAKNESS IN THE ALIENS WE CAN EXPLOIT.
KLAATU BARADA NIKTO.
EXCUSE ME?
IT'S FROM THE OLD MOVIE **THE DAY THE EARTH STOOD STILL.**
THOSE WERE THE WORDS THAT KEPT THIS "GORT" THING FROM DESTROYING THE WORLD.
IT WAS LIKE A SECRET WEAPON TO STOP THE UNSTOPPABLE.
YOU AND MY BROTHER WOULD **REALLY** GET ALONG.

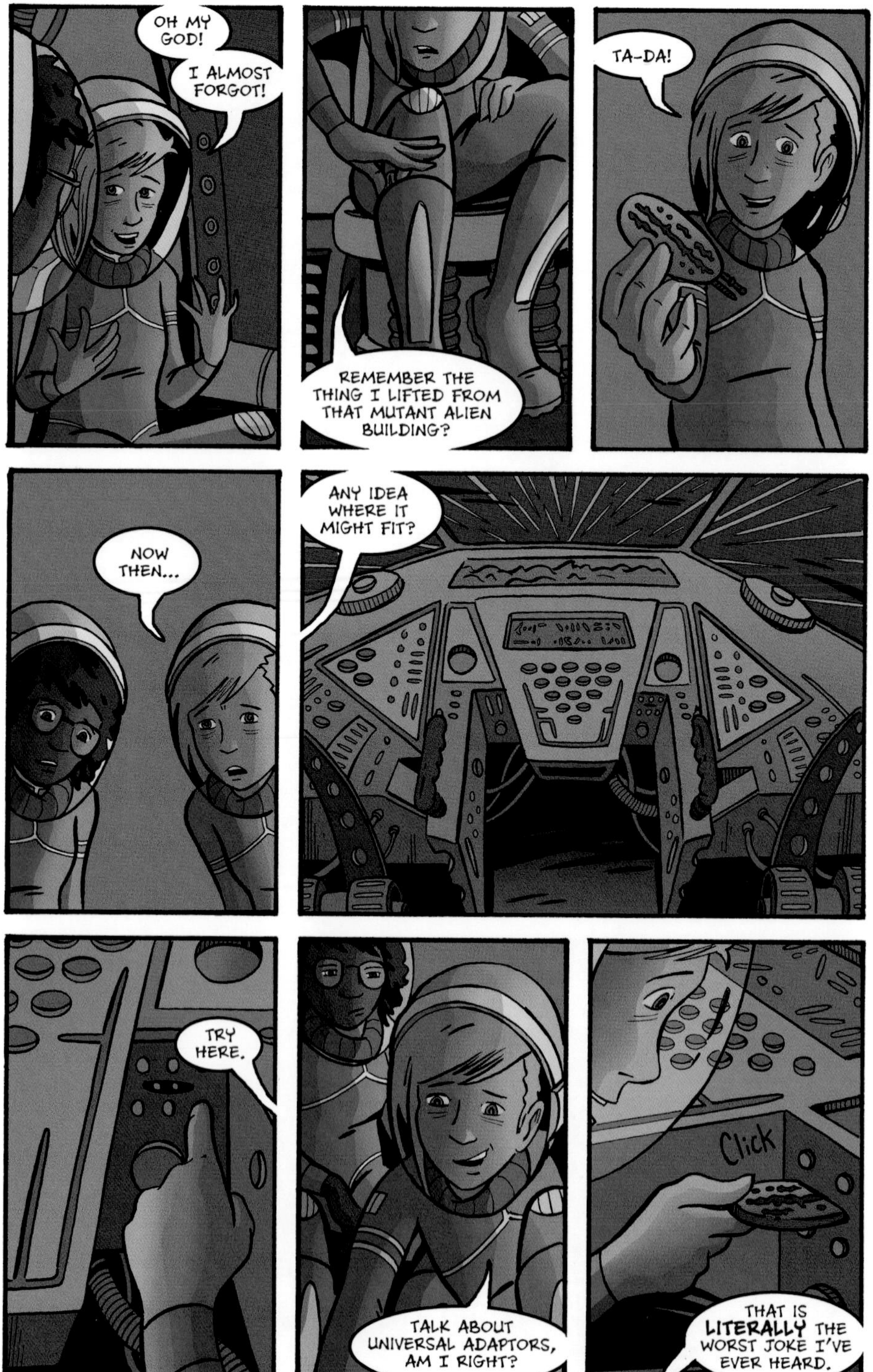
OH MY GOD!
I ALMOST FORGOT!
REMEMBER THE THING I LIFTED FROM THAT MUTANT ALIEN BUILDING?
TA-DA!
NOW THEN...
ANY IDEA WHERE IT MIGHT FIT?
TRY HERE.
TALK ABOUT UNIVERSAL ADAPTORS, AM I RIGHT?
Click
THAT IS **LITERALLY** THE WORST JOKE I'VE EVER HEARD.

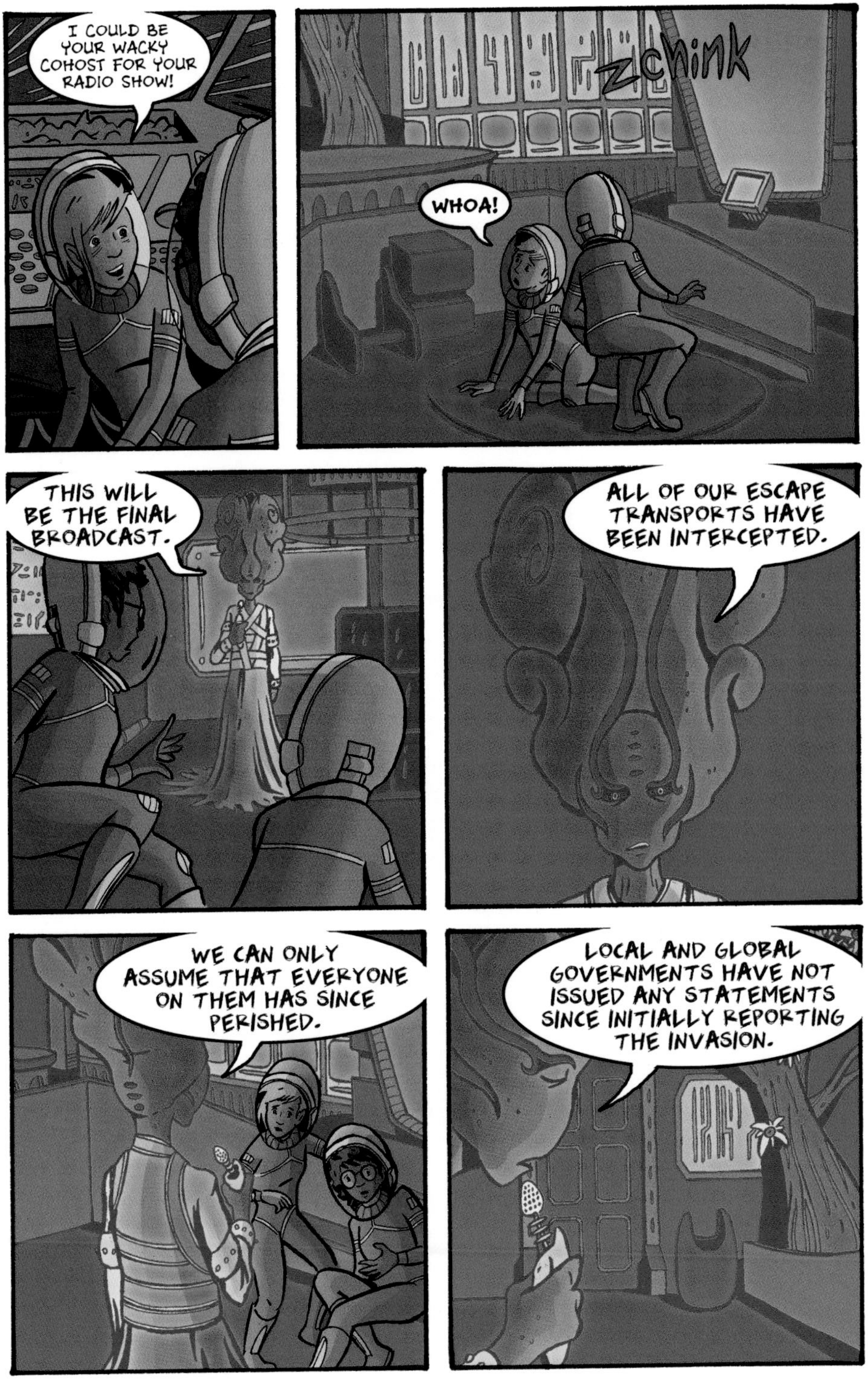
I COULD BE YOUR WACKY COHOST FOR YOUR RADIO SHOW!
ZCHINK
WHOA!
THIS WILL BE THE FINAL BROADCAST.
ALL OF OUR ESCAPE TRANSPORTS HAVE BEEN INTERCEPTED.
WE CAN ONLY ASSUME THAT EVERYONE ON THEM HAS SINCE PERISHED.
LOCAL AND GLOBAL GOVERNMENTS HAVE NOT ISSUED ANY STATEMENTS SINCE INITIALLY REPORTING THE INVASION.

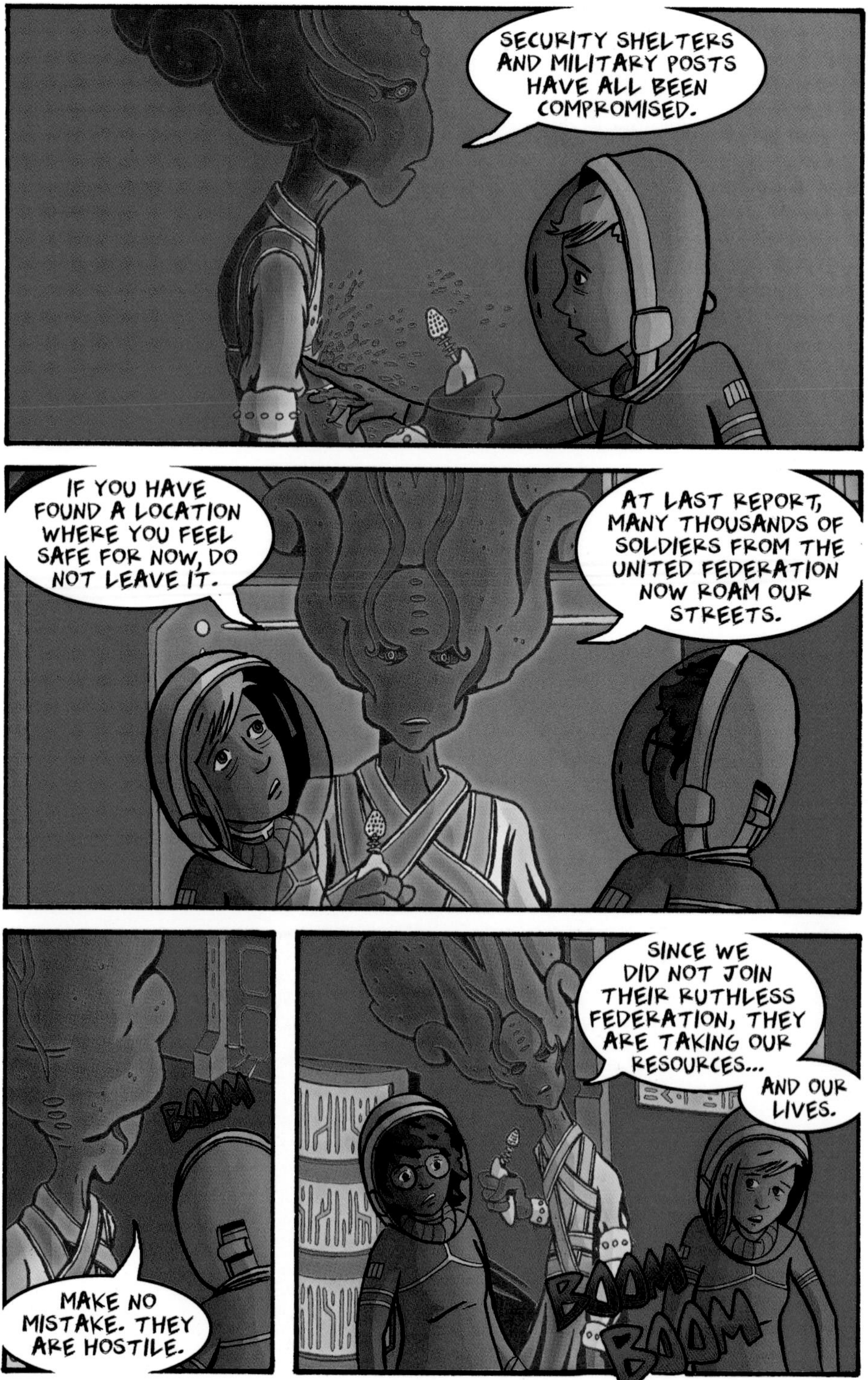
SECURITY SHELTERS AND MILITARY POSTS HAVE ALL BEEN COMPROMISED.
IF YOU HAVE FOUND A LOCATION WHERE YOU FEEL SAFE FOR NOW, DO NOT LEAVE IT.
AT LAST REPORT, MANY THOUSANDS OF SOLDIERS FROM THE UNITED FEDERATION NOW ROAM OUR STREETS.
BOOM
MAKE NO MISTAKE. THEY ARE HOSTILE.
SINCE WE DID NOT JOIN THEIR RUTHLESS FEDERATION, THEY ARE TAKING OUR RESOURCES...
AND OUR LIVES.
BOOM BOOM

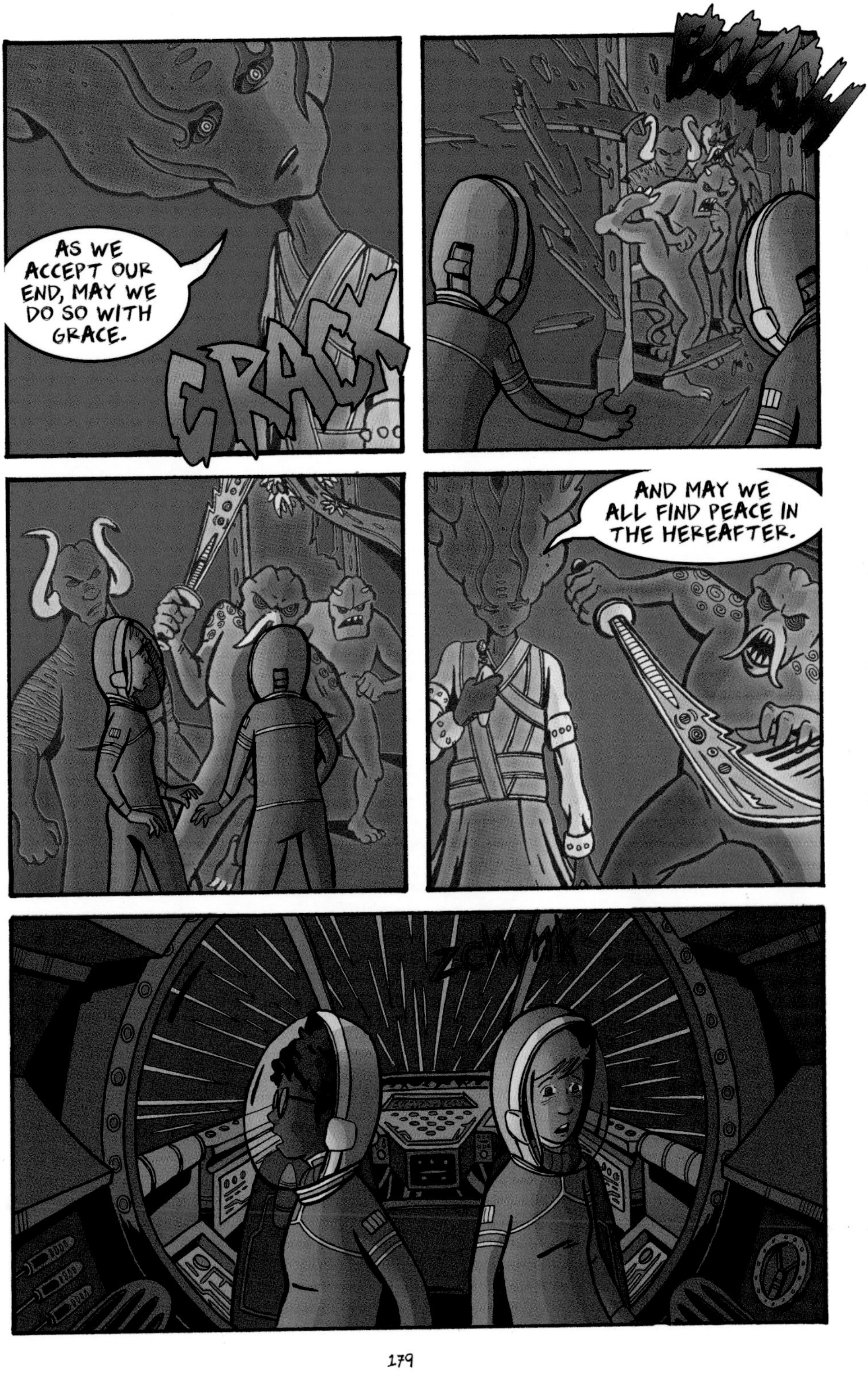
AS WE ACCEPT OUR END, MAY WE DO SO WITH GRACE.
CRACK
AND MAY WE ALL FIND PEACE IN THE HEREAFTER.

WHAT **WAS** THAT?

ARE YOU OKAY?

IT'S JUST...

THERE'S SO MUCH DEATH.

THEY KILL EVERYONE AND EVERYTHING THAT'S NOT OF USE TO THEM.

WE'RE GOING TO MAKE THEM PAY FOR EVERY LAST ONE OF THOSE DEATHS.

WE'RE LOST IN SPACE WITH NO PLAN, AND WE'RE OUTNUMBERED LIKE A MILLION TO ONE.

HOW CAN YOU BE SURE?

I...

I DON'T KNOW.

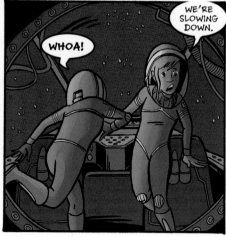

WHOA!

WE'RE SLOWING DOWN.

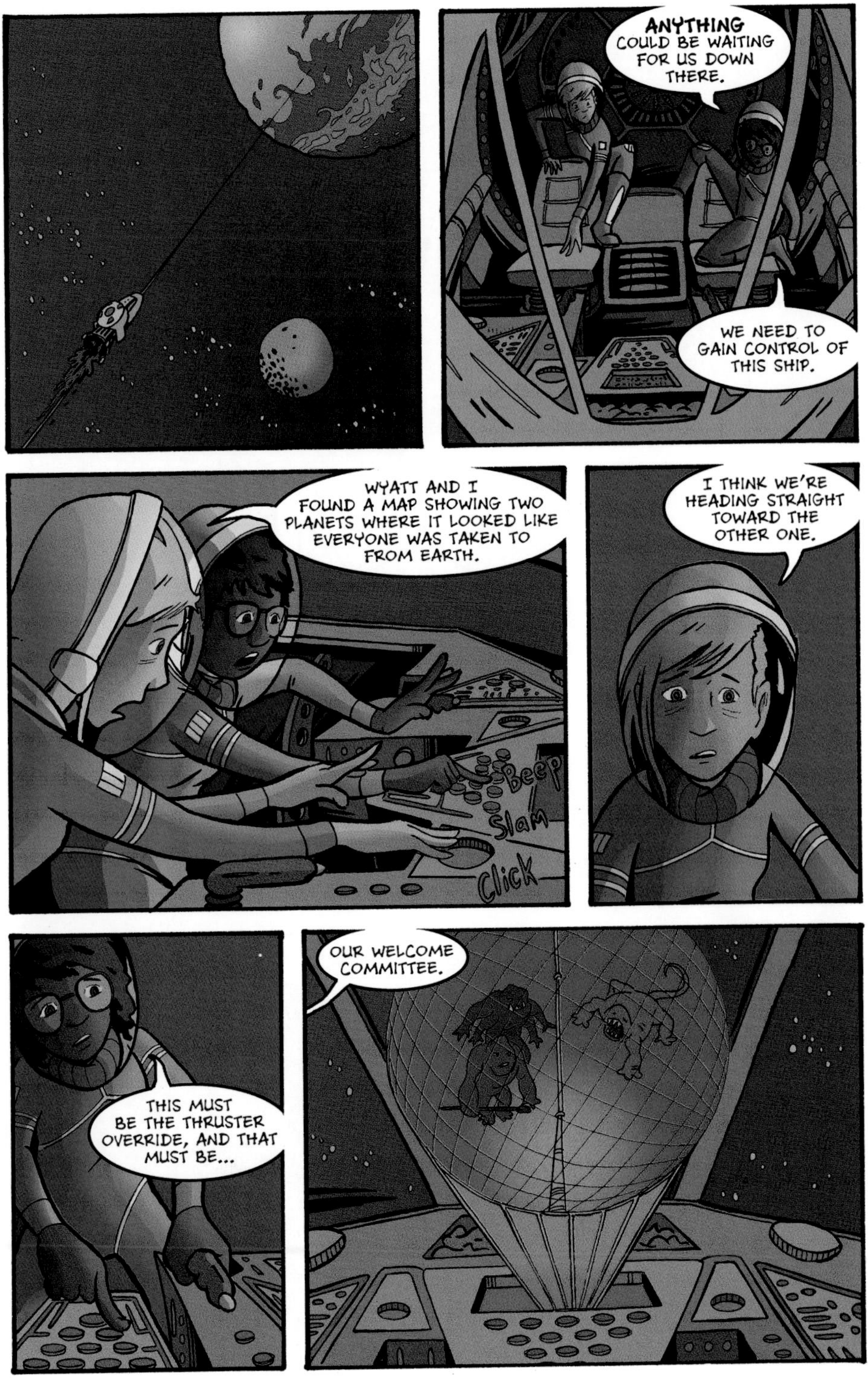
ANYTHING COULD BE WAITING FOR US DOWN THERE.
WE NEED TO GAIN CONTROL OF THIS SHIP.
WYATT AND I FOUND A MAP SHOWING TWO PLANETS WHERE IT LOOKED LIKE EVERYONE WAS TAKEN TO FROM EARTH.
Beep
Slam
Click
I THINK WE'RE HEADING STRAIGHT TOWARD THE OTHER ONE.
THIS MUST BE THE THRUSTER OVERRIDE, AND THAT MUST BE...
OUR WELCOME COMMITTEE.

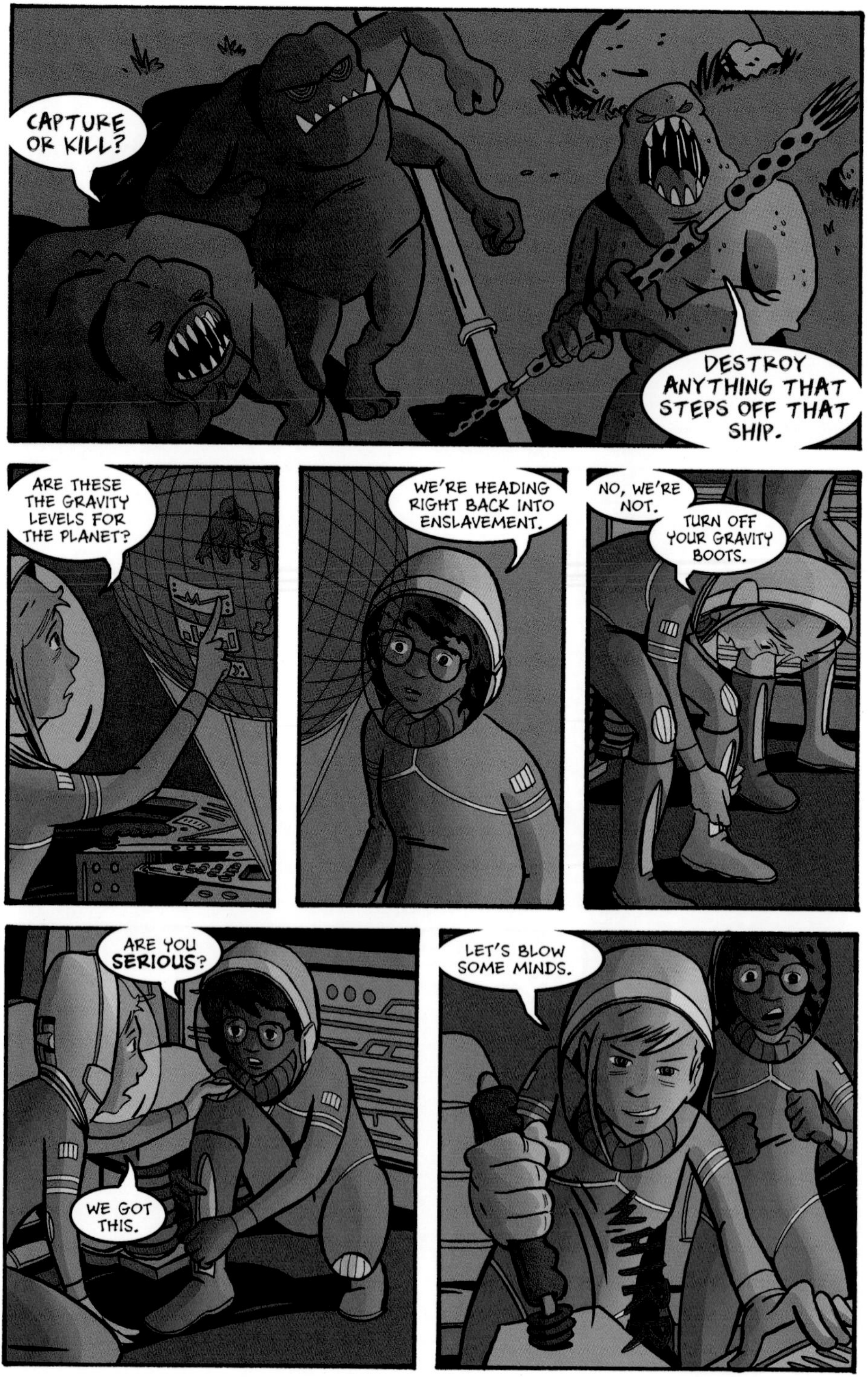
CAPTURE OR KILL?
DESTROY ANYTHING THAT STEPS OFF THAT SHIP.
ARE THESE THE GRAVITY LEVELS FOR THE PLANET?
WE'RE HEADING RIGHT BACK INTO ENSLAVEMENT.
NO, WE'RE NOT.
TURN OFF YOUR GRAVITY BOOTS.
ARE YOU SERIOUS?
WE GOT THIS.
LET'S BLOW SOME MINDS.

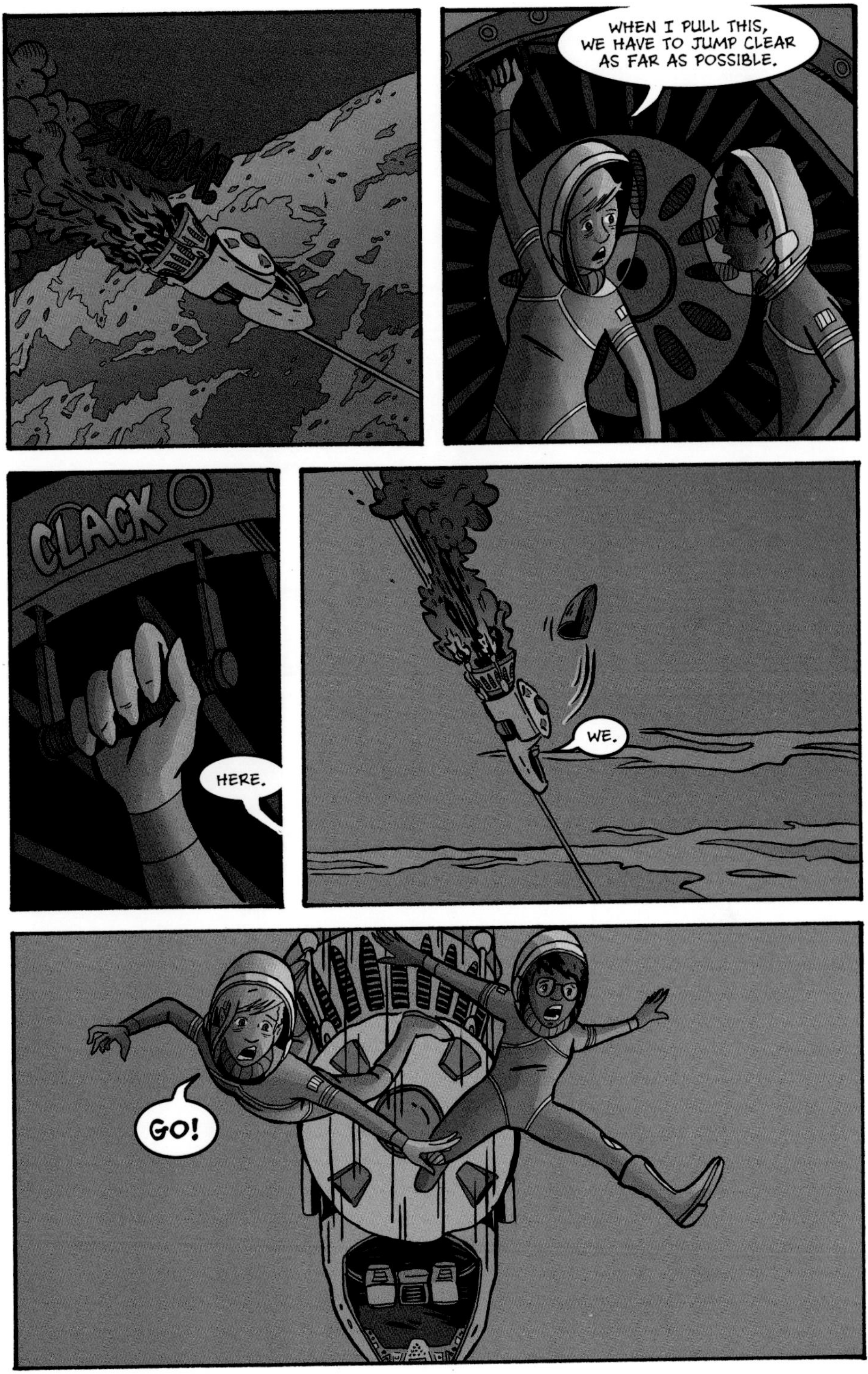
WHEN I PULL THIS, WE HAVE TO JUMP CLEAR AS FAR AS POSSIBLE.
CLACK
HERE.
WE.
GO!

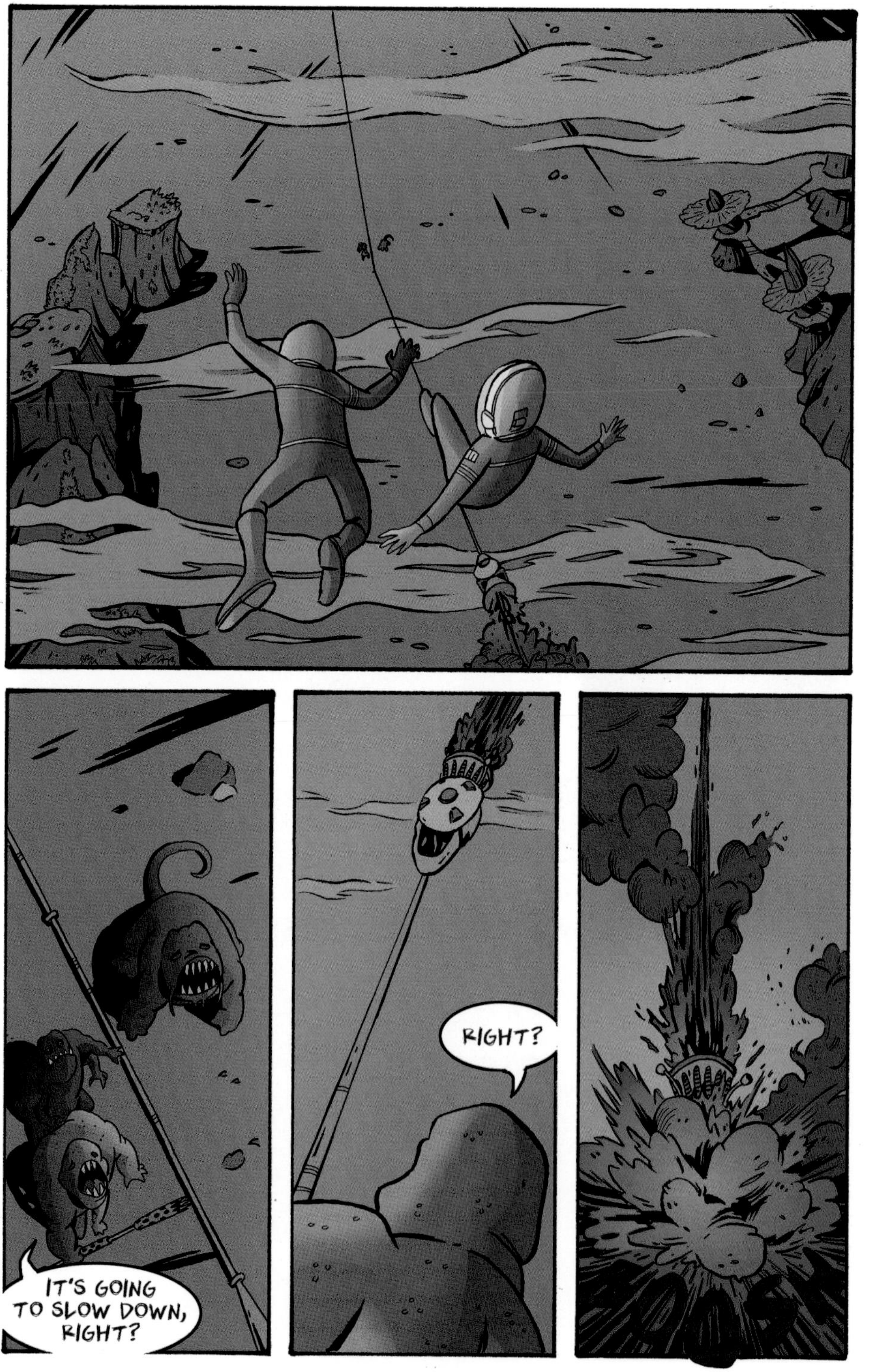
IT'S GOING TO SLOW DOWN, RIGHT?
RIGHT?

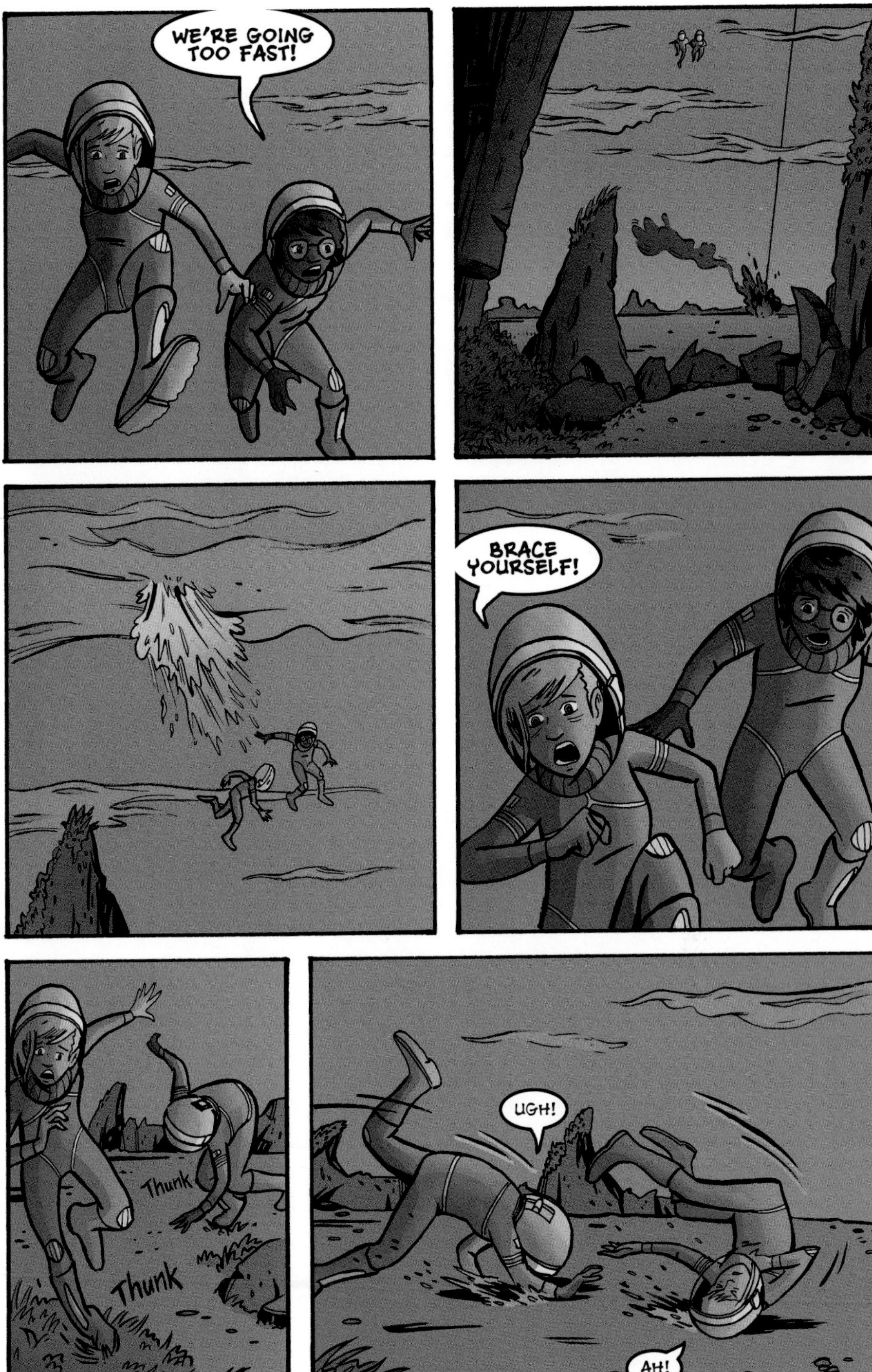
WE'RE GOING TOO FAST!
BRACE YOURSELF!
Thunk
Thunk
UGH!
AH!

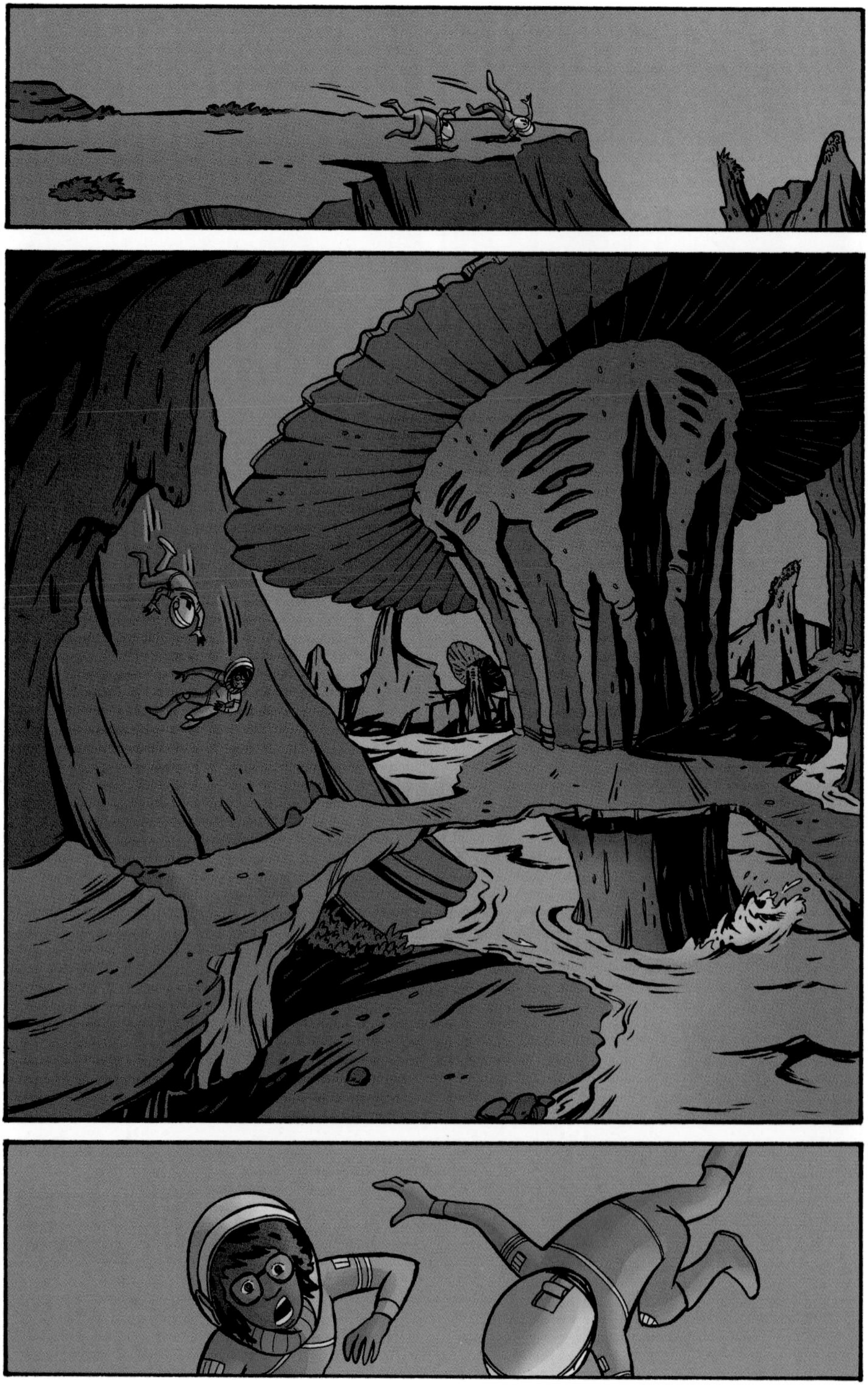

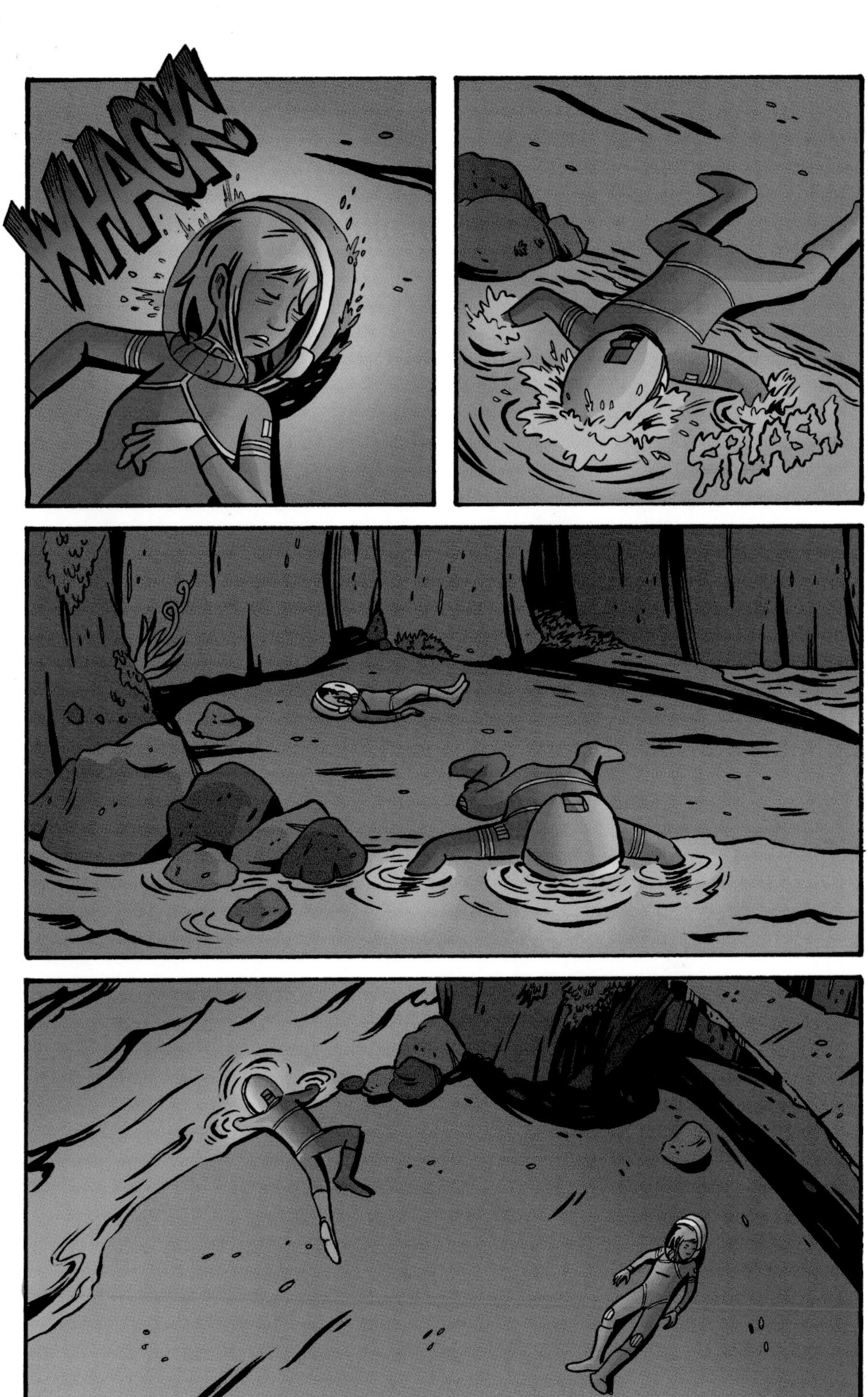
WHACK!
SPLASH

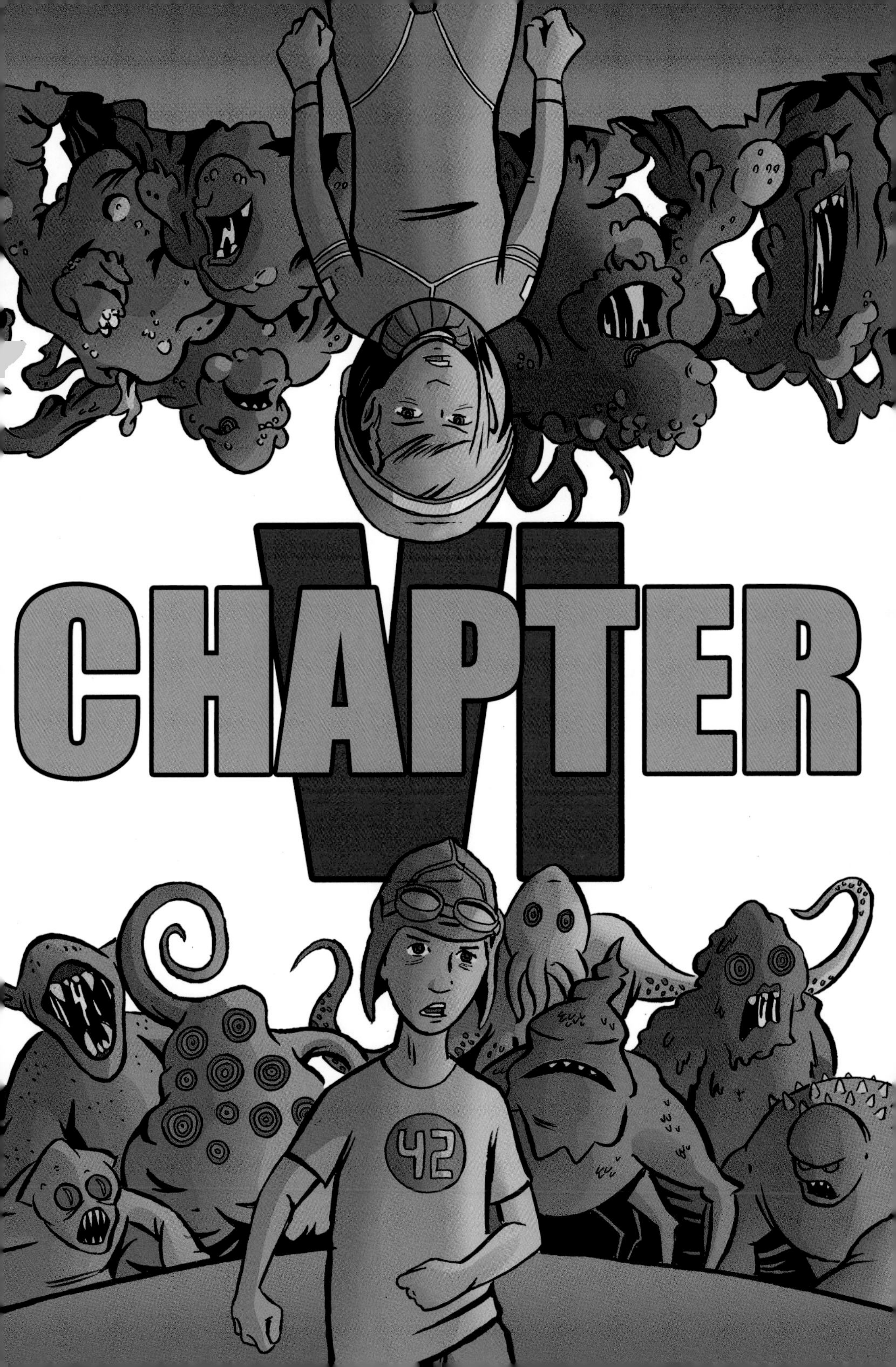
CHAPTER
VI
42

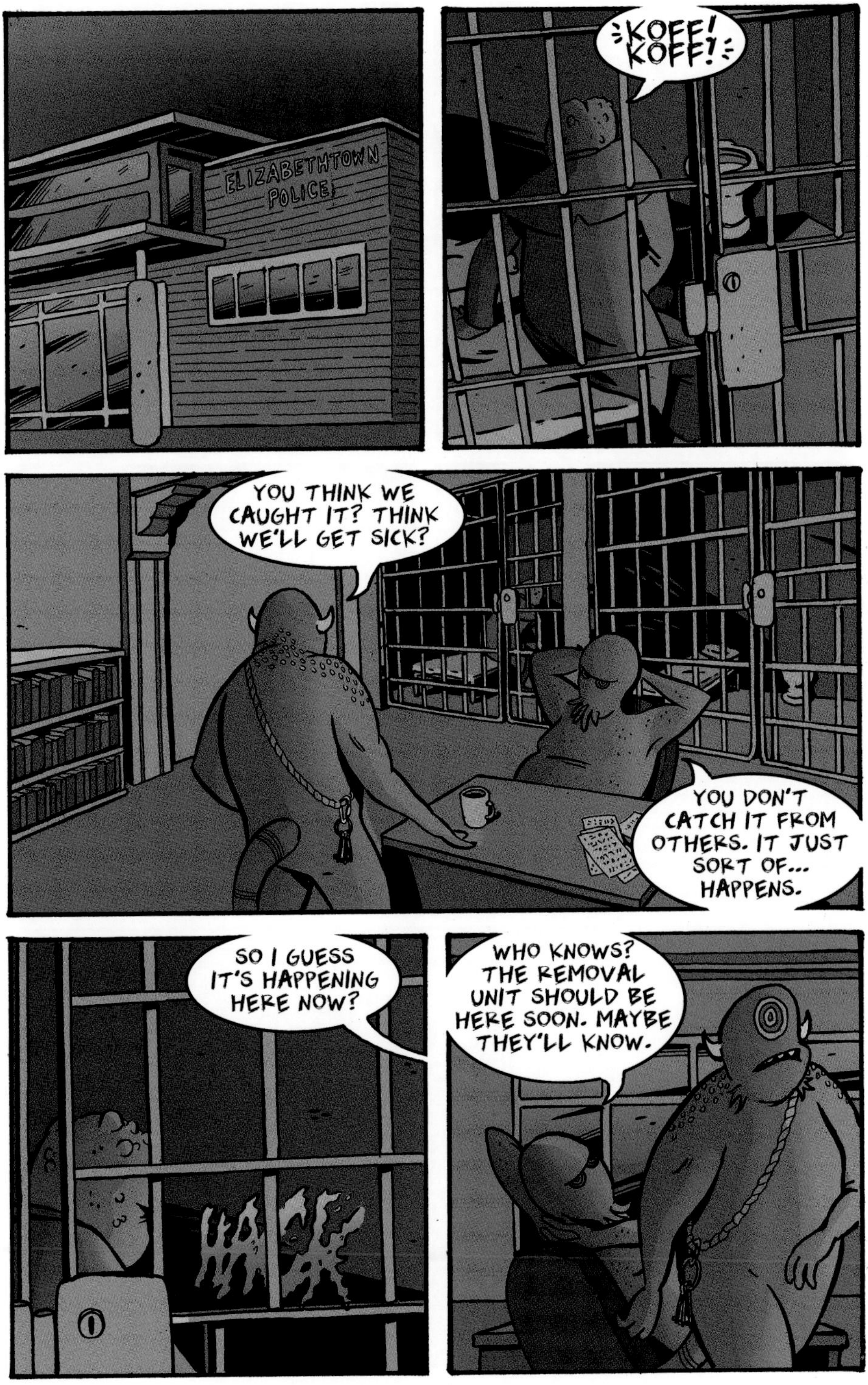
ELIZABETHTOWN POLICE
KOFF! KOFF!
YOU THINK WE CAUGHT IT? THINK WE'LL GET SICK?
YOU DON'T CATCH IT FROM OTHERS. IT JUST SORT OF... HAPPENS.
SO I GUESS IT'S HAPPENING HERE NOW?
WHO KNOWS? THE REMOVAL UNIT SHOULD BE HERE SOON. MAYBE THEY'LL KNOW.
HACK

THEY WON'T KNOW ANYTHING, EITHER.

IT'S TOO UNPREDICTABLE.

KOFF

EVERYONE MUTATES DIFFERENTLY.

FOR SOME, IT TAKES YEARS, FOR OTHERS, JUST DAYS.

KOFF

AAAAAGH!

KOFF

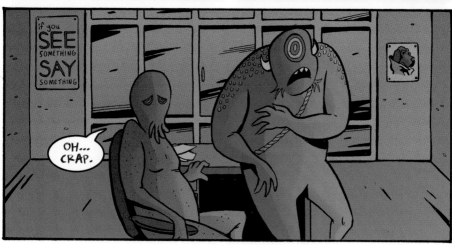

if you SEE SOMETHING SAY SOMETHING

OH... CRAP.

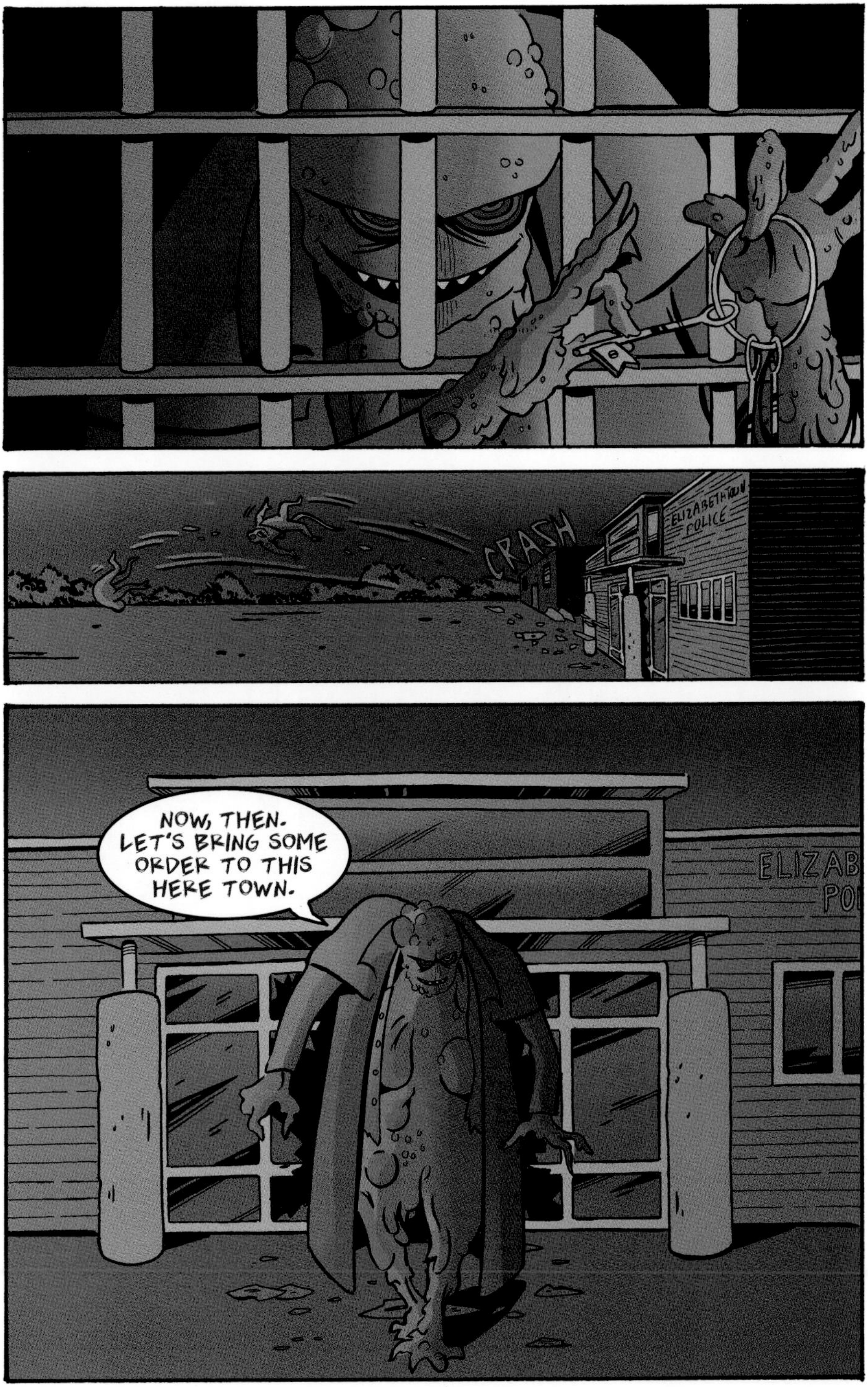
CRASH
ELIZABETHTOWN POLICE
NOW, THEN. LET'S BRING SOME ORDER TO THIS HERE TOWN.

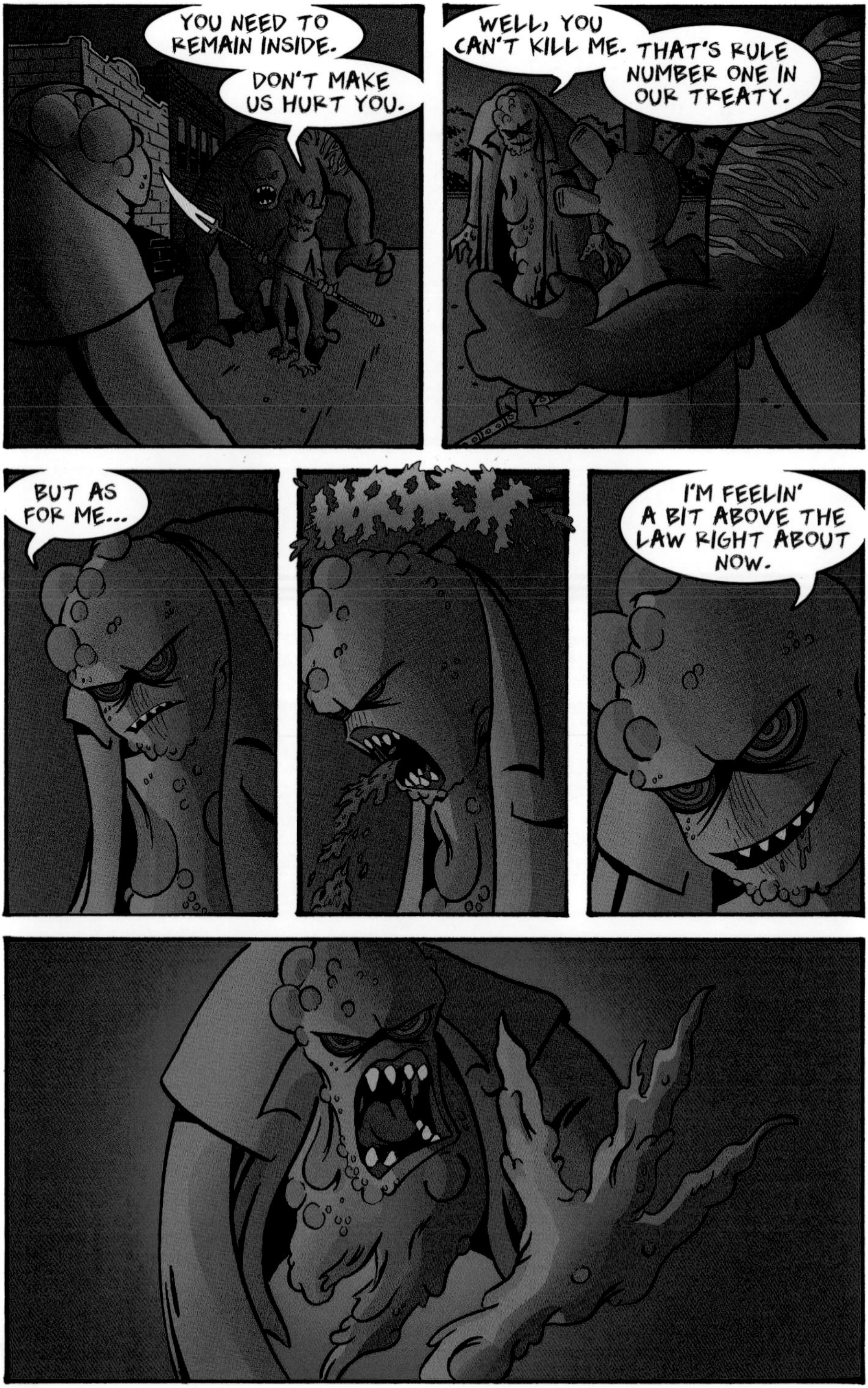
YOU NEED TO REMAIN INSIDE.
DON'T MAKE US HURT YOU.
WELL, YOU CAN'T KILL ME.
THAT'S RULE NUMBER ONE IN OUR TREATY.
BUT AS FOR ME...
I'M FEELIN' A BIT ABOVE THE LAW RIGHT ABOUT NOW.

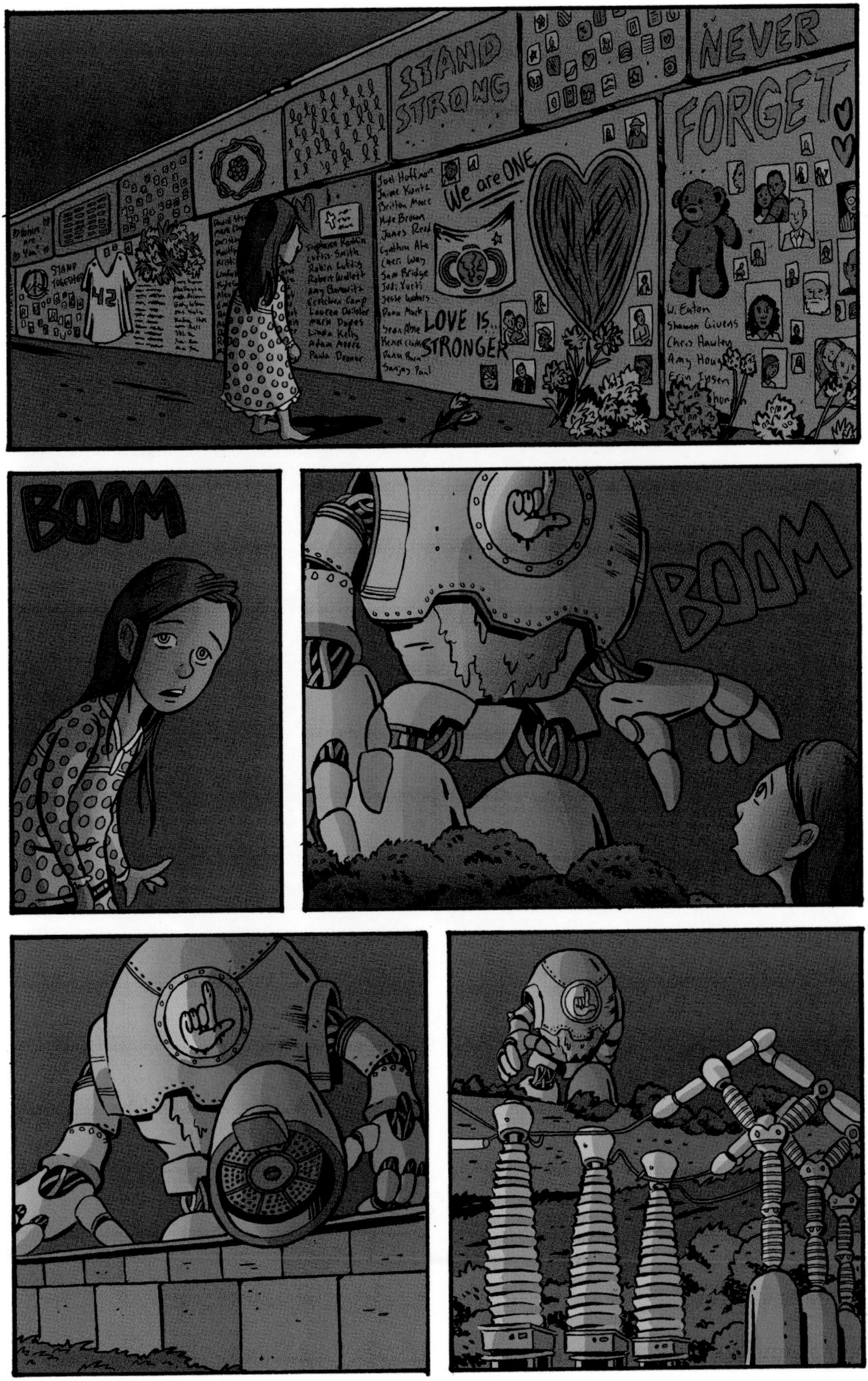
STAND TOGETHER
42
STAND STRONG
NEVER
FORGET
We are ONE
Joel Hoffman
Jaime Kuntz
Britton Moore
Kyle Brown
James Reed
Cynthia Ate
Cheri Way
Sam Bridge
Stephanie Rankin
Curtis Smith
Gretchen Camp
Linda Kelly
Adam Moore
LOVE IS...
STRONGER
Sanjay Paul
W. Eaton
Shawna Givens
Chris Hawley
Erin Ipsen
BOOM
BOOM

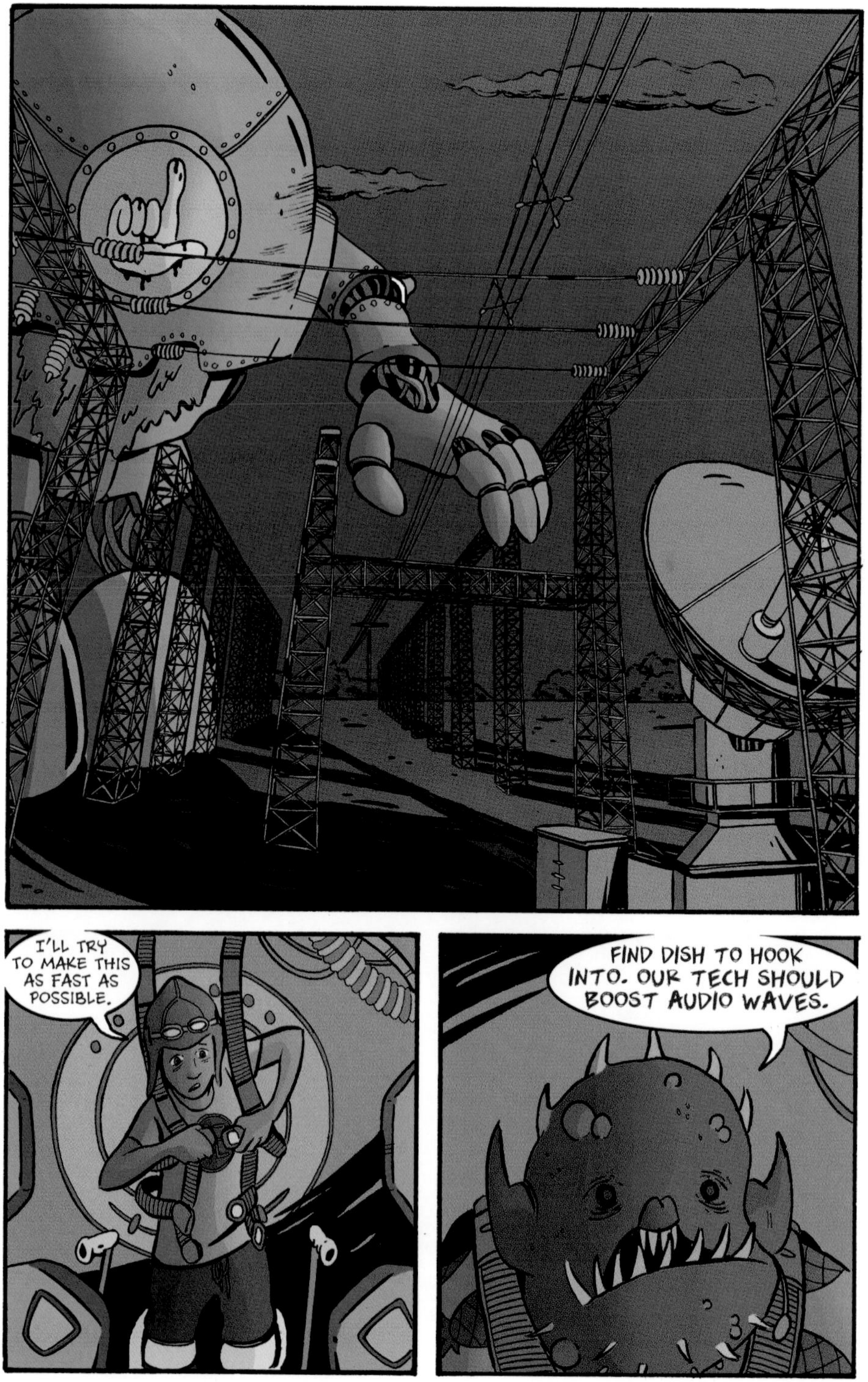
I'LL TRY TO MAKE THIS AS FAST AS POSSIBLE.
FIND DISH TO HOOK INTO. OUR TECH SHOULD BOOST AUDIO WAVES.

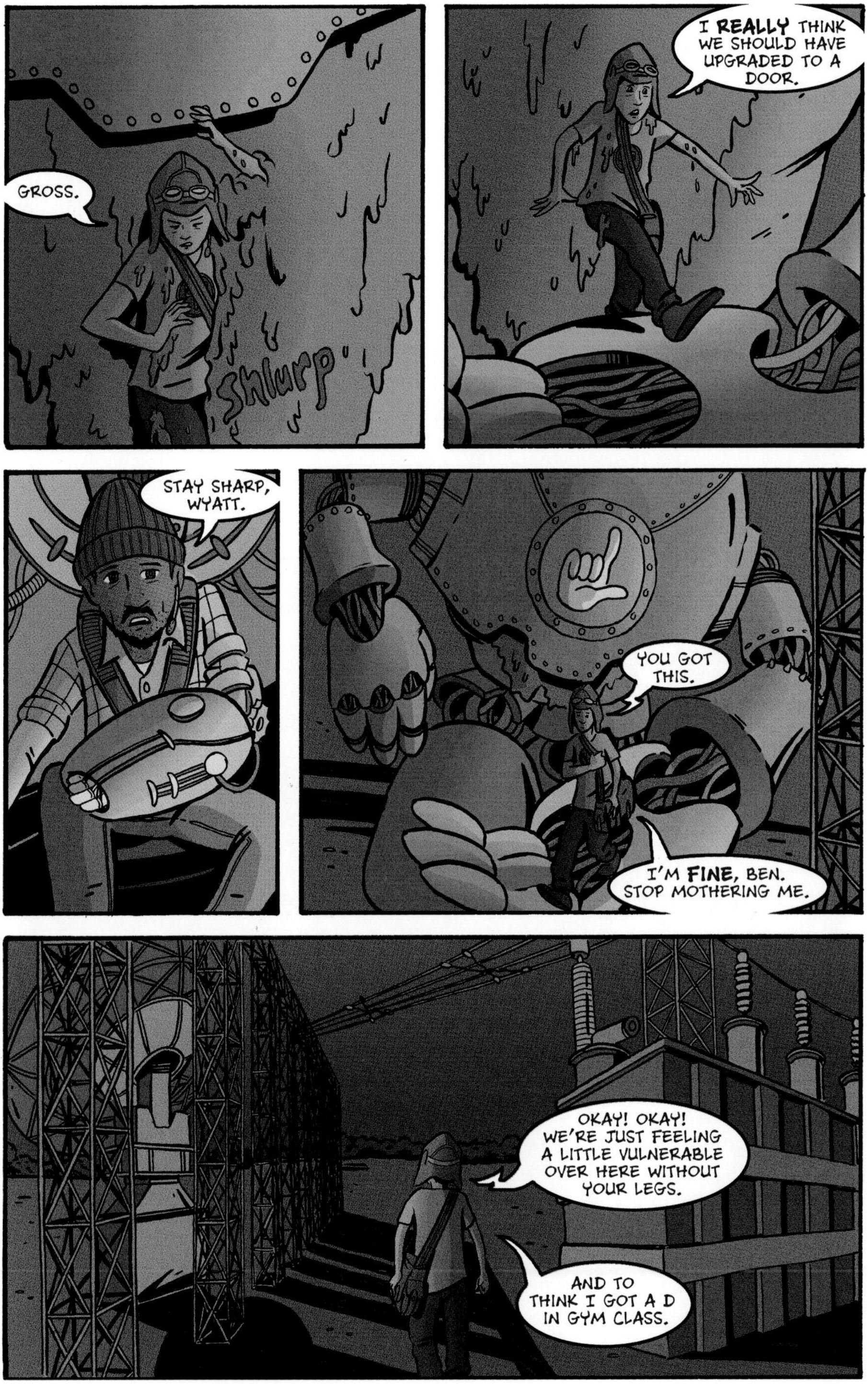
GROSS.
Shlurp
I REALLY THINK WE SHOULD HAVE UPGRADED TO A DOOR.
STAY SHARP, WYATT.
YOU GOT THIS.
I'M FINE, BEN. STOP MOTHERING ME.
OKAY! OKAY! WE'RE JUST FEELING A LITTLE VULNERABLE OVER HERE WITHOUT YOUR LEGS.
AND TO THINK I GOT A D IN GYM CLASS.

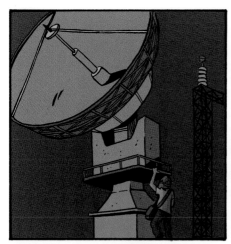

ONCE I'M IN, WE SHOULD BE ABLE TO USE ANY OF THEIR CHANNELS.

WHAT IF THEY DISCOVER WHAT WE'VE DONE?

IT WON'T MAKE ANY DIFFERENCE. OUR TEAM WILL HAVE CONTINUOUS ACCESS WHETHER IT REMAINS CONNECTED OR NOT.

LIKE AGENT SMITH IN *MATRIX.*

A BETTER COMPARISON WOULD BE INVITING A VAMPIRE INTO THE HOUSE.

OR MAYBE FLYNN FROM *TRON.*

WHEN HE WAS IN THE GRID, HE COULD—

BOYS! CAN WE FOCUS?

CHECK THE READINGS TO SEE IF WE'RE GETTING ANY CONNECTION.

≳KOFF!≲ CONNECTION IS GOOD.

I JUST NEED TO LINK TO THE SATELLITE, AND WE CAN GET OUT OF HERE.

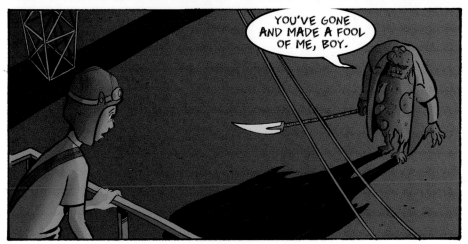

YOU'VE GONE AND MADE A FOOL OF ME, BOY.

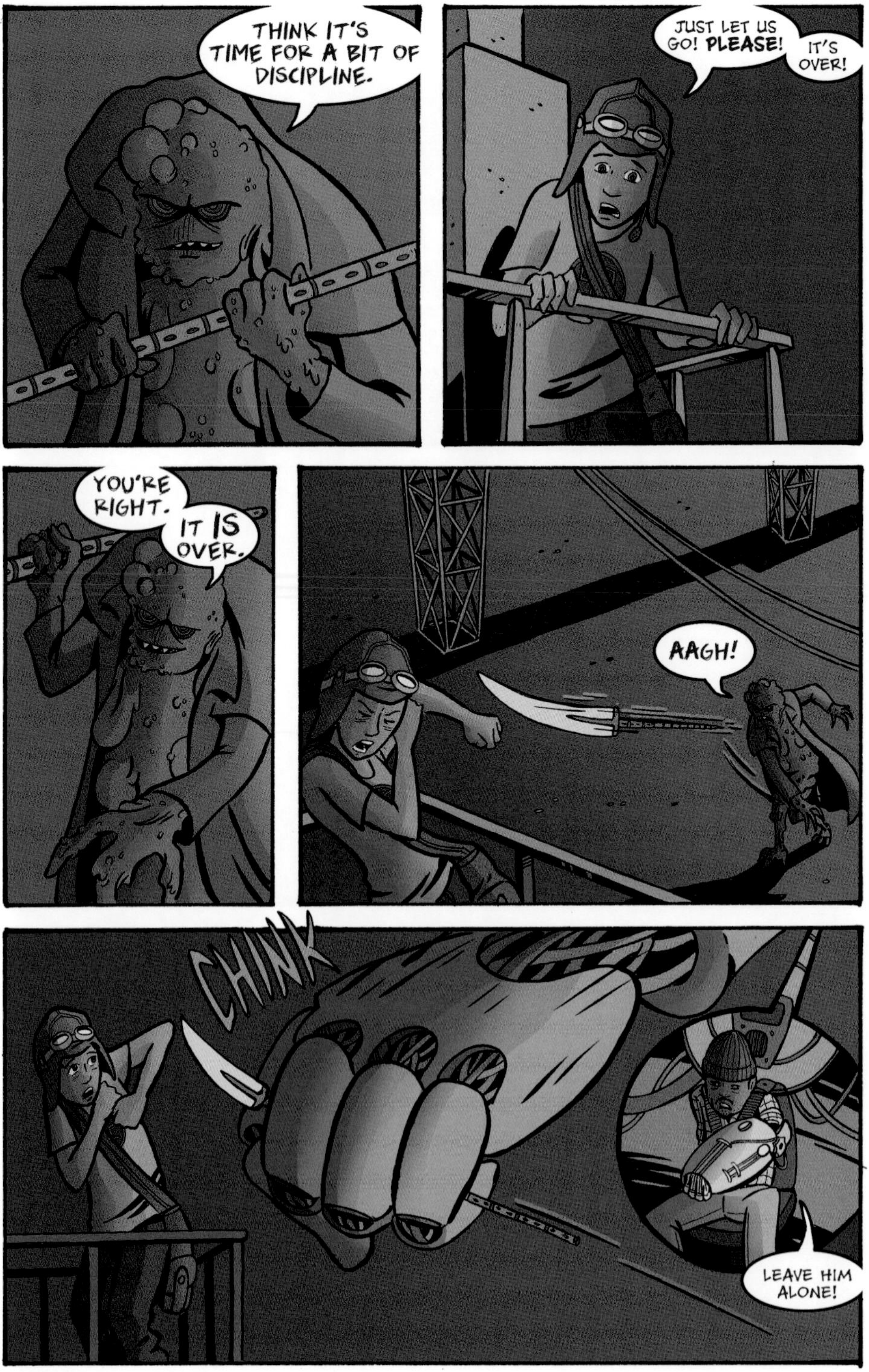
THINK IT'S TIME FOR A BIT OF DISCIPLINE.
JUST LET US GO! PLEASE!
IT'S OVER!
YOU'RE RIGHT.
IT IS OVER.
AAGH!
CHINK
LEAVE HIM ALONE!

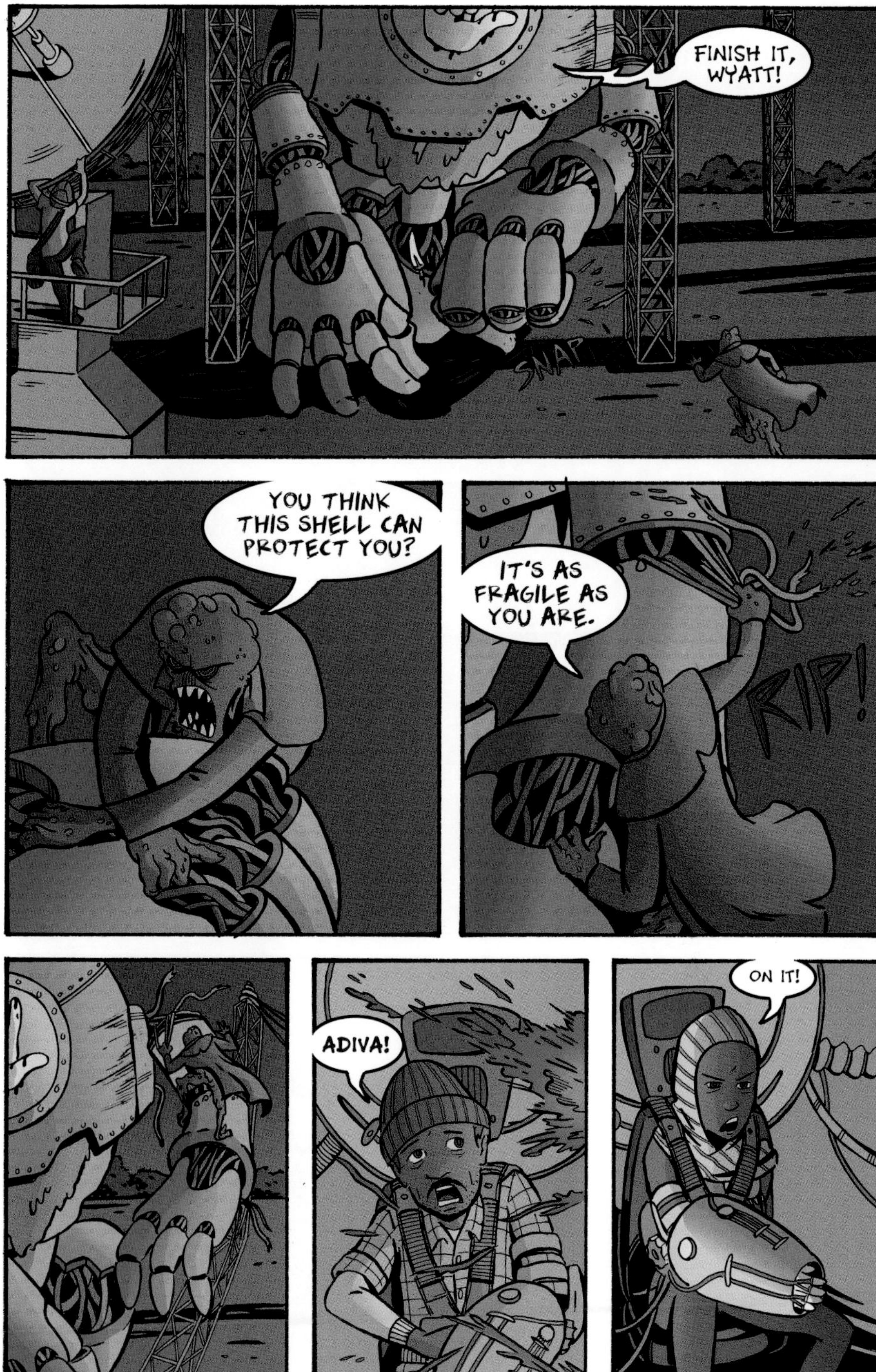
FINISH IT, WYATT!
SNAP
YOU THINK THIS SHELL CAN PROTECT YOU?
IT'S AS FRAGILE AS YOU ARE.
RIP!
ADIVA!
ON IT!

TOO CLOSE.
NEED TO GO.
ALMOST GOT IT.

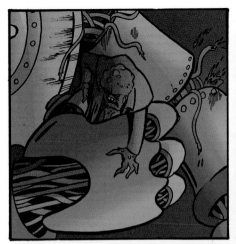

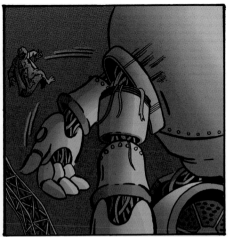

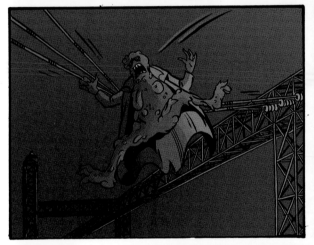

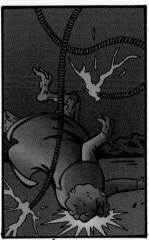

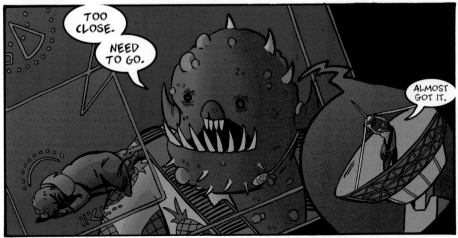

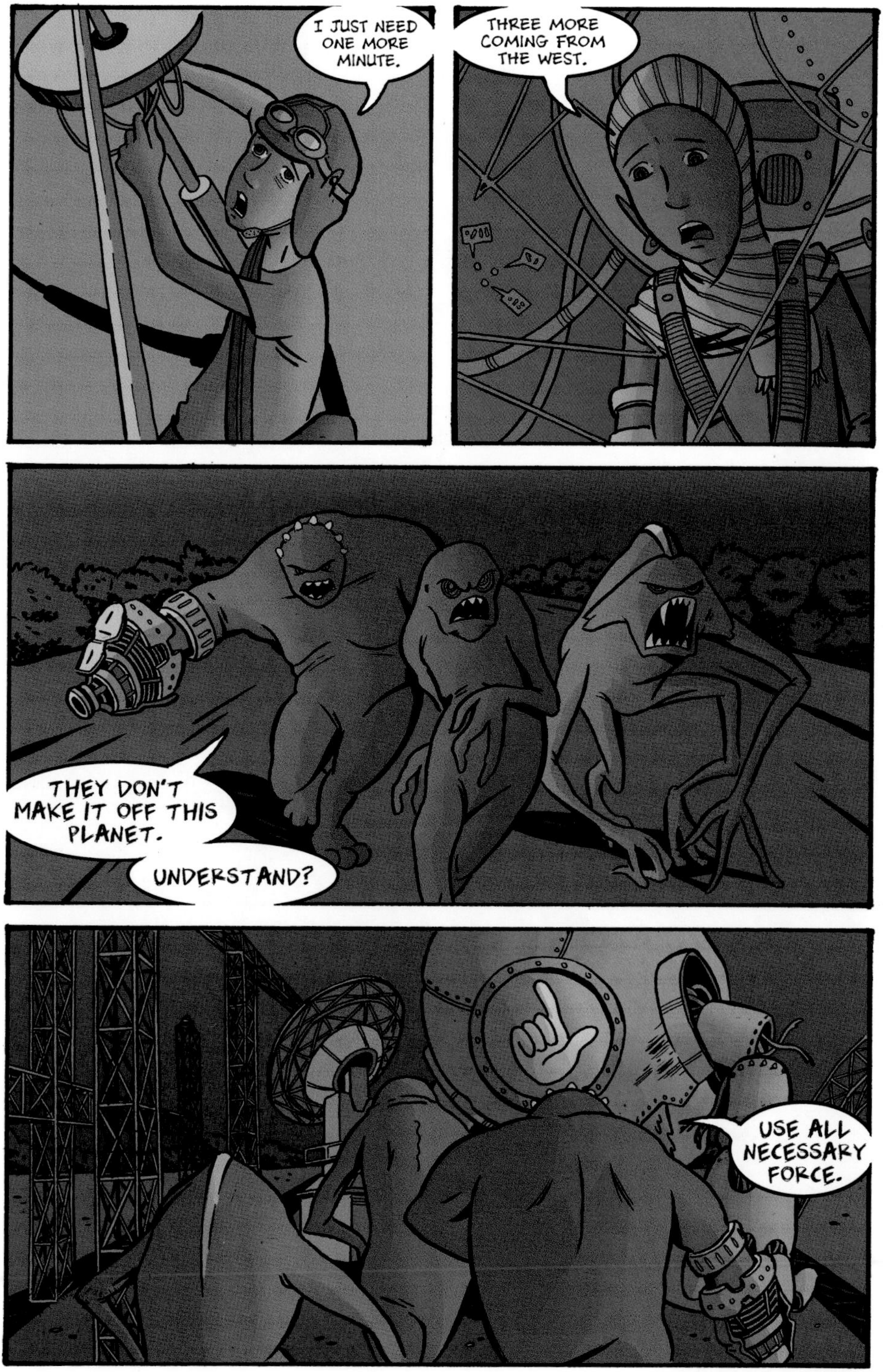
I JUST NEED ONE MORE MINUTE.
THREE MORE COMING FROM THE WEST.
THEY DON'T MAKE IT OFF THIS PLANET.
UNDERSTAND?
USE ALL NECESSARY FORCE.

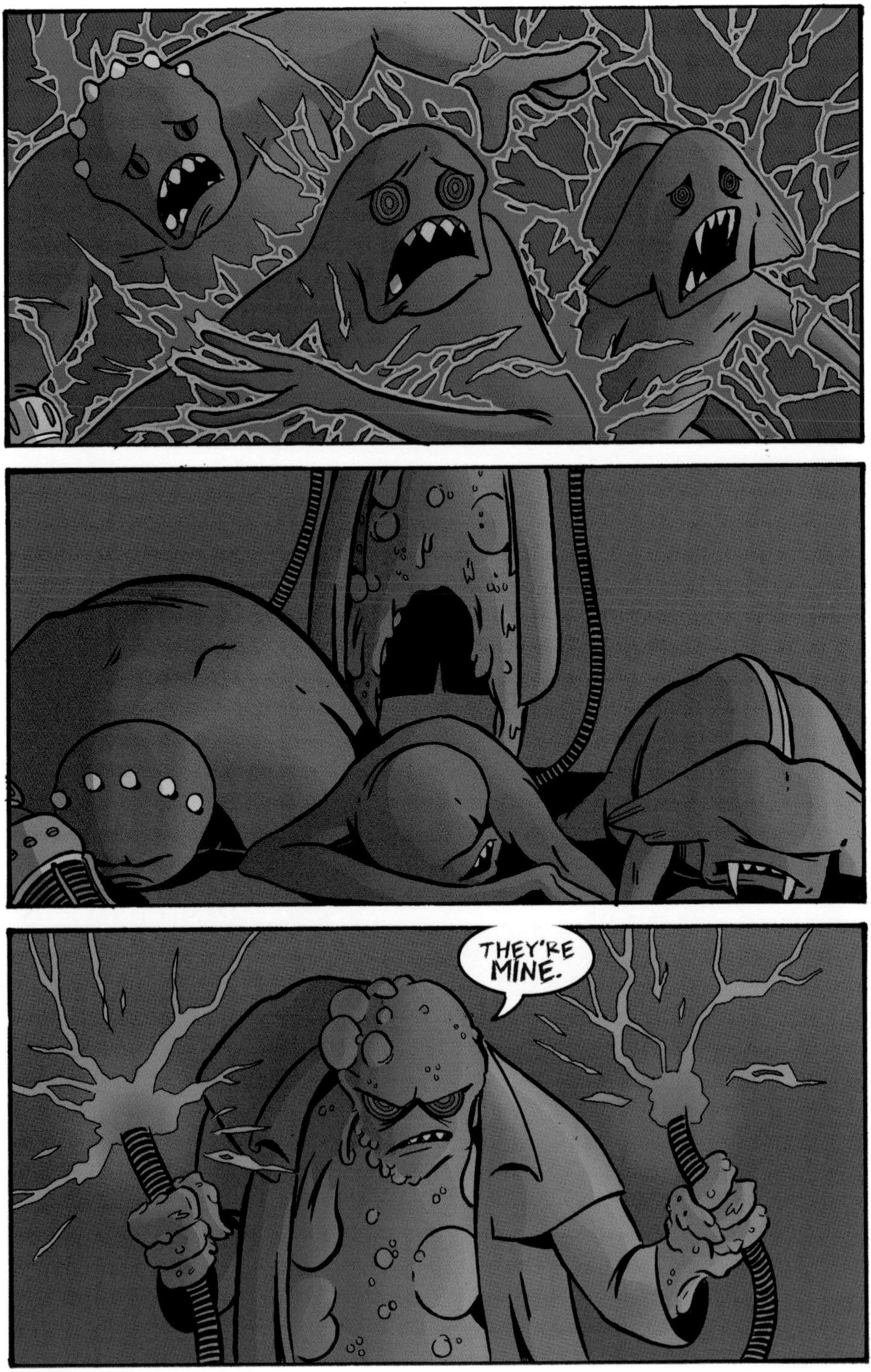
THEY'RE MINE.

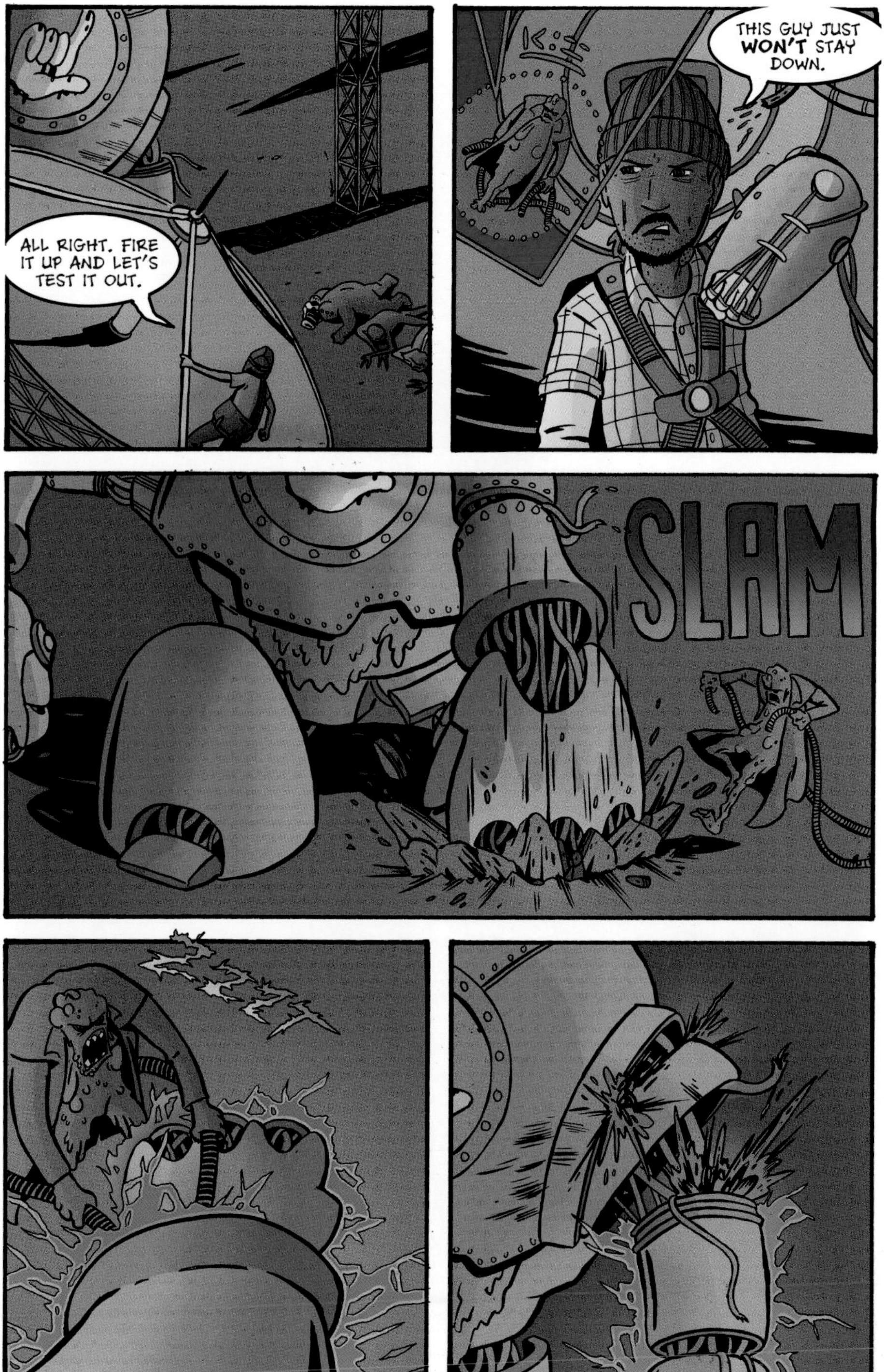
ALL RIGHT. FIRE IT UP AND LET'S TEST IT OUT.
THIS GUY JUST **WON'T** STAY DOWN.
SLAM
ZZZT

AAAAGH!

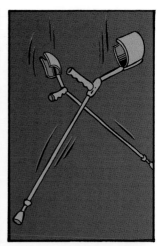

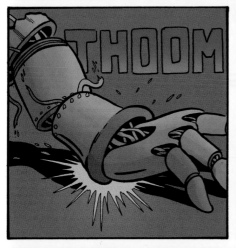

THOOM

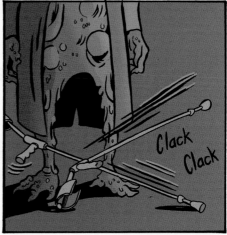

Clack
Clack

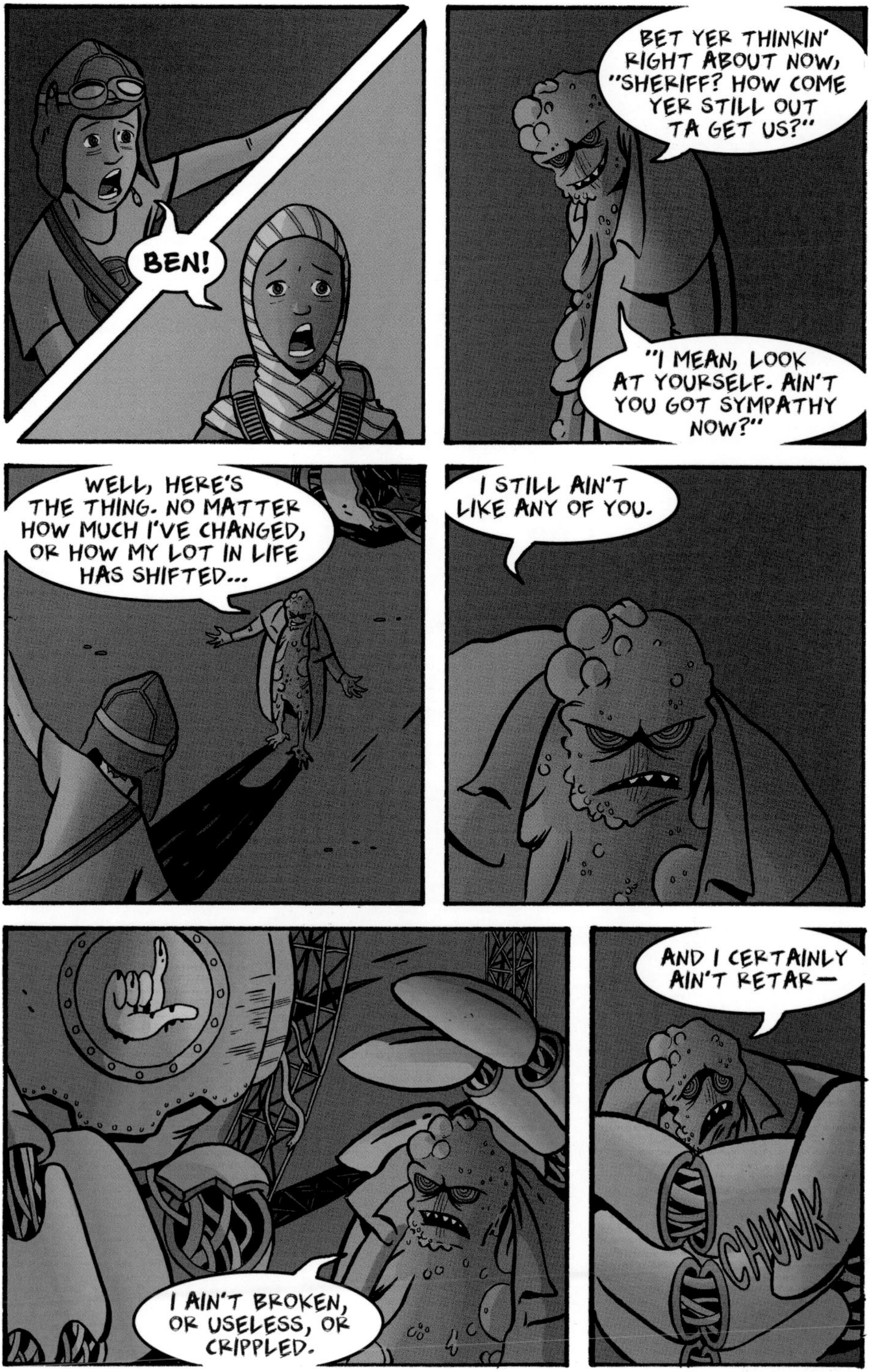
BEN!
BET YER THINKIN' RIGHT ABOUT NOW, "SHERIFF? HOW COME YER STILL OUT TA GET US?"
"I MEAN, LOOK AT YOURSELF. AIN'T YOU GOT SYMPATHY NOW?"
WELL, HERE'S THE THING. NO MATTER HOW MUCH I'VE CHANGED, OR HOW MY LOT IN LIFE HAS SHIFTED...
I STILL AIN'T LIKE ANY OF YOU.
I AIN'T BROKEN, OR USELESS, OR CRIPPLED.
AND I CERTAINLY AIN'T RETAR—
CHUNK

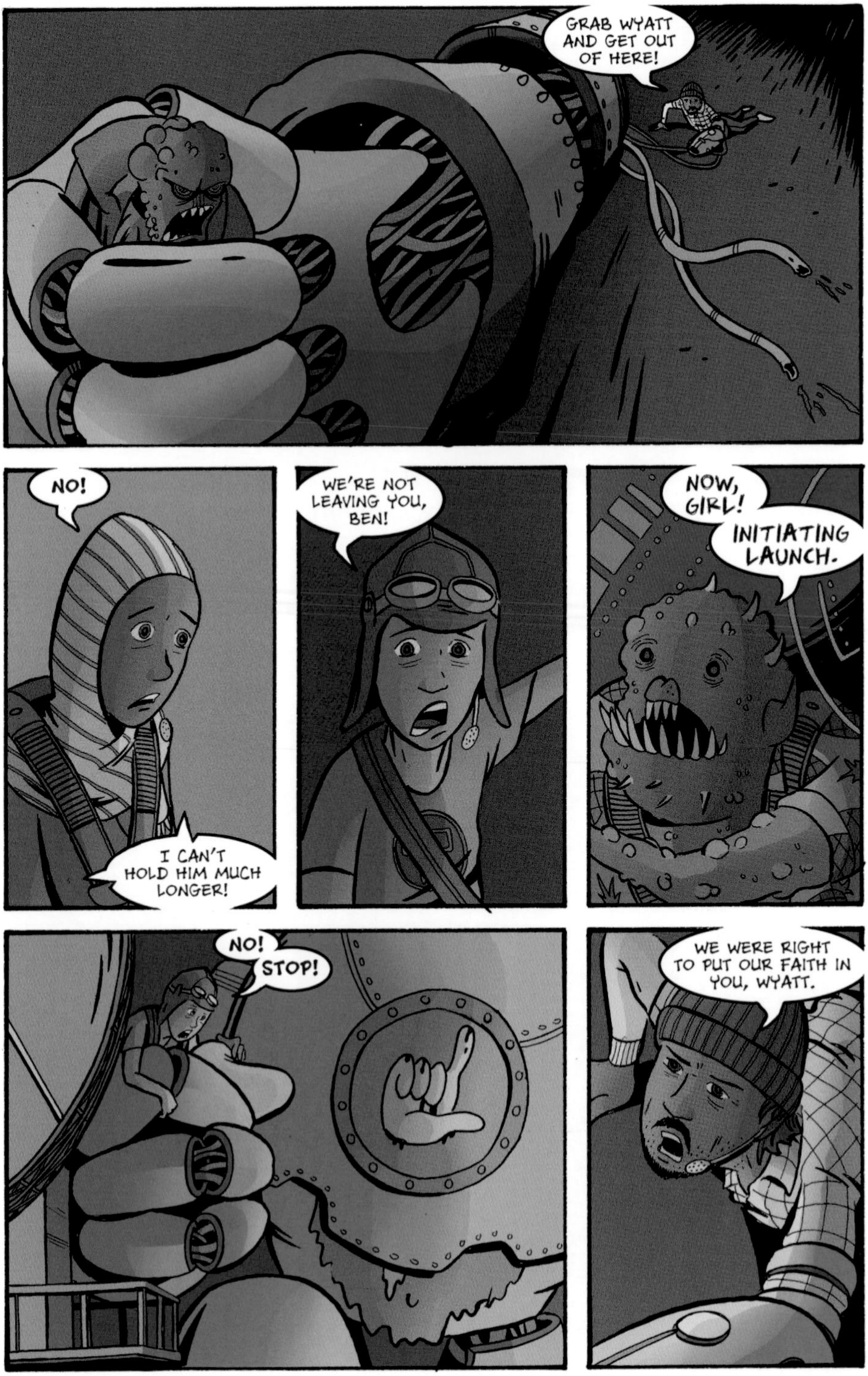
GRAB WYATT AND GET OUT OF HERE!
NO!
I CAN'T HOLD HIM MUCH LONGER!
WE'RE NOT LEAVING YOU, BEN!
NOW, GIRL!
INITIATING LAUNCH.
NO! STOP!
WE WERE RIGHT TO PUT OUR FAITH IN YOU, WYATT.

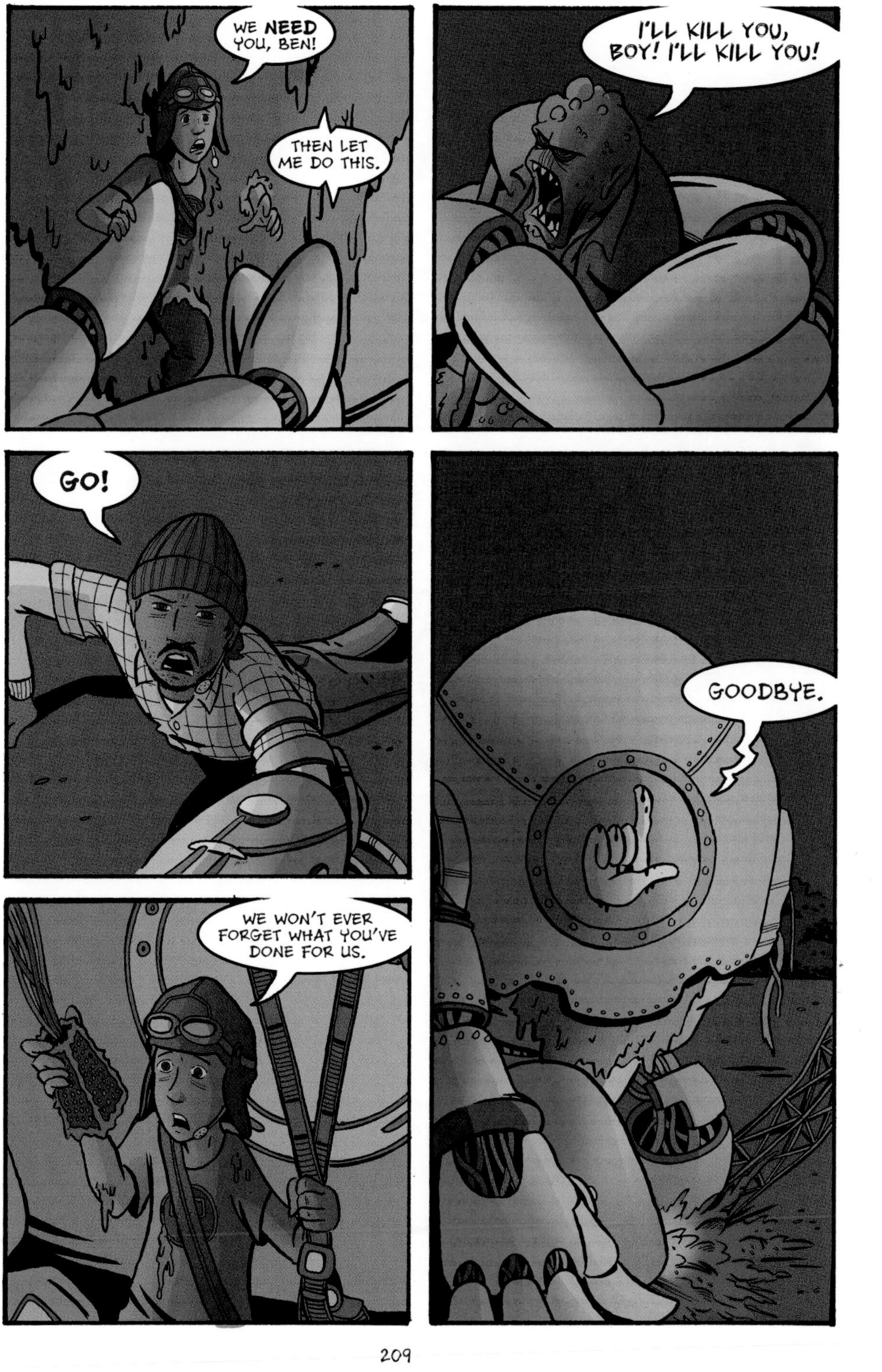
WE **NEED** YOU, BEN!
THEN LET ME DO THIS.
I'LL KILL YOU, BOY! I'LL KILL YOU!
GO!
WE WON'T EVER FORGET WHAT YOU'VE DONE FOR US.
GOODBYE.

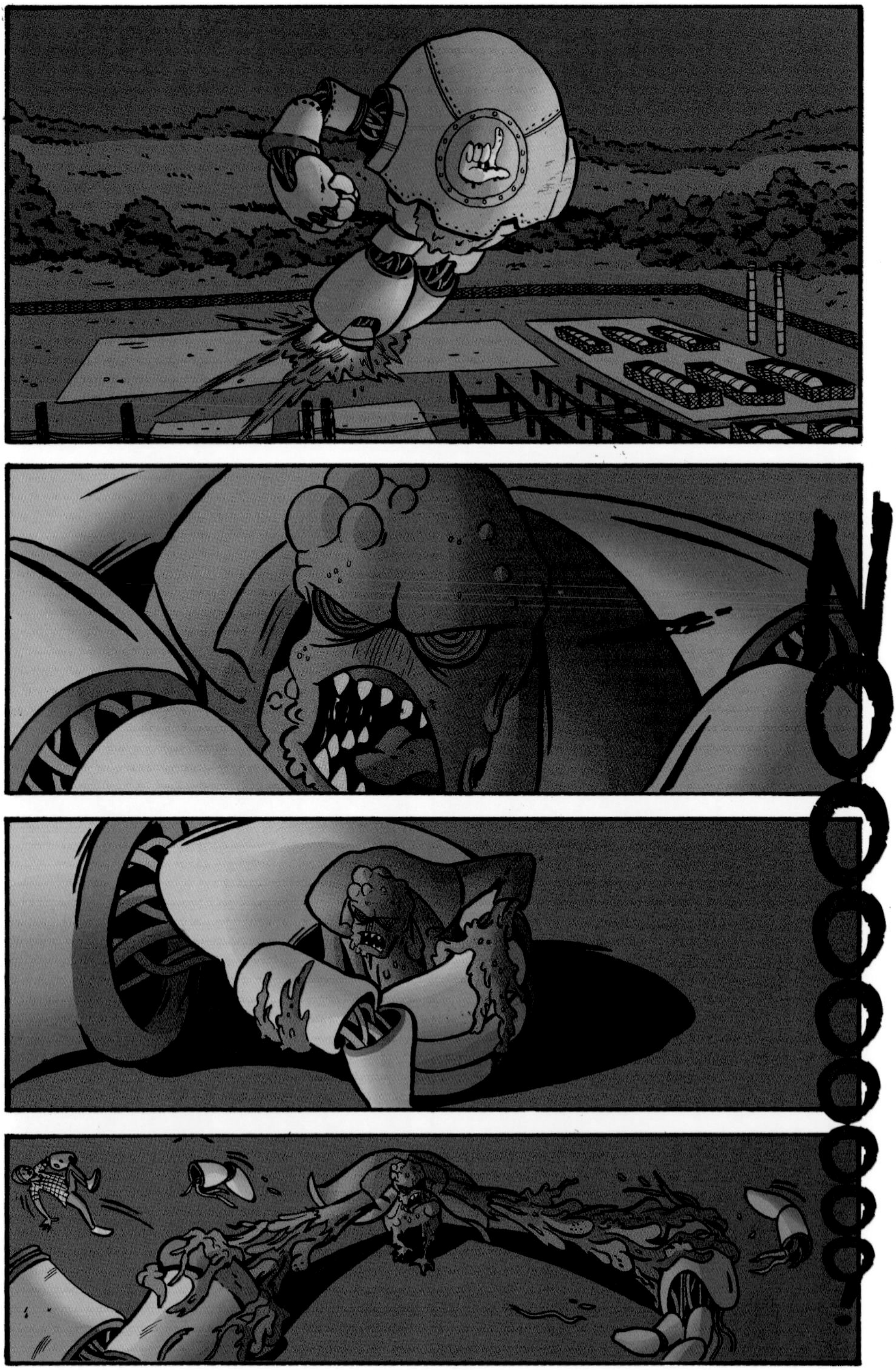
NOOOOOOOO?

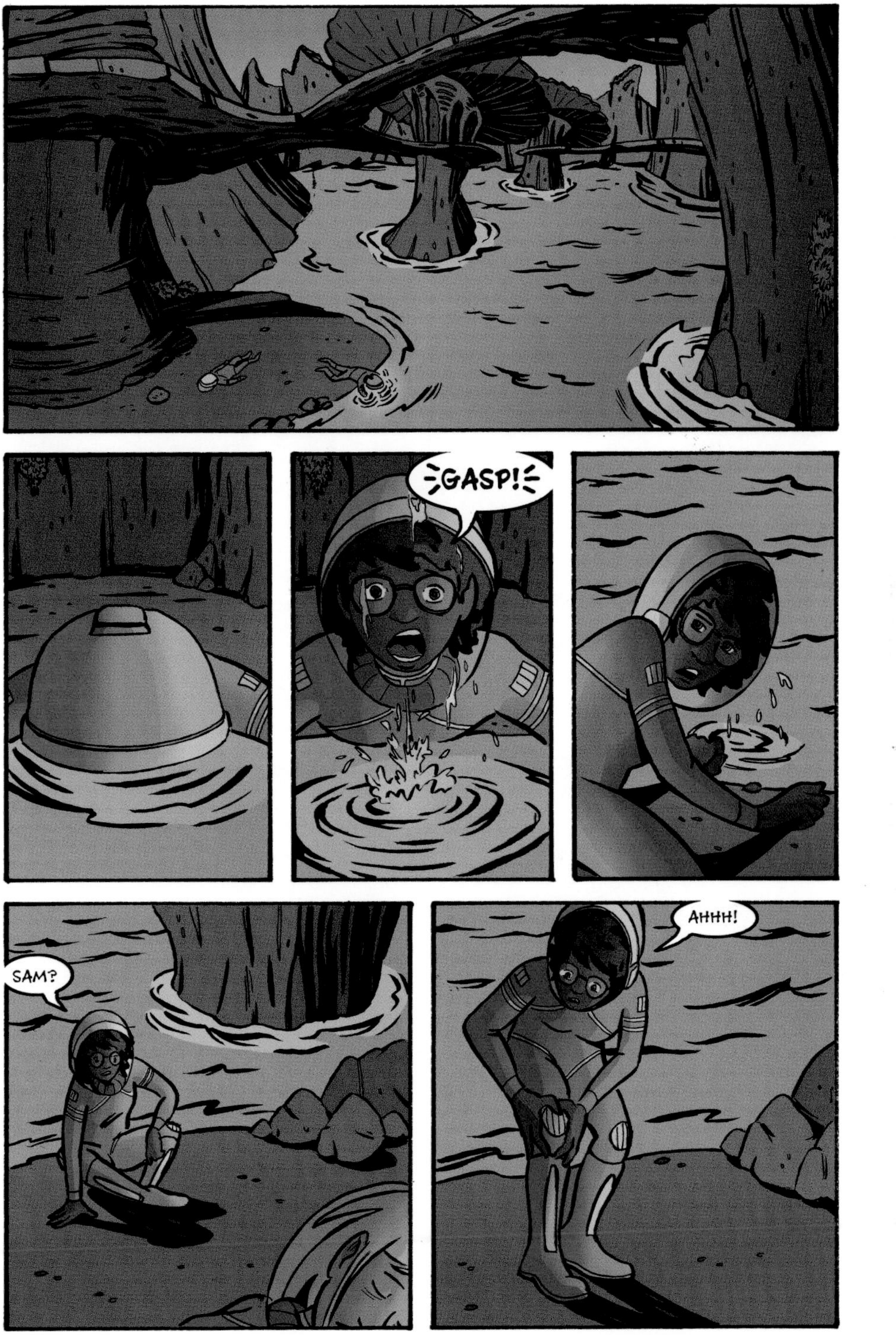
GASP!
SAM?
AHHH!

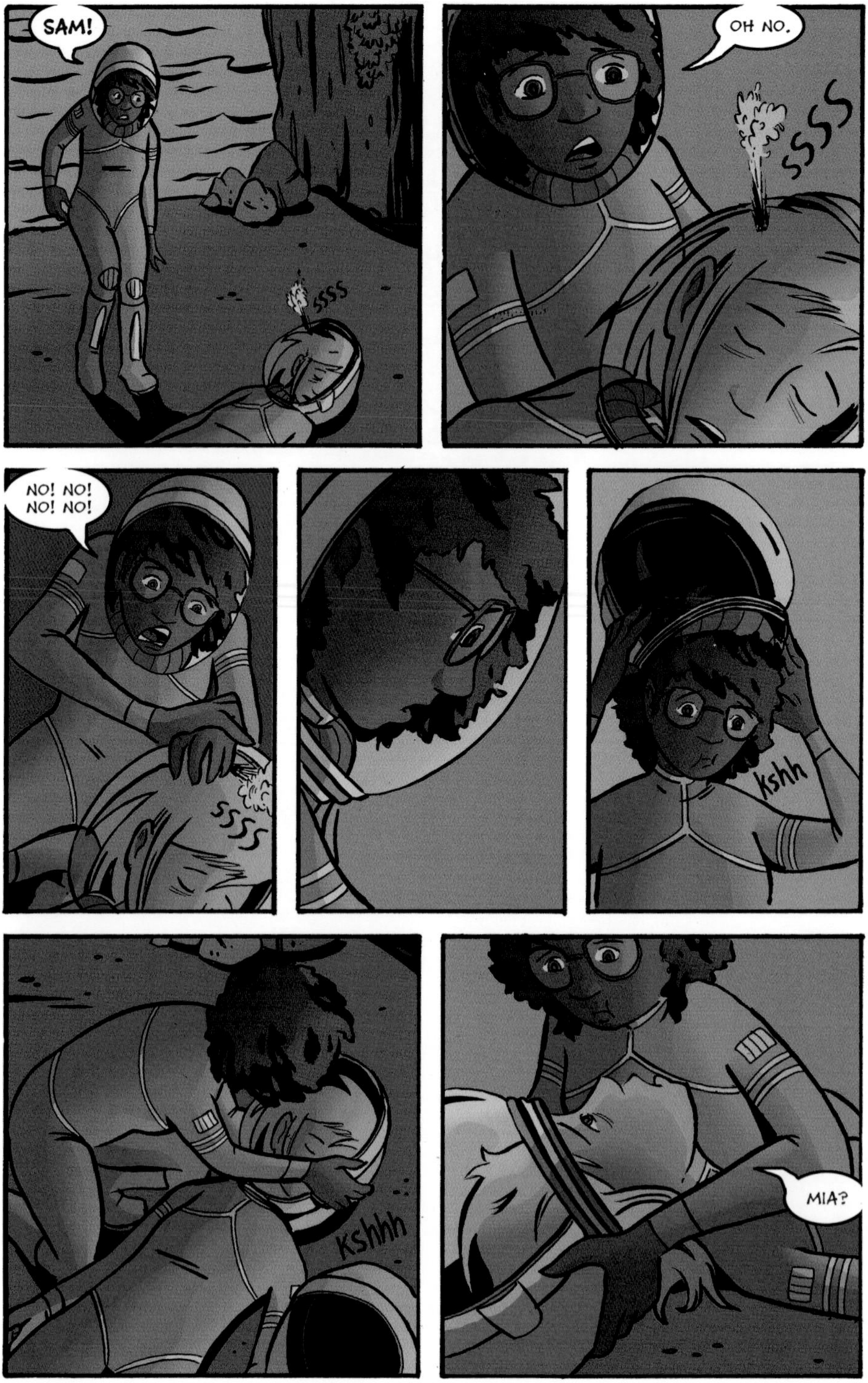
SAM!
SSSS
OH NO.
SSSS
NO! NO!
NO! NO!
SSSS
kshh
kshhh
MIA?

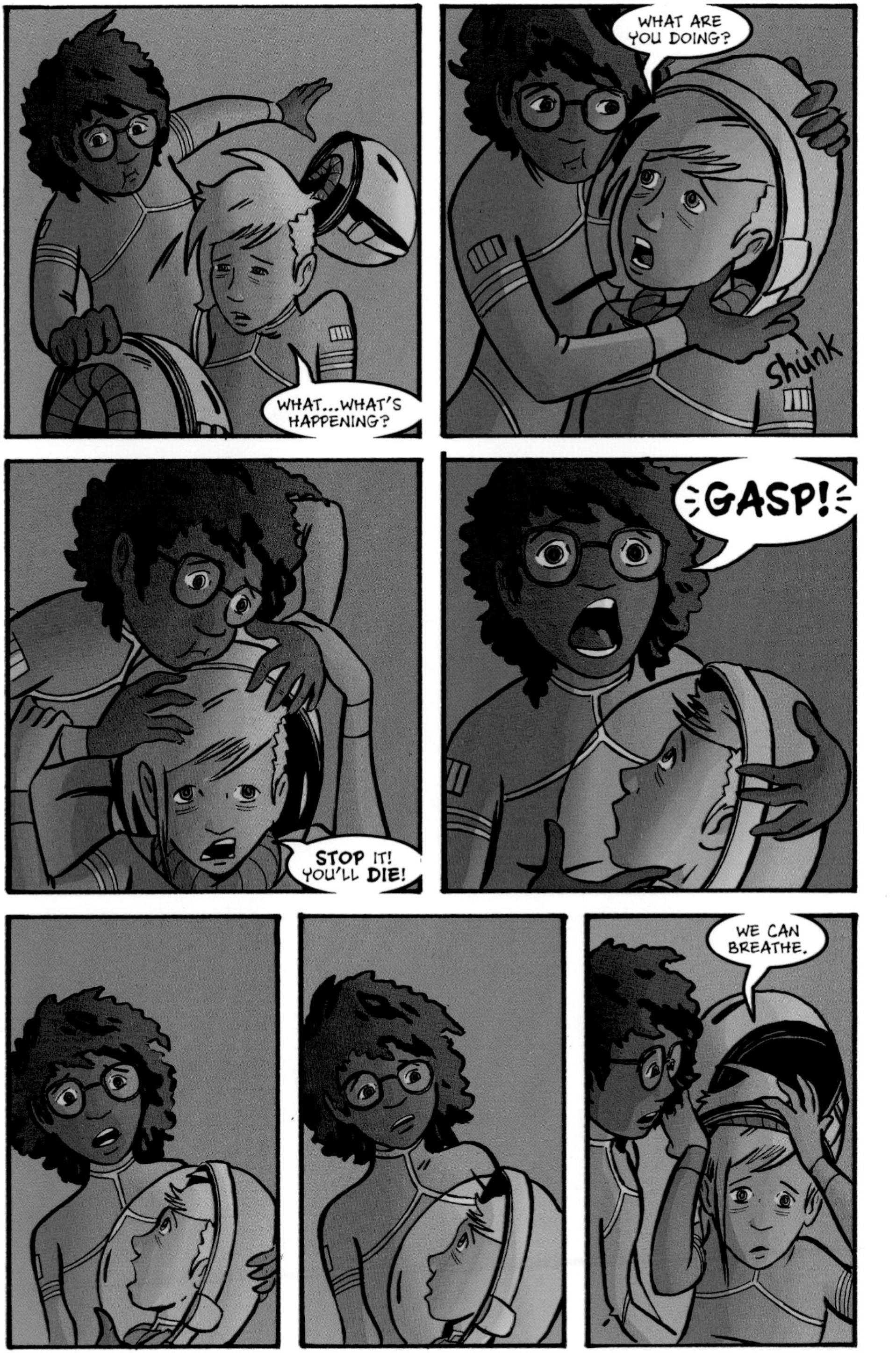
WHAT...WHAT'S HAPPENING?
WHAT ARE YOU DOING?
Shunk
STOP IT! YOU'LL DIE!
GASP!
WE CAN BREATHE.

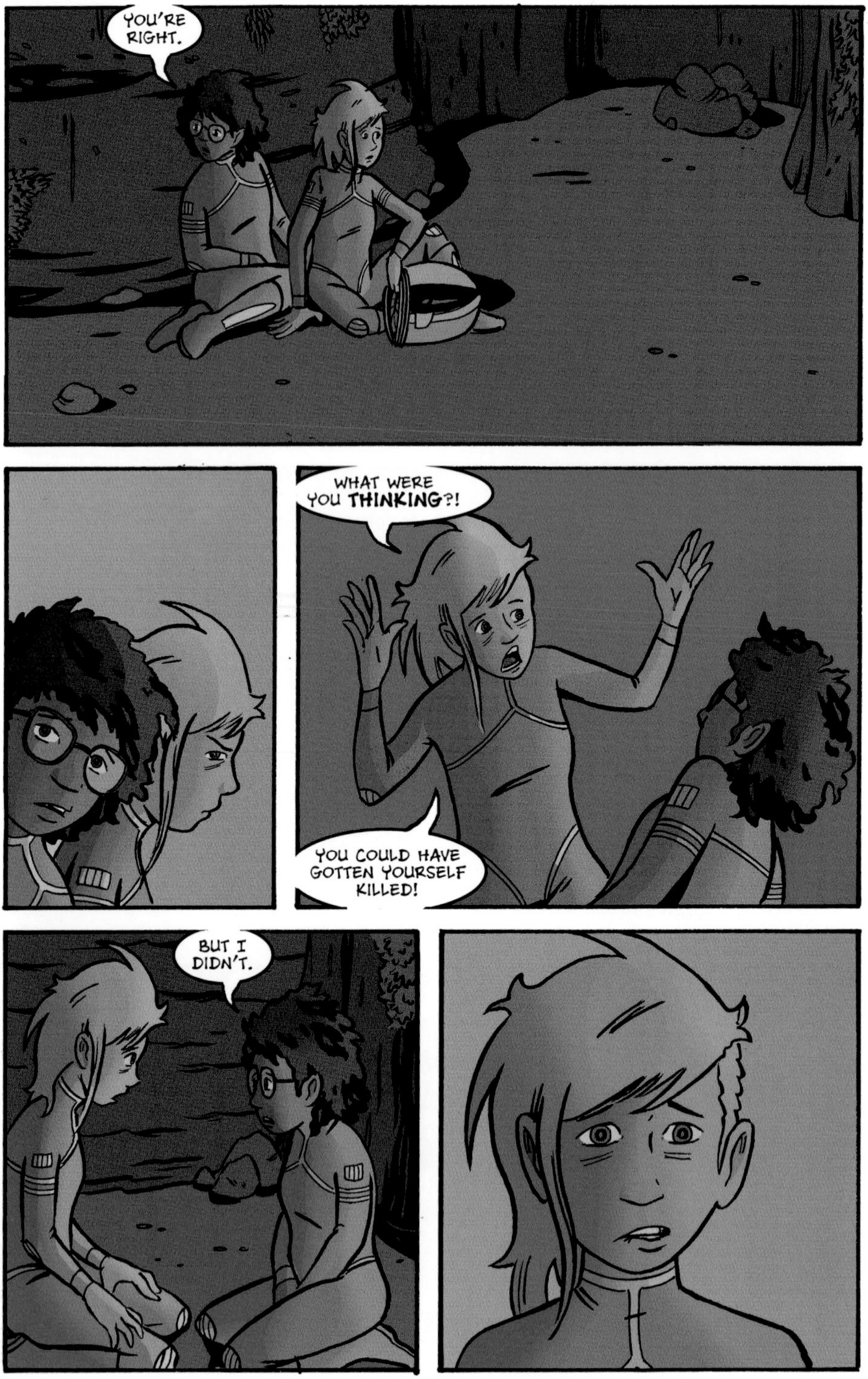
YOU'RE RIGHT.
WHAT WERE YOU THINKING?!
YOU COULD HAVE GOTTEN YOURSELF KILLED!
BUT I DIDN'T.

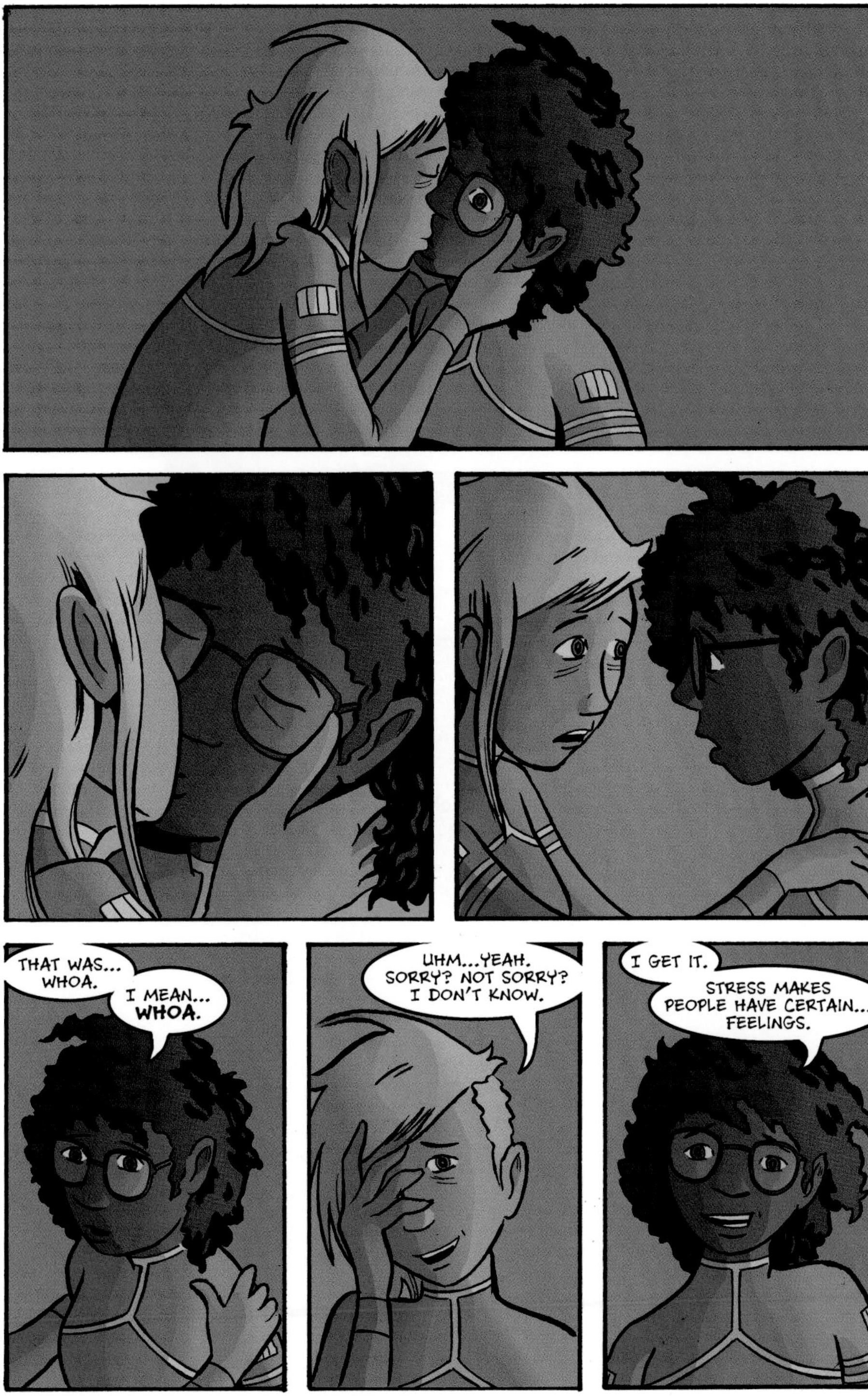
THAT WAS... WHOA.
I MEAN... **WHOA.**
UHM...YEAH. SORRY? NOT SORRY? I DON'T KNOW.
I GET IT.
STRESS MAKES PEOPLE HAVE CERTAIN... FEELINGS.

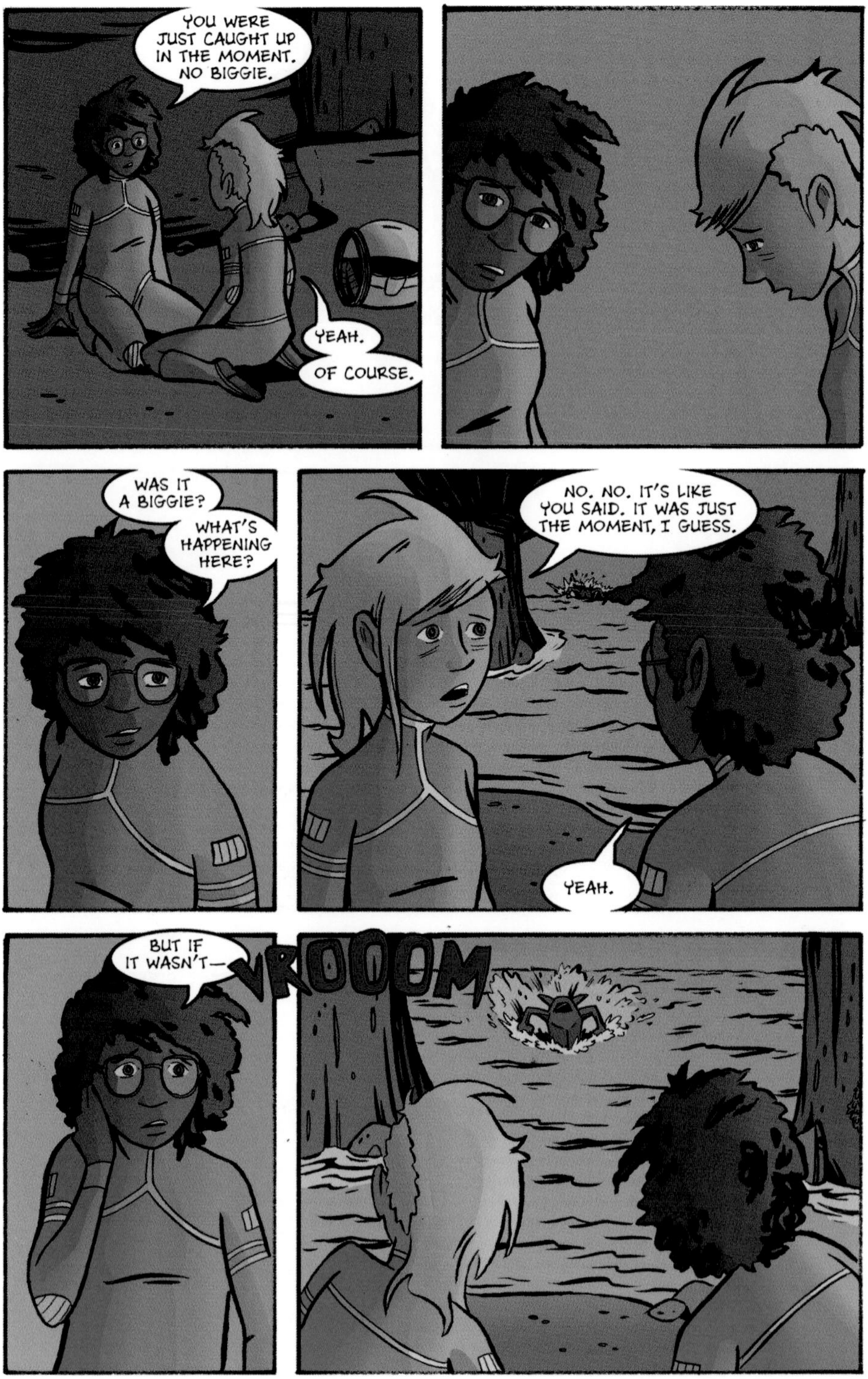
YOU WERE JUST CAUGHT UP IN THE MOMENT. NO BIGGIE.
YEAH.
OF COURSE.
WAS IT A BIGGIE?
WHAT'S HAPPENING HERE?
NO. NO. IT'S LIKE YOU SAID. IT WAS JUST THE MOMENT, I GUESS.
YEAH.
BUT IF IT WASN'T—
VROOOM

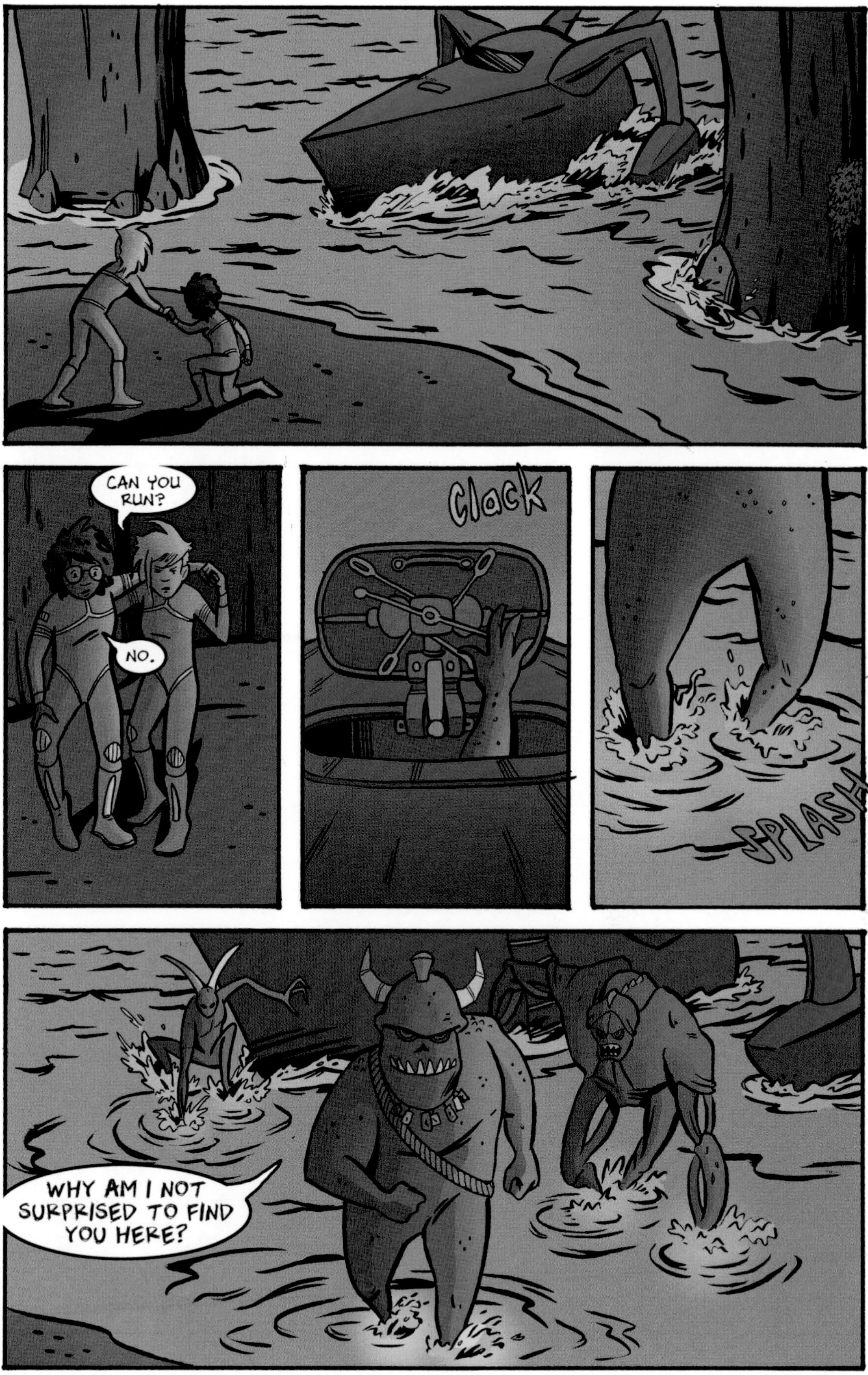
CAN YOU RUN?
NO.
Clack
SPLASH
WHY AM I NOT SURPRISED TO FIND YOU HERE?

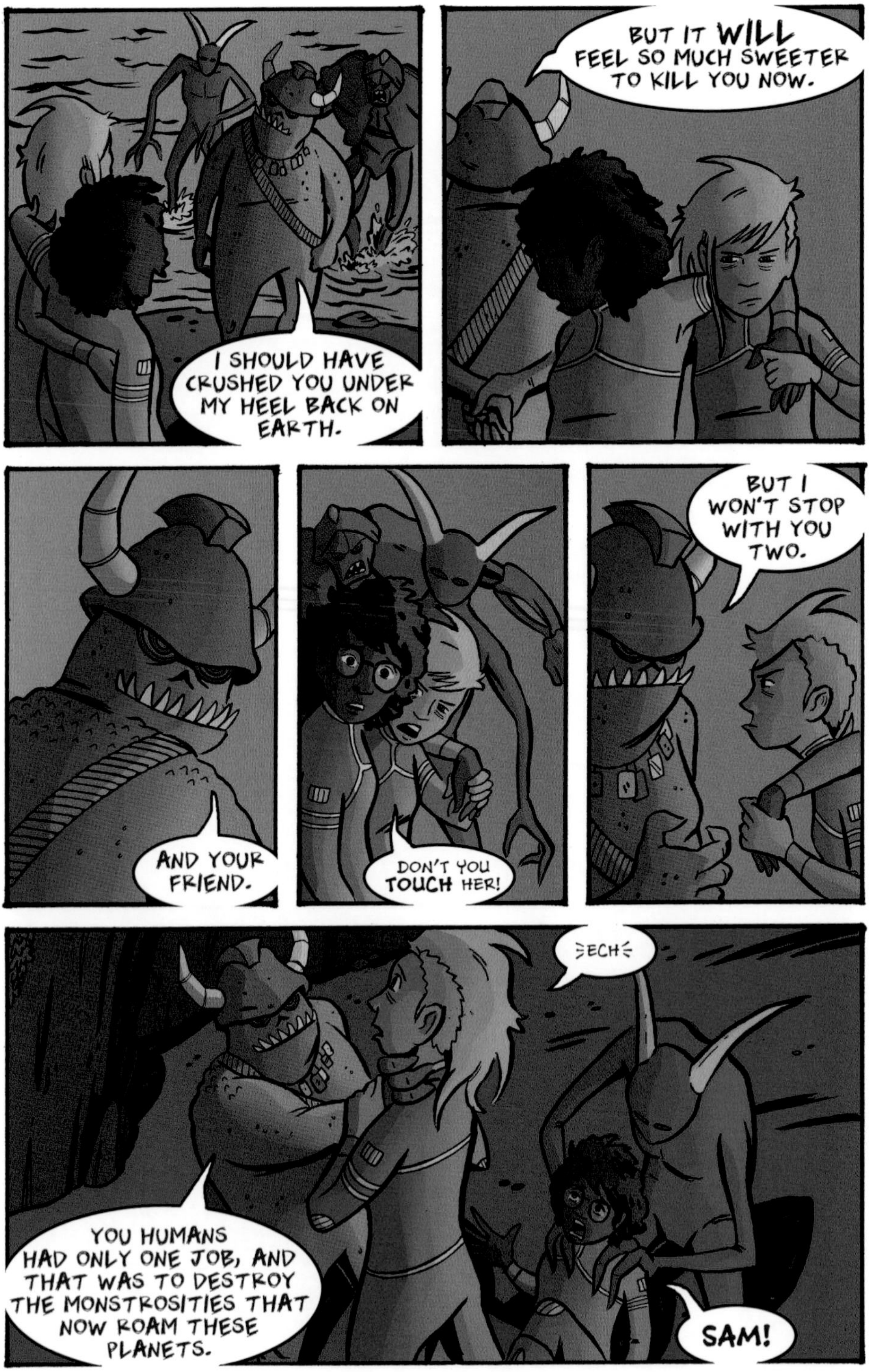
I SHOULD HAVE CRUSHED YOU UNDER MY HEEL BACK ON EARTH.
BUT IT WILL FEEL SO MUCH SWEETER TO KILL YOU NOW.
AND YOUR FRIEND.
DON'T YOU TOUCH HER!
BUT I WON'T STOP WITH YOU TWO.
ECH
YOU HUMANS HAD ONLY ONE JOB, AND THAT WAS TO DESTROY THE MONSTROSITIES THAT NOW ROAM THESE PLANETS.
SAM!

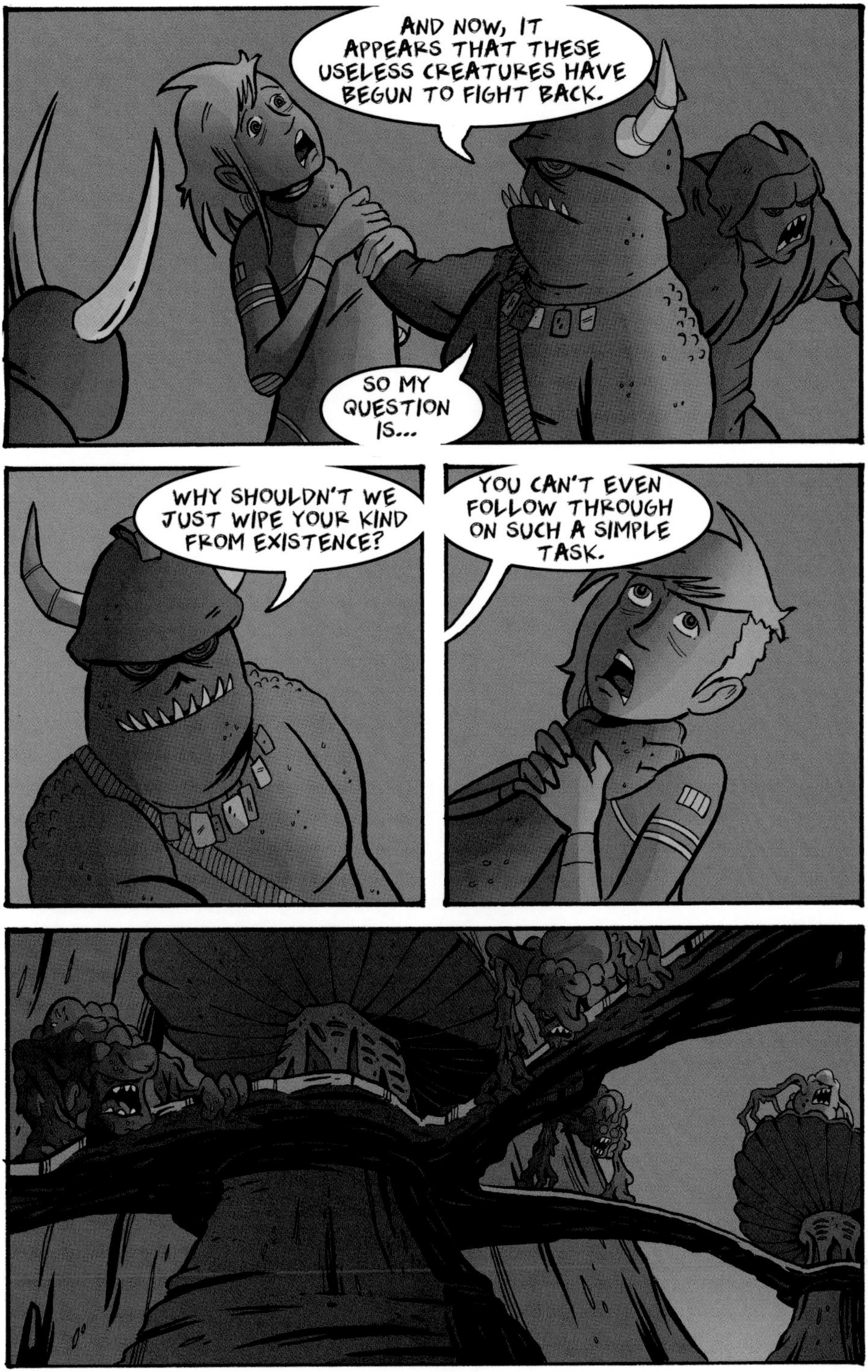
AND NOW, IT APPEARS THAT THESE USELESS CREATURES HAVE BEGUN TO FIGHT BACK.
SO MY QUESTION IS...
WHY SHOULDN'T WE JUST WIPE YOUR KIND FROM EXISTENCE?
YOU CAN'T EVEN FOLLOW THROUGH ON SUCH A SIMPLE TASK.

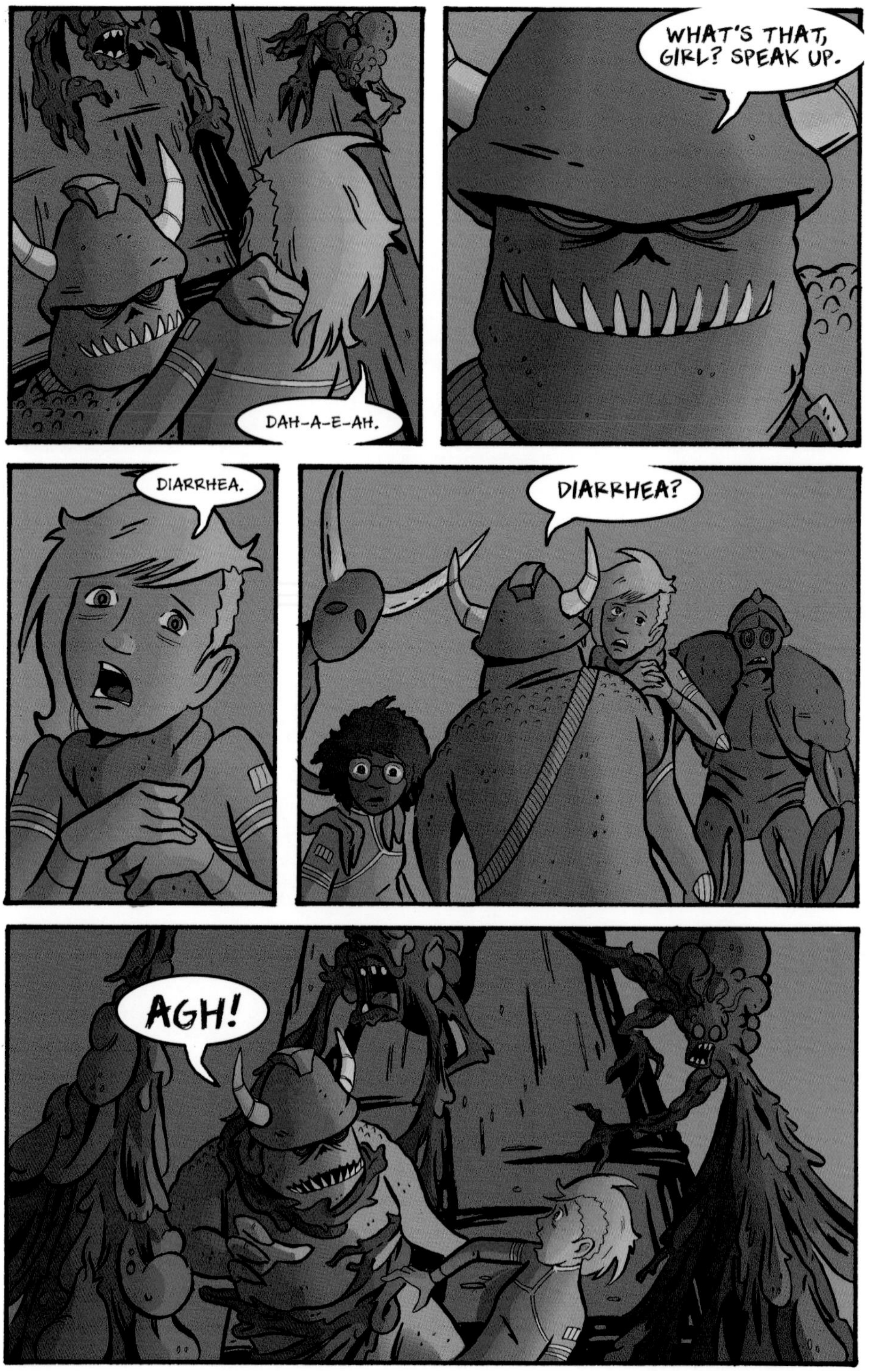
DAH-A-E-AH.
WHAT'S THAT, GIRL? SPEAK UP.
DIARRHEA.
DIARRHEA?
AGH!

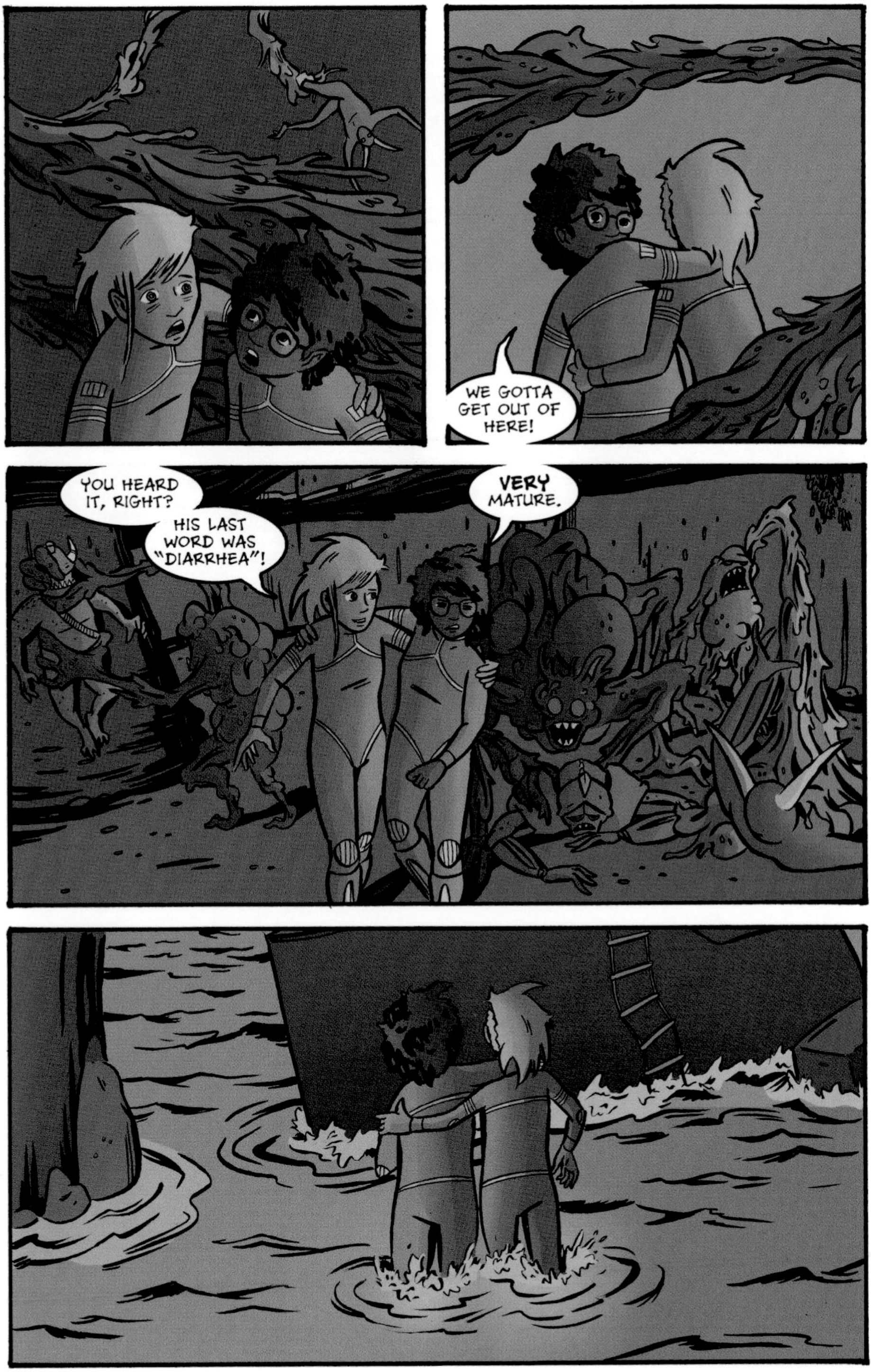
WE GOTTA GET OUT OF HERE!
YOU HEARD IT, RIGHT?
HIS LAST WORD WAS "DIARRHEA"!
VERY MATURE.

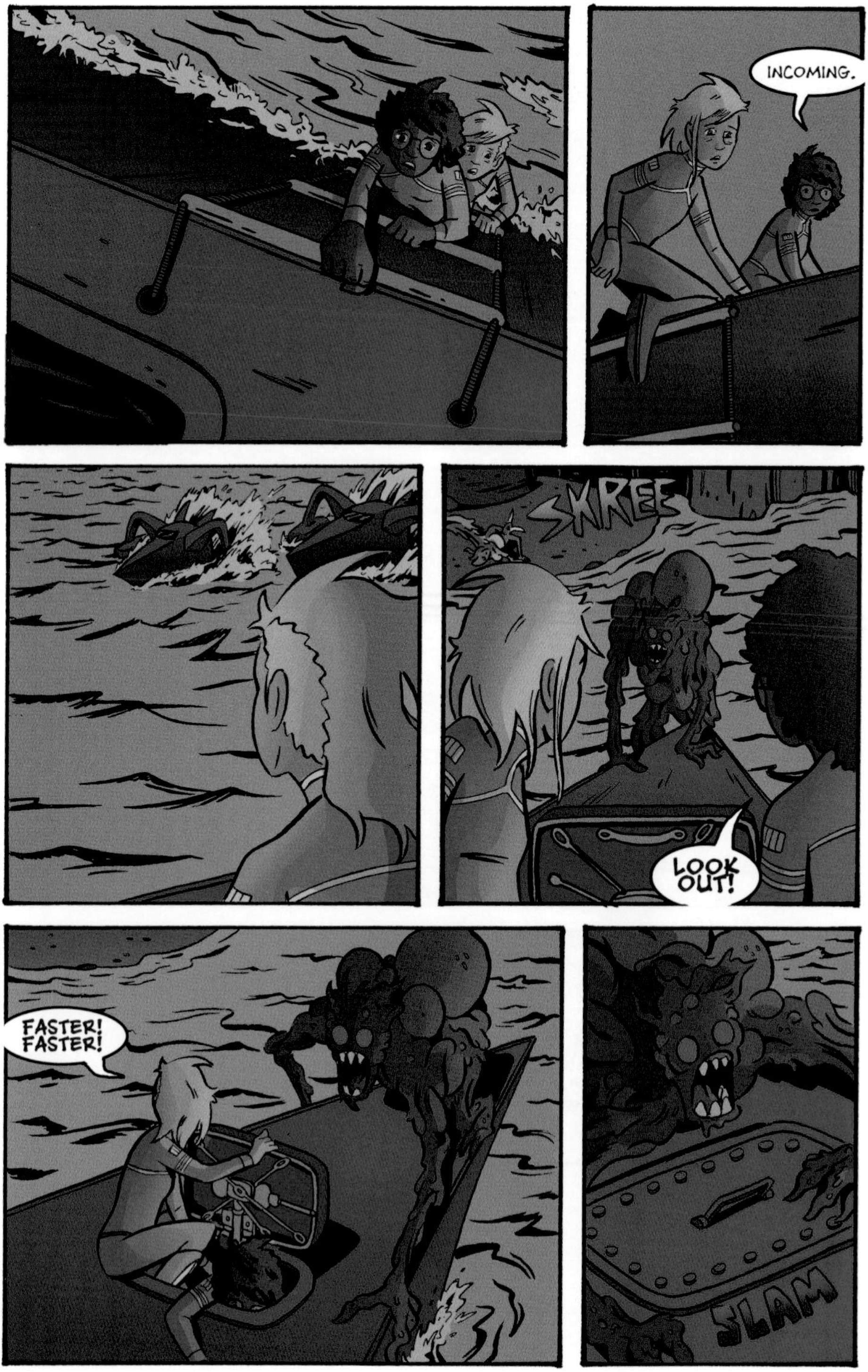
INCOMING.
SKREE
LOOK OUT!
FASTER! FASTER!
SLAM

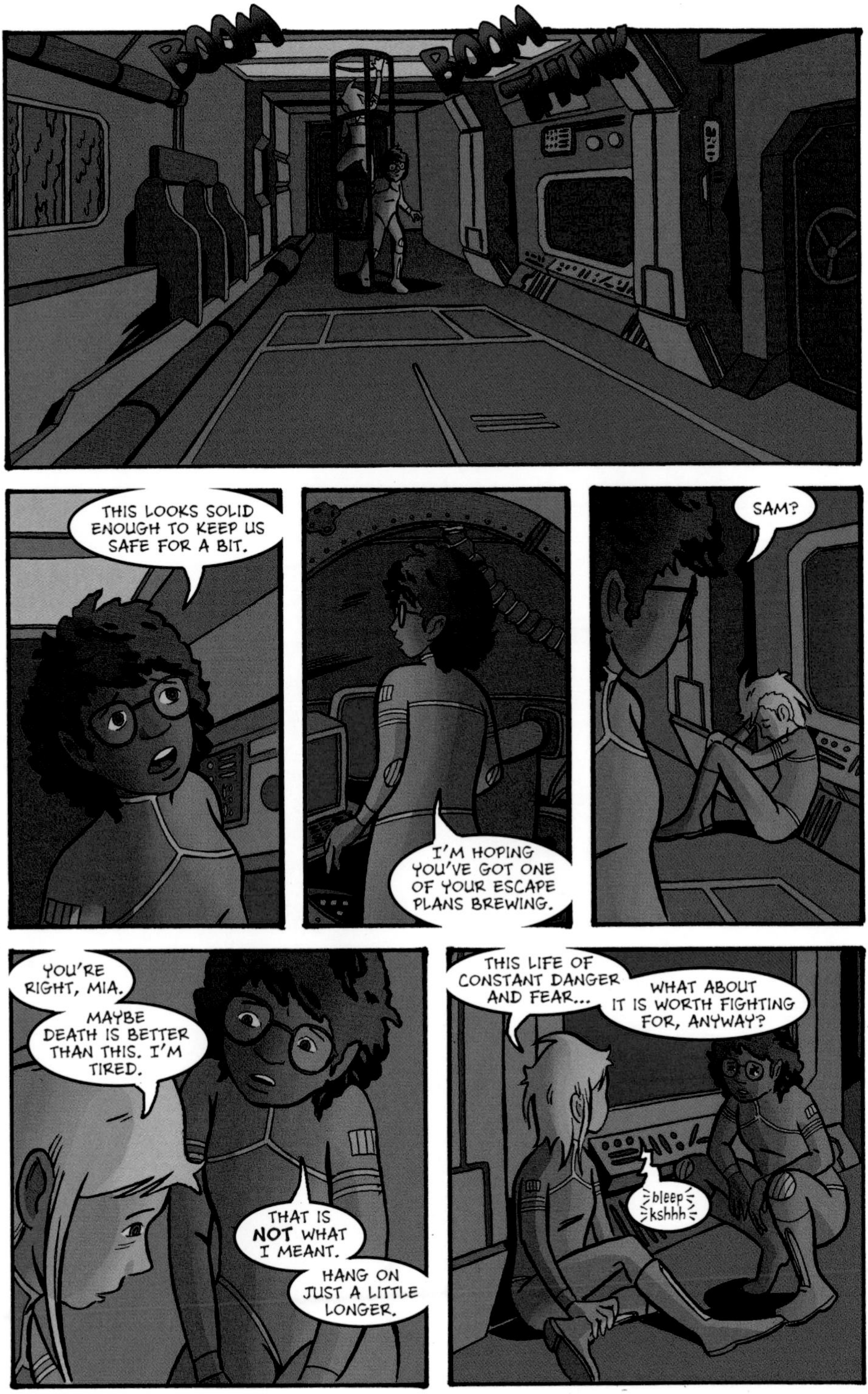
BOOM
BOOM
THUNK
THIS LOOKS SOLID ENOUGH TO KEEP US SAFE FOR A BIT.
I'M HOPING YOU'VE GOT ONE OF YOUR ESCAPE PLANS BREWING.
SAM?
YOU'RE RIGHT, MIA.
MAYBE DEATH IS BETTER THAN THIS. I'M TIRED.
THAT IS **NOT** WHAT I MEANT.
HANG ON JUST A LITTLE LONGER.
THIS LIFE OF CONSTANT DANGER AND FEAR...
WHAT ABOUT IT IS WORTH FIGHTING FOR, ANYWAY?
bleep
kshhh

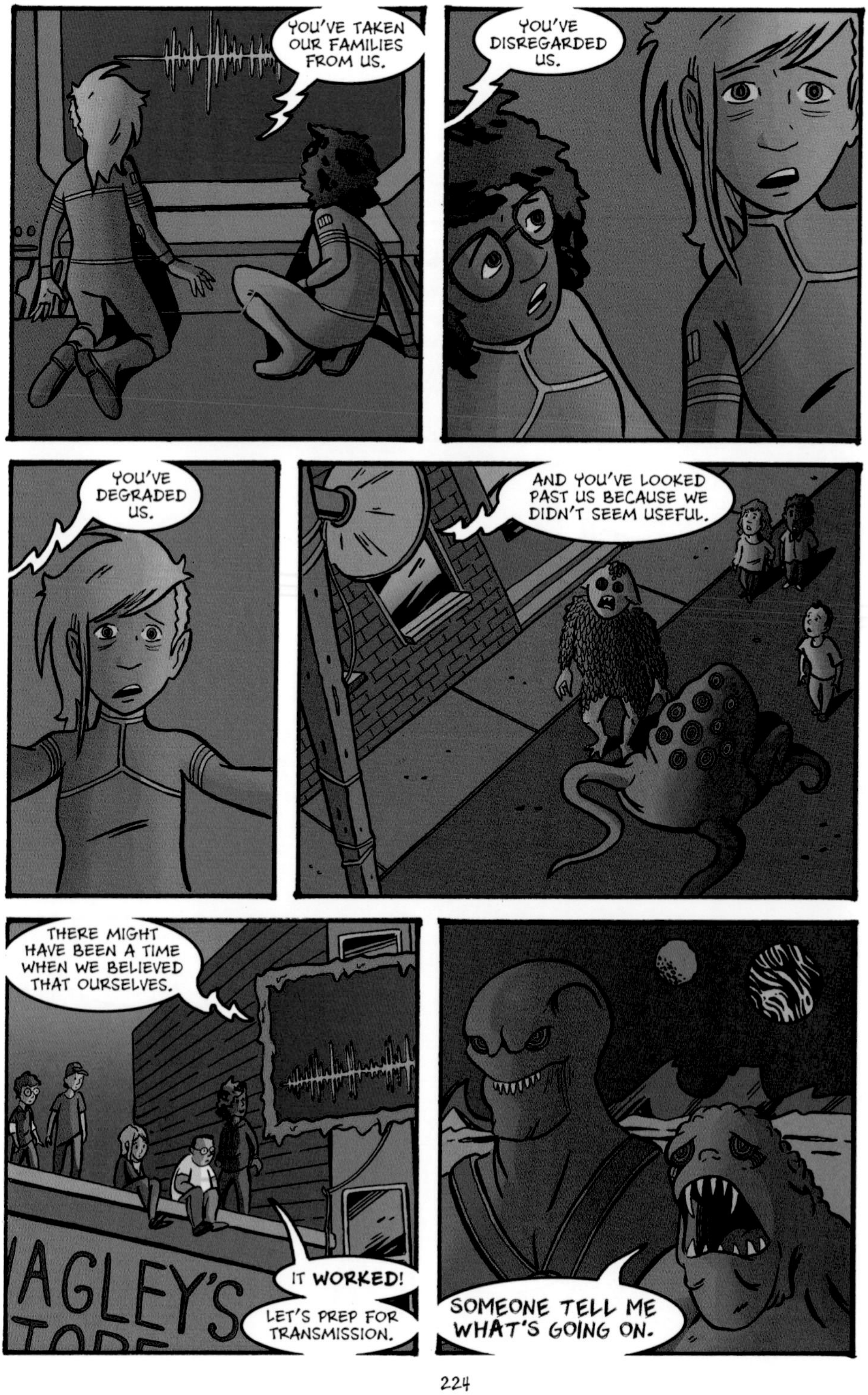
YOU'VE TAKEN OUR FAMILIES FROM US.
YOU'VE DISREGARDED US.
YOU'VE DEGRADED US.
AND YOU'VE LOOKED PAST US BECAUSE WE DIDN'T SEEM USEFUL.
THERE MIGHT HAVE BEEN A TIME WHEN WE BELIEVED THAT OURSELVES.
AGLEY'S
IT WORKED!
LET'S PREP FOR TRANSMISSION.
SOMEONE TELL ME WHAT'S GOING ON.

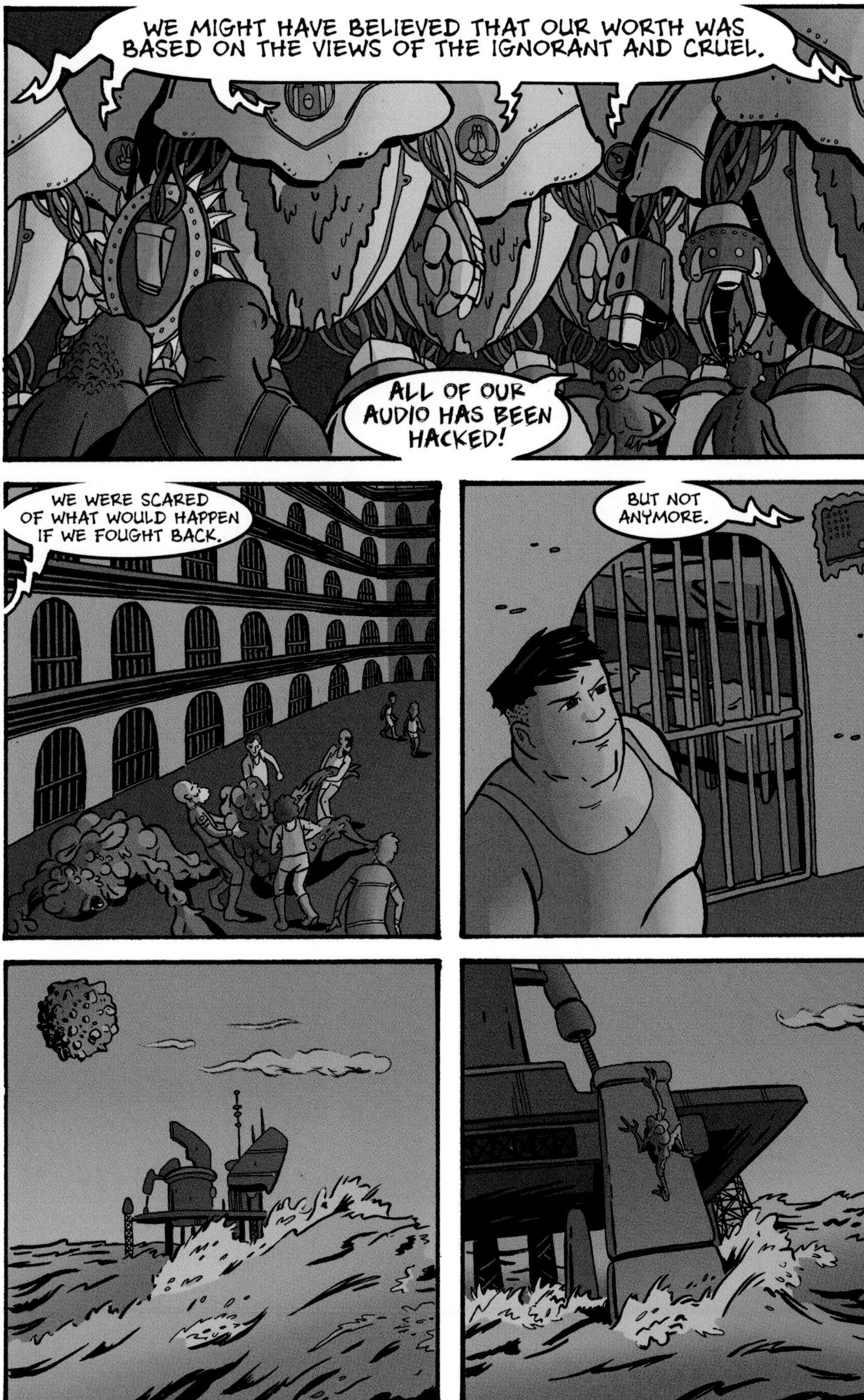
WE MIGHT HAVE BELIEVED THAT OUR WORTH WAS BASED ON THE VIEWS OF THE IGNORANT AND CRUEL.
ALL OF OUR AUDIO HAS BEEN HACKED!
WE WERE SCARED OF WHAT WOULD HAPPEN IF WE FOUGHT BACK.
BUT NOT ANYMORE.

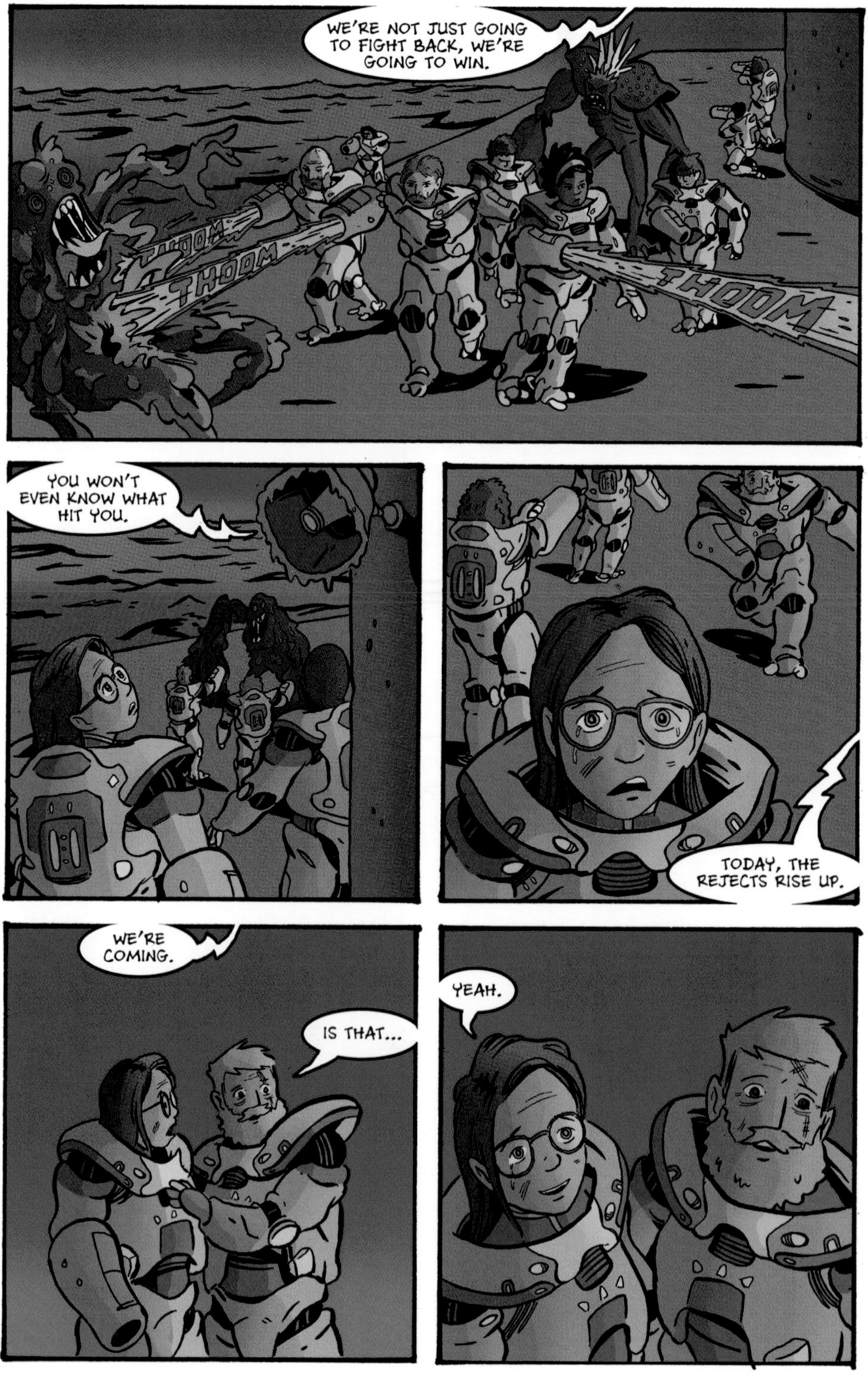
WE'RE NOT JUST GOING TO FIGHT BACK, WE'RE GOING TO WIN.
THOOM
THOOM
THOOM
YOU WON'T EVEN KNOW WHAT HIT YOU.
TODAY, THE REJECTS RISE UP.
WE'RE COMING.
IS THAT...
YEAH.

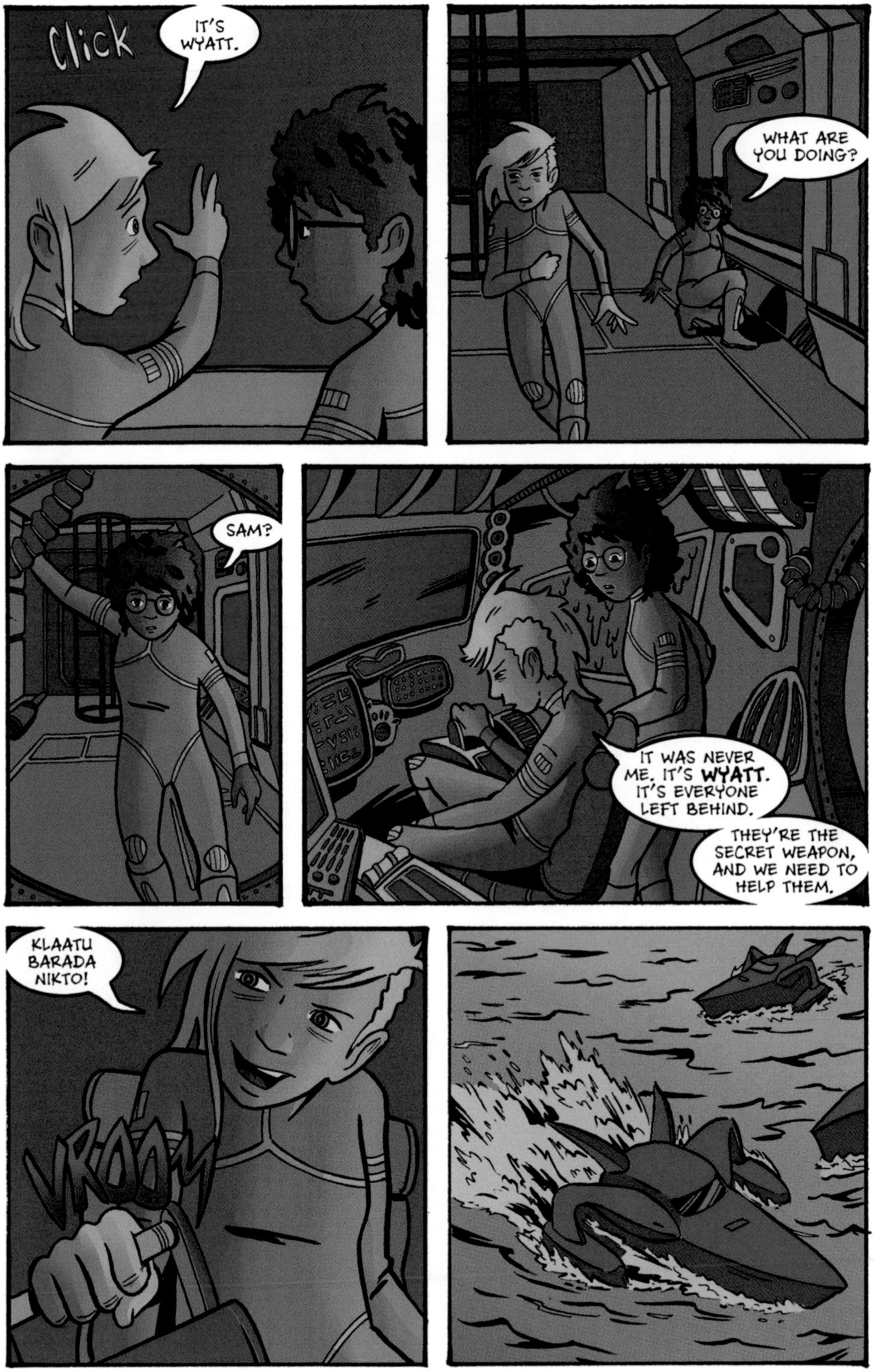
CLICK
IT'S WYATT.
WHAT ARE YOU DOING?
SAM?
IT WAS NEVER ME. IT'S **WYATT.** IT'S EVERYONE LEFT BEHIND.
THEY'RE THE SECRET WEAPON, AND WE NEED TO HELP THEM.
KLAATU BARADA NIKTO!
VROOM

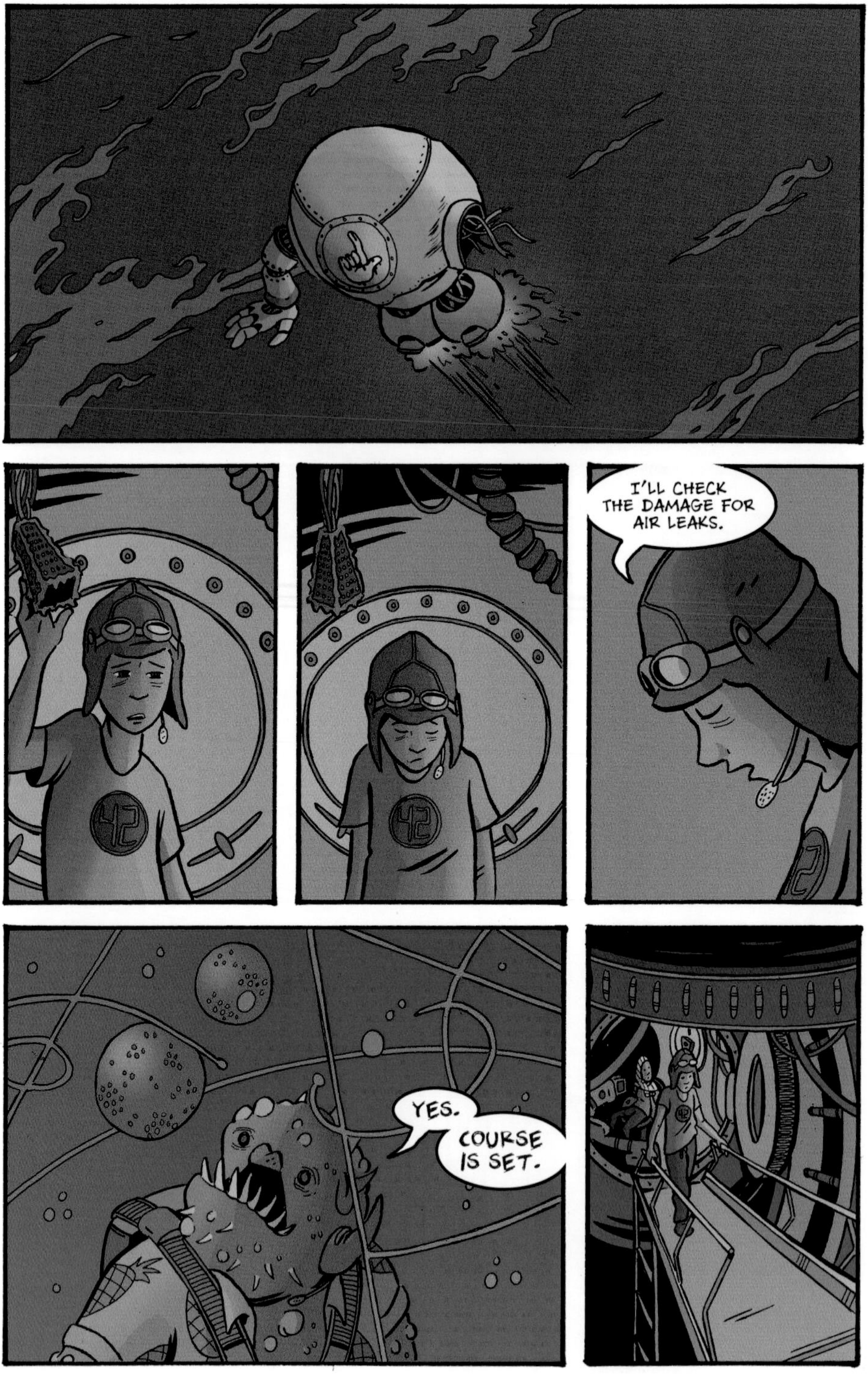
I'LL CHECK
THE DAMAGE FOR
AIR LEAKS.
YES.
COURSE
IS SET.

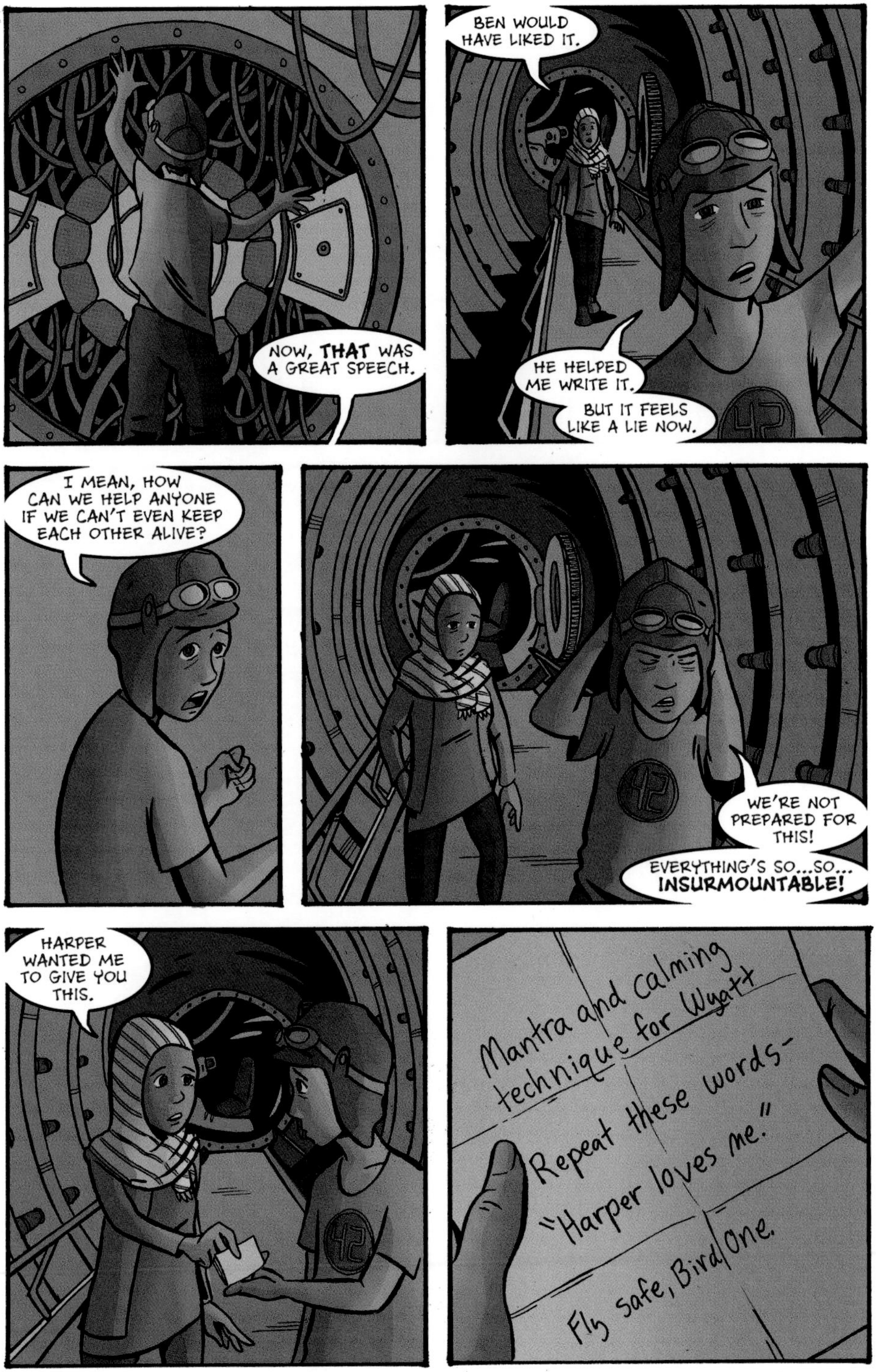
NOW, **THAT** WAS A GREAT SPEECH.
BEN WOULD HAVE LIKED IT.
HE HELPED ME WRITE IT.
BUT IT FEELS LIKE A LIE NOW.
I MEAN, HOW CAN WE HELP ANYONE IF WE CAN'T EVEN KEEP EACH OTHER ALIVE?
WE'RE NOT PREPARED FOR THIS!
EVERYTHING'S SO...SO... **INSURMOUNTABLE!**
HARPER WANTED ME TO GIVE YOU THIS.
Mantra and calming technique for Wyatt
Repeat these words-
"Harper loves me."
Fly safe, Bird One.

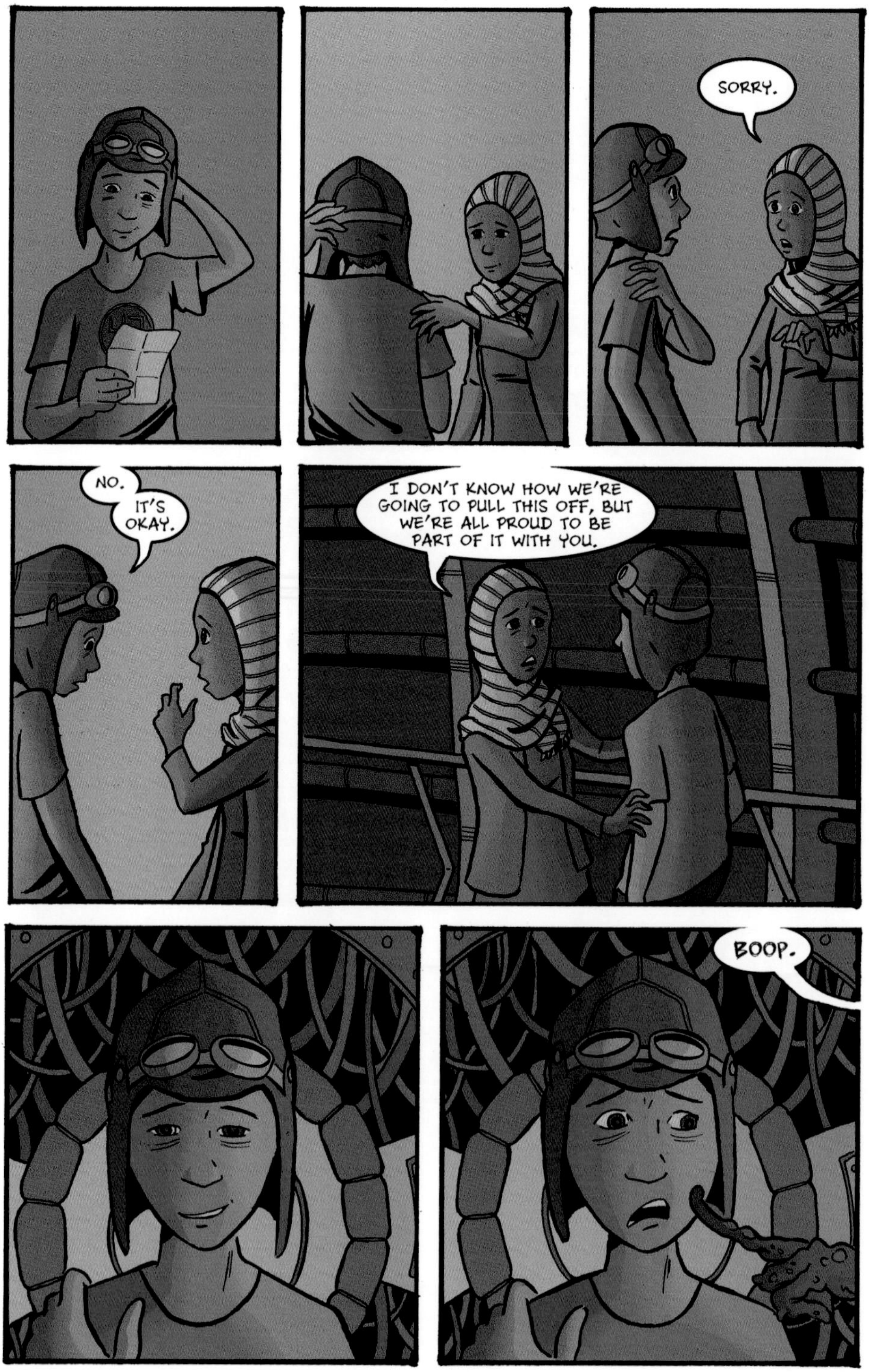
SORRY.
NO. IT'S OKAY.
I DON'T KNOW HOW WE'RE GOING TO PULL THIS OFF, BUT WE'RE ALL PROUD TO BE PART OF IT WITH YOU.
BOOP.

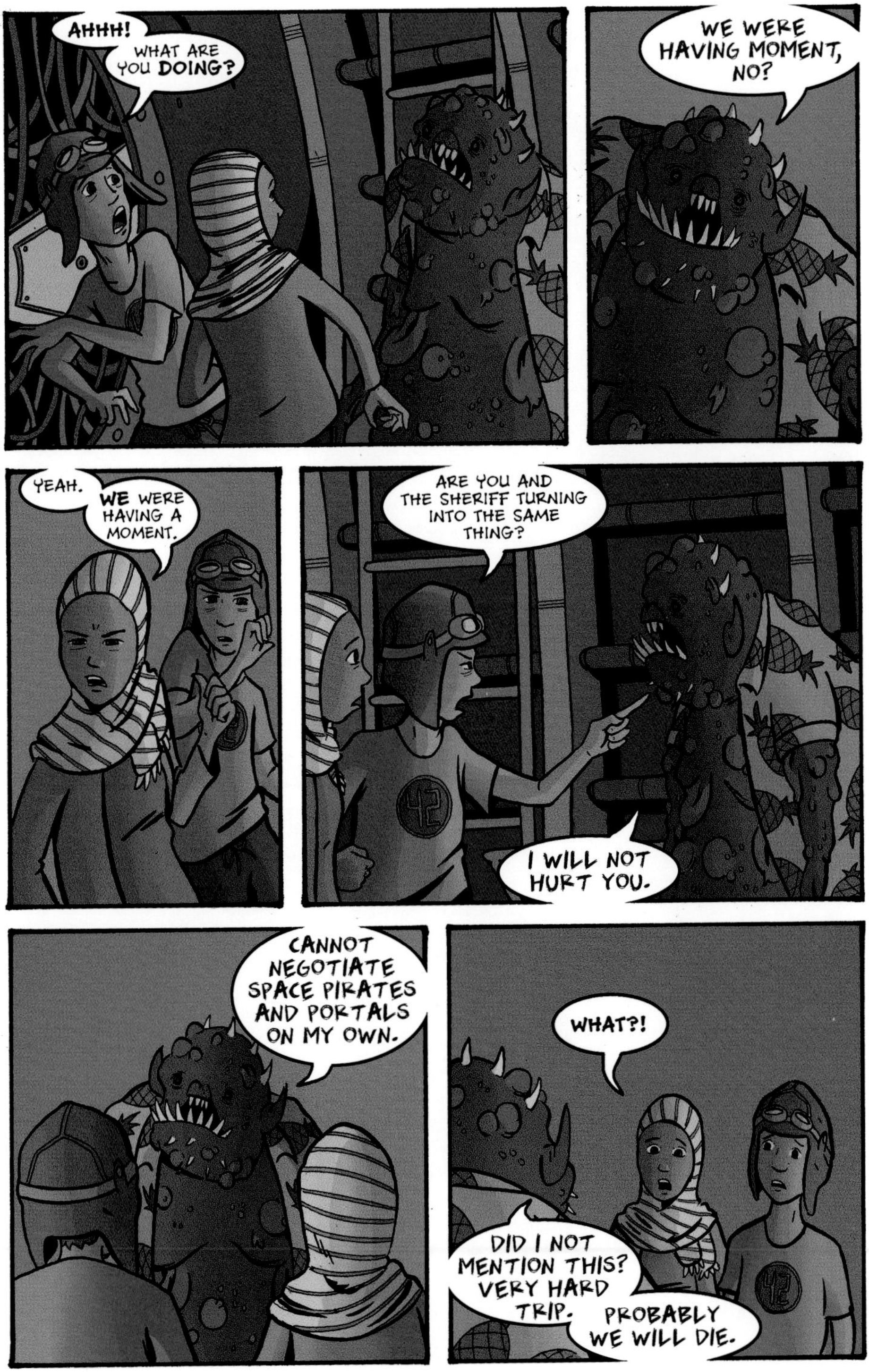
AHHH!
WHAT ARE YOU DOING?
WE WERE HAVING MOMENT, NO?
YEAH.
WE WERE HAVING A MOMENT.
ARE YOU AND THE SHERIFF TURNING INTO THE SAME THING?
I WILL NOT HURT YOU.
CANNOT NEGOTIATE SPACE PIRATES AND PORTALS ON MY OWN.
WHAT?!
DID I NOT MENTION THIS? VERY HARD TRIP.
PROBABLY WE WILL DIE.

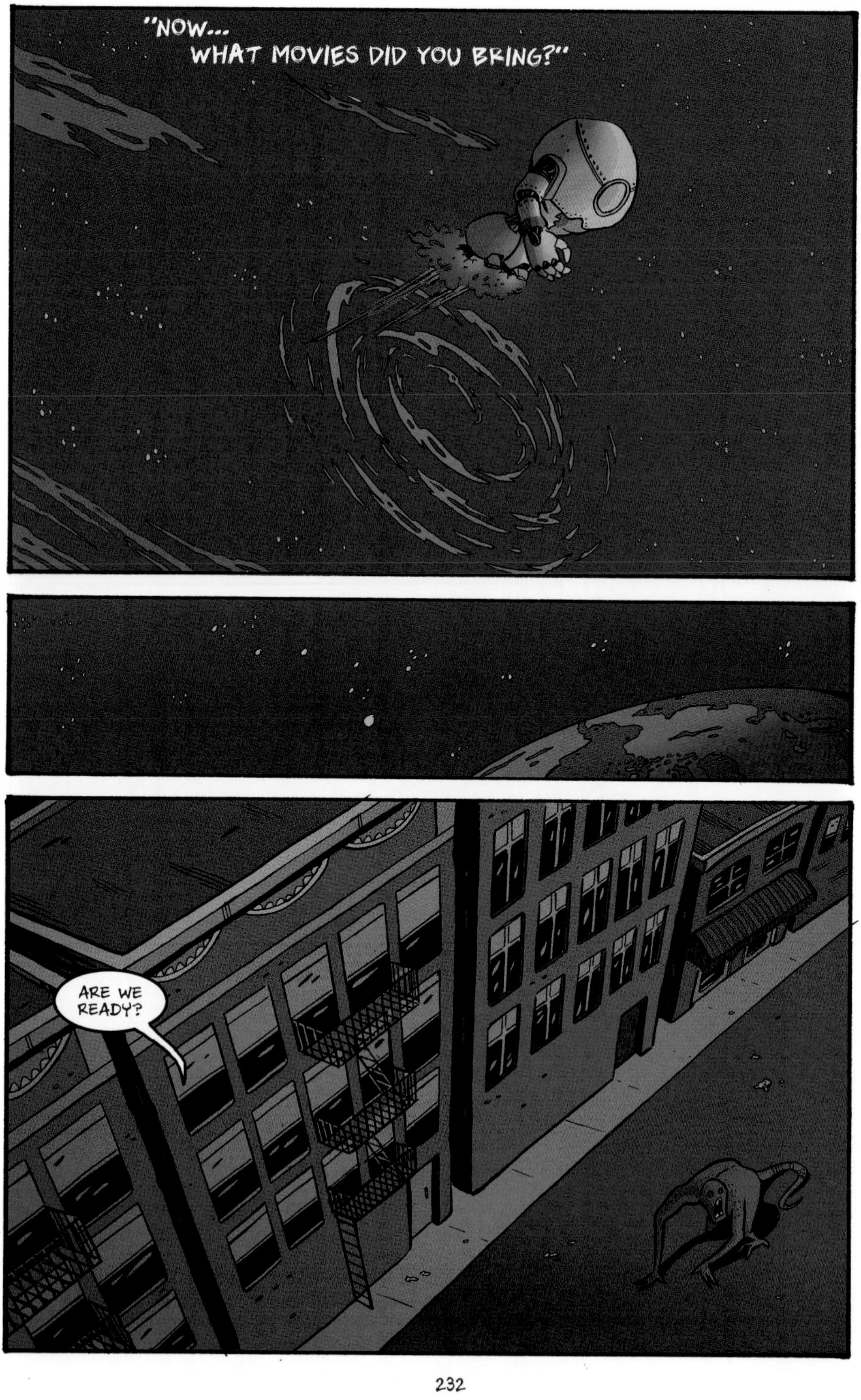
"NOW...
WHAT MOVIES DID YOU BRING?"
ARE WE READY?

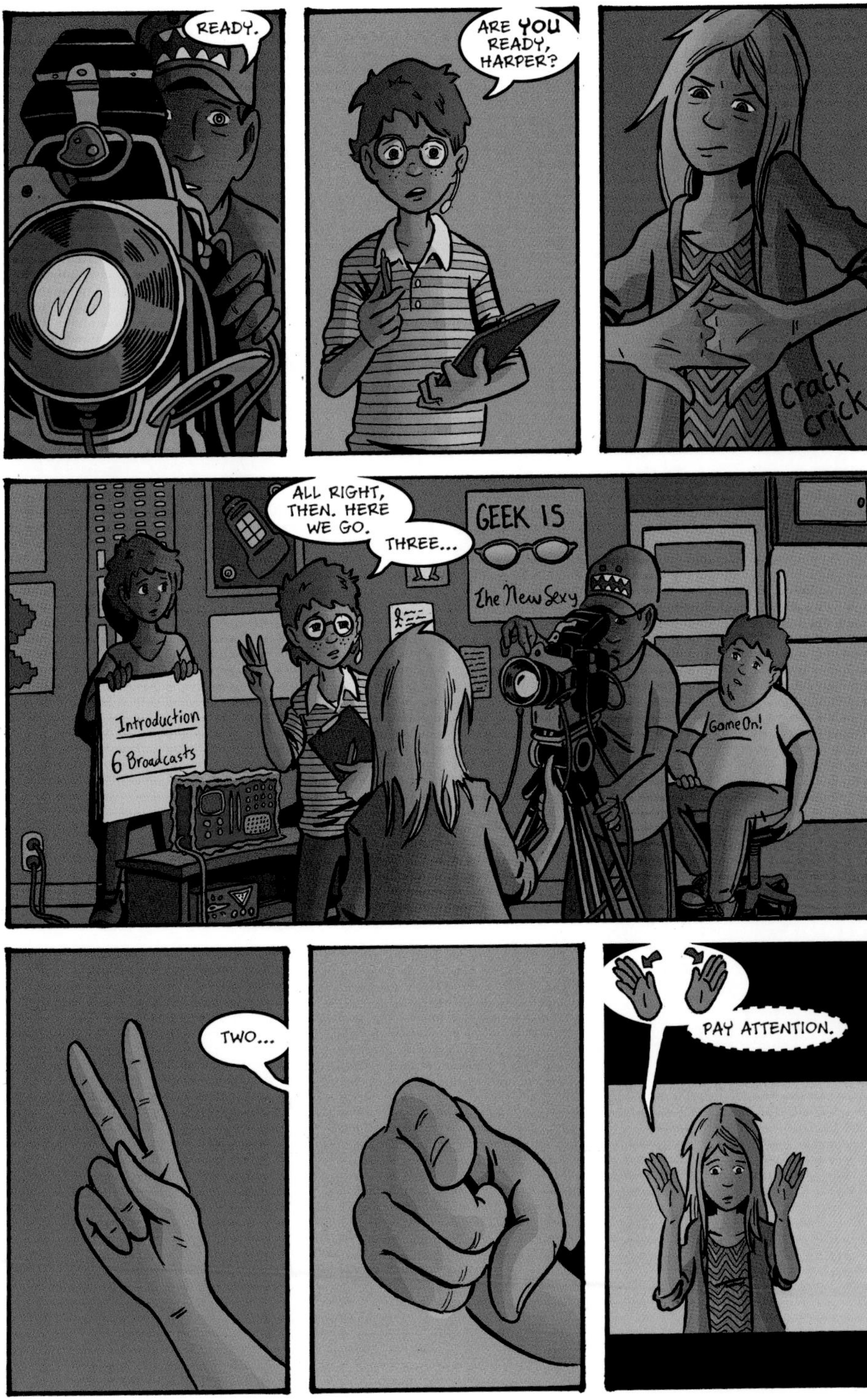
READY.
ARE YOU READY, HARPER?
Crack crick
ALL RIGHT, THEN. HERE WE GO.
THREE...
GEEK IS
The New Sexy
Introduction
6 Broadcasts
Game On!
TWO...
PAY ATTENTION.

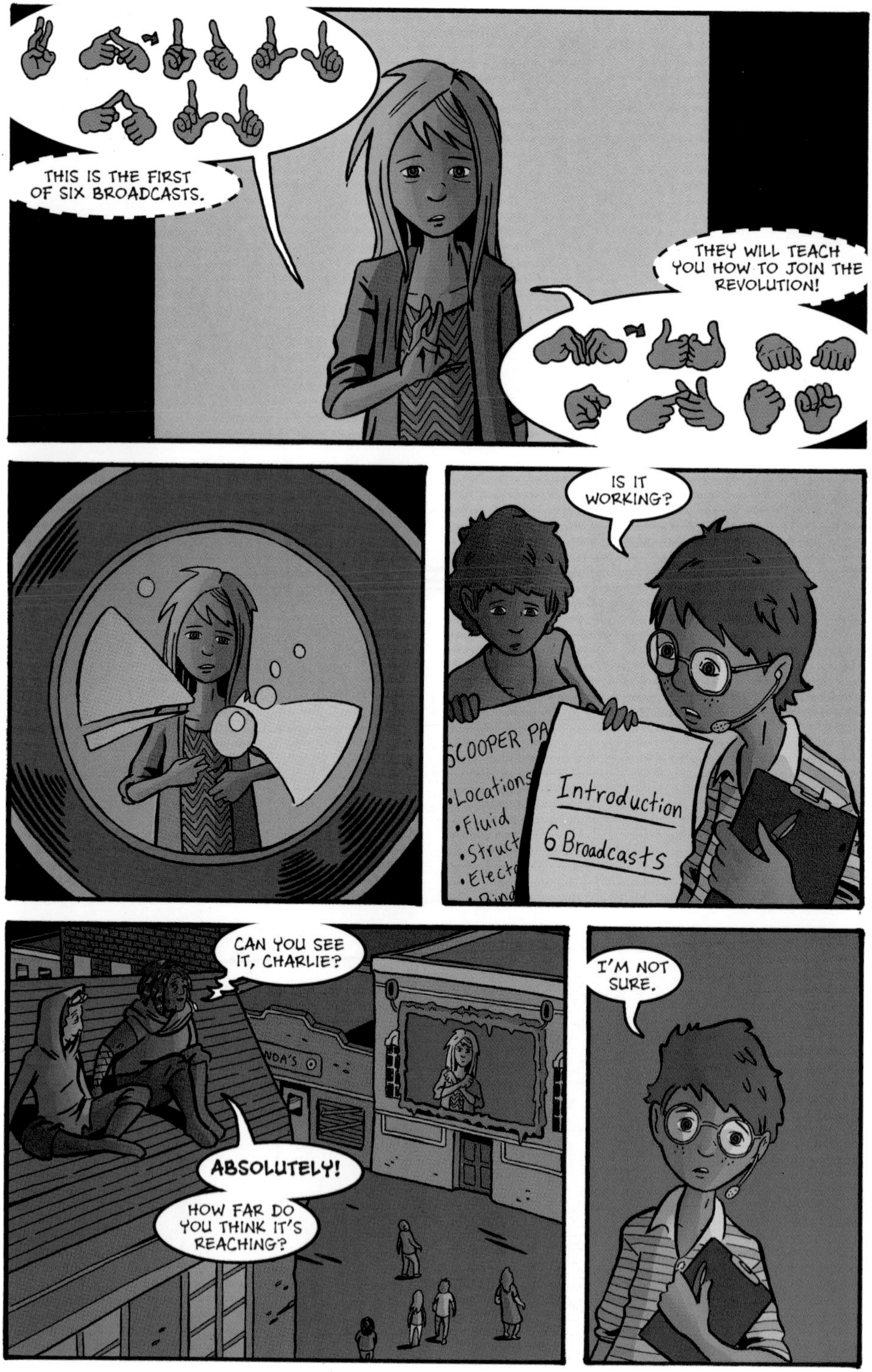
THIS IS THE FIRST OF SIX BROADCASTS.
THEY WILL TEACH YOU HOW TO JOIN THE REVOLUTION!
IS IT WORKING?
SCOOPER PA
•Locations
•Fluid
•Struct
•Elect
Introduction
6 Broadcasts
CAN YOU SEE IT, CHARLIE?
ABSOLUTELY!
HOW FAR DO YOU THINK IT'S REACHING?
I'M NOT SURE.

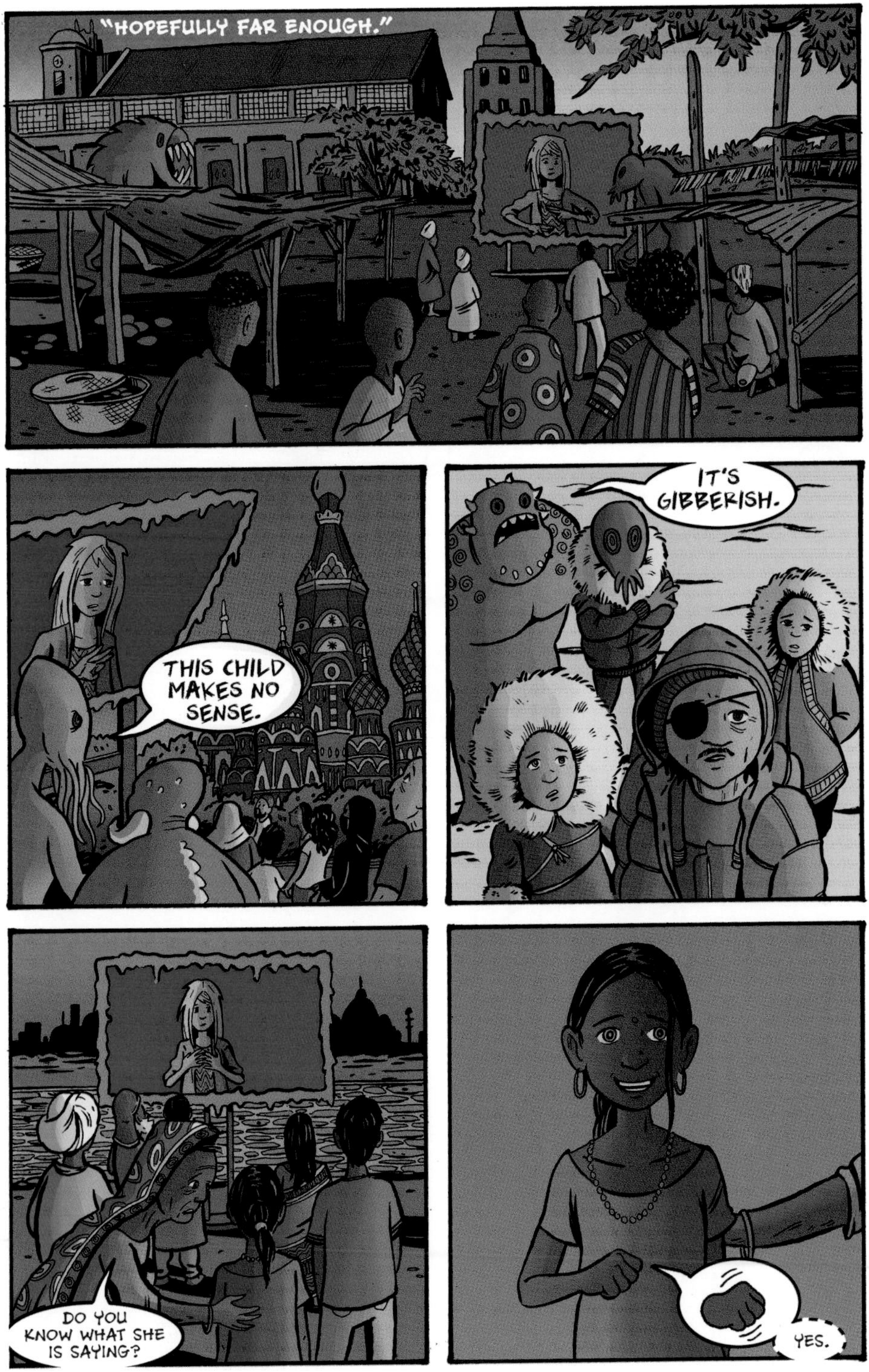
"HOPEFULLY FAR ENOUGH."
THIS CHILD MAKES NO SENSE.
IT'S GIBBERISH.
DO YOU KNOW WHAT SHE IS SAYING?
YES.

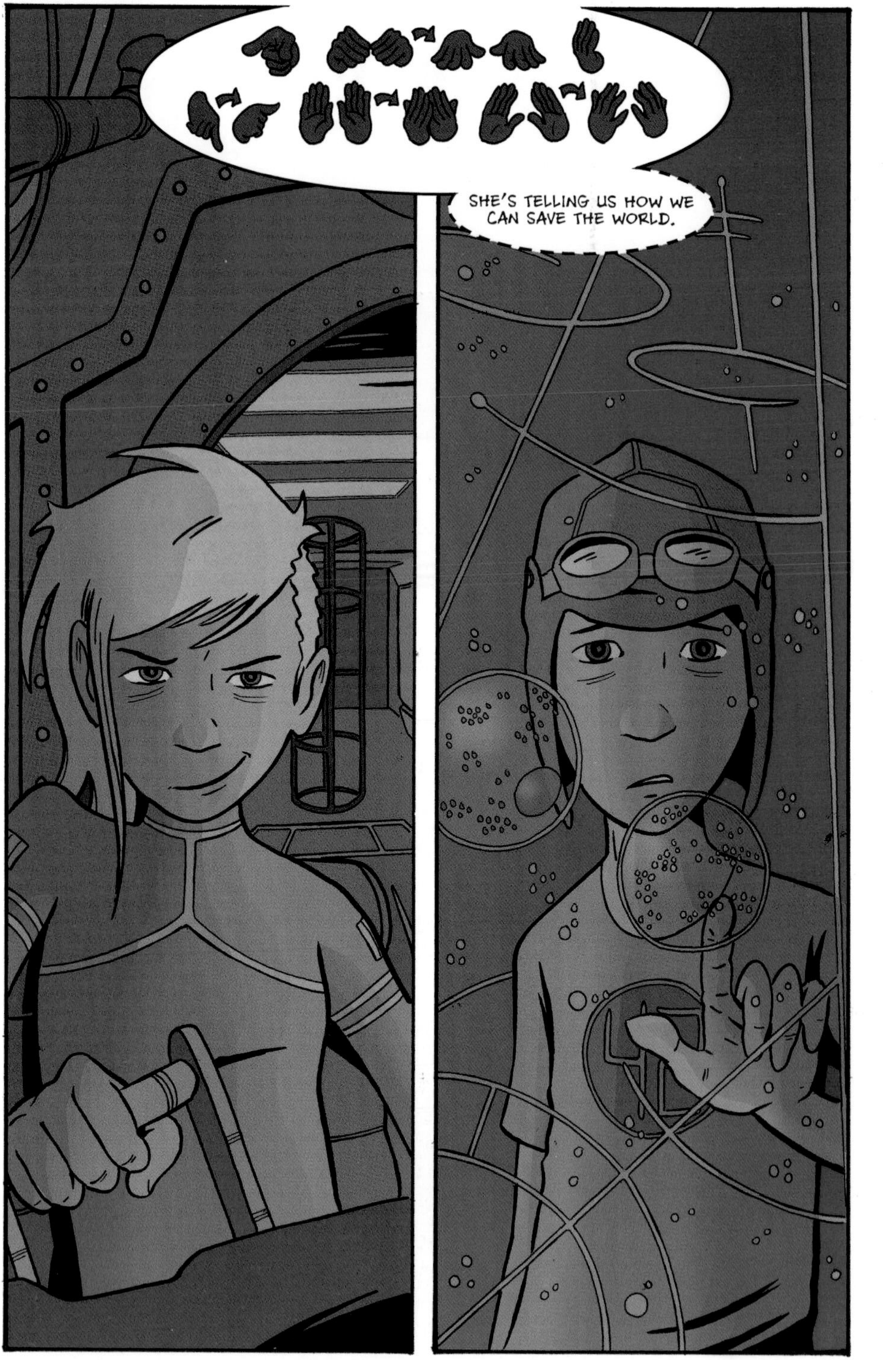
SHE'S TELLING US HOW WE CAN SAVE THE WORLD.